MVFOL

HIGH PRAISE FOR KATHERINE GREYLE!

NO PLACE FOR A LADY

"Katherine Greyle creates a delightful story peopled with engaging characters . . . sizzling sensual tension and an exciting mystery. The pace barely slows down from beginning to end."

—*Romantic Times*

MISS WOODLEY'S EXPERIMENT

"Katherine Greyle writes with humor and crafts an enjoyable, fast-paced read."

—*Romantic Times*

"*Miss Woodley's Experiment* is just the ticket for anyone who wants to kick back and relax."

—*All About Romance*

"An engaging Regency romance."

—*Midwest Book Review*

MAJOR WYCLYFF'S CAMPAIGN

"A splendid, witty romp complete with a few eccentric characters and highly amusing antics."

—*Romantic Times*

"Katherine Greyle's writing has a definite spark."

—*All About Romance*

RULES F̶O̶

"Kathy Greyle alw̶ ̶ ̶ ̶ ̶ ̶ ̶ ̶ ̶ ̶ ̶ ̶ ̶ ̶ ̶ parkles with humor, wit, ̶
—Cath̶ ̶ ̶ ̶ ̶ ̶ ̶ ̶ ̶ ̶ ̶ ̶ ̶ ̶ ̶ ̶ntract

"Greyle's smooth ̶ ̶ ̶ ̶ ̶ ̶ ̶ ̶ ̶ ̶ ̶ ̶ ̶ead."
—*Romantic Times*

MVPOL

CAROLLY'S FATE

"I do not want love or a wife," James said firmly.

"Everyone wants love, James."

He looked closer, finally seeing the small red blood vessels in Carolly's eyes and the slight puffiness in her cheeks. Just as he feared. She had been crying. "What about you?" he pressed. "Do you want love?"

"I'm dead, James. Dead people don't love."

"You breathe," he whispered. Then he lifted his thumb to caress her beautiful neck. "Your skin is warm." He pushed aside her high collar to stroke the pulse at her throat, wishing he could press his lips to it instead. "Your heart beats. You are alive."

She pushed away from him, but not before he saw new tears form in her eyes. He moved to follow her, but her obvious pain kept him from doing so. He did not wish to hurt her by forcing his attentions on her; and so he watched helplessly as she walked unsteadily away from him, half falling into a large maple before steadying herself with one hand on its rough bark. When she spoke, her voice held such flat certainty that part of him wanted to believe her.

"In the last ten years, I have died six times. First in a car crash, then of TB. I've been beaten, stoned, and shot in the back. And I've suffocated from pneumonia." She turned, pinning him with her angry, wounded gaze. "I'm dead, James, and I will keep dying until I become an angel. And nothing you or I can do will change that."

Other *Love Spell* books by Katherine Greyle:

NO PLACE FOR A LADY
MISS WOODLEY'S EXPERIMENT
MAJOR WYCLYFF'S CAMPAIGN
RULES FOR A LADY

ALMOST AN
ANGEL

KATHERINE GREYLE

LOVE SPELL NEW YORK CITY

LOVE SPELL®

November 2003

Published by

Dorchester Publishing Co., Inc.
200 Madison Avenue
New York, NY 10016

If you purchased this book without a cover you should be aware that this book is stolen property. It was reported as "unsold and destroyed" to the publisher and neither the author nor the publisher has received any payment for this "stripped book."

Copyright © 2003 by Katherine Grill

All rights reserved. No part of this book may be reproduced or transmitted in any form or by any electronic or mechanical means, including photocopying, recording or by any information storage and retrieval system, without the written permission of the publisher, except where permitted by law.

ISBN 0-505-52548-8

The name "Love Spell" and its logo are trademarks of Dorchester Publishing Co., Inc.

Printed in the United States of America.

Visit us on the web at www.dorchesterpub.com.

A cloud does not know why it moves in just such a direction and at such a speed, it feels an impulsion . . . this is the place to go now. But the sky knows the reasons and the patterns behind all the clouds, and you will know, too, when you lift yourself high enough to see beyond horizons.

—*Richard Bach*, Illusions

ALMOST AN
ANGEL

Chapter One

May 20, 1815—England

Carolly stumbled and fell into the grass, letting its cool, sweet scent envelop her. She tried to move her right arm, but pain shot through her ribs and she groaned into the dirt. Thank God she always healed quickly at the beginning of each life.

Another life. Another incarnation. That could only mean she hadn't done enough or learned enough or given enough in her last life. So, now she had to start all over. Maybe this time she could earn her wings.

She didn't know how long she lay there, her body throbbing with agony, but eventually the steady thud of hoofbeats penetrated her consciousness. Someone was riding. On a horse. Coming toward her. If only she had the strength to lift her head to see. With a grunt of effort, Carolly managed to roll over to stare at the sky. Once upon a time she'd thought being dead meant she didn't have to hurt any longer. Boy, had she been wrong.

The hoofbeats pounded through the ground, adding to the steady thrum of her pain. Carolly remained still, unable to work up the enthusiasm to rise and grab the person's attention. If whoever it was rode on by, then it was his loss. If he stopped, he'd get his reward. That, at least, she'd managed to figure out in her first few incarnations: The person she met first needed her the most.

Except, she reminded herself sternly, *she* was the one working at something. She had to earn her wings. She sighed. *Time to go to work.*

Carolly pushed upright, moaning as she did, trying to see beyond the grassy hill where she lay. Off in the distance, she heard a shout and turned toward the sound. A man on a horse: He'd seen her and was riding fast straight at her.

Her strength gave out, and Carolly dropped back onto the ground. She waited.

Before long, a man knelt beside her. Carolly saw dark hair and pale blue eyes, so light they were almost gray. She saw a stern jaw in a face unused to smiles.

"Good God, what happened? Where does it hurt?" His voice sounded rough, but not ungentle as he carefully slid his arms beneath her. "Tell me if this hurts."

She smiled through her pain, enjoying the warmth of his touch. Then he lifted her up, and she had the briefest impression of a muscled chest broader than she might have guessed from her first glimpse. He held her firmly, and she smelled the musky scent of horse and leather and man.

Carolly sighed, this time with delight. Some pleasures never faded. "Thank you," she whispered.

Then she slept.

James Oliver Henry Northram, Earl of Traynern, did not like surprises. He liked half-naked and battered women who collapsed on his near lands even less. Which was reason enough, he told himself, to perform his Christian duty by calling for medical help, and then—*now*—wash his hands of the situation. His staff and the doctor would see to the woman's care. He need not think of her again beyond a simple order to make sure she did not steal anything. Yet, here he stood, glowering at both physician and patient, as the examination continued.

He ought to look away. The doctor had to inspect the lovely young woman; he did not. Still, for some bizarre reason, James felt the strong need to stand here, watching the doctor push into obviously broken ribs and press the woman's thick, black bruises. Couldn't the man see she'd been beaten to within an inch of her life? Did he truly need to prod her more?

"Will she live?" James's voice was harsh even to his own ears.

The doctor shrugged. "Perhaps" was his only comment.

James should quit the room. He did, in fact, order his feet to perform that task. They remained grounded, frozen, immobile, his legs aching from his wild ride back to the house. Why, oh why, did he insist on torturing himself?

The answer, of course, remained both obvious and illogical. He stayed because the unknown woman was fair-haired and polite. Many women in England possessed those qualities, he knew. But despite all reason, the echo of a battlefield haunted him, memories of another young person—a teen with flaxen hair and a chest that bullets had torn asunder. Daniel. James had failed to save him. He had tried, even gotten himself wounded as he dragged the boy's body back to safety. But it had been too late.

Danny's last words had been, "Thank you." As if James had done enough.

Now, here James stood over another fragile blond who'd given him thanks, and he knew that fate had decided to kick him again. God, how he hated surprises.

"You say you just found her?" interrupted the doctor, his second and third chins quivering. "Lying in the field? Like this? She's probably a highwayman's doxy. I suggest you send for the runners immediately."

James shifted, finding a victim for his ill humor. "What do

you suppose the runners will find? That she was nearly beaten to death? That she ran from her attacker?"

The doctor flushed a dull red, but did not hold his tongue. "Do not let sentiment interfere with your judgment, milord. She is likely a cheap—"

James cut him off. "Doctor! I suggest you treat the woman and leave my *sentiments* to me."

But he didn't understand his own ill humor. Certainly the doctor merely voiced what everyone believed. After all, no respectable woman simply appeared in such a state without someone, somewhere raising a cry of alarm—a husband or father, likely in grave distress at her disappearance. And this doctor, whose profession carried him great distances, had obviously heard nothing.

Since only ruffians kept silent when one of their kind disappeared, the man's beliefs had merit. And yet, James could not bring himself to damn a lone, lost woman, no matter what her past associations.

His thoughts were cut off as the strange woman moved. Her breathing hitched and her eyes shifted beneath her lashes. "I believe she's waking," he said.

"I shall bleed her, for safety's sake," the doctor proclaimed, ignoring the change in his patient. He tugged at her slender arm, heedless of the bruises. But, just as he pressed his instrument against the crook of her elbow, the woman gasped, scrambling backwards.

"Stay away from me!" she cried, gasping and cringing as her other hand moved to press against her bruised ribs.

"You are awake," the doctor said.

The woman looked up, her beautiful blue eyes shifting between her rescuers. She was obviously nervous, and James stepped forward, hoping to reassure her.

"Welcome," he began—but was interrupted as the doctor fought to bring his cupping instrument to the crook of the woman's arm.

"Remain still!" the physician snapped. "I am a doctor!"

With surprising strength, the woman wrenched her arm away. "I don't care if you're Hawkeye Pierce, you're not cutting into me!" She matched him glare for glare.

James stepped between them before the situation could worsen. "Perhaps, Dr. Stoneham, as she is awake now, you could leave off cupping her." He turned back, expecting to see a quivering, terrified woman. Instead, the patient seemed to have gained control of herself. Her light blue eyes sparkled with intelligence, and she boldly surveyed not only her surroundings but him.

"I must be allowed to work," the doctor said darkly.

"Not on your life!" the woman replied. She took a deep breath, obviously trying to calm herself. "Look, doctor," she said, though from her tone James could tell she doubted the man's credentials. "Cupping doesn't help anyone, least of all me."

"It will bleed off your ill humors."

"Not possible," she shot back. The quick sparkle of her laughter surprised both James and the doctor with the sound of its bitter mirth. "Look, the sad truth is there's nothing wrong with me that a little time won't cure."

She looked away, and James was once again struck by her vulnerability. With her flaxen hair making a soft halo about her face, she seemed like a lost angel. He stepped closer before even realizing his intention.

Fortunately, the doctor interrupted. "You will draw an infection!" the man stated, puffing up with outrage. "Mark my—"

"Thank you, Dr. Stoneham," James interposed, once again regretting that this was the nearest physician within three hours' hard ride. "I will send for you immediately should she take a turn for the worse."

Stoneham nodded. "I shall be waiting." He spoke as if pronouncing her doom, then stomped out the door.

The woman snorted in derision. Flipping back the covers, she climbed out of bed. She wore a baggy white nightgown three sizes too wide and about five inches too short. The hem flapped just below her knees, but she did not seem to care that her trim ankles and shapely calves were exposed.

"Great. He's gone," she said as she once again looked about the room. Her rosy toes wiggled against the chill floorboards, and she looked healthier than James expected. Her stomach growled—a loud, low rumbling that made her press her hand to her belly and giggle in embarrassment. "Oh, my," she said by way of apology. "Um . . . I know this is really rude, but could I possibly have something to eat? I'm absolutely starving. I swear I will work off double what it costs."

James felt his jaw go slack. The woman stood completely unabashed before him, her curves enticingly outlined by the light from the window. Once again, he was appalled by his lack of discipline. He should not even be in her room, much less standing there staring at her long shapely legs, perfectly rounded bottom, or at the perkiest breasts he'd seen in many a year. She could not have aroused him more with a deliberate seduction. Unfortunately, she seemed completely oblivious to her charms—which made her all the more interesting and him all the more irritated by his reaction.

"Madame," he began, his voice tight.

"Call me Caro," she answered, searching the room. For her clothing, no doubt, since she crossed to the wardrobe, opening it to find it empty.

"Please, Madame, you have been—"

"Caro or Carolly. Not Madame." She bent over, tugging open one drawer after another in the wardrobe. She found nothing, while James had to forcibly restrain himself from moving directly behind her and fitting her body to his in a most ungentlemanly manner.

"You have been severely—"

"I can't stand formality. It gets in the way of things," she went on from her bent position. She opened the lowest drawer. "It's important you feel comfortable with me."

James closed his eyes. He had to close them, otherwise the

sight of her upraised bottom would have completely undone him. "You were severely injured," he reminded himself more than her.

"Really, I much prefer Caro."

"And I strongly—"

"Caro."

"Urge you—"

"Caro."

His eyes shot open and he glared at her, funneling all his frustration into his stern tone. "*Miss Carolly!*"

She turned, smiling beatifically up at him. "Yes?"

He ground his teeth. "I run a formal household, madame."

"But 'madame' makes me sound like my mother!"

He regarded her silently for a moment, totally confounded. Finally he snapped, "I do not like surprises!" God alone knew why those words came forth. "Perhaps you should return to bed while I contact someone regarding your accident."

She obviously wasn't listening. She continued to inspect the room, poking at the escritoire and then heading back toward the window. He had to stop her. God only knew what he would see if she stood directly in the sunlight. The hard tips of her breasts already stood out whenever she moved. If the sunlight revealed their color, James doubted his ability to control his baser instincts.

Good God, he realized, he had been far too long without a woman if a strange female tempted him almost beyond reason! But she truly was beautiful, and . . .

With two swift steps, he caught her, being careful to touch only her arm. Her eyes widened at the contact, and she instinctively cringed away from him. He had not gripped her hard, but even so he instantly released her, belatedly remembering her bruises. She had been beaten to within an inch of her life. How loathsome of him to touch her at all, to think such lascivious thoughts about her, to want . . .

"Madame, you must return to bed," he said, "while I send a message to your family."

She shook her head, her eyes wide and her voice suddenly muted. She gazed up at him. "Sorry, no family."

"None?"

"Nope. Nada."

He stood directly before her, and though she was tall for a woman, he still needed to look down to see into her face. A bare shift in his gaze would reveal the dark shadows of her nipples. "Perhaps a friend?" he managed to say through his constricted throat.

"I'm afraid I'm all alone in the world." She lifted her shoulders in a casual shrug, and he nearly groaned at both her words and her movement. He was losing the battle. He knew it. No man could resist temptation for so long, and certainly not one who had lived virtually as a monk since returning from the battlefield.

"I may be all alone in the world," she continued, "but I'm not a doxy like that quack physician said. That's a whore, isn't it? A harlot?"

For the first time in years, James was completely non-plussed.

"Well, I'm not one." She glanced up at him, and he made a conscious effort to regain control of his body and mind. "Look, I know things seem odd right now."

He raised an eyebrow—the only movement he allowed himself for fear of giving into his lust.

"I'm not handling this very well, am I?" she asked. Then she sighed.

He had no response except for the obvious. "Please return to bed, madame. I can only surmise your . . . behavior is due to a serious injury. Perhaps you shall feel better after a short rest."

"Pooh."

"I beg your pardon?"

"I said, pooh."

"But—"

Suddenly, she laughed. It was a gentle cascade of notes like water falling onto pebbles. He could only catch his breath at the sound, praying he would hear it again.

"Look. Thank you so much for your concern, but I feel much better," the woman said. She stretched her arms high above her head and wiggled her toes. "However," she continued with a yawn, "I'm always hungry at the beginning of one of these adventures."

As if to emphasize the point, her abdomen released another loud groan.

"*Madame!* Please cover yourself!" James didn't know where he found the strength to bellow out his order, but somehow he did. And in such a way as to communicate the danger this strange woman courted. She abruptly scrambled away from him, flushing cherry red, then scrambled back into bed and tugged the coverlet up, over her body.

"Perhaps I could suggest a bargain, madame," he said in his coldest tones. "If you will keep yourself properly covered for a week while you heal, I shall have Cook send up a bowl of gruel."

"Gruel!" She had begun to settle back onto the bed, but twisted around at his suggestion.

"You would prefer chicken broth?" He forced himself to keep his tone hard. Though she now sat in bed, her body covered, the memory of what he'd seen, of what he'd wanted to do, still burned in his blood.

"I'll expire from starvation on chicken broth!" she exclaimed. She tilted her head and peered at him. For a moment, her eyes actually shone. "Make it one day of bedrest and the whole chicken," she said.

"Two days," he haggled, "provided Dr. Stoneham says you can leave the bedchamber." Then he forced himself to take one step backwards, away from temptation.

"That quack wouldn't say I could breathe if you held a gun to his head. A day and a half and a steak."

"Three, and gruel."

She groaned. "You're supposed to go down, not up."

"You are supposed to act like a lady, not a child."

That silenced her, albeit only for a moment. She settled onto the bed, folded her legs beneath her, and looked at him. He felt himself grow quite warm beneath her gaze—as if she sought to see the real him, the man without his accoutrements. The concept intrigued as much as it terrified him.

"You're too serious," she said, her gaze almost unnaturally focused.

"And you are too impertinent," he retorted.

She laughed, and once again James was struck by the beauty of the sound. "Well, at least we agree on something." She sighed, her features settling into a guileless smile. "How about this? I promise to spend the next two days in bed if and only if you send me a real dinner—no gruel or porridge or broth— and if you solemnly promise to visit me at least once tonight and twice tomorrow." She lifted her eyebrows as he considered. "How about it? It's the best deal you're likely to get."

He waited, considering his options. He already regretted riding in the east field this morning. Had he gone west, he never would have encountered her, never would have brought her to his home, and would certainly not be standing before her now, his body betraying him in the most embarrassing way. He shook his head at his own ridiculousness.

Yet, who was this strange woman and where did she come from? No man, least of all himself, could resist such a mystery.

"I accept your proposal," he finally said. "Now, if you will please remain in bed, I shall find you dinner. Good evening, madame."

She straightened. "You have to call me Carolly!"

He gave her his most formal bow. "That was not part of the agreement." Then he left the room, quietly shutting her door behind him.

Laughing, Carolly left her bed and paced the confines of her room. She was beginning to feel more oriented. She was in pushing it open to look outside. She was apparently in one wing of a large, very imposing estate home. Just outside her window ran a wide ledge that traveled the full length of the house. If she needed to, she could easi—

ange,

But Lord, h

Focus! she ordered room. Truth be told, she adore pretty cream-and-blue fabrics. She tran luxurious four-poster bed and its damask drape ways wanted to sleep under a canopy!

Next, she inspected the few other pieces of furniture in the room. She'd already explored the wardrobe—a desperate move to keep herself from drooling all over Mr. Aristocratic Hunk— but now she studied the chair, the dressing table, and the desk with its dozen tiny drawers. She spent a good five minutes pulling open each hidey-hole to inventory the contents— which unfortunately were nothing except a bottle of ink, a quill, and some crisp linen paper.

Finally, Carolly sat back and added up what she knew. Given the style and fabrics she saw, she had to be sometime later than the 1600s. Add to that his lordship's clothing: buff pantaloons neatly hugging his narrow hips, a stark white shirt, waistcoat, coat, and of course a tie—no, it was a cravat— stunningly outlining his broad shoulders. He also sported dark unpowdered locks that curled with cute abandon around his frowning face. All in all, it seemed she'd probably landed somewhere in the 1800s.

Or so she guessed. History had never been one of her passions.

Oh yes, and it was spring. Carolly wandered to the window,

walk along it. In fact,
to do just that to get a better view of the
around her, but she suppressed the urge. Instead she
noted a large stable, formal gardens, a green forest, and a glimmer of a lake. Everything she saw was enchanting, enticing, begging her to go outside and explore.

But she was stuck inside.

Carolly sighed. If only she had a newspaper. Even a book would give her an idea of the date, but her room remained bare and she'd promised to stay here.

She chewed on her lower lip, and her stomach released a particularly loud growl. She was really hungry. What harm could there be in looking around a bit, maybe going in search of dinner? After all, she'd be helping out by getting her own food instead of having someone bring it to her.

She tiptoed to the door, opened it a crack and peered out . . .

To find herself staring at the gold buttons of a black waistcoat. She gasped and looked up, only now realizing how tall her host was. And how grim-faced.

"Hi," she said. Her mouth was dry, and she felt the steady heat of guilt rise in her face. "I was just, um, looking to see how long before that food arrived." She backed up, opening the door a little wider. "What are you doing there?"

He leaned against the balustrade, his arms crossed over his chest, his expression forbidding. He didn't say a word.

"You're not standing guard, are you? That would be silly."

"I might be waiting to see if you keep your word."

Carolly felt her flush creep higher on her face. "My word? About not going out and around the house?"

"About staying in bed."

"Oh." She looked down at her bare toes. "Oops."

"Just so." Then he turned and walked away.

"Wait!" she called.

He stopped, his back rigid.

"Please, what—what day is it? And where am I?"

He turned back to her, and she saw his expression soften. "My apologies, madame—"

"Caro."

He raised an eyebrow, and she sighed in resignation. "Miss, then. Madame makes me sound old and married."

"You are not married? You said you had no one, but . . ." He sounded faintly surprised.

She supposed she understood. The women he knew probably married at eighteen. Had she lived, Carolly would be about twenty-nine. At first it had astounded her that she kept her own body each incarnation, aging as she would normally. Or rather, she kept what she remembered as her own body. Sometimes she wasn't entirely sure. Her memory wasn't perfectly clear.

"No, I never married," she answered softly. It was one of the things she hated most about being dead—no longer having the possibility of a husband and a family.

"So, you wish it *known* you are unmarried?" he asked.

She stared at him until understanding crystallized in her sluggish brain. He didn't expect her to be married. In fact, he clearly thought her alone. But he'd expected her to lie about it, pretending to be some poor widow instead of a young maid wandering around unchaperoned.

"Of all the Neanderthal . . ." She cut off her muttered curse when she noticed his raised eyebrow. She took a deep breath. "No, I've never been married. I'm a strong, independent woman who never felt the need to shackle myself to a man." She lifted her chin, challenging him to deny her that right.

He merely shrugged. "That no doubt explains your current . . . unusual circumstance."

She felt her face heat in embarrassment. Okay, so she was apparently a lone woman beaten within an inch of her life who had collapsed practically on his front doorstep. That didn't mean she needed a man's protection. "I can take care of myself!"

"Clearly."

She scowled at him.

He ignored her and leisurely pushed away from the banister. "Very well, Miss. . . ." He raised an eyebrow, waiting for her to fill in her last name.

She opened her mouth to answer, but nothing came out. What *was* her last name? "I . . . I'm Caro. Carolly . . ." She bit her lip. Had she been dead so long she couldn't remember the basics? She never expected to recall names of presidents or rock stars—especially since she was constantly moving around in time. But her name? How could she forget her name?

She looked up, feeling her blood run cold. "I can't remember." Suddenly her legs wobbled, and she had to clutch the doorframe to stay upright. Her host was beside her in an instant, gently leading her back to bed.

"Why can't I remember my name? I'm Carolly . . . Carolly . . ."

"It does not signify. I expect—"

"It sure does signify! It's my name!"

"If you like, I could send for the surgeon."

That got her attention as nothing else could. "No." She shook her head, still struggling to fight through the gray soup of her recollections. "He'll just want to bleed me, and I'll want to punch him."

At his look of horror, she sighed. Really, after years of hopping through time, she ought to have learned how to handle it better—and that meant watching her mouth.

She took a stab at explaining her behavior: "As you can see, I'm feeling a bit disoriented."

"You should rest," he agreed. "You have had a trying day."

She looked up, searching his face as he stepped away, but he'd carefully blanked it of all expression. He did say, "Perhaps I should introduce myself."

She smiled in relief. "That would probably be helpful."

"I am James Oscar Henry Northram, Earl of Traynern. At your service." He bowed slightly while she reeled from all his names.

"An earl," she muttered to herself. "That's below a duke and above a count. No, an earl *is* a count. I mean a viscount, right?" She glanced up at him. "This *is* England, isn't it?"

He obviously had no idea how to respond to her ramblings. Lord, she must sound like an idiot. Still, his voice remained level as he responded. "Yes, this is England. Staffordshire, to be exact."

"As I said, I'm a bit disoriented, uh, sir. I mean, my lord." She felt her face grow hotter. Why, oh why, hadn't she been trained in this stuff before landing here? There ought to be some sort of heavenly prep school. "Or am I supposed to say 'your grace?' "

She never would have guessed it, but apparently her dour host did indeed have a sense of humor. His lips twitched in an almost-smile, and Carolly found the expression absolutely charming. Her host sobered then and said, "Perhaps, Miss Carolly, as I am forced to use your given name, you could call me James."

She grinned. Had he just taken the first step in accepting her? God willing, this might just be her easiest incarnation yet!

Before she could say more, James Northram stepped abruptly away from the bed. "Please excuse me, Miss Carolly. I will go check on your dinner." He gave her a pointed stare. "You will oblige me by remaining in bed." It was not a question.

She tilted her head, eager to continue with her heavenly task, wanting to keep James by her side. After all, the more time she spent with him, the faster she could discover how best to help. "Will you visit me."

He shook his head. "I believe I just have."

He was being difficult. She thought quickly. "On the contrary, *I* visited *you*. Or rather, you caught me in a moment of weakness when hunger overcame my reason." Her eyes dropped to his feet. "I'm sorry about that, by the way. I'm usually good about my promises. I'm an honest person. Almost angelic, you might say."

She couldn't tell if her apology made any headway. Her host's expression gave absolutely no clue. "Good evening, Miss Carolly," he responded formally. Then, after another polite bow, he departed.

When he was gone, Carolly dropped backwards onto her bed, and into her pillow. All in all, she decided, she'd made a good beginning. James had agreed to use her given name, and he'd even smiled once. That was a coup with this man, she imagined. As for forgetting her last name, she dismissed it with a depressed sigh. She'd long gotten used to losing bits of her memory—pieces of who she was, tiny snatches of her childhood that could never be recovered.

What was a last name? She never really needed one anyway.

Carolly rolled onto her side and pretended she wasn't crying.

Chapter Two

Some time later, James looked up to see his housekeeper step silently past the library. "Mrs. Potherby!"

The woman stopped and backed up, keeping her eyes downcast, her posture stiff. "Yes, milord?"

"Did you take a tray up to our guest?"

She bobbed in a curtsy. "Yes, milord."

"A cold collation, as I directed?"

"Yes, milord."

James frowned, wondering what exactly it was he really wished to ask. "What did she do? Did she eat it?"

Mrs. Potherby hesitated, and when she chanced to glance up at her employer, she flushed. "Uh, no, milord. Not exactly."

James straightened in his chair. "What exactly did she do?"

"Well, milord, as to that, she did not do anything. I, uh . . ."

"Please endeavor to explain yourself, Mrs. Potherby." His voice was sharp, and it startled him almost as much as it unnerved his housekeeper.

"I am not sure she knew the tray had arrived, milord. When

I went to her room, she was lying down. She . . . That is to say, I did not wish to disturb her."

"Disturb her?" James pushed out of his chair to pace in front of the cold fireplace. "Mrs. Potherby, she was practically begging for something to eat the last time I saw her. I cannot imagine her not noticing a full tray."

His housekeeper fidgeted, and James narrowed his eyes on her twisting hands. "What are you leaving out, Mrs. Potherby?"

"She was *lying down*, milord." The woman stressed the words as though trying to get him to understand some secret message, but that only made him more impatient.

"Mrs. Potherby, I will ask you one more time, and this time I expect a clear and direct answer. Why did she fail to notice the tray?"

The woman continued to stare at the floor, looking for all the world like a prisoner giving over secret military information. "She was crying, milord. Quiet-like and into the pillow. The kind of tears a body cries when she does not wish others to know."

James felt his insides grow chill. He stared at the older woman. Carolly was crying? "Why? Why was she crying?"

Mrs. Potherby lifted her chin. "I do not know milord. But she is a young woman, apparently alone in the world. And those bruises . . . Who's to know what kind of cares she has been forced to endure." Her tone held some reproof.

James found himself suspicious, given the girl's earlier good humor. "Are you sure they were real tears? Did you see them?"

Mrs. Potherby sniffed in disdain. "Of course they were real tears. I have raised three children, milord, and taken care of more than one young girl in distress. If I cannot spot false tears then I do not belong here as your housekeeper!"

James was startled by her vehemence, and he quickly reassured her. "Of course, Mrs. Potherby. I did not mean to suggest that you . . . or rather, that she . . ." He took a deep breath, then drew himself up to his full height. "Thank you, Mrs. Potherby. I appreciate the information."

He returned to his desk, barely aware of the housekeeper's stiff curtsy before departing the room.

He frowned. Carolly was crying. His gut clenched at the thought, and he stared unseeing at the papers in front of him.

Why? What had happened to make the vivacious if bruised young woman bury her face in a pillow and sob? All the women of his acquaintance, with the possible exception of Mrs. Potherby, seemed to enjoy crying in full view of the world. They relished the drama of it. James would have guessed that if anyone fit that mold, it would be Carolly, with her outrageous behavior and complete lack of decorum. Oh yes, she would sob loud and long, completely heedless of who was about.

But she had not. She had been lively with him; then, when he left, she had buried her face in a pillow and silently sobbed.

James pushed away from his desk, intending to see for himself, to see her tears. Then he stopped. What would he say to her? Should he extend comfort, perhaps pat her shoulder?

No. James shook his head. He did not wish to be presumptuous. She had obviously not wished him to know of her unhappiness. He returned to his desk. Perhaps he could visit her after she felt better. Maybe she would have eaten by then, and they could discuss what had brought on the tears. Perhaps he could help.

He nodded to himself. He would wait.

James leaned back in his chair and watched the ormolu clock tick until precisely one hour had passed.

Carolly felt much improved. She should have known better than to indulge in tears when food sat within arm's reach. She began to smile as she licked sauce off her fingers. Who knew an angel could be guided by her stomach?

Her amusement was interrupted by a knock at the door.

Quickly wiping her hands on the linen napkin, she called a loud, "C'mon in!" before composing herself in her bed. Strangely, no one entered.

She was about to call again when the door opened. It revealed James, standing iron-bar erect. "May I enter?" he asked stiffly.

Carolly felt her smile expand. She found his awkwardness charming, even while she silently devised ways to tease him out of it. "Of course. Pull up a chair," she agreed.

He stepped inside the room and turned to her. She had the distinct impression he was steeling himself for battle, but then he stopped, and stared at her face.

"What?" she asked. Her hands went immediately to her cheeks. "Do I have sauce on my—?" She reached for her napkin.

His voice stopped her. "No, no. Your face is fine. Quite lovely, in fact."

To her horror, Carolly felt herself blush. She'd been complimented before—mostly in her real life or original life or first life or whatever she was supposed to call it—but something about James's delivery made her insides quiver. He truly thought she was lovely. Even if he said so in his strange, flat way. "Uh, thank you," she stammered. "Please sit down."

She had meant on the corner of the bed, but he went to the chair tucked against the wall across the room.

Seeing the distance between them, Carolly shook her head. "If you're going to sit all the way over there, I'm going to have to join you. We can't talk if I feel like we're shouting across the Continental Divide."

"The what?"

"What what?" Carolly carefully set her tray of food down and started to get out of bed.

"Madame, I suggest you remain under the covers."

Carolly froze, one semi-exposed leg pushed out toward the floor. She turned to James, making sure her expression was completely innocent. "Don't worry, I'm just going to join you over there."

"There's no other chair," he protested.

She shrugged. "I'll stand. I'm feeling fine, and I refuse to talk to you if I have to yell to be heard."

"You don't have to yell." He sighed, clearly exasperated. "Perhaps I could bring the chair closer."

She grinned. "What a lovely idea." Then she settled back under her covers, demurely folding her hands in front of her.

She watched as James casually lifted the heavy chair. He wasn't an especially large man. Like a gymnast, he was lean and wiry, his movements fluid and graceful without the clunkiness of a body builder. "So," she began once he'd gotten settled. "Have you come to cheer me up, or was there something on your mind?"

He seemed taken aback by her admission of previous sorrow. "Oh, er . . . yes. I came to see how you fared. I see you discovered Cook's tray."

"Oh yes, James—and I do feel much better now that I've eaten. Thank you. And thank Cook for me."

He nodded and stared intently at her face, then abruptly relaxed into his chair. "Splendid. A good meal always lifts my spirits as well." Carolly nodded, not knowing what to reply. She wasn't given time to ponder, because James suddenly leaned forward, pressing his elbows into his knees and regarding her intently. "If you feel better, perhaps I could trouble you with a few questions."

Inwardly, Carolly cringed. She doubted he was ready to hear her answers. Still, looking across at his angular face, she saw James wasn't the kind of man to shy away from anything, even answers he didn't like.

She smiled bravely. "Ask away. I'll do my best to answer you."

"Very well. First, forgive me if I touch on delicate matters, but have you remembered your surname?"

Carolly looked down at her hands. "No." The one word was

all she could say without tears welling up in her eyes.

"I understand." Though his face hadn't gentled, his tone had, and she knew he was sympathetic to her pain.

She lifted her chin and tried to smile. "Anything else?"

"Yes, actually. Everything else. Do you remember where you are from? Do you have *any* relatives? You are unmarried, you said?"

Carolly nodded.

"Please forgive the impertinence, but I searched your clothing. You carried nothing at all. No papers or money even. Can you tell me anything that will give me a clue as to your identity?"

Carolly sighed. This was always the hardest part—knowing how much to say. She pleated and repleated the coverlet while she considered her options.

"My lord—"

"Please, I thought we agreed on James."

Carolly looked up, pleased that he insisted on the less formal name. She saw it as a good sign that he'd become more comfortable around her. She took a deep breath. Time to begin.

"Actually, James, I know exactly who I am and why I'm here."

The earl raised an eyebrow, and Carolly suddenly felt the full intensity of his gaze.

"First, let me tell you that I never lie. It's the one part of me I've been able to hold on to over the years, and I've found it makes things much easier. If I can't answer a question truthfully, I'll just tell you that. Do you understand?"

He nodded, his expression carefully blank.

"Yes, I can see that you think you do. But in my experience . . ." She stopped, seeing his jaw muscles clench. She swore silently to herself. She'd insulted him. Damn. Nobles were always so touchy, and male nobles even more so. She took a deep breath. "I'm sorry, I didn't mean to suggest anything rude. Just try to remember that I don't lie, I'm not insane, and what I'm about to tell you is absolutely true."

James remained silent a moment, then finally said, "Go ahead."

She watched his face carefully. She often learned quite a lot about a person from his or her reaction to her news. She stared straight at James, keeping eye contact as she steeled herself to say the words: "I'm an angel, James. And I'm here to help you find love."

"Did you hear me, James?"

His guest's voice sounded uncertain, hesitant, as though *she* were the one who had just been told something astounding. "Yes," James said, working hard to keep his voice level. "You said you never, ever lie. Then you told me you are an angel here to help me find love."

Carolly nodded, though the movement seemed jerky. She stared at his face. James knew she was trying to read his expression so he took extra care to keep it blank.

"James, you're not reacting. I know what I've just said is a little, um, surprising."

"To say the least."

"Usually people argue or laugh. Actually, most just go pale and glassy-eyed, then start talking to me like I'm a two-year-old. You seem to have jumped straight to some heavy-duty denial."

He raised an eyebrow. Her strange way of talking, along with everything else about her, deepened his determination to get to the bottom of the mystery she embodied. "You are an angel," he repeated, needing to say the words aloud one more time. "And you intend to help me find love."

She shifted uneasily. "Actually, I don't think I'm an angel yet. I'm more of a pre-angel."

"A pre-angel. And you said you never lie."

She frowned and bit her lip. "I'm not lying. Although . . . about the pre-angel thing, I don't truly understand it myself."

That, at least, was quite clear. In fact, James realized with a deep sense of sadness, he now knew she was quite mad. Still, he recognized her madness, and for the first time he understood why the Divine Maker had sent her to his door. It was odd, but this bizarre, misguided creature was the answer to his prayer, the very redemption he had longed for but never expected. She was his chance to atone for Danny.

"Perhaps," he began, "if you gave me the facts I could help you ascertain the truth."

She stared at him, hard, but when he kept his face impassive she shrugged and launched into her story. "I was rather selfish in my first life—my *real* life." She sighed. "Actually, I was so selfish, I managed to kill myself and maybe my sister as well."

"I see," James said. But he did not see. Not at all.

She went on, "And now, I've come back, and I think I have to learn how to be selfless. I have to help people, and when I finally learn how to be selfless, I'll go to Heaven."

"As an angel?"

"I hope so."

"And if not?"

She looked down at her hands where they clenched the coverlet, and suddenly her veneer of good humor evaporated. A terribly frightened young woman was left behind. "I continue working at it until I earn the right."

James studied her bowed head, reading the tension in every line of Carolly's body. He wanted to comfort her, to soothe the torment of her unbalanced mind. But, he did not know how. He only knew that arguing had not helped before, with Danny.

But there was more time now. He would simply encourage her to talk. Eventually some truth would emerge, or he would think of a better approach. James settled back into his chair, feeling the unaccustomed hope for the future spark within him.

"Tell me," he began, "do you make a habit of telling everyone you are an angel?"

She smiled, briefly. "No. Actually, after the first time I stopped altogether. You're a rare exception."

He tilted his head in a slight bow. "I am honored. May I ask why you have favored me with such distinction?"

"Because I get the feeling you wouldn't be content with the usual I'm-just-passing-through bit."

He frowned, a little thrown by her language. "I do try to investigate unusual situations—especially when they occur on my lands."

"And I suppose I'm as unusual as they come," she quipped. James felt himself almost begin to smile at her humor, but then silence descended and Carolly evidently became uncomfortable with the quiet. "Help me out, James," she said. "I need some sort of reaction from you. Some way to know what you're thinking."

"Why?" He had not intended to speak, but once he did, he did not regret it. The trick was to keep her talking, to quietly guide her toward reality.

"Why?" she echoed, frowning. "Because I need to know how to proceed with helping you."

"Helping me find love?" James clarified. He tried not to wince at the statement. Danny, in his madness, had decided simply to bring peace to all of Spain. That had been an unreasonable goal, but this woman's focused intent on him and him alone, made James far more uncomfortable. But, he could not choose her delusions, so he supposed he would simply have to make do.

"No, James, I'll help you find your socks. Of course, how t—" She cut her sarcasm off mid-sentence. Her mouth snapped shut with an audible click. She took a deep breath. "I'm sorry. I shouldn't be yelling at you. I had just so hoped that my last assignment would be just that: my last. I tried so hard." She shrugged, but the movement seemed forced. "Oh, well. I guess I'll just have to learn to be more angelic, more holy." She quirked an eyebrow at him. "How am I doing?"

He paused, wondering what to say. He decided on honesty.

"I am afraid you do not, as yet, meet my notion of an angelic messenger."

She paled slightly and began chewing on her lower lip. "Okay . . . I mean, all right, what would convince you that I'm an angel?"

He leaned back in his chair and contemplated the ceiling. "Perhaps a heavenly choir. A miracle of some sort."

She shook her head. "Sorry. No can do. No choirs. No miracles. I'm just an ordinary Joe. Or rather Jane."

"I see," he said, wondering just how far this incredible conversation would go. "Then I have to take you on faith?"

She tilted her head, studying him with such lively intelligence that he found it hard to accept she believed her own fabrication. But then, Danny had appeared sane as well. "You sound like you don't much believe in it," she said. "You don't think miracles happen every day?"

He shrugged. "Let's just say I prefer the comfort of solid fact." He leaned forward in his chair, watching her expression closely. "What makes you think you are an angel—or rather a pre-angel? You do not possess wings, you cannot do miracles. What leads you to the conclusion that you are a heavenly creature?"

She didn't answer right away, and he knew she was searching for an answer.

"You need not be frightened, Carolly. I simply want to examine your conclusion. Perhaps, together, we can find a more logical one."

"You think I'm crazy." He did not respond, but from the expression on her face, Carolly clearly understood his thoughts. Finally she started speaking, her words reluctant but still clear. "I think I'm an angel—or rather a pre-angel—because I keep dying and appearing somewhere else."

James kept his eyes focused on her face. "I beg your pardon?"

"I was born in 1978 A.D., died in 2000, but I didn't go to Heaven. I was suddenly in 1902 in New York. I mucked about there for a while feeling really confused, eventually died of TB, then showed up in 1585, in England."

"Here?"

"Well, not in Staffordshire, but in England."

"And did you die then as well?"

She nodded, her face taking on a gray cast. "Yes." Apparently she did not wish to elaborate. She shrugged, as though pushing off unwanted thoughts. "Anyway, I've died four times." She frowned. "Or was this five?" She started counting silently on her fingers, only reaching the number three. "Maybe it's been less. I tend to forget . . ." Her voice trailed off.

"How extraordinary." There seemed to be no end to this woman's imagination, and James was hard put to decide whether to be impressed or appalled. "You are a pre-angel because you die, then appear again in another place and time," he repeated.

"It's that or I'm a ghost. Or someone with a really messed-up reincarnation schedule. Overall, I prefer thinking I'm trying to earn my wings."

"By helping people find love." He wanted to say it out loud just to make sure he had her twisted logic correct.

"That's my guess. Like I said, I really messed up my first life. I figure I have a lot of good deeds to do to make up for that. Why else would I be hopping through time, except to help the people I meet? I think of this as my job," she continued, blithely unaware of his thoughts. "That sort of takes away from the depressing being-dead part."

"Yes, that would be depressing."

She sighed, no doubt recognizing the cynicism in his voice. "You know, when I first decided I was here to help people, I imagined myself as this glorious figure hopping through time, setting everything to rights. I imagined songs written to me, a place in holy texts, followers hounding me left and right for a touch of my hand—that type of stuff."

James caught the strains of loneliness in her voice, and he

wondered if perhaps he'd already divined the root of her problem. Isolation tended to prey on a person's mind. "But people have not been following you around?" he asked. "You do not have a packet of devoted followers?"

She snorted. "Oh, yeah. I do. Most carrying stones.

She abruptly pushed herself out of bed and paced to the window. Fortunately for James, she brought the coverlet with her, wrapping it around her. She looked like a lonely Greek goddess staring forlornly out at his estate. "Those people are why you're the rare exception," she continued. "At the beginning I used to tell everyone, but now . . ." Her voice trailed into a sigh. "Nothing dies faster than innocence. Or in my case, naiveté. I've worked damn hard to help some of these people, and no one has ever appreciated it."

He stood up and crossed behind her, wanting to touch her but uncertain whether she would welcome the intrusion. "How did you get the bruises, Carolly?" he asked as gently as he could. "Did they throw those stones at you?"

She shrugged, the gesture rigid and painful despite her nonchalance. "Stones, torches, rotting fruit. What does it matter?"

"It matters to me." And he meant it.

She turned, her gaze rising to his. They were so close. James could smell the faint scent of meadow grass, fresh and clean, as it clung to her skin. He heard her gasp at his nearness, and he felt the heat of her body seep into his, invading his senses and clouding his judgment.

He stepped back.

"Wh—what did you say?" she whispered.

He cleared his throat, then decided to return to his seat. "The bruises. How did you get them?" He made his voice impersonal again.

"Oh." She looked down at her wrist, running her hand along a fading dark patch that had been vivid purple just that afternoon. He was surprised how quickly it had faded. "Uh, I wasn't stoned by your villagers or anyone around here," the woman said. "The stoning happened years ago." She released a short laugh. "Both literally and in my life." She looked up at James, chagrin twisting her face. "I know this doesn't make any sense. I don't know why I'm telling you."

He didn't know, either. "Perhaps you need someone to talk to, and a stranger is often better than a friend."

She looked at him again, her eyes bright spots of light even in shadow. "No, James. A friend is always better. Perhaps that's what *you* need to learn."

He felt suddenly vulnerable under her strange gaze, and went over and gripped his chair as he sought to regain control of the conversation. "Shall we talk more about you? What can you tell me about you?" He was fishing for information in the crudest manner possible, but he did not want to let her focus on him.

"I told you," she said in exasperation. "I just showed up in this time. Yesterday I was in 2035 ordering burgers and fries on a new touch panel at Mc—" She cut off her words abruptly, her eyes downcast in confusion. "McDon . . . I can't remember the name."

James felt completely thrown. He understood the words individually. At least most of them. But she hadn't mentioned any of this before, and altogether her words made no sense. Perhaps she was speaking a new dialect of Scottish? McDon was maybe a relative or a friend. She did not speak with an accent, though.

"Tell me about McDon," he tried.

"He's a clown with big red feet that panders to kids while secretly hardening their arteries."

"I beg your pardon?"

"Never mind." Carolly turned away, her eyes suddenly bleak. Then, to James's complete surprise, she climbed back into bed.

"Are you feeling ill?" he asked, concerned.

"No. Just discouraged. This angel business isn't all it's cracked up to be."

"No, I don't suppose it would be," he said.

He knew in his heart that words were not enough. He had seen Mrs. Potherby comfort girls on his staff. The woman was warm and motherly, putting her arms around the maids and plying them with biscuits and honey. For a moment, James had an irresistible urge to do just that to Carolly. He wanted to hold her in his arms and soothe away the confusion in her mind. But he dared not. The sexual attraction he felt for her was nearly overwhelming. He had no explanation for it, only knew that it existed and he could not give in.

"Shall we talk more about your supposed divinity?" he said instead.

She leaned forward on the covers, and her sudden grin took him by surprise. "I'd rather talk about your marital status. Are you married?"

James frowned. The woman's mood shifted with lightning speed. Yet James felt an excitement he had not experienced in years. He felt intoxicated with the challenge and found himself relaxing into his chair, crossing one booted foot over the other with casual disdain.

"No. I have not yet had that—"

"Dubious honor?" She was clearly mocking him.

He let his foot drop heavily to the floor. "Madame, if you are applying for the position, let me assure you that I have no intention . . ."

He ground to a halt as she laughed. The sound was as clear as before, but this time it held true tones of warmth and maybe the slightest touch of sadness. "Me? James, how delightful a proposal! Except, I don't do that. I can't do that if I want to earn my wings. No, I'm more interested in the local women. Anyone you have a particular fondness for?"

James rose stiffly to his feet. As much as he wanted to help this poor woman, he had to draw the line somewhere. That line stood black and bold, right in front of his personal life. "I believe you have had enough excitement for one evening, madame. If you need anything further, the staff can assist you. I bid you good-night."

He gave her another formal bow, for which he was again surrounded by her sweet laughter. "All right, James," she said when she finally regained control of herself. "I suppose I've harassed you enough for one night. But, believe me,"—she shook her head—"in all my lives, I've never met a man who needed a good woman more than you do."

Her laughter followed him through the door as he departed, its echo haunting him even as he sauntered to the library and his nightly brandy. It was only later, as he opened his favorite volume of Horace, that he realized he was grinning.

Chapter Three

Carolly woke to a beautiful morning and a body well on its way back to complete health. Not that she would be able to convince anyone else of that. People saw and believed what they wanted, no matter the facts. She'd figured that out during her first reincarnation.

She folded her hands over her stomach and began her morning recitations: "Carolly . . . Carolly H . . . Carolly Ha . . ." She sighed and decided to skip that part. "Born 1978. Died 2000. Sister named Janice. I died in a car crash that was my own stupid fault. I was selfish and arrogant. Next came 1902, New York. Everyone thought I was a sickly Karen somebody . . ."

She went on, carefully cataloguing everything she could recall about her different lives. She did it in the mornings when she was most likely to remember. It was her way of recollecting who and what she was—and most especially, why she was here: to help people, to be selfless and good and to atone for her sins. When she had done enough, she would become an angel and this whole nightmare would be over. She hoped.

Twisting her head, she looked out the window. It was a little after dawn and she was already awake—something unheard of in her original life. Still, it felt good to greet the new day, and she scrambled out of bed to throw open the window.

James was up, too. She saw him below, standing in the stable yard next to a magnificent jet stallion who snorted in the slightly chilled air. He looked resplendent in dark riding clothes, and he faced a smaller person while a groomsman held his horse.

Carolly narrowed her eyes, trying to distinguish his companion. It was a child—a red-faced girl in a light brown dress. She was probably the child of some servant. Carolly thought the girl was speaking to James, but perhaps she was mistaken because James walked away without even a nod. He swung onto his stallion and rode away, chasing the dawn.

Carolly followed the magnificent sight with her eyes, watching hungrily as man and beast thundered across the open fields. She longed to go with them. She'd taken some riding lessons as a child, and though not a great horsewoman, she wouldn't disgrace herself. Then her eyes drifted back to the stable, and Carolly saw the little girl kick unhappily at the dirt and slink away. Poor kid. Like Carolly, she'd probably wanted to go riding.

Well, they couldn't. Carolly had promised to stay in bed another day, and the kid apparently wasn't of a status to enjoy the privileges of James's estate. Heck, he hadn't even answered her request, if Carolly interpreted correctly what had happened. Poor kid, she thought again.

With a dispirited sigh, Carolly pretended she was James, mentally riding with him, feeling his magnificent stallion beneath her, the wind streaming through her hair, the sun bright and warm on her face. What a glorious morning! A wonderful day to be alive!

Her fantasy ended abruptly. She wasn't outside; she wasn't having a great morning ride, and she most certainly wasn't alive. Taking herself to task, she turned toward the bed, but couldn't stomach getting back under the sheets. At last she dragged the chair to the window and perched there, wrapping one of the bedcovers around herself for warmth. Then she stared out the window like a caged bird.

James found her there two hours later, still staring.

"Good morning, Miss Carolly."

"Morning, James." She turned her back on the delightful day to greet the more tempting sight of a man in tight-fitting trousers. "You have a beautiful horse. And the way the two of you ride . . ." She stopped, searching for a way to express her thoughts. "It's like you're one creature, like you read each other's thoughts."

"Shadow and I have been together a long time," he explained.

"I can tell. I watched you all morning."

"I know." He sounded annoyed. "I felt you. Even after I topped the rise, I could feel your thoughts following me, like a falcon giving chase."

Carolly felt her eyebrows shoot up in surprise. "Why, James, you have the heart of a poet!"

"I do not."

Carolly blinked.

"Is this one of your 'angel talents'?" he asked finally. "Following me wherever I go?"

His question was serious, and Carolly didn't know how to answer. Finally, she just shrugged. "I don't know. Perhaps you're especially sensitive to the divine."

He snorted and turned to leave, but Carolly scrambled off her chair and across the room. "Don't go. Not yet. I'm bored to tears, and we have so much more to discuss."

"Discuss?" He held himself stiff. "I was unaware we had anything to discuss."

"Oh, but we do. I've told you why I'm here. We've got to talk about the best way to find you love. It doesn't have to be a woman, you know—although I'm a great believer in that." He made a strangled sound in his throat, and she rushed on before he regained power of speech. "It could be a dog for all I care. Just a little crack, a tiny opening in your heart. That's all we need."

"A dog! You wish me to love a dog?"

She giggled. "Not that way! My word, for a stuffed shirt, you certainly have a perverse turn of mind."

"I beg your pardon!" His jaw nearly dropped to his chest.

"Oh, don't get so huffy. I'm only teasing. I know you didn't mean it that way. What I'm saying is, a little shift in your heart will open the whole world for you."

If possible, James drew himself up even taller. He spoke softly. "I will say this once, madame, and I expect you to listen. I do not need you to find me a woman, or a dog, or anyone. I am an earl with everything I need. Your interest in my personal life is not only unnecessary, it is entirely and unequivocally unwanted!"

He clearly expected her to bow her head and mumble some sort of apology, but, true to her perverse nature, she couldn't resist provoking him a little further. Carolly dropped onto her bed, crossed her legs beneath the coverlet, and smiled up happily at him. "They *always* say that, you know. Without fail, every soul I've tried to help has always said it's none of my business."

He rubbed a hand over his forehead. "Perhaps you should listen."

"But then who would teach you to love?" she asked. She stretched out her legs until her bare toes showed. "Look, it's probably my task to get you to love someone. After you experience love—and real love, not just sex—then I'm outta here. So, if you want to get rid of me, you'll have to help me do my job."

"Your job?" he asked.

"Yes." She looked up at him, her expression slowly changing to uncertainty. "Well, that's my best bet. You look like you need it. Please, James, let me help you learn how to love, then

I swear I won't bother you ever again. With any luck, I'll be in Heaven learning how to play the harp," she added happily.

He sighed. "Learn to love? Very well, Carolly, you may get dressed and be on your way, because I have a young niece that I love very much."

She'd been fussing with her nightgown, but she stopped dead at his words. "A niece? A little girl? You have a little girl?" Her mind flashed to the little girl by the stable, but she quickly dismissed the thought. Even if James were cold enough to treat his niece so abysmally, she couldn't believe he would dress her so shabbily.

"One would think an angel," he said quietly, "would be better informed."

"Don't I wish," Carolly muttered.

James stepped forward suddenly, dropping to one knee before her, and Carolly was startled by the earnestness in his blue-gray eyes. "Listen, Carolly, what if you are actually a normal human? What if you are lonely and confused, and you wish to feel special?" She shivered at his words and tried to draw away, but he wouldn't let her. He rose, put his hands on her shoulders and held her still, forcing her to listen. "Maybe you wish to feel special, so you pretend to be divine."

"And dead? Would I want to feel dead, too?"

He shook his head, dismissing her question. "Try to think logically."

She pushed him away. Wrapping herself in the coverlet, she turned her back on him. "You think *too* logically, James. Sometimes you've got to look in your heart." That was where she'd found all of her own answers. Or most of them.

His response was cold. "The heart is a remarkably contradictory organ. I find life only makes sense when you use your head."

She rounded on him. "You're wrong, James. Now I'm sure you have to find love." She grinned up at him. "And I won't leave until you find some way to open your heart."

He regained his feet, brushing nonexistent lint off his trousers. "Then perhaps you should meet my niece and be on your way."

"Very well," she said with a sigh. It was a place to start. "Let's go see your niece."

James walked to the door. Turning, he said, "If you're going to stay, I took the liberty of acquiring you some new clothing. I believe it arrived this morning. I shall send Mrs. Potherby to assist you in dressing."

"Thank you," Carolly responded. Looking down, she was reminded of how inappropriately she was garbed, and she was genuinely warmed by his unexpected thoughtfulness. "That was quite nice of you."

"Nothing of the kind, Miss Carolly. As you seem insistent upon walking about my house, it is my obligation to see you appropriately attired."

She stared at him, suddenly overcome by the ridiculousness of it all. Here she was, a dead woman who thought she was an angel, she was going to meet his niece and show him how to love, and he was worried about keeping her appropriately attired.

Chapter Four

"You want me to wear that?" Carolly eyed the corset with distaste. A long tank top with bone slats, it seemed perfectly designed to torture the female body. "I'll never be able to sit!"

"You will sit like a lady," came Mrs. Potherby's firm response.

Carolly shook her head. "I'm not a lady, Mrs. Potherby. Never have been, never will be. Look, can't I just stand up tall and pretend? Without actually having..." Her voice trailed off. She could see by the older woman's face that she was getting nowhere. If she wanted to leave her room and meet James's niece, she'd have to wear the instrument of torture. "Oh, all right. Show me how to put it on."

She was wrong about it being uncomfortable—excruciatingly annoying described it better. Carolly felt like she'd just put on a tight barrel. Her breasts pushed up almost to her chin and as for breathing, her only choice was a delicate pant. On the up side, panties apparently hadn't yet been invented. She felt deliciously naughty walking around without them.

Carolly grimaced as Mrs. Potherby tied her tights, just under her knees. She would have done it herself, but she hadn't figured out how to bend. She'd never thought she'd miss elastic, but here she was, wondering how on earth she would keep her stockings tied, especially when she couldn't reach them.

"All right," she said with a groan. "What's next?" Carolly had hoped they were done with the underclothing. No such luck. Mrs. Potherby brought out a dove-gray petticoat.

"It's a beautiful day," Carolly began. "A *hot* day. Surely I don't need—"

"Please raise your arms."

So much for avoiding the petticoat.

"It's like the layered look, only in reverse, right?"

Mrs. Potherby didn't answer. Instead, she dropped the rough fabric over Carolly's head.

"Ugh! It's stiff." Some sort of paste had been applied to the skirt to keep it full. "I'm going to have to practice walking so I won't knock over tables or beat some poor dog senseless."

"I am sure you will remember soon enough."

Carolly lifted her head, fixing Mrs. Potherby with a pointed stare. "How can I remember something I've never done?"

The older woman refused to answer. She turned away and shook out a light gray dress with a high neckline and a lace collar. Carolly stopped the woman, taking her arm and not letting go until the housekeeper looked directly at her, but the woman said simply, "His lordship is waiting. Come. I still have to fix your hair."

She buttoned Carolly into the gray gown, tied her into the flimsiest slippers Carolly had ever seen, then pushed her onto a stool and began brushing out her hair with a vengeance.

"Ow! Go easy, will you?" Carolly gasped.

"Hush. Hand me that ribbon."

Carolly did as she was bid, wincing.

"It is beyond me," commented Mrs. Potherby, "why a woman with such beautiful hair would want to have it cropped almost to her ears."

"*I* like it short. It's easier to ignore that way." But even as she spoke, Carolly watched the mirror in fascination. The housekeeper tied the ribbon deftly, neatly pulling the hair up and away from Carolly's face.

"Add a few more inches and think of what we could do with it," coaxed Mrs. Potherby.

Carolly shook her head. "Short and sassy. That's me."

"Aye," agreed Mrs. Potherby sadly.

Carolly frowned. "Why do you say it like that?"

The older woman shook her head, then abruptly pushed Carolly off the stool. "His lordship awaits."

Carolly dug in her heels. "Let him wait. I want to know what you mean."

Mrs. Potherby only shook her head. "You are arrogant through and through, Miss Carolly. But you must remember, you reside in an earl's house, are here by his leave. He could toss you out this afternoon if he had a mind. Then where would you go?"

"I . . ." Carolly shut her mouth. She'd wanted to laugh and say she would find a way. But she had spent her first life doing just that: shrugging off others' concerns, allowing problems to get worse because she was too lazy to change. Now she was working toward becoming an angel. She had to be good and responsible.

Which meant heeding Mrs. Potherby's advice. Carolly *was* here on James's good will. It would be best to remember that.

"I'm sorry, Mrs. Potherby. I'll try to act better."

Her resolve lasted for exactly two and a half minutes.

James stood in the door to the nursery and bristled.

Carolly had groaned. Actually groaned. He'd heard it quite distinctly.

He glanced around the pristine room. Everything appeared in order, every toy in its allotted place. Margaret sat at her desk holding open a book of edifying sermons for girls. But she was not looking at that; she was staring at him, her blue-green eyes open wide with surprise, her chin lifted in quiet defiance. To her right, the governess Miss Hornswallow, a beanpole in austere black, rose from behind her desk with regal formality.

"My lord, you did not inform me you intended to visit the nursery this morning." There was only the slightest hint of censure in her voice.

Then he heard it again: another of Carolly's groans. Or maybe it was one of those sighs that seemed to start from her toes, gathering momentum as it traveled through her system in search of escape. Whatever it was, it annoyed him greatly.

"Is there something wrong, Miss Carolly?"

"Hmmm? No, of course not. Whatever could be wrong?" Her tone clearly indicated the opposite.

James's eyes returned to his niece, and finally he divined the source of Carolly's dismay. Margaret had on one of her most shapeless brown dresses, the same one she had been wearing this morning when he refused to allow her to join him during his morning exercise. He had not been averse to sharing the ride with her, but her attire had been completely inappropriate. The light fabric she wore would not protect her from scrapes and bruises as her riding habit would. And now, looking at his sullen ward, he realized her dress was not only completely inappropriate for riding, it made her look like a formless lump.

His frown deepened as he tried to recall Miss Hornswallow's exact reason for dressing his ward in such ugly attire. She'd said something about neutral colors quieting a distressed child's mind. James had become so used to seeing Margaret in such clothing, he had initially missed how it must look to an outsider. "Miss Hornswallow, have you been allowing Margaret to eat sweets again? I distinctly told you she seems to be gaining."

The governess opened her mouth to respond, but she never got the chance. Carolly spun on her heel and began screeching: "James, what a cruel thing to say! And you said you love her!"

"But—"

"No, I don't want to hear it. I just don't! You men are impossible—hear me, impossible—when it comes to even the basics of raising a girl."

"*Carolly*." This time he infused his voice with all the annoyance he felt. That always controlled even the most unruly of his subordinates. It had worked marvels on the soldiers in Spain. As for his domestic staff, the tone had once reduced his impeccable butler to near blubbering idiocy.

But it seemed to have absolutely no effect on Carolly. Or rather, it appeared to have the opposite effect of the one he intended. Instead of bringing the woman into an acute awareness of her failings, it pushed her to further excesses of emotionalism.

"Don't try to freeze me out, James. It won't work. Not this time." She made a sweeping gesture at the nursery. "This is even worse than I feared! What could you be thinking, James, raising a little girl like this for the last four years?"

"I was caring for my ward—"

"You were *ignoring* her. Oh!" She cut herself off, whirling back to face the room like a soldier preparing for battle. As she spun, her soft gray skirts twisted and flared around her ankles in a most distracting display, but her aggrieved tone did not allow James the luxury of appreciating it. "I thought she was a servant, James. I saw you both this morning and I thought she was some servant's child. That's how you treat her."

James felt his words freeze in his throat. Was it possible? Could Carolly truly have thought his niece a servant?

Meanwhile, Carolly continued, her hands waving about in agitation. "What could you have been thinking? You can't throw her in a dull room with ugly clothing and hope no one will notice. *I* notice. *She* notices. James, think!" And when he did not immediately respond, she once again threw up her hands in disgust. "Oh, just leave me alone while I talk with her. And take Miss Hornwigging—Hornsweeney—"

"Hornswallow," corrected the governess in a cold tone of her own.

"Whatever. Take her with you."

James shook his head. "Carolly, if you wish to be alone, I suggest you return to your room."

She twisted around, once again presenting him with a magnificent view of her flushed face and heaving bosom. Initially he'd thought the dove-gray dress too drab for her, but now he saw she infused whatever was around her, whatever she wore, with vibrancy. Though the hastily-obtained gown's color was almost grim, its fabric clung to Carolly's curves with anything but modesty. He could not think for watching the lace around her breasts rise and fall with her agitated breathing.

"I will not be bullied, James. It's my job to rescue this situation, and I take that very seriously."

"Carolly," he repeated. He made his voice a near whisper. "You are overwrought. I suggest you return to your room. Now."

She stared at him, her mouth falling open in surprise. He could tell by the shock on her face that no one had ever refused her when she spoke so forcefully. In fact, she looked so completely thrown, he gave a small smile of pure masculine satisfaction.

It was a mistake.

Within seconds of his self-congratulation, her expression changed. He saw the look. He had seen it before in the few men he openly admired. An unshakable determination, a certain steel of the soul.

His smile faded.

Carolly snapped her mouth shut and lifted her chin. "My room? An excellent idea, James." She turned and smiled sweetly at the young girl. "Margaret, I am Carolly. Will you please come with me? I would like very much to talk with you for a few moments, and I believe his lordship is correct. We will be much more comfortable in my bedroom." She released a soft snort. "Lord knows, my prison can't be much worse than yours."

Margaret stared at her, clearly torn between admiration and fear. James could readily sympathize. He often felt that way himself around Carolly. But true to the girl's innate good sense, she turned to her uncle seeking his opinion.

He deliberated. Given Margaret's mood lately, she was likely to rush headlong into outright disobedience if he told her to stay put. Then again, the last thing his recalcitrant ward needed was the added influence of his unstable guest.

James was still contemplating his response when Miss Hornswallow stepped forward. "My lord, truly I must insist. I cannot have Margaret's day disrupted. As you yourself have told me, structure and schedule are exceedingly important in the rearing of young children."

Carolly did it again. She groaned, only this time she did nothing to disguise the sound. "By all means, James, stifle the poor girl. At least if you break her spirit, you won't have to worry about her acting out."

James felt his fury grow. So, while he still had some control of himself, he made a final stab at resolving the situation. "Miss Carolly, I find your meddling impertinent and exceedingly—"

"Yes, yes. We've already established that I'm impertinent, totally insane, and let's not forget immodest." Behind her desk, Miss Hornswallow gasped, but Carolly only rolled her eyes. "Henceforth we can add stubborn, intemperate, and . . ." She waved her arms, searching for another adjective. "And . . ."

"And you are an inappropriate role model for Margaret."

Carolly snorted. "That has yet to be seen. One would think my, uh, chosen profession would make me . . ." She fell silent at his raised eyebrow. "All right, we'll leave a discussion of my profession for another day."

"Yes, do. Or perhaps we should continue our discussion in the library and leave Margaret to her lessons."

He opened the nursery door, clearly indicating it was time to leave. Out of the corner of his eye, he saw Margaret sink an inch lower in her seat. Miss Hornswallow sniffed in victory as she too settled back into her chair. Everyone, it seemed, had come to the conclusion that he was the victor.

Everyone, that is, except Carolly.

Carolly folded her arms across her chest and stared at him, her expression almost pleading. "Look, James. Really look. Does your niece look happy? Does she ever seem happy?"

James felt his shoulders tense. Indeed, no, he thought. He had been aware for some time that his niece seemed out of sorts. But for the life of him, he could not understand why. Was it possible that his mad guest somehow knew—had determined in the space of a few seconds, no less—what was missing in his ward's life? Something he and a score of governesses had not discovered in months and years of concerted effort?

The thought set him back on his heels. Yet he could not discount the possibility. After all, madness had its own logic. Perhaps the answer to Margaret's difficulties merely required a new perspective. Carolly's thoughts certainly were . . . unusual.

As if sensing his indecision, Carolly stepped forward. Her tone became soft and pleading. "James . . ." she began, but he glared at her, effectively telling her that feminine wiles would get her nowhere. She sighed and turned away from him, apparently deep in thought.

Relaxing against the doorway, James found himself admiring the delicate curve of her neck, smiling at the childish way she chewed on her lower lip, even feeling mesmerized by the simple play of her fingers in her hair. He found himself pleased. Her temerity inspired him. He had forgotten the sheer joy of a real hell-for-leather argument. The only other person to fight him like this had been his older brother. They had done it with the daily frequency possible only for siblings, and had driven their nanny close to distraction. That had been half the fun. Glancing over at the outraged face of Miss Hornswallow, James could not help but feel a similar childish glee.

Carolly's soft voice interrupted his reminisces, bringing him abruptly back to earth. She'd moved nearer to him. "This is fun," she said in a low tone, startling him. Could she read his mind? "I love challenging you, trying to make you think." She gave him a glance filled with wonder. "I like arguing with you. But you know, James, there are so many less important things we could fight about. I'd rather not do it over Margaret."

James stared at her. Would she ever cease to surprise him? "I agree," he said slowly. "I suggest we remove to the library and leave Margaret to her lessons."

Carolly sighed and shook her head. "I'm determined to talk to her." She shifted to look directly at him. "It's important."

"Why?" he asked. His voice was harsher, more abrupt than he intended. "So you can disrupt her routine, upset her delicate emotions, and generally throw her life into chaos?"

"No. That's what I'll do for you." Carolly said, her light blue eyes shimmering with . . . glee? "Yes," she continued. "I can see I already do. I disorient you. I challenge your neatly ordered world." She lifted her chin with clear pleasure. "Good. Maybe there's hope for you after all." Turning back to Margaret, Carolly suggested, "I know! Why don't you stay with us, James? Be with me when I talk to her. See how harmless I can be." She slanted a sideways look at him. It was filled with devilry and mischief, but despite all his mental warnings, James found himself warming to the excitement her eyes promised him. "I truly am trying to help," she added.

He was going to give in. He felt it in his bones. She had a way of setting his blood on fire that he found absolutely irresistible.

Yet something held him back.

Margaret. She was still very young. He was a man. He could walk with his eyes open into the disaster Carolly would no doubt visit on his head and have no one to blame but himself. But Margaret was a child. He would be remiss in his duties if he allowed her to be influenced by such a strange woman. And letting Carolly talk to the girl would just be the beginning. It was a slippery slope.

Reluctantly, he hardened his heart and shook his head. "I cannot allow Margaret's life to be disrupted."

Carolly snorted. "I'd say Margaret's life could use a good disruption. Oh James, look around. Can't you see how stifling this room is?"

James let his gaze wander around the room. The walls were a pristine white; the hard wood furniture, though sparse, appeared more than sufficient for Margaret's needs. The only other objects in the room were three books of sermons stacked neatly in front of Mrs. Hornswallow. The fourth lay open in front of Margaret.

Things did seem a *bit* dull.

"I see nothing wrong with this room," he lied. He didn't want to promise too much too quickly, especially since Margaret was prone to flights of fancy. The last thing he wished to do was promise the child something vague only to see her disappointed. He smiled at niece. "Though perhaps we can get you a few new books." And maybe he'd even paint the room a different color.

Carolly sighed. "Books aren't going to cut it. She needs excitement. Playfulness. A childhood in her childhood." As James was trying to puzzle out those words, she grinned at Margaret. "Well, since we can't meet now, how about a midnight rendezvous? I'll climb along the wall tonight to meet you. Sound like fun? Then we'll talk boys or clothes or whatever you want. Truly. I promise."

James gave in. He told himself his capitulation had nothing to do with the image of Carolly's small body flattened against the manor as she tried to inch her way to Margaret's window. He ignored the imagined sight of her broken body lying on the ground after she inevitably fell to her death.

No, he was thinking only of Margaret.

"Very well," he groaned. "Margaret, you may come with us to the library." He ignored Miss Hornswallow's gasp of outrage. Rounding on Carolly he added, "But you will not—I repeat, *not*—walk along the wall. Tonight or ever! Is that clear?" His voice brooked no disobedience.

Carolly responded with a laugh: that joyful cascade of notes which never failed to stir his soul. "Relax, James. Don't you remember my . . . chosen profession? I couldn't possibly be hurt unless it was time for me to leave anyway."

Moments later, the three of them marched quietly into James's library. James led the little procession, then immediately crossed to his desk and sat behind it like a judge. Carolly shook her head at him, then left him alone behind his barricade.

Margaret followed, a precise three steps behind her uncle. Despite her obvious resentment toward her guardian, she had apparently learned her place in his household quite well. She stood at attention in front of his desk, looking very much like a prisoner about to be sentenced.

Carolly bit her lower lip as she stood to one side and tried to think. The problem wasn't that James didn't love his niece; it was that he had no clue how to translate that warmth into real life. He obviously hadn't had any guidance on how to love, so he merely repeated the patterns of his own childhood—which had apparently been bleak.

Carolly spared a moment's grief for the child James must have been. It broke her heart to imagine him so alone, even while she recognized it was probably that very adversity that had molded him into the commanding figure she saw today.

But now she had her chance to shine. Now was her opportunity to show him just how to handle a young girl. She sauntered around the library, conspicuously letting her gaze travel over the sumptuous ceiling and walls. "Beautiful," she breathed. "Absolutely beautiful."

Whatever poetry James possessed, he'd clearly lavished on this room. It was quite large, easily holding eight huge mahogany bookcases with openwork silver panels, each filled almost to collapse. Interspersed between each case were huge windows that let in the sweet spring breeze and illuminated the thick mattresslike carpet. Most amazing of all was the painted ceiling.

Drawn in bold lines above their heads was an exquisite painting of Prometheus descending from Mt. Olympus with the gods' fire. Everywhere Carolly looked in the scene, she saw something new and amazing—whether the shock on the face of the gods, or the awe of the primitive humans. It was incredible, and Carolly knew she could spend hours staring at the painting and still see something new in it the next day.

Compared to this room, the nursery was a dungeon.

"Tell me, Margaret. How do you think your uncle would feel if you two traded rooms for a week or so?"

Margaret, smart girl that she was, didn't answer. But the comment hadn't really been directed at her. It had been aimed at James, and from the sudden frown on the earl's face, Carolly knew she'd made her point.

Now all she had to do was establish a rapport with Margaret. She decided to start with seating arrangements. She settled onto a velvet couch angled just enough away from James's huge desk that she and Margaret could have the illusion of privacy without actually excluding the earl. After all, he was the one who'd sat behind his desk. Let him come out from behind his fortress if he wanted to talk.

Patting the seat beside her, Carolly smiled at Margaret. "Come and sit here, dear. There's no reason for you to stand at attention. Your uncle will let me run this particular show." She directed a pointed glance at James, praying he wouldn't contradict her.

The seconds ticked by as both Margaret and Carolly held their breath, waiting for James's verdict. Finally he nodded, and the girl hesitantly joined Carolly on the couch. Immeasurably relieved, Carolly took a deep breath and decided to plunge right in. "First off, Margaret, please allow me to apologize."

She saw the little girl's shock. She couldn't quite see James's face, but she guessed he wore a similar expression of astonishment.

"You seem surprised, dear," Carolly continued. "Is that because no one has ever apologized to you before? Well, rest assured, when I make a mistake, I try to apologize immediately."

"Do—do not regard it, madame." Margaret's voice was high and uncertain, and Carolly could already see that, just like a wall, just like her uncle, Margaret had a great deal of reserve. It would take nothing short of a full-blown force of nature to break through.

Fortunately, Carolly thought with a smile, she was up to the task. Or so she hoped.

"Thank you, Margaret. But you have not yet heard what I'm apologizing for. For all you know, I could be confessing to murdering your parents."

Margaret gasped, and James shifted angrily in his seat. Carolly suddenly understood the magnitude of her blunder. She'd forgotten the girl's parents were dead. Margaret was an orphan.

"Oh, no! I'm so sorry, Margaret. That was completely tactless of me. I didn't . . . I wouldn't . . ." She grimaced as she accidentally bit down hard on her lip. "I'm not very good at talking to children, you know. Adults simply ignore me, but children—well, they often take what I say too seriously or not seriously enough." She paused a moment. "Well, that's pretty much the way the whole world treats me, so I guess children aren't very different, are they?"

Margaret looked completely at a loss, so Carolly simply continued babbling, silently praying God would put the right words in her mouth.

"Let me try again. I wanted to apologize for that scene in

the nursery. I fought with your uncle over you without asking what you wanted. I practically ordered you downstairs, and that wasn't very nice of me. I'm sorry."

Carolly waited for a response, but the girl simply pressed her lips together. Glancing at James, Carolly was struck by the resemblance between the two. Physically, of course, they were almost complete opposites. James was powerful, handsome, and very male. Margaret was young, a shrinking violet, and too aware of her place. And yet both had wills of steel.

Well, it was time to make Margaret feel important.

"From now on, Margaret, there will be new rules. They are very simple, really. First, if you don't want to be with me, you may leave. But," Carolly hastily added, "I hope you will stay."

For one heart-stopping moment, Carolly thought the girl would get up and leave just to be difficult. Fortunately, Margaret's only other alternative was probably the nursery.

"Good," Carolly said, once it became clear Margaret was staying. "Second, you are free to say anything you like, ask anything you like." She leaned over and lowered her voice. "You can even swear if you want to, and it won't bother me."

"It will bother *me*," James said, his rich voice descending on them like a pronouncement from the Greek gods overhead.

Carolly turned with a grin. "Then you needn't join us."

"Carolly—"

She turned back to Margaret, ignoring him. "And third, we may do anything you like when we're together." She caught James's angry glare and decided to amend her statement. "Within reason, of course. It can't be dangerous or take us too far away from your uncle's lands." James continued to glower, but Carolly ignored him. She would deal with him later. "So," she said brightly to Margaret. "How does that sound to you?"

"It is fine, madame," came Margaret's cool response.

Carolly squelched her disappointment. Obviously, given the girl's expression, Margaret didn't believe a word of it.

Well, thought Carolly with renewed determination, she would just have to prove she spoke the truth. "All right, Margaret. Now that we've established the ground rules, we should go on to introductions. My name's Carolly, but you can call me Caro." She felt James's disapproval, and squared her shoulders in defiance. "Now, shall I call you Margaret? Maggie? Peggy? What?"

In her first show of collusion Margaret turned to her uncle and spoke, her words as much a challenge to him as if she'd thrown down a gauntlet. "You may call me Mags."

Carolly felt her eyebrows rise at the odd nickname, but her surprise was nothing compared to James's reaction. His face became a thundercloud, and he boomed, "Your name is Margaret Amanda Northram—"

"But I shall call her Mags," Carolly interjected.

"Carolly," he thundered, "you do not understand—"

"I don't need to understand, James. She wants to be called Mags."

"But that was her mother's name!"

"Oh." Carolly understood. She smiled sadly at Mar—no, Mags. "My mother's name was—" She closed her eyes. What was her mother's name? Oh, yes. "—Gloria, but my father used to call her Gold." She looked at the still-defiant girl. "You can call me Gold, if you like. Or Caro."

She didn't get the reaction she anticipated. She'd hoped to win a smile from Margaret, or at least a slight softening in the girl's demeanor. Instead she got a sneer of derision. "What a stupid name."

"Margaret! You will apologize immediately," barked her uncle, startling them both. But before Margaret could respond, Carolly rounded on him.

"Really, James. Can't you stop being domineering for five minutes and let me talk with the girl like a civilized person?"

"I will not allow her to insult a guest in my house!"

"I wasn't insulted. And even if I was, James, I'm perfectly capable of standing up for myself. If Margaret insults me, I'll tell her so. And if she keeps insulting me, then I won't be her friend."

James's eyes bored into her. They glittered like coal in the sunlight, and Carolly quailed under the force of his anger. She swallowed nervously, knowing James didn't like being contradicted, especially not in front of his ward. But it was too late now. She couldn't back down. And kindness, she was sure, was the way to the little girl's heart.

She lowered her voice, but didn't soften her tone. "I'm sorry I snapped at you, James, but I truly would like to get to know your niece. And I can't do that if you keep yelling at her. Even if she does something unkind. Now, do you think you can stay out of this for five minutes? Or should I find some other time to speak with her?" Her threat was clear. She would do whatever it took, including sneaking around the outside of the building at night, if it meant she could talk to Margaret unhindered.

James glowered. His eyes narrowed, his jaw clenched, and Carolly waited, expecting him to lash out angrily. But he didn't. To her immense relief, he glanced at Margaret then settled back in his chair.

Carolly exhaled, slowly releasing her pent-up fear. She wasn't fooled into thinking he'd given up. They both knew he was merely biding his time until they could speak in private. But in the meantime he was letting her proceed.

With a shaky smile, she turned back to Margaret. "Now, Mags, is there anything you'd like to do or ask?"

The girl thought for a moment, her blue-green eyes narrowed. Carolly held her breath, her stomach knotting tighter as the seconds ticked by. The girl was clearly trying to think of the most outrageous thing she could, something she hoped would unsettle the adults.

Carolly was determined to remain sanguine no matter what.

"Are you an angel or a tart?" the girl finally asked.

Carolly nearly choked. James exploded out of his chair. "Margaret—"

"Five minutes, James. Can't you be silent for five minutes?" Carolly asked.

He rounded on her. "Madame—"

"Your niece's question is reasonable, and you've no doubt been wrestling with it."

"Hardly," he responded in dry tones.

"Uncle thinks you are an escaped Bedlamite. He has already sent inquiries."

"Really?" Carolly responded, raising an eyebrow. James suddenly became sphinx-like. He settled into his chair, his features carefully blanked of all expression.

"Oh, yes," continued Margaret, clearly imparting as much outrageous gossip as possible. "Henry, the footman, overheard you telling Uncle you were an angel, but Miss Hornswallow says you are just a cheap tart. Cook thinks you are a tart, too. One who has been beaten many times about the head."

"Oh, my!" Carolly was stunned. Obviously Margaret knew all the household gossip. But what was even more fascinating was how the girl became much more lively, much less of a stifled lump, as she spoke. Her eyes sparkled in quite a lovely fashion, plus she began to bob up and down on the couch as she spoke, shifting her shoulders left and right even though she was still too repressed to move her hands.

"Don't stop," urged Carolly. "What else do they say?"

"Well, the footmen just talk about . . . about your legs." Margaret grimaced.

"Men can be so singled-minded at times." Carolly didn't dare look at James. He was probably on the verge of a stroke.

"And the stablehands all want to meet you."

"They're probably hoping I'm a tart."

Margaret appeared to consider this, then nodded. "Probably," she said sagely.

There came a choking sound from James.

"What about you, Mags? What do you think?" Carolly asked.

The young girl silently considered, tilting her head as she inspected Carolly from head to toe. It was hard sitting still for such a thorough examination, but Carolly did her best, all the while trying to remember what genteel nineteenth-century women looked like.

"I think," began Margaret, "that I agree with Mrs. Potherby."

"The housekeeper?"

Margaret nodded. "She thinks you are just a lonely lady who is pretending to be an angel so you can poke your nose into other people's business."

"Oh." What could she say to that? She could tell that the little girl felt sorry for her, that deep down Margaret didn't want her to be lonely.

"So which are you?" the little girl pressed. "An angel or a tart?"

James pushed away from his desk. "I think we have had enough of this for now."

Carolly sighed, sensing James had reached his limit. The man obviously didn't want her confessing to being a pre-angel to his impressionable niece. But she planned to do it. Children tended to be much more accepting of miracles than adults. She couldn't do it now, though. James would only confound her explanation and muddle the whole thing up.

She reached out and touched Margaret's hand. "I'll answer your question, Mags. But not right now." She glanced significantly at James. "Don't worry," she said, looking back to the child and investing her voice with the strength of a vow, "I won't fail you."

Then she smiled, deciding to arrange another visit while James was still tolerant. "So when shall we meet next? Perhaps tomorrow afternoon? We can do anything you like." She folded her hands in her lap, imagining a long giggling chat about boys and clothing. It was one of the things she missed most now that she was dead—curling up with her sister and talking ad infinitum about the male gender.

Margaret hesitated, glancing nervously at her uncle. "I can really pick whatever I want?"

Carolly grinned, already envisioning wonderful times. "Absolutely."

"Providing it is not too dangerous," declared James.

Carolly made a face at him, then turned back to Margaret with an encouraging smile. "Come on, Mags. What is it you want to do?"

Clearly screwing up her courage, the young girl took a deep breath. "Insects."

"What?"

"I want to go collecting insects."

Carolly felt as if she'd been kicked right in the stomach. "You're kidding, right? Don't you want to talk about boys and dresses and make-up?"

Margaret shook her head, her eyes shining. "No. I want to collect insects and put them on pins in a box, like I saw at Baron Lansford's estate."

"Bugs," Carolly repeated. "You want to go collecting bugs?"

Margaret lifted her chin, clearly daring Carolly to prove she was just as unreliable as every other grown up. "You said I could pick whatever I wished," she accused.

Carolly sighed. "Yes, I did. And if bug hunting is what you truly want, then I suppose that's what we'll do." She paused, glancing hopefully at the girl. "You're just teasing me, though, aren't you? Wouldn't you much rather sit and sip cocoa by a fire and talk about . . ." She waved her arms. Her favorite topics had always been rock stars or movie idols. What was the equivalent of a television hero in the 1800s? She couldn't think of anything.

"I want to collect insects."

Carolly felt her last fantasy of girl-talk die. "All right, Mags. Bugs it is."

James released the first true laugh she'd heard from him. She couldn't help but glare.

"So, will you do it?"

"What?" Carolly looked up from where she sat, staring into

the cold library grate. James had just sent his niece back to the nursery, then returned to the library to finish grilling her. He closed the door behind him.

"Will you insect-hunt with Margaret?"

"Well, of course, I will. I said I would, didn't I?"

"Yes, you did."

"But you thought I'd think up some excuse not to."

James shrugged, and Carolly couldn't help but notice how incredibly handsome he looked as his broad shoulders shifted within his coat. She laughed nervously. "You're testing me, James. You both are. You want to know if I'll welch on my promise." She looked up at him, challenging him without moving from the couch. "I do confess to hoping it will rain tomorrow. But short of an act of God—" She glanced toward the heavens, wondering just how much pull she had with the Lord. At last she sighed. Despite her firm belief that she was a pre-angel, or something like that, heavenly miracles even in the guise of a thunderstorm seemed as elusive as ever. "—I'm going bug hunting with Mags," she said firmly. "Because I never welch on my promises."

"Perhaps I'll join you."

A cloud seemed to pass from her heart. Suddenly Carolly didn't remember her less than spectacular performance with Margaret. She didn't think about being dead or having lost her memory. All she could think of was wandering around the English countryside with James and Margaret.

Perhaps bug hunting wouldn't be so bad.

Chapter Five

"Dumb. Dumb. Dumb. This is really dumb." Carolly sucked in her stomach, leaned against the cold stone wall and peered through the darkness. She didn't dare glance down, knowing she'd see a two-story drop to a very hard stone walkway. Sure, she was almost an angel, but that didn't mean she could fly. At least she'd taken off her corset, which would have made traversing this ledge downright suicidal.

"Doesn't the man know to keep his ledges clear?" she asked the stars. Her gentle and relatively safe stroll along the ledge that separated her window and Margaret's had suddenly become frightening when she came upon a good seven-foot stretch of tangled ivy. But she wasn't willing to give up yet.

Sighing, she reached out and grabbed a fistful of greenery. "Please, don't let me touch some creepy crawly thing." She could probably keep her balance, even with the thick vines, but not if some disgusting insect started crawling up her arms.

"Crrroak!" That came from the frog she carried, protesting his location wedged into the pocket of her dress. She didn't blame him. She wasn't too happy either. She'd found the hapless creature in her bedsheets just ten minutes ago. He'd probably been put there by a certain eight-year-old.

"More tests," Carolly muttered, worming the toe of her now very wet slipper into a gap in the foliage.

She'd seen the poor frog and couldn't help but laugh. She appreciated all the signs that Margaret's spirit wasn't totally squelched. A child needed to be mischievous. She planned to find some way of nurturing that bit of Margaret's personality. And what better way than to return the frog at a midnight rendezvous?

Well, it had seemed logical at the time. In one brilliant move, she'd not only prove herself trustworthy, a person who kept her promises—even ones no one expected her to keep—but she would also show she was daring and not the least bit prissy about slimy creatures. That had been the plan five minutes ago, before she had discovered this huge expanse of ivy clogging the ledge.

Carolly grabbed another vine only to have it pull loose from the wall. "Aiee!" She scrambled for another handhold, found one, then stood still while her heart pounded like a kettle drum. She felt lightheaded from the adrenaline, but she hadn't split her skull open yet, so she supposed she ought to be grateful.

Did God protect fools? She certainly hoped so.

She took another cautious step and had to jerk her head away from an annoying leaf that flapped her in the face. It tickled her nose, and she had the strong urge to sneeze—which would certainly pitch her over the edge.

It was at that moment she realized she might possibly be in over her head.

"Oh, Lord," she prayed. "This was really dumb, wasn't it? I'm sorry. Please don't kill me yet, I'm not done here."

She pushed further along and was grateful to see the window and its recessed alcove looming just ahead. She was almost there. Another step, another handhold.

Then she stopped. This was Margaret's window, wasn't it? She recalled the hallway in her mind's eye, carefully recounted the doorways down to the bedroom just off the nursery. Sure enough, she'd passed the right number of windows. But doors and windows didn't always coincide.

Carolly sighed. This *had* to be Margaret's bedroom—she'd die of mortification if she suddenly dropped in, frog and all, on that prissy governess Miss Hornswizzle . . . or Hornswatter, or whatever her name was. She bit her lip. No going back now, not with six feet of tangled vines behind her. She took another careful step.

As a breeze picked up, Carolly couldn't stifle a small moan. Sure it was spring, but the night air cut through her already damp dress, chilling her. Her fingers, cramping from the strain of clenching the ivy, grew clumsy as she slowly turned into an icicle.

"Once again, almost-angel Carolly, ten-year veteran of the afterlife, astounds Heaven with her stupidity. Photo, page seven." Carolly didn't know if Heaven had a newspaper, but if it did, she was sure this stunt would become a feature article, probably in the humor section.

Just a few more feet. One more foot. Inch along, she told herself.

Hallelujah! She'd made it.

Carolly took a deep breath, appreciating the safety of the recessed alcove. She had enough room to turn around. If absolutely necessary, she could probably even sit down.

Sliding up to the window, she peered inside. Unfortunately, she couldn't see a blessed thing. The full moon bathed everything outside in a delicate bluish white, but only a few stray beams found their way into the bedroom.

Flattening her face against the glass, Carolly did her best to peer in.

She saw Margaret's bedroom all right. It had to be. Lace furbelows abounded everywhere she looked, including the bed curtains. But no sound or movement came from within. The girl was probably asleep.

As carefully as she could, Carolly tried to open the window. No go. "Come on, you stupid piece of eighteenth century architecture. Open up!" Carolly tugged and pulled, pushed and rattled, nearly losing her balance half a dozen times, but the window refused to budge.

"Margaret . . . I mean Mags, wake up. I'm freezing out here."

"*Crroak!*" added the frog.

Carolly rapped on the window. "Please, please, wake up."

Nothing. And to her total frustration, the breeze increased, rattling panes up and down the house. If Margaret did hear something, she'd assume it was the weather.

Carolly knocked harder. "Come on, Mags. Any louder, and I'll have Miss Hornswooper on me. Or worse yet, your uncle—"

"Have you lost your mind!" James's stentorian tones rang out above the mournful sound of the wind.

Carolly spun around, flattening herself against the window as she tried to become invisible. She couldn't, of course—and even if she could, James wasn't the type to forget what he'd seen.

"Get back inside this instant!" he bellowed at her from below.

Carolly looked down to see James standing on the stone walkway, hands on his hips. He glared up at her. What a disaster! Not only had she failed to wake up Margaret, but she'd been caught, too. Carolly leaned forward, letting her frustration seep into her words. "Can't I do anything without you constantly interfering? Why don't you just go to bed like a normal person?"

"Good God, woman, get back against that window. Do you want to die?"

"I'm already dead!"

"Then be so good as to lie down in a grave and stop confusing the rest of us!"

Carolly was so startled by his unexpected humor that her bad mood evaporated. Or perhaps it had something to do with how handsome he looked. For the first time ever, she was seeing James in something less than formal attire. He'd pulled off his cravat, and his shirt front was slightly unbuttoned. Even his dark hair had been tossed by the wind until it curled in reckless disarray about his face. Add to that the loving touches of moonlight, and he looked something like a pirate from a romance novel.

It softened her heart to look at him, and she couldn't help but smile.

"Carolly, please."

She heard anguish in his voice, and she bit her lip in consternation. "Please what?"

"Get inside!"

"Oh." She glanced back at the window. "I can't," she told him. "The window's locked and Mags won't wake up. I've got to slide back to my room."

"You shall do no such thing! Do not move. I will open the window."

"No! You can't just barge into Mags's room. She'll never forgive me. Eight-year-olds are very sensitive about their privacy."

"Privacy? Do you mean to tell me you really crawled around to visit Margaret?" He took a deep breath. "Did you find the hallway impassable?"

Carolly chuckled. "Of course not. But I did promise to walk along the ledge to her window. She won't wake up, though. I had no idea she was such a deep sleeper."

"She is not. She sleeps across the hall."

Carolly stared at him, momentarily dumbfounded. "Oh," she said softly, glancing back inside at the dark room. "That's probably why this room looks so neat."

"It is also why the window's locked," he said dryly.

Carolly nodded. "Makes sense."

"I am glad something does. Now stay put. I shall be there directly."

"Wouldn't you rather just catch me as I fell into your arms?" she called. The romantic image had definite appeal.

"If you try, I shall let you plummet to your death."

"Hmmm." She eased down until she sat on the edge, her legs dangling over the precipice as if she were preparing to jump. "An interesting thought. Would you, the most honorable, chivalrous person I know, actually let me fall?"

"Without a doubt." And with that, he started toward the house.

Carolly felt something wriggling in her dress. "Wait!"

He stopped dead, then moved back to see her better. "Is there something wrong? I mean, other than the obvious."

"Uh." She paused. "Catch."

"What?"

She didn't give him time to object. "Just don't drop it, okay?" She hauled the hapless frog out of her pocket and as gently as possible let it drop.

"*Croooak!*"

"What the—?" He nabbed it neatly out of the air.

"Don't squeeze!"

"Ugh! This is a toad!"

Carolly leaned further out over the edge. "Really? I thought it was a frog. How can you tell the difference?"

"This type of toad gives off a noxious smelling poison when frightened." He glared up at her. "Like when it is dropped two stories."

"Oh." She watched in silence as he lowered the poor thing into a nearby bush; then she called: "He'll be all right there, won't he? I mean, I'd hate to have to tell Margaret that I'd killed her fr—her toad."

James carefully wiped his hands on a handkerchief. "I would think you might be more worried about whether I'm about to die from the poison."

She looked at him in surprise. "You're not serious, are you?

You're not really poisoned." The idea of that made Carolly ill.

"No, I am hagridden by a woman determined to take me back to Bedlam with her."

She decided to ignore his rude comment, even though it hurt. He was surely just frustrated by her whimsical nature. But he needed to be loosened up. "Maybe you should go wash your hands just to be sure."

He sighed and looked back up at her. "I shall be there in a moment. Do not under any circumstance move from that location."

She smiled at his softened tone. "Take all the time you need."

He paused, mid-step. "I am quite serious, Carolly. Not an inch."

"I'm a stone statue."

"If only that were true. Then I could put you out in the garden with the toads and be done with it." Then he disappeared. A moment later, she heard him enter the house.

Carolly smiled and leaned back against the window pane behind her. She felt totally at ease now that she wouldn't have to cross the ivy back to her bedroom, not to mention sweetly reassured at the thought of James coming for her. Despite his gruff words, she knew he would do whatever he could to get her safely inside.

She sighed happily and let her eyes travel over the scenery. There was something ethereal about an English garden bathed in moonlight. She took a deep breath, drawing it all in: the smells, the sights, even the taste of the breeze. Then she closed her eyes and imagined herself with a lover, a handsome man with dark tousled hair who stole kisses from her beneath a silver-tipped bough.

It was enough to set even a dead woman's heart fluttering.

Then James was there, behind her, softly rapping on the glass to get her attention.

She turned and smiled. For a moment she believed her fantasy. For a desperate second, she looked at James with all the

longing and secret passion she'd thought she'd buried long ago.
What would it be like to love?

Inside, James stood transfixed. Never in his life had he seen
anything so beautiful as the woman poised just outside the
window. Her hair was a golden brown, but in the moonlight
it became a halo of liquid honey and light. Her gown was
gray, but the wind molded it to her curves, outlining her delicate frame, her sweet breasts.

Looking at her face, he gasped. Why had he not noticed
her eyes before? They were a very dark blue with tiny gold
flecks like fine grains of sand stirred up from the bottom of a
deep pool.

He touched the thin pane separating them, and she mirrored his movement. Their fingers were separated by the cool
glass, but a part of him knew he touched her, just as a part of
her touched him.

"Hold tight," he warned, his voice thick with desire. "I shall
open the window."

He waited until she had grabbed two fistfuls of ivy to anchor
herself, then carefully, slowly, he pushed open the window.
She arched backward to let it swing wide, and he forgot to
breathe as he watched her hang out over the stone below.

"Give me your hand." Much to his surprise, she obeyed
immediately, flattening up to the window as she peered
through.

The sill came to just below her breasts, and, as she leaned
in, the fabric pulled taut over her body. Her nipples were
puckered from the cold, and he could feel his body respond
to the sight.

"You'll have to help me," she breathed. "I'm afraid I'll slip
if I try to jump on this ivy." She looked up at him, and his
whole body throbbed with protective instinct.

"At least you have *some* sense," he commented. Making a
swift decision, he stepped forward and grasped her ribcage just

below her arms. Then he braced himself as best he could and pulled her in.

She felt so soft in his hands, so delicate. But there were muscles beneath her curves, muscles that held him while together they maneuvered her inside. She pressed against him, her breasts flush with his chest. He could smell the fresh scent of the heather outside mixed with the heady scent of her.

She had almost cleared the window, so he stepped backward to drag her across the opening. Then it happened. His bad knee gave out, and he stumbled as he tried to shift their weight completely to his other leg. The strain was too much, their balance too precarious.

He went down, and she tumbled on top of him.

She might have banged her head, but he held her solidly against his chest. She might have braced herself with her hands, stopping their rolling tumble, but he pinned her against him and allowed their movement to carry him over on top of her. They ended with his hips and most of his weight to one side, with his bad leg and his arms resting firmly atop her.

"Why, James," she teased. "This is all so sudden." But her smile faded when he did not respond. Just moments before he had been fantasizing about capturing her beneath him; now fate had literally placed her there. He was not about to lose this opportunity.

Supporting himself on his elbow, he looked at her, enjoying the fresh blush of her cheeks and the sparkling clarity of her eyes. He had to touch her. He'd been denying himself too long. And she seemed willing. Using his free hand, he touched her face, gently brushing the curls away from her eyes. Her skin felt soft, like angel down, surrounded by short gossamer strands of spun gold.

"What a crime to crop your hair so short."

"What?" Her response was breathy and almost inaudible, and he felt it pass his cheek on a whisper of air.

"The poets say a woman's hair is her crowning glory. Who cut yours so short?" He played with it, drawing the silky stands over his fingers, delighting in the feel of each lock as it tickled the back of his hand.

She tried to pull away, but he would not release her. Not before he had explored the smooth planes of her face. Not until he had tasted the ruby bow of her lips. But as he leaned forward, he felt her skin flush with new heat. Looking down, he witnessed her enchanting blush.

"Carolly?" he whispered.

"In my past incarnations, I had to pass myself off as a boy. It was a bloody mess trying to get all that hair into a cap, so I cut it off. I've kept it short ever since."

He felt his eyes widen in shock. Though his attention had been focused on her face, he could not deny the exquisite feel of her left breast pressed intimately against his chest, its point a tiny pebble of heat. Lower down he felt the yielding indent of her waist before the hard flare of her hipbone.

"How could anyone mistake you for a boy?" he asked, his voice already thick with desire.

Her blush deepened, and he decided he liked the idea that he could affect her. "I, uh, I didn't do it often and not for very long."

"I should say not." He let his fingers pull away from her hair to trail across her soft cheek and gently caress her full lips. "Your curves are decidedly feminine."

He would kiss her now. He knew it with a profound sense of inevitability. No force on earth would prevent him. And so he lowered his head to touch his mouth to hers, but she shifted beneath him, her long body sensitizing his with her every movement.

"Uh, James. I think you better get off now." Her voice remained breathy, and he could hear the regret in her voice. She wanted his kiss as much as he wanted to give it. And yet, inherent modesty forced her to twist her hips away from him, to push at his shoulders. She could not know that her very movements inflamed him all the more.

He pressed his bad knee downward to hold her steady. God,

to feel a woman beneath him again, warm and lovely and aching for his touch. She moaned slightly, a desperate, hungry sound of both surrender and desire. All he required for completion was *motion*, so he lowered his head and at last touched his lips to hers.

Lord, she tasted sweet. Innocence and wonder were pale descriptions of his feelings at their first tentative touch. He felt Carolly's mouth tremble beneath his, even as her entire body seemed to soften, surrounding him in heat and beauty.

"I can't do this," she whispered. But her mouth clung to his, her hands trailed upwards to stroke his arms, his back.

"It's just a kiss," he lied. "One, single, sweet . . ." His lips descended again, and this time he opened her mouth with his tongue, exploring deeper. He felt his blood surge as he began to take control, his mouth slanting more fully over hers, his body angling between her thighs, opening her to his touch, encouraging her surrender.

He went too fast. He knew it and so did she, and he felt her stiffen beneath him. "No!" she cried. "I can't!" Then she tried to shove him away. But he was too heavy, his bulk too much for her slender frame.

He shifted, twisting to remove his weight from her. But as he did so, she jostled him and his bad leg strained to support his weight. Suddenly it slipped, slamming him down onto the hard wood floor with just enough force in just the right place to completely immobilize him. Pain sliced through his limb like a hot nail had been driven deep through his kneecap.

"Lie still," he gasped, his voice harsh. He tried to lift himself up, but his muscles locked up and her every breath jostled him further, bringing fresh waves of torment.

Unfortunately, she thought he was continuing to take advantage of her. "Get off, James."

"I cannot."

"Then let me help you." She abruptly shifted her leg out from under him, unwittingly wrenching his knee again as she did.

"Caroaiiiiiiee!"

"James?" She tried to sit up, and he obliged her by rolling backwards, nearly fainting from the shooting bolts of anguish.

"My knee," he managed to gasp.

"Oh, God, you really are hurt. What happened?"

"I injured my knee . . . in Spain." Shallow, panting breaths kept the worst of the pain at bay.

"Oh, Lord," Carolly moaned. "That's why we fell down. You have a bad knee!"

He opened his eyes, trying to keep his breathing steady. "I apologize for accosting . . ." His words faded as fresh waves of agony punished him. Nevertheless, he forced himself to roll onto his side, intending to stand up and apologize for his heinous actions in the proper manner. His leg did not cooperate. "Damn," he grunted.

"What are you doing? Lie still!"

"I should not have done that," he responded through clenched teeth.

"What can I do?" She was frantically looking about the room. Suddenly, she jumped up and grabbed a pillow from the bed. "You shouldn't have pulled me in the window. I could have made it myself."

"I have insulted you," he began again, but she wasn't listening. Instead, she focused on sliding the pillow beneath his knee.

At last she said, "It's God's way of punishing you, you know. For being so macho." She stood again, reaching into the bed curtains for another pillow.

He shook his head. "It is the Lord's way of telling me I should not kiss lunatics," he snapped.

She was lifting his head, intending to slide the second pillow beneath, but she froze at his words. He watched her eyes, and he saw them grow glittery as they filled with tears. "Oh God, you're right. Oh, James, I'm so sorry." She set his head down on the pillow. "I won't let it happen again."

"What are you talking about?" The pain was subsiding into

an aching throb of misery, and the whole experience had made him curt and irritable. "You should be demanding *my* apologies," he said.

"Shhh. Don't try to talk."

"Damn, woman, I—"

"I said, shut up!"

He stared at her, torn between shock at her tone and amusement that she was trying to keep him silent because of a knee injury. But then she leaned over him and brushed a lock of hair from his brow, and he forgot everything. He gazed into the deep swirling pools of her eyes.

"I'm well aware that in your culture a woman is responsible for her own virtue," she said.

Her words took a while to reach his brain, but when they did, they made him furious. He jerked away from her touch and glared at her. "Do not be ridiculous. I tried to take advantage of you, and I most heartily beg your forgiveness for such reprehens—"

"Shhh." She pressed her fingers against his lips, but he shook them off.

"I will not be quiet. I was in the midst of begging—"

"My forgiveness. I know." Then she dropped her hand into her lap and regarded him silently. He tried to shift to see her expression more clearly, but a sharp pain in his knee kept him still. When he finally could see her, he wondered at the strange expression on her face. She seemed remote, as if she were afraid he would see too much of her thoughts. Compared to the openness he usually felt with her, her current lack of expression was like a bucket of ice water in the face.

"What has happened?" he asked. "What are you thinking?"

"James," she began, speaking slowly as though carefully weighing her words. "Do you often force yourself on unwilling servant girls or unprotected guests?"

He stiffened in outrage. "Of course not!"

"Then, I was your first?"

"Madame, this conversation is highly improper!"

"So is trying to force yourself on me," she responded tartly. "Now answer my question."

He lifted his head off the floor, but she pushed him back onto the pillow. "I was not forcing you," he snapped. "You only needed to say no!"

"So, which is it, James? Am I responsible for my own actions or not? If you weren't forcing me, then I must have been willing. And it was just a kiss."

"But—"

"I *was* willing, James." Her eyes darkened. "It's been so long. And for the first time in forever, I felt. . . ." She gestured vaguely with her hand. "Womanly." She touched his cheek. "Alive." Her fingers trailed longingly over his lips. "I let myself get carried away. I'm so sorry. It won't happen again."

She pulled her hand away and began to stand, but he grabbed her wrist, kept her beside him. "You *are* alive, Carolly. Perhaps more alive than anyone I have ever met."

She shook her head. "I'm different, James. I was born in the twentieth century, and now I am forced to be an angel—"

"No!" He shook his head, trying to make her focus on the rational, the here and now—anything but her strange delusions. "There is nothing wrong with what we did. I was merely jesting before. God is not punishing me. Kissing is perfectly natural. And as for your culpability, I simply overwhelmed your maidenly sensibilities."

"Not a prayer," she said. "You could never overwhelm those." She grinned at him, and for a moment he was lost in the brilliance of her smile. But then her expression faded as she grew serious. "Of course there's nothing wrong with kissing—provided you do it with a living person. I'm dead, James. I want you to fall in love, but necrophilia wasn't what I had in mind."

He was shocked. Necrophilia? She should not even know such a word, much less understand it. Certainly such words were not taught to gently bred girls. Yet, neither would a common laborer have learned it. In fact, most educated men did not even know it.

Ignoring the pain in his leg, he pushed himself upright to confront her. "Who are you?"

"I've already told you, James. When are you going to start believing me?"

He had no answer.

She passed a hand over his swelling knee. "I better get your valet. You'll need to ice that before it becomes a grapefruit. Even so, you may have to cut your trousers just to get them off." At his look of astonishment, she chuckled and pushed to her feet. "Good Lord, James, you don't mind rolling around on the floor with me, but you're shocked when I talk about taking off your pants? Don't be such a prude." Then she dropped a chaste kiss on his forehead and disappeared, leaving him more frustrated and confused than ever.

Back in her room, Carolly sat on her bed and listened to James and his valet shuffle by. The valet murmured something polite, but James responded with a string of curses that made Carolly giggle. She hadn't thought he knew how to swear, but obviously she'd been wrong. Obviously James possessed a rough edge that he rarely revealed to anyone.

Carolly dropped onto her pillow, her thoughts spinning back to that moment on the floor. He'd kissed her. She touched her fingertips to her lips, still feeling them tingle. She'd never wanted a man more.

Abruptly, she pulled her hand away. She couldn't give in. She was working her way toward being an angel, and angels didn't seduce their charges. Besides, with luck she'd only be around a few more weeks, a couple of months at most. She was finally getting the hang of this time-travel business. Her last life had been very short. If she worked hard, then this one would go equally quickly. It wasn't fair to James to start something that would end so soon.

Yet her legs still trembled with wanting, and her heart beat triple-time with every thump as James's valet helped him to his master suite.

She had to do something fast, had to get him interested in other women. Her chest squeezed at the thought, but she refused to be stopped. True angels didn't lose their focus. She had a mission, a purpose here, and she wasn't going to welsh on it no matter what the personal cost.

But how? It wasn't like eligible women were beating down James's door.

Carolly bit her lip and wondered what was wrong with the local females. James was a handsome, well-dressed man. She sighed in wistful memory of tonight's dinner. He'd worn a dark maroon evening coat contrasted with a white linen shirt and a single diamond to anchor his cravat. Carolly's mouth watered even now. If only other women could see him like that. They'd climb in the windows to get to him. Surely then he'd find one to his liking, one who could change his life and make him happy.

Carolly flopped over in bed. How? How would she get women here? As far as she could tell, no one ever came to visit. Obviously, a person had to be nearly beaten to death to be invited in.

The answer came suddenly. It was like a divine whisper in her mind, and she knew immediately that it was the perfect solution. And so simple!

A *ball*. Just like the one where Prince Charming finally met Cinderella. A huge ball for all the eligible ladies in the land, or at least from the surrounding area. Given James's title and wealth, they'd be crammed into the rafters.

Organizing would be a lot of work, of course. And she'd need Mrs. Potherby's help every step of the way. But this was still the perfect solution.

The only problem was how to convince James. Worse yet, she had to convince him without giving in to her baser instincts. Without throwing herself into his arms in the most shameless fashion. It would be a difficult task, because more than anything else—more than throwing a Cinderella ball, and perhaps even more than gaining her angel wings—Carolly desperately longed to finish what they'd started on that bedroom floor.

Chapter Six

Carolly tried not to run. She tried not to streak through the house on the way to the library, but it was hard to restrain herself.

The mail had arrived.

Mrs. Potherby had told her quite clearly: The post had come. And with it came the London Times. Finally, she had a chance to find out exactly when and where in time she'd landed. Sure she knew the date, but Carolly needed to fit herself into world events.

Plus, she was desperate to get an idea of modern fashions. After all, she didn't want to disgrace herself at James's ball.

She barely checked her speed at the closed library door, pausing only to throw it open before she sailed through. "Good morning, James!" she called sweetly.

He sat in a comfortable leather chair, one that might have been a recliner if they were a hundred years in the future. As it was, it seemed big and warm and very elegant—the perfect backdrop for James in his superbly fitted, tightly clinging coat and pantaloons. Geez, didn't the man ever look bad? After last night's disaster with his knee, he could at least appear a bit disheveled. But no, he had to look like a Greek god. An annoyed Greek god. One with a fearsome scowl.

"Goodness, Carolly, has no one ever taught you to knock?"

She grinned at him, her eyes hungrily taking in both him and the newspaper spread across his knees. "Of course I know how to knock. I was trying to catch you doing something scandalous."

"In the *library?*" He seemed more shocked by the suggested location than by anything else.

She gave an airy wave. "If you prefer, I can burst into your bedchamber."

He carefully set down his paper. "I would rather you not burst in on me at all."

She crossed the room to drop into a chair. "I'll try, of course, but my mother used to say I have the manners of a barnyard animal. Is that the newspaper?" She leaned across to lift if off his knee, but he neatly folded it up out of her reach.

"Is there something you wanted, Miss Carolly?" His tone of annoyance finally broke through her fixation, and she realized she'd have to cajole him out of his ill temper just to get her hands on his paper.

She sighed and flopped back into her chair, then looked at the difficult man across from her. "How's the knee?"

"My leg is recovering quite nicely. I shall no doubt be able to ride as early as tomorrow."

She nodded, suddenly understanding. "You're in a bad mood because you couldn't go riding today."

"I am in a perfectly normal humor."

"Which for you means a bad mood, especially when you can't ride in the morning." She dropped her chin onto her hand, her gaze straying longingly to the newspaper. "Unless it was something you read. What's happening in the world? I'm desperate for a peek."

To her surprise, he seemed to soften toward her. His lips

lost their pinched look. The change was as startling as it was subtle. "I would not worry about Napoleon, Carolly," he said gently. "We managed him before, we shall manage him again."

"Napoleon?" Carolly perked up. Of course, the Napoleonic wars! "Is he doing something?"

James flipped the paper to the front page, his expression grim. "He has escaped."

"Escaped St. Helena?"

He gave her a sad look, the one men reserved for particularly ditzy women. "From Elba."

"No . . ." She frowned, sifting through her dim memories of history class. "Oh, right. He's doing his hundred-day thing." If she remembered correctly, Napoleon marched through France bent on a glorious re-instatement as supreme emperor. It took the English a hundred days to defeat him.

"I beg your pardon?"

She curled her legs up beneath her as she settled into her chair. "You have to remember that for me the Napoleonic wars happened over a hundred years ago. The most I can remember about him was that he died on my birthday."

"He is still alive, Carolly."

She tried not to laugh at his solemn expression, but it was hard. He took everything so very seriously. "Well, of course he is, silly. He will die on my birthday. May fifth, by the way—in case you want to get me a present." She was teasing him, but he seemed to take the comment as proof of her idiocy.

"That was two weeks ago," he said repressively.

She sighed with her own special dramatic flair. "Oh, well, can't blame me for trying. So what were we talking about?"

"Napoleon." He said the word as if he didn't really want to hear any more of her nonsense, but couldn't stop himself.

"Right. If memory serves," she said, gazing sweetly at him, "and believe me, it wasn't all that reliable even before this reincarnation stuff." He clearly didn't know how to respond to that, so she just kept talking, ticking off the facts on her fingers: "First, Napoleon escapes from Elba. Then he marches around terrifying everybody for a hundred days before he gets it at Waterloo."

"Where?"

"Waterloo. Oh, you mean, where is Waterloo. Gee, I don't know." She shrugged. "What exactly is Napoleon doing?"

James glanced down at the paper, and Carolly noticed how tightly he gripped the pages. "He is gathering another army."

"Oh." Slowly she began to fit the pieces, not into a world order, but into the way they fit James personally. She eyed his injured leg, now stretched in front of him, all hint of last night's accident totally masked. "You were wounded in the army, weren't you?"

"Yes." The word came out almost as hard as the planes of his face.

"You must be worried about your military friends."

He didn't answer, but she saw the anguish in his eyes.

"Well, don't worry. The British perform brilliantly at Waterloo."

"Carolly—"

"I know, I know—where exactly is Waterloo? Let's see. Where do you think he'll march first?"

James shook his head, and she wondered briefly how involved he'd been in military strategy. Probably deeply. He seemed born to command. "It must be really hard for you to be out of the loop, so to speak."

"I beg your pardon?"

"Well, you're stuck in the countryside far away from the most important battle of the century."

"Carolly—," he began, but she cut him off.

"Oh, stop thinking so much and just play along for a moment. Where do you think Napoleon will go first?"

He sighed, but his gaze grew abstract as he started thinking. "Probably into Belgium to reestablish France's so-called natural borders."

She nodded. "Well, there you have it. Waterloo must be on the way to Belgium."

He frowned at her. "Or perhaps he will cut south into Spain, or expand westward toward Italy."

She shrugged. "Whatever. Waterloo is in Europe somewhere. I'm sure of it. Unless it was that big naval battle . . ." She shook her head. "I really wish I could remember. Mostly I remember reading Tolkien's *Lord of the Rings* through history class. Elven battles seemed much more interesting at the time."

"Of course," he agreed, his voice completely deadpan.

Carolly glanced up, then suddenly fell backward with a peal of laughter. "Oh, James, lighten up. I promise, Napoleon rules for a hundred days, gets beaten at Waterloo by . . . um . . . beef . . . beef Wellington, and then gets sent off to St. Helena."

"To die on your birthday. Which has already passed." His tone remained excruciatingly disbelieving.

"Well, he obviously doesn't die this year." She laughed. "It's in ten, twenty years or so. Does it really matter?"

He took a long time to answer, but when he did it was with infinite sadness. "No. I do not suppose it does."

Carolly felt her good mood slowly evaporate. The man across from her was the most handsome she'd ever met. In fact, he was a lot of "mosts." The most sexy, the most infuriating, and the most sweet. But he thought she was completely insane.

"James—"

"Perhaps you should go rest for a while, Carolly. We will have a busy afternoon hunting insects with Margaret."

"I'm not crazy, James."

"I never said you were."

"But you're thinking it." Carolly bit her lip, wondering exactly how she could bring him around. Then she remembered the other reason she'd come here this morning. Putting on the smile that had always worked wonders on her father, she clapped her hands as if suddenly getting a brilliant idea. "I know, we'll make the ball a Waterloo theme party! Naturally, it's going to be the topic of the hour. It'll be great."

"Ball? What ball?"

Carolly tried to look shocked. Her best strategy was to pretend he'd forgotten, even though she'd never mentioned it to him. "Why, *your* ball, of course. You're going to have a party. With dancing and food and lots of champagne."

He leaned forward, and Carolly was relieved to see the lines of strain ease from his face. Unfortunately, he shifted to a severe frown. "I am not going to have a party, Carolly. I do not give balls, I do not dance, and I do not have champagne."

"Wine, then. Or ale. It doesn't really matter what people drink," she said, focusing on the easiest of his objections.

"Carolly—"

"Oh, come on. It'll be fun."

"I sincerely doubt—"

"How else are you going to meet all the eligible young women in the land, hmm?"

"No."

"Let me think." She jumped up and began pacing, pretending she hadn't heard his refusal. "All I have to find out is when Napoleon lands in France, add a hundred days, and voila, we have the Battle of Waterloo."

"No, Carolly."

"I'll make all the arrangements. With Mrs. Potherby's excellent guidance, of course. Cook will be thrilled, I'm sure. She'll get to show off her culinary arts. Maybe we could even get Mags—"

"No."

"Just think of it, James."

Suddenly he stood, his injured leg rigid as he grabbed her shoulders. "I do not dance, Carolly. I do not need to meet any more women. Believe me, those already in my life are more than enough."

He glared directly at her. She made a face back at him.

"And I will not allow a rout or an endless parade of husband-hungry women through my parlor."

"But—"

"End of discussion!"

Carolly could see she was beaten. James's eyes blazed gray lightning. If she pushed any more, she risked being tossed out on her ear. At last, she sighed in defeat. "All right, James."

"Good. Now I suggest you go to your room and rest for a while. You have had an extremely taxing morning."

"You mean you've had an extremely taxing morning," she said airily. "I've just gotten started."

He groaned. It was a sound made of frustration and dread. She loved it. Finally, she was breaking through his cold reserve. Perhaps this morning hadn't been a total loss after all.

"I believe I shall go sit in the garden," he ground out.

"Good idea," she agreed, flashing one of her best smiles. "And I'll look at the fashion pages for ball gowns." She winked outrageously at him. "Just in case you change your mind."

He stared at her in open-mouthed shock. Then with a curse, he stomped out of the room. She didn't stop laughing until after she heard the front door slam behind him.

"Mags, tell me about your uncle." Carolly lowered her butterfly net and sidled closer to the young girl. "Does he have any lady friends? Maybe some woman that he talks to a lot?"

The girl didn't look up, but her snide voice carried easily. "He will not marry you. You are not proper enough."

Carolly winced as the words hit home; then she quickly covered her pain with a false laugh. "Oh, how sweet of you to think of me," she said gaily. "But no, I'm talking about another lady he might get interested in." Why did the words taste like dust in her mouth?

"He sometimes goes to London." Margaret glanced up, her large eyes serious as she awaited Carolly's reaction. "Mrs. Hornswallow says all men have needs. Uncle James goes there to take care of them."

Carolly wrinkled her nose. "Ugh. Sounds like he's going to get his tooth pulled or something."

"No, he goes to have carnal relations with a woman."

"Uhh . . ." Carolly let her voice trail away. What could she say to that?

"Miss Hornswallow says we have to be practical about understanding men's baser instincts."

"Everyone has baser instincts," Carolly returned. "Men just don't bother to hide them." She let Margaret chew on that while she turned her attention to Mrs. Hornswigger, who was sitting rigidly correct under a nearby tree just up the hill. The woman seemed happily occupied with James, discussing Greek poets as if the subject truly intrigued her.

Carolly sighed. She hated to admit it, but Mrs. Hornsipper was rising in her esteem. The woman seemed quite intelligent and apparently spoke bluntly to her charge about every possible subject, including sex. Carolly couldn't help but admire such honesty. She knew how rare that was, especially in the 1900s. Unfortunately, from what Margaret had been saying, the woman's views tended to be somewhat bitter. Her attitude on men's baser instincts seemed typical of the governess's general outlook.

Carolly shook her head. Any woman who could speak so bluntly was either a realist or had been badly hurt. Glancing over at the thin governess, currently conversing with regal formality with James, Carolly judged it a little of both. The genteel poor suffered a miserable lot. Mrs. Hornswoffer was lucky to find so fair a boss as James. Yet, fair or not, her existence certainly couldn't be one filled with much joy.

Carolly sighed, mentally adding Miss Hornswallow to her list of people to assist.

"Look! Look, I got one!"

Carolly turned as Margaret held up her butterfly net to show what looked like a huge black grasshopper. It jumped around in the net, scrambling for an opening, but Margaret cut off the poor creature's escape.

"That's wonderful," said Carolly, suddenly feeling a kinship for the little thing, trapped as it was in delicate gauze, suddenly snatched from its peaceful world without explanation. "Now what do we do with it?"

"Miss Hornswallow! Miss Hornswallow! I got one." Margaret scrambled up the grassy hill. Both governess and guardian turned at the child's scrambled approach, each with a fond smile.

As Carolly watched, Miss Hornswallow pulled a glass jar with a wet rag at the bottom from the picnic basket. She moved with innate grace, and Carolly was startled to see James watching the governess with a puzzled expression. Suddenly, Carolly felt her heart clench within her chest, seeing what James must now be noticing.

Miss Hornswallow was beautiful!

True, she still had hawklike features and a tight pinched look to her face. But right now, as she fiddled with the jar, the sun danced in her dark hair revealing blue highlights hidden beneath her tight bun.

Carolly narrowed her eyes, picking out the carefully obscured features of the woman's figure. Where before she had seemed iron-rod thin, Carolly now noticed the governess's slender bone structure. She'd thought the woman's face severe, almost harsh, but it also possessed pearly skin tones and a high aristocratic bearing.

All the poor woman needed was a little push—some new clothes, a new hairstyle, and a few lessons in smiling—and bam, she'd make the perfect countess.

"Uncle James, I dropped it! Get it!"

Carolly saw James start in surprise, his attention suddenly pulled to his niece who pointed at the grass near his knee. Quicker than she thought possible, he swooped down as he tried to catch one very terrified grasshopper. He very nearly succeeded, but then it jumped up over his hands, straight at his nose. James reared back, and Margaret squealed happily before chasing after it, bowling over her governess and uncle in her eagerness. Then came a rollicking, pell mell battle of three humans against one grasshopper. Laughter filled the air as they chased and tumbled over one another.

After a few moments, Carolly turned away, unable to watch the free-for-all anymore. She ought to be pleased, she told herself. In one flash of sunlight, she'd seen her goal revealed with sparkling clarity.

James and Miss Hornswallow were perfect for each other. With Margaret to bind them together, they could build a wonderful aristocratic family. It might not turn out quite as casual and bubbling over with hilarity as Carolly would have preferred, but clearly, they would be happy. And that should make her happy. She'd be able to get her wings.

But she wasn't happy. She was lonely.

For ten years, she'd been shifting around in time, trying to do good deeds, straining to make up for her very selfish first life. But ten years was a long time to be engineering other people's happiness without doing anything for her own. Sure, Carolly liked helping people, but she also wanted a rest, a place where she had friends, a place where everybody knew her name.

Carolly groaned and kicked a stone. She was spouting television slogans. She always did that when she got depressed. It reminded her of who she was, where she came from, and most of all, that she was as superficial as the boob tube that had helped raise her. She wasn't meant for long-term relationships. She'd known that growing up. She knew it now.

That's why she'd make a great angel. She would come in, be angelic while helping people, and then leave. Except for the last few lives. With each incarnation she'd found it harder and harder to escape her emotions. And this life felt the worst of all.

Glancing back at the happy trio of man, woman, and child, Carolly forced herself to be grateful she had this special gift. How many people got to affect others in such a profound way? She was going to make a great angel.

So why didn't the thought make her happy?

* * *

James saw Carolly wander aimlessly away. He glanced over at Margaret, who was happily chasing another grasshopper while Miss Hornswallow observed. A tolerant smile was on the governess's austere face. Odd how he had never noticed how beautiful, how very regal the governess was. She had natural dignity and the cool demeanor necessary for an aristocratic life. With the right clothes and lineage, she would make a perfect countess. And he had never even noticed before.

A whole world suddenly opened up to him, a whole life he had never bothered to see because it did not fit into his orderly—rigid, Carolly would call it—schedule. He could not even remember the last time he'd gone for a walk in the afternoon, much less had a picnic luncheon and enjoyed the sweet tempo of a spring day like he was doing now.

And it was all because of Carolly.

In just three days, she already had him cavorting around after grasshoppers and noticing the beautiful women who were his servants. What would he be like after a week in her disruptive, delightful, and totally confounding presence?

He watched her wander toward a copse of trees, idly kicking at the grass. Without thinking why, James stood up and strolled after her. He found her a few minutes later. She sat cross-legged on the grass, absently stripping wildflowers of their petals.

"Never let my gardener catch you doing that. He thinks every plant is his sacred charge."

"What?" Carolly looked down and flushed at the ripped petals in her lap. "Oh. How does he ever pull weeds?"

James leaned down and picked up one of her discarded stems. "Well, there are plants, Carolly, and then there are upstarts."

She looked into his eyes, her face soft and glowing in the sunlight. "My goodness, James. Was that a joke?"

He twirled the denuded stem, hating himself for how unsure he felt. "I cannot tell. Was it funny?"

She started to chuckle, and he felt his face flush with embarrassment. "Yes, James, it was funny."

They remained silent a long time, the awkwardness growing between them like a dark, twisted vine. He tried to break through it, searched for something to say, only to have his true thoughts escape his lips.

"I saw you walking away."

She looked down as her fingers shredded more flower petals, tearing them into minuscule bits.

"Why did you leave?" he pressed.

"I thought you three could use some privacy."

He frowned, both confused by her words and confounded by the sight of her long legs outlined by her skirt. "The *three* of us?" he pressed.

Carolly nodded, looking anywhere but at him. "Have you noticed how beautiful Miss Hornswallow is? With the right clothes and hairstyle, she would make a fine earless. Uh, wife of an earl—"

"Countess."

"Right. Well, she could be a fine one."

James studied Carolly's bent head. The sun seemed to sparkle in her hair, making it a shimmering crown. But, beautiful as the sight was, he did not like it. He wanted to see her face, needed to watch her eyes and study every twist of her lips. But she didn't look up.

"James? Did you notice her?" she asked again.

"Yes, I noticed." He also noticed the long curve of Carolly's neck. He had never thought a woman's neck particularly sensual, but Carolly's looked soft and creamy white. Would her skin be warm or cool to the touch, he wondered.

"The two of you have so much in common," Carolly went on. "She's very learned, or so I gather from Mags. How's her lineage?"

James blinked, startled. "Lineage?"

At last she looked up, and he could see the soft pink bow

of her mouth. "Her parents and forefathers and that sort of stuff," she said.

He settled down on the grass beside Carolly, feeling a physical pull, drawing him inexorably to her side. "Mrs. Hornswallow comes from an excellent family, though her grandfather gambled their fortune away."

"How sad," Carolly commented. Her voice betrayed genuine regret. Then she turned toward the sun and, in the light, her blue eyes became the color of a bright robin's egg. They flashed merrily up at him even as she turned away. "She must have led a very hard life."

James grunted in frustration. Despite his earlier thoughts about her attractiveness, he had no wish to think about Miss Hornswallow. He wished to understand why Carolly suddenly sympathized with a woman whose name she could not remember ten minutes ago. He wanted to know her thoughts. He wanted her to laugh again, to tease him with her smiles, not to hide herself away.

"She truly likes Margaret," Carolly continued, shifting to look at the two. "Have you noticed that? I think she'd be a good mother, if given the chance."

James narrowed his eyes, this time forcing himself to focus on things other than the attractiveness of Carolly's body. As a deliberate choice, he watched not the exquisite curve of her neck, but the tight clench of her shoulders. He no longer wondered at the golden texture of her hair, but at the way her head seemed to droop, as if she carried a great weight.

"Carolly . . ." he began, but she forestalled him.

"Have you given any thought to your name, James? I mean, isn't it important that the title carry on?"

James clenched his teeth, at last realizing the direction of her thoughts. She wished to match him with his governess! He was not surprised. Indeed, Carolly had stated her interest in finding him a wife. And yet, an irrational anger flowed through him. Despite his own similar thoughts earlier, he had no wish to have Carolly match him up with Miss Hornswallow. "I have an heir," he stated. "A cousin with a squat nose and freckles, but he loves town life and is seen with all the right people. He will make a respectable earl."

Carolly's gaze returned to him, her eyes darkening. "He loves town life? What does that mean? That he gambles and wenches and goes to cockfights or something?"

"Er, essentially, yes." He felt his skin flush at such openness, but he was becoming accustomed to such with Carolly. Indeed, he found himself smiling with grim satisfaction. Then he shook his head at his folly. Why would he invite such an impertinent line of discussion?

As he puzzled at his own illogic, Carolly continued to focus on him, frowning in disgust. "So, cockfights and wenching trains one to be a good earl?"

James shifted, stretching out his bad leg. "I really could care less. I shall be dead when he inherits."

She cut off a sigh. "But, James—"

"Let us be clear, Carolly. Are you perhaps suggesting I marry my governess?"

His cold and implacable tone didn't seem to bother Carolly. And there, James realized, lay the source of many concerns. If he, with a reputed coldness, could not discomfit or discourage this woman, then what *had* bothered his odd charge? What could possibly have led her to wander off alone and disconsolate?

A spark returned to her eyes, and she challenged him, "Why *not* marry Miss Hornswimper? Just because she's a governess doesn't mean—"

"To be honest," James snapped, "I would not care if she were my bootblack or the queen." His eyes focused on the way Carolly clenched another flower, rending its tiny petals with her fingertips. "I will not marry her."

"But—"

"Enough!" James pushed up from his seat, intending to stomp away, his irritation getting the better of him. What was it about this woman that always had him running, his composure in tatters?

"I didn't mean to insult your honor," she said, her voice carrying a clear note of pique. "I just thought she'd make a good wife."

"She would, if I were looking for one," he admitted. Then he sighed, still wondering at his own ineptitude. Why did he seem to bungle every conversation he had with this woman?

Carolly exhaled loudly. It sounded very much like the word "pooh," but James chose to ignore that. Instead, he shifted, kneeling down in front of her so he could take her by the shoulders, turning her to face him. She resisted, but he was relentless and finally he gazed into her wide blue eyes.

"I do not want love or a wife," he said firmly.

"Everyone wants love, James."

He looked closer, finally seeing the small red blood vessels in Carolly's eyes and the slight puffiness in her cheeks. Just as he feared. She had been crying. "What about you," he pressed. "Do you want love?"

"I'm dead, James. Dead people don't love."

"You breathe," he whispered. Then he lifted his thumb to caress her beautiful neck. "Your skin is warm." He pushed aside her high collar to stroke the pulse at her throat, wishing he could press his lips to it instead. "Your heart beats. You are alive."

She pushed away from him, but not before he saw new tears form in her eyes. He moved to follow her, but her obvious pain kept him from doing so. He did not wish to hurt her by forcing his attentions on her; and so he watched helplessly as she walked unsteadily away from him, half falling into a large maple before steadying herself with one hand on its rough bark. When she spoke, her voice held such flat certainty that part of him wanted to believe her.

"In the last ten years, I have died six times. First in a car crash, then I died of TB. I've been beaten, stoned, and shot in the back. And I've suffocated from pneumonia." She turned, pinning him with her angry, wounded gaze. "I'm dead, James, and I will keep dying until I become an angel. And nothing you or I can do will change that."

They stared at each other, and James had the sudden feeling they stood on opposites sides of a huge gulf. Perhaps a gulf large enough to incorporate life and death.

"Carolly—"

"Don't." The tree she leaned on seemed to support her entire body. "Don't say anything. Just go back." She gestured wearily toward the top of the rise where Margaret and Miss Hornswallow were bent over some poor insect. "Your life is there, James. Live it. Now, before it's too late."

James followed her gesture, seeing the sunlit hill, hearing the earnest voices of the two people up there. He felt an urge to follow Carolly's command, not because he wanted to, but because she wanted it. And he wanted to make her happy.

But then he saw Miss Hornswallow stand, her body stiff and cold, her whalebone corset making her movement awkward. He remembered Carolly's body as it had been the night before, warm and yielding beneath him. She hadn't worn a corset. Indeed, the thought of encasing her energy, her passion, in cold whalebone seemed criminal to him. If anyone was dead, it was the excruciatingly correct Miss Hornswallow, not this strangely compelling Bedlamite.

"You are not dead, Carolly."

She did not answer, only turned away. He knew she was crying. He could hear her tiny gasps and could see the tiny spasms that shook her shoulders. The compulsion to go to her, to hold her, nearly overwhelmed him, but he did not. He could not. Emotion would not help her.

Worse, perhaps the attraction he felt for her would somehow push Carolly further into madness. Any sort of strong feeling was perilous. Passionate debate had aggravated Danny in Spain. He did not want to see the same thing happen to Carolly.

How did one quietly, calmly convince a woman that she

lived? James nearly gave up. He nearly gave in to his frustration and walked away. But he could not. His mind replayed the memory of Danny calmly walking out onto that battlefield to declare peace. His arms had been outstretched, sweetly blessing all who lived. And seconds later . . .

No, he could not allow Carolly to suffer a similar fate. Though not a battlefield, England was equally dangerous to a lone, confused woman. It was vitally important that she understand reality. He would put her through anything, fight with her until they stood knee deep in her tears, force her through countless memories, if only at the end, she understood the truth.

"Carolly," he ordered, his voice loud and firm. "You are not dead. And you are not an angel."

Carolly felt the change in James. Moments before she had watched his eyes turn vague as he focused on Miss Hornswallow's figure. His posture relaxed as he looked at Margaret, and his expression had softened.

But then something had happened. Before he could take that first step toward his now future, his jaw clenched and his eyes hardened. He'd turned back to Carolly, his dark eyes stones glittering beneath the black slashes of his brows, and suddenly she saw determination harden his expression.

The old resolved James was back.

But it wasn't until he ordered her to live that she realized the purpose of his resolve, and that he had changed in a major way. Three days ago, the Earl of Traynern had been a cold man, determined to remain isolated, emotionless, and empty. Now, hearing the intensity of his words, Carolly realized he had abandoned his defensive position.

"Please don't do this, James," she begged softly.

She heard him shift his position, settling on the ground, stretching out his legs one by one. She knew he wouldn't leave her alone. He was simply taking his time while he chose the method of his attack.

"I'm tired," she said. "Perhaps we should go back."

"We still have some time, Carolly. Sit down, and we shall talk."

Carolly tensed. Whatever he planned, she knew it wasn't good. "James—"

"Tell me, how exactly did you die that first time?"

Carolly felt her legs weaken beneath her. "James—"

"I want to know," he continued. "I want to understand why you think you are dead. The only way I can do that is if you explain it to me. Tell me about your other lives."

She turned away from him, wondering if she could run, knowing she could not. James held the key to her afterlife. She had to help him before she could move on, before she could end this nightmare of hopping from life to life. But James did not wish her help. For whatever perverse reason, he wanted to torment her.

She whirled back around, her anger finally breaking free. "Why? Why should I tell you anything?"

He answered calmly, quietly. "Because you want to tell someone. You need to tell someone. Good God, Carolly, you need to talk about your delusions. It is the only way to get past them."

She shook her head, fighting the tears. "They are not delusions."

"How do you know?"

"Because I lived them. Every life, every breath, every death, just like I'm . . ." She cut off her words, seeing the trap he'd laid for her.

"What, Carolly?" He leaned forward, eagerly pressing his point. "Just like you live them now?"

"It's not the same as being alive as you are!"

He stood, advancing on her. "Why not? What is different?"

She pushed away from her tree, her sight wavering with those hated tears she couldn't stop. "Because I always die!" she cried. "I try to fix things, and then I die. One month, ten months, a year and a half, it doesn't matter. I'm someplace, I do what I can to help, and then I die."

He caught her, his movements quick and sure as he gathered her into his arms. "We all die, Carolly. One way or another, we all die."

She wanted to shake her head, but he held her so tight that she couldn't move. "It's not the same. It's not."

"It is," he whispered, and as he spoke, she felt him tremble as if he, too, remembered dying. As if he knew the pain of losing everything because of his own failing. If only she'd been a better person. If only she'd said or done the right thing, then maybe she could have saved those she tried to help. Maybe they would have found happiness, and she would at last rest in peace.

But she'd failed. And she'd died. Only to live again, repeating the miserable process another four times. "I'm not crazy," she whispered to the enveloping comfort of his strong chest.

He stroked her spine in a mesmerizing caress. "Tell me what you remember," he coaxed.

She wanted to do it. She wanted to lie in his arms, to hear the steady beat of his heart, to feel relaxed and content and oh so safe. She would even tell him all her secrets, catalogue every one of her failures for him just so she could remain tucked tightly in his embrace. But then how would she earn her wings? She couldn't turn him toward Miss Hornswapper if he lavished his time and his attention on her.

And yet, for all her strategizing, Carolly remained quiet in his arms, allowing her tears to soak into his shirt, selfishly hoarding his every touch.

Guilt finally forced her to push him away. "I won't fail you," she said. She directed his attention up the rise to where Margaret and Miss Hornswallow walked in the opposite direction, butterfly nets in hand. "You will be my first true success," she continued, her voice growing stronger with every word. "I will help three lives in one masterful stroke. Then I'll get my wings. I'll really be an angel."

He spoke softly, but he left no doubt in his voice. "I will not marry Miss Hornswallow."

"I can't leave until you do."

James sighed, and Carolly was surprised to realize the sound seemed almost happy—as if he wanted her around. Still, his voice remained devoid of emotion when he spoke. "Then we are at an impasse."

Carolly leaned forward, her tears drying as she saw an opening. "Not necessarily. I just need to find you love. If you have a ball, you can meet all the eligible ladies you want. You'll have your pick of hundreds."

"Carolly—"

"You don't have to love Miss Hornswallow, although I think she'd be a good choice. Think of it. Now that your heart is opening up to Margaret, I'm sure there's room for a woman, too."

James shook his head. "How did we get back on this topic? I thought I already—"

"You wish to end this impasse, right?" she coaxed. "Merely fall in love, and you shall be rid of me."

"No!" They both seemed startled by his sudden exclamation, but James was the first to recover. He moderated his tone even though his face remained flushed. "Perhaps that was the problem. You were shuffled from one relative to another until each departure seems like a death to you, each new situation another life."

"It's hard to confuse heavy stones cracking your skull with a tearful good-bye at the front door," she said dryly.

"But that is exactly my point. Maybe they were not cheerful goodbyes. Maybe they chased you away with torches—"

"No." Lord, he was like a dog with a bone. He would not leave off this line of inquiry.

"Maybe they threw rotting vegetables at—"

"No."

"Maybe—"

"Damn it, James, I'm not confused. I'm not a lunatic, I'm not schizophrenic, manic-depressive, or delusional. Hell, I don't even have athlete's foot. James, I'm just dead. And I'm trying to make up for my miserable first life by helping you find happiness. When I do, maybe God will release me from this purgatory and let me be an angel. In Heaven. Now, if you'll excuse me, I'm going to help Mags catch grasshoppers."

She reached over and grabbed her butterfly net, but he stopped her, his large hand suddenly hard and inflexible on her wrist. "I will not stop, Carolly."

She looked at him, her heart beating double at the determination in his eyes. "I know," she whispered.

"We will talk more. Tonight."

She shook her head, then slowly straightened, pulling away until he released her wrist.

"I do not concede easily," he continued. "Some claim I never give in at all."

Carolly looked up into the pure blue sky and wondered where in all that expanse was God. Where was He when she needed His guidance most?

She didn't see Him, so she looked back at James and spoke the thought uppermost in her mind. "One of these days you'll realize I'm not lying. What's going to happen to your orderly world then, James? How will you feel then?"

His expression flattened out. "It will not happen. It cannot happen."

She sighed. "But it will, James. And the reasons I've failed before . . . You want to know about how I died? Each and every time, someone figures it out. Someone finally realizes I am so different that I don't fit into their world concept. So they kill me. Sometimes it's quick and in a rage. Other times I go slowly, by neglect or my own stupidity. But always, I die because someone finds out I am an angel—or almost an angel—and it frightens them so much they have to be rid of me."

James's hands clenched into large, white fists. "I will not kill you."

"It doesn't have to be with a gun, a knife, or even with your fists. You're a civilized man who will find some quiet way."

"I will not kill you!" His denial echoed across the landscape, loud and startling in its intensity. And in that moment, Carolly saw the pain he kept locked inside. She did not understand its source, only that the wound ran deep. She wanted to touch him, to soothe the agony that had become like a wall around his heart, but she knew he'd never accept her comfort. Just as he'd never accept the truth about her. And so . . .

"It's all right, James," she said softly. "That's the way life is for me. For angels, I suppose."

"You're not an angel yet!" he said, the statement aimed like a blow.

Carolly didn't care. She knew the truth. "No, I'm not," she responded calmly. Then she smiled, though the movement felt unnatural and awkward. "But I will be as soon as I find you a wife."

Chapter Seven

Dinner was a somber affair. Carolly sat in silence at one end of a long table while James gestured imperiously at the servants from the other. They sat like two strangers in a restaurant, eating in silence at separate tables. She wasn't sure where Margaret or Miss Hornswallow were.

Carolly didn't even try to speak to James, and he certainly didn't do anything to bridge the gap.

It wasn't until after the meal, long after the servants had been dismissed for the evening, hours after night had settled around the huge house, that she finally got up the nerve to approach him. He sat in the library staring at his brandy. He'd discarded his cravat on a nearby table and was apparently reading some book of Greek something-or-other—except that it lay ignored on his lap.

She knocked lightly, though the door was already open. "James?"

He looked up, his expression unreadable.

"I, uh, I just wanted to apologize for that scene this afternoon."

He raised an eyebrow in surprise, but made no other comment.

"I've always had a stubborn streak." She gave him a wry smile. "No doubt you've noticed."

He set his brandy down on the table beside him, his motions slow and precise.

"Anyway, I hate it when people don't agree with me about something I'm positive is true."

He looked up, his gaze sharp. "You are *positive?*"

She shrugged, taking a deep breath. "I'm positive I'm right, and you're positive I'm wrong. But you know . . ." She wandered further into the room. "It doesn't really matter. *Que sera, sera.*"

"I beg your pardon?"

"Whatever will be, will be. It's a song—uh, never mind. Anyway, we don't need to fight about it."

James leaned back in his chair. His eyes remained hooded, his expression casual, but Carolly could feel the tension between them. It snaked up her spine, making her scalp tingle and her mouth go dry. But she stood her ground and tried not to twist her fingers in the folds of her skirt.

"Tell me, Carolly, did you come here just to apologize? Or did you have some other purpose in mind?"

Carolly squirmed. How did he do it? How did he see so clearly into her thoughts and motives? She sighed. There was no going back now.

"Well, now that you mention it, I did hope to ask you to reconsider about the—"

"No."

She took another step forward, trying to get him to understand. "James, it won't be so bad. It might even be—"

"I said, no."

Carolly held her breath a moment, desperately searching for a way to make him change his mind. Then she looked at his hard face, the angry clench of his jaw, even the smooth way he swirled his brandy. It all added up to one thing.

No.

With a heavy sigh, she collapsed into a chair. "James, you can be such a stuffed shirt sometimes."

"A stuffed shirt?"

"A prig, a killjoy, the guy who always looks down his aristocratic nose at the rest of us while we're having a good time. A—"

"There is no need to elaborate further."

She glanced up. If anything, his expression was even more forbidding. "No, I don't suppose there is."

The silence descended between them, thick and heavy, stifling in its intensity, so that Carolly nearly choked on it. In the end, she settled for a mockery of a laugh. "I guess I'm not very good at apologies."

There was a brief silence. Then, "Tell me about your first life," he said.

Carolly blinked, then burst out laughing. "You're not going to give up, are you?"

"Are you going to stop asking about a ball?"

She thought long and hard, then finally admitted the truth. "No, I'm not."

"And I wish to know about all your lives."

She dropped her chin on her palm and chewed on a fingernail. "How about a trade? I'll answer any question about my previous lives if you let me host a Waterloo ball."

He didn't budge. "I will not host a ball."

"A card party?"

"No."

"A luncheon?"

"No."

"Tea, then."

"No."

"You're a stubborn man, James."

"Yes."

"We're at an impasse." She sighed, her eyes wandering over his slightly disheveled appearance. She loved the sight of him in evening clothes, but even more than that, she loved it when he wore them in disarray. It truly brought out the pirate in him. It was hard to look at him and still argue. Just the sight of his curly chest hairs peeping out between his open collar left her insides weak.

Her gaze wandered outdoors to the breezy night. Maybe a little exercise was what she needed to get a new perspective. She certainly felt like she had energy to burn. She hadn't fidgeted this much since her Aunt Grace's wedding in an un-air-conditioned church when she was six. Er, seven. Maybe she'd been ten.

She sighed and pushed out of her chair. "I think I'll take a walk."

He glanced at her in surprise. "Now?"

She gave him her most devilish smile. "Of course now. You may recall, I'm fond of late night walks."

He grumbled something unintelligible. "I trust you to keep both feet firmly planted on the ground this time."

"Ground?" She waved him off, unable to resist teasing. "Ground, rafters, rooftop. Who knows?"

He pushed out of his chair. "Then I believe I shall go for a walk as well."

Carolly had been about to torment him some more, but the words caught in her throat as she saw him carefully straighten his injured leg. "Um, perhaps you better stay put. I—"

"It helps to exercise it." His voice was low, cutting off her sympathy. "In fact, if I don't walk every day, it gets decidedly worse."

She lifted her eyebrow. "You walked quite a lot this afternoon."

He lifted his head and skewered her with his gaze. "I will go for a walk. With you."

She clicked her heels. "Yes, sir! Anything else, sir?"

He didn't crack a smile, but she thought she saw some glint of amusement in his eyes.

"Yes. Get a coat. It is brisk out, and Mr. Wentworth says it will rain."

Carolly laughed and left in search of a shawl, her good humor inexplicably restored.

"Tell me about your first life."

Carolly sighed happily and let the wind blow her closer to James. "That's what I like about you. You know how to enjoy a peaceful walk in the woods. You don't let some meaningless bit of information rule your every waking thought, pursuing it like a dog after a bone."

James didn't answer except to take her arm to help her over a thick tree root. They were wandering through the woods near his home, listening to the toads and the whispering leaves. When he finally did speak, his voice was pleasant and urbane, its low masculine notes blending perfectly with the higher-pitched gurgle of a nearby stream.

"I wonder why you so studiously avoid speaking of it. Is it perhaps because there is nothing to tell?"

"I avoid talking about it because I don't like thinking about it." She sighed, swinging herself around an aging birch. "Very well. I'll talk, but only because I feel good tonight."

He seemed vaguely startled. "You do?"

"Yes. It's a beautiful night, I'm in a deep, dark, enchanted wood, and I'm with a rakishly handsome pirate. How could I refuse anyone anything?"

He stiffened slightly. "I am certainly no pirate, Carolly, and I sincerely doubt the Traynern wood would be so un-British as to be enchanted."

Carolly felt laughter bubble out of her, flowing easily from her heart. "My goodness, James, I believe you have a sense of humor."

"Only when conversing with Bedlamites."

She swung back around the tree trunk to come nearly eye

to eye with him. "Then I hope you are surrounded by mad-women until the end of your days."

He pressed his hand against his lips in horror, then let it slip to his heart as he began an earnest plea to heaven. "I swear, my Lord God, I swear by all that is holy, that I will donate five thousand, no ten thousand pounds to the church if only you will keep this wretched fate from me!"

This time there was no stopping Carolly's laughter. It surrounded them as sweetly as the night air as they continued meandering through the wood.

"You still have not answered my question," he said.

"Answered your question? Why don't you just say 'Tell me what I want to know or I'll break your legs?' A threat should work."

James slowed, clearly insulted. "I am a gentleman, Carolly."

"I know. More's the pity." Then she sighed with more feeling than she wanted to admit having.

Realizing she was joking, James chuckled and put his arm around her waist, guiding her over a rough part in their make-shift trail. "Carolly—"

"Oh, all right. What do you want to know about my past life?"

"Anything. Everything. Did you have any brothers or sisters?"

"I know what you're doing, you know. I warn you, James, you're about to get more than you bargained for."

"I will endeavor to survive."

The hazy moonlight played in his dark hair while the wind tousled it from its customary perfection. He seemed relaxed. More relaxed, in fact, than he'd been all day. But Carolly knew his easiness was deceptive. He had never been more alert, never more dangerous than now.

She tugged at a maple leaf, yanking it off a tree. Could she tell him everything? She had never told anyone everything before. Not since her second life when they'd locked her up in a loony bin for it.

But there was something about James, something that got to her down deep and made her *want* to explain. Actually, it was more than that. When she was with him, she wanted to tell him all about everything so that together they could figure out her entire messed-up, confused life. Lives. Except she also wasn't sure she wanted to expose all her failings to him. His opinion mattered much more than it should.

She glanced at James. He waited patiently for her decision, his face stoic, but his eyes—those hard, black eyes—challenging her to tell him everything.

She looked away. She'd already told James she was going to be an angel—what harm could there be in the rest? It might be nice, after ten years, to finally have a confidant.

"I had a sister," she began. "Her name was Janice. She reminds me of you." She paused. "Or you remind me of her."

He cocked an eyebrow at her, so she elaborated.

"She was so serious and shy. Always studied, never played."

"And what did you do to torture *her?*"

She grinned. "Same thing I do to you. I forced her to go to parties."

"She did not like them?" He seemed surprised a girl would refuse parties.

Carolly turned so that she faced him. "Actually, James, once I got her there she always had a great time. It was just the 'getting there' part that was a pain in the tookas."

"The what?"

"Pain in the ass, James. Tush. Butt. Hindquarters." She started walking along, shaking her rear for emphasis. She grinned when she heard his strangled choke.

"Your language is most colorful." His voice was clearly strained.

"You should have heard me in my last incarnation," she said over her shoulder. "I was downright disgraceful."

"Why am I not surprised?" His voice was dry, but she could tell he enjoyed their easy banter. It was something he'd never experienced. "What about your parents?"

"Oh, they were good folk—worked hard, devoted themselves to their children. The usual."

He stopped, reaching out to keep her from continuing on. "Was it so very bad?"

Carolly bit her lip, surprised. She'd thought she'd camouflaged all the clues in her own off-brand of humor. But James seemed to see through her barriers.

"Why did you leave them, Carolly?"

She let him turn her around to face him, but she refused to look up, choosing to watch the dark, shadowed leaves fluttering behind him in the wind. "It wasn't bad."

"Then why did you leave them?"

A thousand answers danced through her head. Things about car accidents and teenage drinking, about New Year's Eve and sowing wild oats. But none of those thoughts made it to her mouth. Instead, she spoke the one horror she'd lived with all her afterlife.

"I hurt them, James. I was hurting them."

"How?"

Carolly shrugged, pushing away from him to wander through the dark. The clouds were getting thicker, the moonlight dimmer. A storm was coming, but she didn't care. He'd started her thoughts on this course, and she found she couldn't turn away from it.

"I was the party girl, the fun one. You have to understand, James. We had enough money to live on, but not much more. My parents worked their fingers to the bone to give us every opportunity for a better life."

"And?"

"And I squandered it. Janice studied. She worked hard. And the harder she worked, the more I partied. And the more I partied, the harder she worked. I was selfish, arrogant, and cruel." She stopped, one hand clutching a gnarled branch. "If I'd lived, I would have broken their hearts. Janice probably would have become a brilliant lawyer or doctor. The best I could have achieved was being the fun-girl scamming drinks between shifts at the factory."

"So you left."

"So I got snockered one New Year's Eve, gave the keys to Janice even though I knew the roads were too icy and I'd forced her to have a drink, too. She couldn't control the car, and I got my face flattened between a truck and the back of my car." She gave a flamboyant stage bow to a tight knot of trees. "A spectacular end to a woman who never did anything without flair."

The woods fell silent. The wind died, if only for a moment, and the crickets no longer sang. Carolly didn't dare look at James. The guilt was hard enough to bear without adding his disdain. But as the silence lengthened between them, she found herself gouging her nails into a tree trunk waiting for him to speak. Finally, she forced him.

"What are you thinking?"

"That you and my brother would have thoroughly enjoyed each other."

Of all the things she had expected him to say, that ranked lowest. She turned around, placing her back against another tree, and peered through the silver leaves at him. "Your brother, huh? Where is he? In London flirting with all the eligible young ladies?"

James looked away. "Bradley died while I was in Spain. He broke his neck when he overturned his phaeton during a race to Bath. He was Margaret's father."

Carolly was surprised. "I'm sorry."

He didn't answer, but then, he didn't need to. She had grown accustomed to reading his silences, learning his thoughts by the tempo of his breathing and the tilt of his chin. "You don't miss him, do you?" She saw him stiffen.

"He was my brother. Of course I grieve for him."

"No, you don't. Not really, or at least not yet. You're too busy being angry with him. And that makes you feel guilty." Carolly shook her head, wondering if Janice felt that way about her death, knowing her sister probably did. "You shouldn't, you know. Feel guilty, that is. We party pals know what a nightmare we are. We breeze in, create havoc in the name of a good time, then disappear leaving you solid ones to clean up our messes." She leaned just the tiniest bit forward. "We're not stupid, you know. Most of us have irresponsibility down to an art. We *expect* you to be angry at us."

James stepped forward into a shadow, becoming nothing but a black silhouette. "You enjoy this, don't you? You work at it—your irresponsibility, your foolishness?"

She knew he was thinking of his brother, but she answered for herself. "Of course. I got to drink and carouse to my heart's content."

"And now?" She felt the sudden intensity of his gaze, and her face heated. He was no longer thinking of a long-dead Bradley. He was focused entirely on her. "What do you enjoy now?"

Carolly laughed, pushing him and her nervousness away with one wave of her hand. "Now? Now, I'm working off my sins. Now I drop in, try to teach the partiers responsibility, show the serious ones how to have a good time, and hope that one day I'll have suffered and sweated and helped myself into a set of angel wings." She looked up at the darkened sky, wishing she could see some stars. "I want this to work out, James. I want it so bad."

He touched her arm, soothing her with the lightest of caresses. "Are you sure about your purpose . . . ?"

"Yes."

"How? How do you know?"

She shrugged, letting her gaze drop to him as she managed a weak smile. "I don't know how I know. I just know that's what I'm doing. I'm working my way to a set of wings."

"Why not just live *here?*" He clearly struggled to accept her explanation, but pushed doggedly on. "Live in the present. In this . . . incarnation."

She shook her head. "I can't."

He grabbed her arm, stopping her from running when she would have ducked under a low branch. "You can."

"I don't want to!"

"Why?"

"Because I don't!" She jerked away from him, but he wouldn't release her. Instead, he leaned close, his body pressing her against the tree trunk, his breath heating the space her lips.

"Why is this life so terrible for you?"

She didn't answer because she didn't know, and that frightened her. Did she want to stay here? Could she stay? Questions burned in her thoughts, and her eyes blurred with tears she couldn't stop.

"Carolly." His word was a whisper. He touched her cheek, catching her first tear on the pad of his thumb. Then he dropped his head to hers and pressed his lips to her temple. "I am sorry."

She had no answers for either him or herself. She knew she was dead, and yet, she had never felt more alive. She felt the rough bark at her back, the lean muscular strength of him in front. She heard the slight rasp of his breath and smelled the scent of wood mixing with the strangely compelling odor of Bay Rum.

How could she be dead when all around her was life? When inside she felt such longing. "James . . ." Her voice was ragged with need.

"I want to kiss you."

"I . . ." She shouldn't. She knew that. But she wanted to.

He leaned forward, barely touching her with his lips, trailing them slowly along her cheeks, the corner of her mouth, to her lips. The air all around was moist and hot, and she tingled as if he were taking tiny nips at her body, tasting her, tormenting her.

She let out a soft moan that was both desire and fear. She couldn't let him closer. She couldn't let him into her heart.

"Oh, James," she breathed, closing her eyes against her tears. "I'm so confused."

"Then let me help you."

She felt the hard planes of his chest where it rubbed against her breasts. Her legs heated where the taut muscles of his thighs pressed against her. But most of all, she was aware of the hunger in him, the incredible power that he restrained for her sake, so he wouldn't frighten her.

That, more than anything else, caused her to weaken. Through her entire life and all her incarnations, she'd met men both weak and strong who blustered and bullied. They used whatever power they had, physical or mental, to force the world to conform to their ideas. Some were effective, others weren't. But none of them had held back, had ever controlled themselves enough to allow her to make the decisions.

Always it had been a battle of wills.

Now, with James, it was different. He was stronger than she was. She knew that. But he did not abuse his position. He held himself apart, controlled himself with such fearsome intensity that she'd initially thought him cold and empty.

How wrong she'd been.

Now he held her pinned against a tree, not to hurt her, but to keep her from running while she made her decision.

"Let me kiss you," he whispered. His breath was a soft caress along her cheek.

She turned, lifting her face to his, her body softening in open invitation. Her mind told her to refuse, to push James away, but her hands traced the rippling muscles of his arms, skimmed the width of his broad shoulders, reached into his hair to pull him to her.

His mouth was as uncompromising as the rest of him. It was demanding, but she opened willingly to the assault. His tongue plunged into her mouth, taking and tasting as though he feared she would change her mind.

She arched against him, awed that nothing in her many lives had ever felt this right, this wonderful. His hunger fed hers, his power invaded her, and she was strengthened even as she submitted to him. She moaned, barely aware that she pushed her hips forward, begging for more than just a kiss.

Bang!

A small chip of wood ricocheted against her cheek. James froze for an instant; then he abruptly threw her to the ground, covering her with his body.

Carolly welcomed his weight, only vaguely realizing his intent wasn't seduction but something entirely different. "James?"

Another shot rang out, mixing with the sporadic tapping of a rainstorm just beginning.

"Was that a gunshot?"

He didn't answer, but then again, he didn't need to.

"Is someone shooting at *us*?"

James shook his head. "A poacher. They have become bolder since I changed things at the mine."

"What?" She started to roll him off of her, but he held her down, his weight trapping her as surely as an iron cage.

The rain increased, a soft *pitter-pat* at odds with the tension in James's body. Then, abruptly, he raised his head, bellowing into the black woods: "The Earl of Traynern is here. Go home. Go home to your fire and your children before I catch you."

Then they both waited, their bodies tense while the musky smell of wet ground rose around them. They couldn't hear anything through the howl of the wind and the sound of the rain on the leaves.

Still James held her down. Carolly twisted slightly, looking around, but could see nothing. The darkness was complete, the world revealed only in sound and nearly indistinguishable shades of black.

"James," she whispered. "We should get home."

"Give them another moment to get away."

"Them?"

He shrugged as he shifted off of her, though he still held her down with one hand. "Him, her, or them. It makes no difference except that they be long gone by the time we get up."

"I didn't think there was much game in these woods. They're thin and so close to your home."

She felt him shift again, a resigned gesture. "When people are hungry, they go wherever they can and hope to find something."

Carolly didn't respond. She was too busy trying to hold back a sneeze. A chill seeped through the ground, straight into her back. Then with a sudden clap of thunder, the clouds opened up, quickly drenching them both.

She sneezed.

He gave her a sharp look then stood, intending to lift her up with him.

"No! Your leg." She pushed him away and got to her feet. Her skirt felt like clammy seaweed that weighed two tons. She took a step then stopped, realizing she'd completely lost her bearings. Nothing looked familiar.

Nothing *looked* at all. It was all black.

"Take my hand."

James's voice was a reassuring murmur, and she groped blindly toward the sound until she found him.

"Do not let go," he ordered gently.

No chance of that. She was attached to his arm like an industrial strength vacuum. He walked slowly and surely. She moved after him, ducking when he said to duck, stepping higher when he told her to. Carolly felt like a blind woman being led through a maze, and she was amazed that even with his injured leg, James never faltered. His step was solid and confident, and she was eternally grateful for his presence.

Soon the ground began to even out. They cleared the woods. The rain continued without pause and the wind picked up as they left the trees, but at least the darkness seemed more gray, less black. Carolly sneezed again, wondering if she might be warmer without the sodden weight of her dress slapping against her legs. The thin wool certainly didn't seem to keep out the icy wind.

"There!" James's voice cut through her misery, and only then did she realize they'd stopped. James leaned against one of the last trees, his breathing loud even through the storm. "Do you see the house?"

Her gaze followed the line of his arm, up the rise she knew was there, until she made out the blackened silhouette of his house. "Yes!"

"Run for it!"

She glanced at him, noting that his breathing had not steadied, finally understanding the ragged edge was from pain. His leg must feel like it was on fire.

"Go!" he repeated, trying to push her away.

She shook her head, grabbing onto his arm. "Not without you."

He disentangled himself from her, his anger carrying clearly through the rumble of thunder. "You will go now!"

"Then come with me!"

"Do not be a fool! You are chilled through."

Carolly turned, planting her hands on her hips, oblivious to the icy drops needling through her thin clothes. "Don't be an ass, James." She grabbed his arm and yanked hard. "Now move it!"

"Damn Bedlamite," was all she heard. But he did move, his limp becoming more and more pronounced as they struggled together up the hill.

Chapter Eight

The morning dawned fair and bright, and Carolly wanted nothing more than to bury herself under the covers for the next week at least. James had been a complete bully as soon as they'd gotten inside. He'd roused the entire household and ordered baths, refusing to care for himself until he'd carried her to her room. *Carried!* But she'd shivered so much she couldn't get the words out to effectively argue with him.

Fortunately, she'd recovered quickly enough to cancel the baths. There was no sense in sending servants out into the rain to get chilled just for that. She'd ended up drying her hair by a roaring fire while sending messages through a maid to Mrs. Potherby on how to properly care for James's knee.

She must have driven the poor woman to distraction.

But now it was morning and time to face another day. Except Carolly hadn't even finished dealing with the night before. It obsessed her so much that she skipped her usual mental catalogue of her lives just to dwell in memory.

She'd kissed him. Again. In fact, if not for the poacher and the storm, they would probably have made love right there against the tree.

Her face flushed, and she buried herself even deeper under the covers. She wasn't embarrassed about what they'd done. In fact, the thought of becoming James's lover had her tingling from head to toe with excitement. If she weren't trying to be an angel, she'd run across the hall straight into his bed right now.

But she did want to be an angel. And even if she wanted to live a normal, mortal life, she couldn't. She was here to help James, not to live out her lurid fantasies. Though what wonderful fantasies they were, she thought with a smile. Her, little Carolly, an earl's lover.

She giggled at the thought, then abruptly clapped her hand over her mouth. She shouldn't be thinking this way. She should be planning ways to throw James and Miss Hornswallow together. But somehow that didn't seem to catch her interest, and she found her attention wandering back to the night before.

"Morning, Carolly! Did someone really shoot at you last night?"

Carolly peeked out from under the covers to see Margaret's face grinning at her. She lifted her chin suspiciously. "Where did you hear that?"

"I heard Uncle telling his steward."

Carolly was torn. On the one hand, she should admonish the child for listening at keyholes. On the other hand, she was consumed with curiosity and she'd always encouraged mischievousness. What would James do about the poacher?

Finally, she achieved a compromise. "You shouldn't be listening at keyholes," she admonished. "But since you were"— she tried to put on a casual air—"what else did your uncle say?"

Margaret smiled, not in the least bit fooled. "Well," she began with dramatic flair, "he will hire someone to patrol the near grounds at night."

Carolly sat up. "Really? A bunch of rabbits mean that much to him?"

Margaret shook her head, quick to defend her uncle. "Oh, no. He said the villagers may hunt on the far grounds, but he cannot allow anyone to get hurt in the near woods."

Carolly nodded, thinking that sounded reasonable.

"Besides," added the girl, "it will provide one more job for someone."

During her short stay so far, Carolly had never gone off the near grounds and never met anyone who wasn't somehow connected to James's household. All of them had appeared clean, well-mannered, and well-fed. It had never occurred to her that the area might actually be in economic crisis. What had James said last night? She searched her memory, skating past the erotic parts, trying to focus on what he'd *said* to her. Something about changes in the mine.

"What did your uncle do at the mine?"

Margaret's eyes twinkled, bursting with information. "Uncle did something bad."

Carolly sat up straighter. "Bad? What did he do?"

The girl leaned forward, milking the information for all the drama she could. "He fired them. Just after I arrived four years ago."

"Fired who?"

"All of them."

"Who?"

"All the women and children. He will not hire any woman or any child under thirteen."

Carolly let out a relieved breath. For a moment there, she'd thought it had been something bad.

"Miss Hornswallow says it is cruel, but Uncle will not change his mind."

Cruel? Cruel to keep the women and kids from dying of black lung disease? From risking a mine collapse, suffocation, or burning? From spending most of their waking hours underground in miserable conditions?

"All the miners hate him. There is even talk of rebellion."

Carolly was flabbergasted. Rebellion? Against James? She twisted her fingers into the coverlet. She'd thought this incarnation might be fairly straightforward. All she had to do was get Miss Hornswallow and James together. Except now she had to add an economic crisis and a mining revolt to her list of problems. Things just seemed to get more and more complicated.

Carolly threw back her covers, startling Margaret with her sudden energy. Match-making James and Miss Hornswallow could wait. She had to check into this other crisis.

"How about showing me around the village, hmmm?"

The young girl jumped up. "Great!" Then her enthusiasm quickly died. "Except I have lessons with Miss Hornswallow. I always have lessons," she moaned in the familiar whine of all schoolchildren.

"You leave your governess to me. This afternoon, you're going to give *me* lessons."

Margaret brightened immediately, but Carolly felt as if a weight had settled on her chest. Why? She should be thrilled. By taking Margaret with her, she increased the chances that Miss Hornswallow and James would meet and go on their own little walk in the woods. Carolly winced, but then she steeled her resolve. Nothing could ever come of hanging on to James. Nothing except heartache all around.

She sighed and motioned to Margaret. "Go on and study hard now. It's early. Then meet me after lunch in the stable. I'll tell Miss Hornswinger that we're to have an outing."

"Hornswallow."

"Whatever."

Margaret grinned. She stopped just before opening the door. "Someone really did shoot at you?"

Carolly smiled. "Yeah. I also walked along that ledge to return your toad—except that you don't sleep in the room I thought."

The girl's eyes narrowed suspiciously. "You did not walk

along that ledge. Uncle forbid you to. I heard him."

Carolly almost laughed. "I've never been able to take orders well. Ask your uncle if you don't believe me."

Margaret stared at her a little longer, still suspicious.

"I climbed out right here onto the ledge," Carolly said, stung that she'd risked her life and the girl didn't even believe her. "It was very safe until I came up against the ivy. Here, look." She threw open the shutters and pointed. "See where that vine is pulled away from the wall? I did that when I almost fell."

Margaret leaned out the window, then started climbing out onto the ledge to see clearer.

"No, no! Don't go. It's not safe." Carolly couldn't believe the panic that clutched her at the thought of Margaret standing out there. Even though she knew the near ledge was fairly safe, she was nearly hyperventilating at the thought.

Margaret, of course, had no qualms. "But *you* did it," she said, her voice muffled as she pushed her torso further out.

"That's different." Carolly firmly tugged the child inside.

"Why?"

Carolly bit her lip. Why? She couldn't really tell Margaret that she didn't fear death because she was an angel. James would have a fit. Instead, she chose her own version of the truth. "Because I'd die of heart failure if I saw you crawling that far above the ground."

"But you said it was safe."

"Don't do it because your uncle would kill me," Carolly tried.

Finally, she'd hit upon something Margaret understood. To Carolly's enormous relief, the girl sighed in agreement. But it was a heavy, heavy sigh, and the child cast longing looks at the window. "Will we still go into the village?" she asked with a long face.

Carolly frowned. "Yes. Why wouldn't we?"

"Because Uncle will not like that either."

"Oh."

"He says it is not safe."

"Hmmm." Carolly thought. James was probably exaggerating the danger. He simply didn't want Margaret wandering off alone. But they should be safe as long as they stayed together. Besides, Carolly had to see the conditions in the village, and for that she needed a guide. Any of the maids or footmen would have to ask for permission, and then James would find out.

She wasn't entirely sure why she was reluctant for James to know of her upcoming adventure. The thought of tooling around town with him sent an excited thrill through her body. But she strongly suspected that James would not want to broadcast the fact that a mad Bedlamite was living at his house, which meant he would refuse the trip. Which meant she would never get to see the village for herself.

Besides, she reminded herself with a sigh, she had to get Margaret and herself out of the house if James and Miss Hornswallow were ever going to get together.

Which meant that she and Margaret would go to town together.

Shrugging off her misgivings, she turned on her brightest smile. "You leave your uncle to me. With any luck, he won't even know we're gone."

Margaret tilted her head, clearly considering her options. Carolly held her breath while the precocious child thought.

"All right," the girl finally said. "But I get to drive."

Drive? It took a moment before Carolly realized Margaret meant a wagon or carriage or whatever they used to go to town.

"Are you sure you can handle it?"

"Absolutely." Margaret spoke with an eight-year-old's certainty. Alarms went off in Carolly's head, but she really didn't have much choice; no matter how bad Margaret was at driving a carriage, she was probably a good deal better than Carolly. She just had to keep the little girl safe.

"It's a deal," Carolly finally said. She could only pray James never found out.

Letting an eight-year-old drive a gig was like letting a teenager play around with a Ferrarri, except there wasn't a seat belt. Margaret apparently knew the basics—the stuff Carolly could have figured out herself. You sat in the front and said something like "giddy-up" and the horses went forward. But Margaret didn't just say "giddy-up." She flicked the reins not once, not twice, but four times until they zipped along a rutted road at what felt like warp speed. Carolly felt like she was going down the slalom without bothering to avoid the bumps.

"Uh, Mags, could we please slow down?"

Margaret had on a wide grin of ecstasy and wasn't listening. Then Carolly looked a little harder at the two brown horses in front of her. Something about them seemed odd. Sure, she didn't know much about team horses, but she didn't think they ought to be snorting and throwing their heads like that. That's what wild horses looked like in the movies.

"Mag—" Her word jolted right back into her throat as they went over another big rut. That's when she started to get a really bad feeling.

She decided it was time to put a stop to this ride before she permanently damaged her tailbone.

"Margaret! Slow down!"

This time, the girl heard. She pulled back on the ribbons. Or at least it looked like she did. Carolly waited for the telltale slowing of the vehicle.

Nothing.

"Maaaaiee!" Another huge bump, and Carolly had to grab the edge to keep from flying out. If they kept this up, they'd lose a wheel for sure. "Damn it, Mags! Slow down!"

"I am trying!" The girl's voice came out as a wail of panic. One quick look told Carolly the only thing keeping Margaret from hysteria was lack of breath.

Without thinking, Carolly encircled the child with her

arms, covering Margaret's hands with her own, and together they pulled backwards, reining in the horses. Except they were on a downhill slope, and the horses and gig gained speed as they went. Even as the two of them pulled back, the weight of the carriage pushed the horses on.

Carolly cursed loudly and fluently while searching the floor. "Where the hell is the damn brake?" She flailed her feet in a wide arc, hoping to hit something, anything that might resemble a pedal. "Mags! Wh—ow! Where's the brake?"

Carolly wasn't watching the girl's face, but she felt Margaret's body jerk with sudden understanding. While Carolly tried to control the now panicked horses, Margaret wormed her fingers free, then reached out and pulled back on a thick stick that Carolly hadn't paid any attention to.

"Right here!"

Carolly didn't have time to sigh in relief, but she did send a brief prayer of thanks to God as they began to slow.

Crack!

"Oh, no!"

Carolly glanced over, only to gasp in horror as Margaret held up the broken brake handle. She looked back at the horses. Something was wrong with them. They were heaving like tormented beasts, headed straight to the curve at the bottom of the hill. All she could do was haul backward on the reins while her mind repeated a movie slogan:

Be afraid. Be very, very afraid.

She didn't have to be told. Coming to a quick decision, Carolly dropped the leads, grabbed Margaret, and screamed, "We've got to bail!"

"What?"

"Jump!"

Carolly wrapped her arms around the young girl and tensed for the right moment.

"Now!"

They leaped together, landing in the muddy ditch at the side of the road. Carolly rolled, doing her best to hold on to

Margaret, but the child was ripped from her arms. Off in the distance, she heard a crash as the gig hit and splintered against the trees at the bottom of the hill. As soon as she tumbled to a stop, she pushed to her knees, ignoring the pain she only now began to feel.

"Mags!" Her voice came out as a soft croak, so she took a deep breath and tried again. "Mags! Where are you?" She'd kill herself if anything had happened to the girl.

Wiping away the mud and leaves, Carolly crawled out of the ditch. Thankfully, she had landed mostly in mud, which meant that, although she was filthy, she was at least alive and generally whole. She could only pray Margaret was equally fortunate.

"Margaret!"

She scrambled up the embankment and stopped to look, scanning the ground, the trees, everything, dreading the sight of blood. Around her, the woods remained in complete silence. Even the wind had stopped.

That's when she heard it. It was soft and quiet, but heartfelt. A muffled sob—one that could only have come from a terrified eight-year-old girl.

Margaret was alive.

Sending her thanks to heaven, Carolly closed her eyes and focused on the sound. When she located it, she opened her eyes and stepped slowly toward it.

She almost tripped over the child by the time she finally found her. Margaret huddled behind a tree, clutching her knees while huge tears streamed down her face. "Oh, Mags, thank God you're all right."

Carolly dropped to her knees beside the child, searching for any sign of injury. Other than a few scrapes, including a very raw knee, Margaret seemed fine.

"Oh, thank you, thank you God." Then Carolly pulled Margaret into her arms and held her close while they both cried their eyes out.

It was some time later before Carolly regained control of

herself. And even longer before she felt strong enough to do more than just hold the whimpering Margaret. But eventually she took a deep breath and spoke, albeit softly and mostly to herself.

"Well, this is a fine sight. Me, a strong modern woman, on her knees sobbing because we're both alive. I'm so sorry, Mags. I never would have allowed this if I thought there would be so much danger. I'm so sorry." Then she buried her face in the child's hair and kissed it, feeling the specter of her many failures rearing up once again.

Yes, Carolly Hansen had failed again because she was just too stupid to think things through.

"At least you're safe. I would have died if anything happened to you." Then she lifted her head, suddenly needing to be extra sure. "Are you sure you're all right? Does anything hurt? Any pain, dizziness, any . . . I don't know, double vision or something?"

She pushed Margaret back, searching her face, but the girl only shook her head, her big brown eyes shimmering with tears.

"You'll tell me if anything hurts, won't you? If you feel weird in any way."

"Weird?" The word was little more than a whisper, but Carolly greeted it as a godsend. Margaret could speak. Carolly didn't know why she was so thrilled by that, just that she was.

"Weird means . . . uh, funny. Uncomfortable. I don't know, just tell me about anything out of the ordinary." Then she glanced at their disheveled clothing. "Or rather, anything *else* out of the ordinary."

That brought a tentative smile from the girl which made Carolly feel immensely better. In the end, the two were grinning together as they slowly pushed to their feet and unsuccessfully tried to brush the mud and leaves off their gowns.

"Thank goodness I left off that ridiculous corset," Carolly announced. "I might have punctured a lung with those whale bones."

Margaret's eyes opened wider. "You aren't wearing a corset?" she asked, her voice filled with awe. "But we are going into town."

Carolly pursed her lips. "I was going to stand up straight so no one would notice."

Margaret looked significantly at the gaping hole torn in the side of Carolly's dress, then at the raw scrape of flesh beneath. "No one will be fooled now."

"Ah, well," Carolly said with a shrug. "What's life without a little scandal?"

Margaret frowned. "Uncle does not like scandal."

"No, I didn't think he did," Carolly said nonchalantly. Her equilibrium was slowly returning. "But then, he isn't here now, is he?"

Then the most amazing thing happened: Margaret giggled. It was a girlish sound that reminded Carolly of Barbie dolls and hot chocolate. It was the giggle of a child who was finally casting off the shackles of nineteenth-century repression in a cold household.

More importantly, it was the sound of a happy child.

It thrilled Carolly so much she couldn't resist hugging Margaret one more time. "Come on, sweetheart. Let's go see what damage we've done to your uncle's gig."

Hand in hand, the two walked the rest of the way down the hill. Carolly was almost afraid to look, but she steeled herself for total disaster.

"Oh, my." That was Margaret. Carolly couldn't draw breath to speak. It was too horrible a sight. The gig was smashed into ragged bits and the horses were nowhere to be seen.

"The traces broke."

Carolly spun around. "What?"

"There." Margaret pointed to the torn leather. "It broke."

"Which means the horses are probably halfway back to the manor by now."

Margaret nodded, her expression suddenly very solemn.

"Well, at least they survived."

"But the gig . . ."

Carolly glanced at Margaret, noting her shimmering eyes and the trembling lip. The girl was on the verge of losing it. Carolly would have to distract her quickly if she didn't want a bawling child on her hands.

"Come on. Let's start walking."

"But Uncle—"

"Don't think about it." She spoke as much to herself as to Margaret. She didn't dare picture James's reaction to this little disaster, or she'd be the one sobbing in the middle of the road.

"It's all my fault," Margaret whispered. "All my fault."

"No," Carolly said quickly. "No, it's our fault. Except that you're a kid. You're supposed to do stupid things. That's part of being a child. I'm an adult. I gave you permission to do a stupid thing, and worse than that, I went along to help." She knelt down to give the girl a hug. "It's not your fault, Margaret. It's mine, and it's past time I started thinking things through instead of just following my impulses." *Especially given my current heavenly task,* she thought with a swift, mental kick to her rear. Angels were supposed to help people, not smash their gigs, nearly kill their nieces, or generally screw things up even more.

Carolly look up and down the empty road. "So, which way to do we go?"

Margaret blinked and looked confused.

"Is there a farmhouse or something close by? How far is the town? It's a long walk back to the manor."

"Uh," the girl began. "The town is close, I think. The first houses should be around the next bend. Maybe."

"Then that's where we'll go." Carolly started to walk, but Margaret held back.

"No!" the girl said with unusual force and a little bit of horror. "We cannot go there dressed like this. We must go back to the Manor."

Carolly stopped and stared at her young charge. "That'll

take forever, and you said there were farmhouses just around the corner."

Margaret folded her arms and looked stubborn.

Carolly tried again. "We've just been in a bad accident. I'm sure they'll forgive a few mud stains."

"But you are not wearing a corset, and we look like . . . like servants. Or beggars." Margaret's whole face quivered with revulsion at the idea.

This from the girl who only a few days earlier had looked like a sullen lump in a shapeless brown dress? "Mags . . ."

The girl drew herself upright, speaking pompously for all her eight years. "I am the ward of an earl. You are his guest. What we do reflects upon him."

Carolly dropped her hands to her hips, thoroughly insulted by the child's attitude. "So we'll have them all over to tea!" she snapped. "But we're not going to walk for hours when a warm fire and dry towels are just around the corner."

"You don't understand! They are already angry at Uncle. If we appear—"

"What I understand, young lady, is that very soon people are going to miss us. They'll worry, especially when the horses get back. Oh, Lord," she moaned, "your uncle is going to be worried sick."

Margaret's face set into a mulish pout. "But we look—"

"We're going. Now."

Margaret shut her mouth, but her outrage remained, plain for all to see. Carolly simply shook her head and began a quick march down the road. For a moment, she thought Mags would refuse to follow, but eventually the girl stomped after her.

Children! Carolly thought with annoyance. Who could figure them? She knew they both looked a fright, but they'd had an accident. Surely the townspeople would stop to help a stranger in need, no matter how disreputable they appeared.

The first person they came across was a large woman with her children in what seemed to be an empty yard. She was stirring something vile in a big cauldron while ragged young children harassed her from all sides.

"Excuse me, ma'am," Carolly began.

The woman merely peered up at them and sneered, "Git on. I cain't 'elp ye."

Carolly stepped closer. "No, you don't understand. We've had an accident—"

"Git on!"

Carolly stopped moving and turned to Margaret to see if the child knew why the woman was acting so strange. But the girl was still in the midst of her preteen sulks, which left Carolly to navigate unfamiliar waters.

She turned back to the peasant woman, who had now stepped out from behind her huge pot while her children clung to her skirts. "Look, we're not beggars," Carolly said. "We're staying with the earl—"

"Wait a moment. I know *'er.*" The woman stared at Margaret, who simply lifted her chin and tried to look disdainful. "Yer the by-blow. Git out! Go git yer high-and-mighty earl to 'elp."

"I am not a . . . a . . ." Margaret was flushed with anger, her hands bunching into fists.

Carolly stepped forward, coming between the two combatants and trying to redirect things before matters got completely out of hand. "There must be some mistake. Look, we've had an accident and—"

"And you be the new earl's fancy-piece. Git out!" To make her point, the peasant grabbed a large and very sharp ax off a tree stump and started advancing.

"Wait!" Carolly cried, appalled that the word came out more like a squeak than a command. "I'm not a—"

"Wot's cracking up 'ere?"

Carolly turned, thankful for any interruption, even in the guise of a grizzled old man stomping out of the hut.

"They's from uphill. Come to steal more from us."

"What?" Carolly took a deep breath, trying to take control

of both the situation and her fraying temper. Why wouldn't these people listen? "Look. We've had an accident—"

"Git on. Ain't we suffered enough from the earl?"

"But—"

"Git!"

Carolly wanted to argue, but the woman was still brandishing her ax. Clearly, neither she nor the man had any interest in helping them, let alone listening to anything Carolly could say about economics, lung disease, or child labor laws. So, with a frustrated glare in the woman's direction, Carolly grabbed Margaret and beat a hasty retreat.

It wasn't until they'd reached the road again that Carolly trusted herself to speak. "Some time very soon, Mags, we're going to talk about what just happened here. But not right now. Right now, I'm much too angry."

Typically, Margaret said nothing. She just sulked.

Great.

Fortunately, the next place they came to was a small coaching inn. "Wonderful." Carolly breathed in relief. At least they could freshen up somehow, and with any luck the innkeeper and his wife would be of a higher, more educated, less judgmental caliber.

"Come on, Mags. They're sure to help us here." She practically had to pull the increasingly reluctant child along with her. But once they reached the relatively empty courtyard, she released the girl's arm, stepping over to one of the younger boys there, presumably a stable boy, who lounged against a barrel of some sort.

"I'd like to speak with the innkeeper, please," she said, trying to make her voice sound aristocratic.

Her answer was a loud hoot of derision from another boy and a small, squat man. "We ain't got nothin' for ye."

Carolly tried again through clenched teeth. "We're not looking for a handout. We've had a carriage accident along the road."

"An' I be the queen o' England."

"Then, your highness, be so good as to fetch the innkeeper so that I may send a message to the earl."

That got their attention. The man stood up and squinted at them. "The earl?"

The small boy gasped. "It's the fancy-piece and the by-blow!"

"I am not his mistress!" Carolly snapped.

"Don't matter." The grizzled man spit contemptuously into the dirt by her feet. "We ain't got nothin' to say."

Carolly ground her teeth in frustration. What was the matter with these people? She could understand anger at beggars, but they knew Margaret. Shouldn't they be falling over themselves to help? Did they hate James so very much?

"What's going on here?"

Carolly heaved a sigh of relief as the innkeeper bustled out of the inn, wiping his hands on his apron. He was quickly followed by a large, red-faced woman carrying a broom, and a couple of early customers, all very old, still holding their ale.

"Finally," whispered Carolly as she stepped forward. "Excuse me, sir, but my carriage has met with an accident—"

"From the manor, Durbin," interrupted the old man.

The innkeeper subjected Carolly to a thorough and insulting inspection, taking in everything from her muddy clothes to her missing corset. Then, with a snort of disgust, he turned his back. "So theys can go on back there."

"Wait!" Carolly was becoming desperate. Humiliation rarely bothered her much. In fact, it had become almost routine in her last few lives. But that was her. Mags, on the other hand, seemed to be shrinking into herself more as each second went by. The girl wouldn't stand up to much more of this. Thus, Carolly took recourse in the only thing left. "I'll pay you," she cried.

At last she was rewarded. The innkeeper stopped and turned, silencing the hooting crowd with a wave of his fist. "Show me," was all he said.

Carolly flushed. "Or at least I'm sure the earl will pay you when he learns of our predicament."

She had barely gotten the words out when the crowd renewed its laughter. Carolly ignored them, reaching instead for the oldest line in the book. She turned to the only woman in the group and let herself look as desperate as she felt.

"Please. In the name of Christian charity . . ."

The effect was immediate. The woman puffed herself up with righteous indignation and stepped forward, brandishing her broom. "Charity? Christian charity, you say? An' why should we 'elp the likes of you when it's because of you and 'er"—she made a vicious stab at Margaret with her broom— "that our babes are starving at our breasts? Our children are crying for milk, an' we ain't got a roof over our heads."

Carolly stared at the woman, feeling totally confused. "How are *we* responsible for your situation?"

"My situation! Did you hear that, Bob? My sit-u-ation. When it's 'er who's been tossed out on 'er ear. Well, good riddance to bad rubbish, I say." A cheer echoed through the courtyard.

"But we haven't done anything to you," cried Carolly. She scrambled for a way to deal rationally with these people.

"You took our jobs," they cried. "You seduced the earl to yer evil ways."

The insults were coming fast and furious, led by the shrewish woman. Carolly tried to shout them down, but couldn't. Her tenuous hold on her temper was slipping, and she was thinking about slugging the woman when she got hit in the face with a gob of mud. It didn't hurt, just surprised her. But some experiences—like being stoned to death—tended to stick with a person. Carolly knew exactly what was happening even as her mind reeled with the horror of it all.

She raised her arm as more mud sailed with painful accuracy right toward her face. Whipping around, she tried to shield Margaret from the crowd. "Run!" she screamed, knowing that the throng would soon progress to throwing stones along with mud.

She was almost too busy ducking and running, her skirts slapping about her legs, to hear the oncoming rush of hooves. Glancing up she saw James, his powerful body astride Shadow galloping into the courtyard. His face was twisted in rage.

If ever she felt grateful that he could look so incredibly terrifying, it was at that moment. The crowd quickly dropped back as he clattered into the yard.

"Stop it this instant! Stop it!" he bellowed. The mud bombs stopped, but James did not. He glared at the people around him and continued to shout: "These people are under my care! Anyone who touches them again will answer to me! Is that clear?"

His only answer was a sullen, angry silence, and Carolly looked back fearfully. True, the people were cowed for now. A furious earl on horseback was a little much for seven unarmed people to fight. But the inclination remained. Hatred and resentment simmered in the afternoon heat.

"Get up."

Carolly blinked, only now realizing James spoke to her, ordering her to climb onto his horse. Margaret, she noted, had already scrambled up in front of her uncle. After one last glance behind her, Carolly quickly grasped James's outstretched hand and swung herself up behind him.

"Are you sure Shadow can carry us all?" she whispered.

"Just hold tight."

He didn't have to tell her twice. She buried her face against his hard back and wrapped her arms so tight around his middle, a hurricane could not tear her loose. She felt the horse's powerful haunches bunch and release as they rode away.

"Are you hurt?" James called back to her.

"No," she said, coloring her voice with false bravado. "I'm an old hand at stonings, remember? But Margaret—"

"She is fine."

Carolly sneaked a peek at the girl in front of James. Mags

was curled tight against her uncle, her face tucked out of view, but she didn't seem to have any cuts or bruises. "Thank God," she said.

Carolly took a deep breath. Even though the child was unhurt, she could tell by James's rigid body and stony silence that she was in serious trouble. She wasn't surprised. In fact, she was in serious trouble with her own conscience. She had acted stupidly again, putting herself and an innocent child at risk without thinking. Whatever dressing down the earl intended was nothing compared to what she was telling herself right now.

But then again, knowing James, he'd probably find a way to make her feel even worse.

She was almost looking forward to it. She certainly deserved it.

Chapter Nine

"So. Aren't you going to yell at me?"

"I beg your pardon?" James settled into his favorite leather chair, and, out of habit, stretched his feet toward the cold library grate. Carolly sat beside him, her hands folded demurely in her lap, her head bowed as though a great weight compressed her shoulders. She sat properly, refraining from her usual sprawl. And if he wasn't mistaken, she wore a corset.

Carolly in a corset. What had the world come to?

He let his gaze travel the length of his strange guest. For a moment he allowed his senses to linger on the golden highlights in her hair, on the sweet curve of her neck, and the soft scent of lemon clinging to her luminous skin. She was beautiful, and she contained a fire that defied God and man alike. An angel, indeed. And yet, if anyone could be what she claimed, it would be Carolly.

Except she was not an angel—or a pre-angel, as she so delicately put it. She was a madwoman. And he had come to care deeply for her.

He turned away, pushing his thoughts toward this afternoon's trauma. At least Margaret seemed unharmed. After a long hot bath, the child had gone straight to bed, not even bothering to eat. He knew Carolly had spoken with her, and he intended to check in on the child later, but for right now, he was content to let her be. The afternoon's events were shocking and frightening, especially for a young child. But she had survived and would be much more wary in the future.

Right now, his attention was drawn to the strange woman at his side.

"Carolly—"

"I was stupid, irresponsible, and idiotic," she whispered. "I didn't think my actions through, and I could have gotten Margaret killed."

What could he say to that? She would not even look at him, her customary directness somehow stripped away. It pained him to see it.

"So, go to it, James," she continued with utter defeat in her voice. "Yell. Scream. Throw me out. Hit me."

He stiffened in his chair. Did she honestly believe he would strike her? He took a deep breath, then carefully made his voice its most gentle. "Will you ever go to the village alone again?"

She didn't hesitate. "No."

"Will you ever take Margaret exploring without speaking to me about it first?"

"Absolutely not."

He paused, wanting to make sure she understood. If only she would meet his eyes. It was hard to be gentle when all he could see was the top of her head. "I do not act without good reason. You are aware of that, are you not? And for Margaret to again—"

"You don't have to worry about it." Her voice was dark. "We're not going anywhere. At least not without an armed escort."

"Then," he said, kneeling down before her and lifting up

her chin, "I shall not lecture you. I have the impression you have been censored too much in your life."

Carolly blinked, and he caught the distinct shimmer of her unshed tears. "You're not throwing me out?"

"I cannot allow a Bedlamite to wander lost and alone about my lands. What would the neighbors think?"

She pressed her lips together, but he saw the betraying tremble of a silent chuckle. She said, "Don't make me laugh, James. I feel too rotten."

He touched her cheek. Her skin was soft and pliant beneath his fingertips. "Please do not leave without telling me again."

"I won't. I promise."

He could not explain the relief he felt. He only knew it washed through him like a breath of fresh air, easing muscles he did not know were clenched. But when he looked at Carolly, he did not see the same ease. If anything, she looked more miserable, more anguished than before.

"Carolly?"

"I'm all right. Really. It's just that . . ." Her voice trailed away as she struggled for the words to express her thoughts.

"Tell me," he urged softly. He took hold of her hands, not to comfort her, but to keep her near him. She always seemed on the verge of running, and just this once, he wanted her to stay. He had come too close to losing her this afternoon to want to risk it again.

"What are you thinking?" he asked.

"I . . . I'm not ready to leave yet." She looked up at him, and he was startled by the pain etched in the fine lines around her eyes and mouth. Had it always been there? She shrugged, twisting her face away when he would not release her hands. "Can you believe that? I don't want to go. There's so much wrong here that I'm not even sure where to begin, but I want to fix it all." She laughed, a short bitter sound. "I'm not ready to die."

Her words left him mystified. There were times when she seemed completely rational. Other times, all he could do was pretend to understand. "Most people do not wish to die," he said gently. "That is perfectly natural."

"Not for me." She clenched her hands, but he held them effortlessly, letting his fingers gently circle her fists. "In all my other lives, I couldn't wait to leave. Everyone thought I was crazy, pretty much. No one really cared, even the people I tried to help. *Especially* them." Her bitter laugh returned. "In the end, death was always a huge relief."

"But not this time?"

She shook her head. "Not this time."

"Good." He had no special knowledge of the mentally ill, but he felt sure this indicated progress. She wanted to live. He almost shouted with glee. Instead, he pressed her for more details, more understanding. "What makes you not want to go?"

"You." Carolly turned back to face him, her gaze meeting his. And for the first time ever, she did not fight his touch. She did not seek to sever the connection to reality or to him. "It's because you care."

He started, surprised by her comment. "Is that so rare a thing?"

She quirked her eyebrow, her expression wry. "You tell me. How many people would do what you have done for me? Who else would let me invade his home, disrupt his life, and endanger his ward—then not throw me out or turn me over to someone else?"

He shrugged, beginning to feel uncomfortable with the shifting emotions she so readily embraced. How could he keep pace with a woman who moved so quickly from guilt to humor to madness to sudden warmth? It disturbed him even as it fascinated him. "Perhaps I am the better candidate for Bedlam," he mused.

She smiled, and her eyes reflected the colors of the fading sunset. "Or perhaps you're just a nice guy." Then she winked at him, wrinkling her nose in the most impertinent manner.

His breath caught in his throat. He knelt before her, their

eyes level, their mouths a scant inch apart. But his focus remained on the sparkle in her eyes, the laughter in her smile, the delight that suffused her entire body. Moments before, he had tried to understand her, tried to ferret out her secrets in an effort to help her. But not now. Now, he wished merely to touch her. To hold her. To kiss her.

And so he did. Without extra thought or planning, he merely leaned forward and claimed her lips. She responded slowly, as if reluctant to give in to the force that seemed to surround them constantly, pushing them inevitably together. But he had no more strength to resist; and as he added his own encouragement, nibbling gently along the edges of her lips, her reluctance seemed to melt away.

He did not press against her, though his entire body urged him on with a power that made his legs shake. Instead, he held himself back, leisurely tasting her mouth, exploring the dark recesses behind her lips while she sighed sweetly, opening herself up to him. And then, guessing her to be a virgin unused to such attentions, he forced himself to withdraw. He did not wish to. Indeed, were her mental state solid, he would have pressed her down onto the carpet. But he feared pushing her into madness, and so he pulled away, his body protesting every inch that separated them.

She spoke, then, her words confirming his worst fear: that his attentions overwhelmed her so much as to further unbalance her mind. "Angels aren't supposed to kiss like that," she whispered. He looked at her eyes, saw the shimmer of regret within them.

"Oh, James, angels shouldn't even think of kisses like that." She swallowed, obviously pulling her thoughts about her. Unfortunately, they were disordered thoughts, steeped in madness. What else could they be? "We must think about what you'll do to help the villagers."

He slid away from her, returning to his seat, while inside his heart sank. He should have known better. He *did* know better. One could not dally with a madwoman. For *her* stability, not to mention his own. Obviously, his attentions had disturbed her so much she'd run straight for her madness, using it as a shield against him.

And yet, even now, he wanted to touch her again. To taste her again. To introduce her to love with the sweetest, most gentle of caresses.

"James,' she repeated, as if trying to get his attention. "We have to help the people who lost jobs because you turned them out."

He sighed, the evening soured, his thoughts buried in defeat. "I will not rehire them, Carolly. I am wealthy enough without having to make money off the sweat of women and children."

She clapped her hands, her grin widening. "Exactly!"

"What?"

She pushed out of her chair, pacing in front of him with sudden enthusiasm. "I think we should start a school. Once we've got the children enrolled, then we can focus on the women. We should give them pigs or goats or something."

"The children?" he managed. "You want to give goats and pigs to children?"

She spun back toward him, her loose hair spilling over her shoulders. "No, silly. The women. But first we should handle the kids."

James shook his head, knowing her madness a direct result of his attentions. And yet, he did not know how to address the situation. The best he could do was ride out her spell and hope she returned to lucidity soon. He reached for his brandy as she resumed pacing.

"Do you know those people actually blame Margaret for losing their jobs?"

"Yes, I know." He'd tried to explain it to them. The timing was the merest coincidence. But somehow Margaret's arrival and the changes at the mines were inextricably mixed in the villagers' minds.

"James! How can you let them think that?"

He sighed. "It is not a question of me *allowing* them to think anything. They chose who they wish to blame, and nothing I say changes that."

Carolly shook her head. "But she's just a child."

"I realize that."

"How can they be so stupid?"

He merely shrugged. He had no answers for the oddities of the human mind, as evidenced by his spectacular blunders with her. She was speaking so quickly, he doubted even she fully understood what she was saying.

"Well, you've got to do something. This can't go on."

James let his brandy glass dangle from his fingertips and stared out the window. "Things were awkward, but not untenable until recently. Two years of bad crops have escalated the tension."

She tugged at her hair, clearly deep in thought. "Mining's horrible, but it's still a job. What we need to do is find the women and children something else, some way to replace their lost income. Something like farming."

He shook his head. "They are farming. But the yields have been poor."

She pursed her lips. "Okay, something for the children. The boys could apprentice with the blacksmith or as stable hands. The girls could learn sewing or become maids."

"I have already hired a blacksmith I do not need. The maids are so plentiful I trip over them, and I have more stable boys than I do horses."

She turned to him, her face aglow with an odd sort of joy. "And here I thought you were being ostentatious."

He shifted, lifting his chin. "I am merely ensuring a well-run household."

"So much so you can't stand it."

He sighed, knowing she could read the truth in his face. "I do prefer a less crowded household."

She smiled. "Can you send any of them off to other homes? Sort of farm them out to your friends?"

He shook his head. "My friends have all the servants they need."

"Hmmm." She frowned as she resumed pacing. "Guess we're back to pigs and school."

"I beg your pardon?"

"All those people you fired, you need to train them, right? Teach them another trade that will earn a living."

"We are speaking of women and children."

She waved that thought aside as if it had no bearing on the situation. "Well, the children ought to be in school. As for the women, there must be lots of things they can do. That's what I meant about pigs or goats. Raising animals is something they can handle at home, at least until we can set up a working day-care."

"Working day what?" He stared at her, unsure whether she jested or was merely insane. Either way, he could not process her bizarre comments. "Pigs?"

"Never mind that," she said, her movements becoming more animated. "The first thing we should do is start a school."

He sighed. Truth be told, he had thought of that. "But it will not recompense anyone for lost income."

Carolly turned and stared at him. "We pay them to go to school."

"We what?"

"Well, that's the only way."

He gaped at her, knowing she was completely mad. "I should pay children for the privilege of going to school?"

"Well, of course. Eventually, people will see the value of an education all on their own. In my time, people will end up paying exorbitant sums to go to school. But we've got to get the first couple generations there first."

"Generations? You want me to pay for generations of schooling?"

She nodded, then gave him a mischievous wink. "Just look at it as an investment. A long, long, long-term investment."

He folded his arms over his chest, the first glimmerings of amusement stirring within him. "And just where am I supposed to get all this money to pay people to educate themselves?"

She shrugged. "You're an earl, aren't you? Rich enough to buy a good portion of the world, I shouldn't wonder.

His gaze shifted to the fire. "But I certainly do not intend to squander it—"

"It's not squandering. It's—"

"Investing," he interrupted grimly. "A long-term investment with no expected return."

"An investment in the future."

He threw up his hands, amazed by her audacity. "I should have made you my mistress," he commented ruefully. "At least a mistress only demands a few baubles every month or so. You want to beggar me for generations."

She grinned. "Yes, but think of the happy, non-violent children you'll be raising."

"I certainly do not—"

"Now, as for the women . . ." Carolly continued, tapping her finger on her lips as she thought. "Is pig farming truly feasible? What we need is a high-yield animal that requires little space." She glanced over at him. "I assume there's no way to find them all a small plot of land."

"You assume correctly."

She suddenly brightened. "What about rabbits?"

"Rabbits?"

"Yes! They breed like . . . well, rabbits. And they're cute. Maybe you could import some Angora bunnies." She trailed a finger across her cheek, her expression dreamy. "It's the softest material this side of heaven."

He frowned, trying not to be distracted by the enchanting sight she presented. "Carolly, we eat rabbits."

She grimaced. "Well, of course you do. But not if you're breeding them for their hair."

He shook his head. "Carolly, can you not strive to return to lucidity? Please?"

"All right, so maybe rabbits aren't a good idea. But you didn't like pigs. Sheep and cows require a lot of room . . . What about bees?"

"Bees?"

"Nah, too dangerous. Hard to be a good beekeeper with a toddler running around. Guess that makes it rabbits." She plopped down on the arm of her chair and leaned toward him. "So, how do you go about getting a bunch of Angora bunnies?"

"I think I need another brandy," James muttered, standing abruptly. Then he looked at her, seeing not only her beauty, but also her madness. There were times he truly believed her sane, her angel nonsense nothing more than an active imagination.

Then came times like this. Bees and pigs and bunny hair, indeed. Obviously, he was not helping her, and his defeat weighed on him all the more painfully because of the echo to Danny. He could not bear to lose another soul to madness, and certainly not Carolly. The very thought cut him to the core.

His best option was a strategic retreat. Perhaps alone, away from his disturbing presence, Carolly would return to a more rational state. And, hopefully, with distance, James would be able to view her more objectively, more rationally, without the constant temptation to touch her.

With a sigh that came from his soul, he bowed deeply to her. "My most sincere apologies for upsetting you. Good night."

Chapter Ten

"She's the oddest woman I have ever met. I honestly do not know what to make of her." James paced the confines of his library, walking first to the cold fire grate, then back to his desk. He barely spared a glance for his cousin and heir, Garrett, who watched him placidly, his lean form folded elegantly into the leather chair.

"You have no idea," continued James. "Her conversation hops around from topic to topic in the most hurry-scurry manner." He spun on his heel. "And she has this insane idea about rabbits."

Garrett arched a slightly ragged red eyebrow. "What about them?"

James shook his head. "She wants to breed them for their hair."

"I beg your pardon?"

"That is exactly what I said!" James stopped to pour himself a sherry that he did not drink. "But she is prepared to write to Turkey for these . . . these bunnies, as she calls them."

Garrett dropped his quizzing glass into his lap and stared at James. "Bunnies?"

"It must be some odd expression from the Colonies."

"Then she is from America?"

"I had thought so," confirmed James as he stared into his full glass. "She had an accent when she first arrived, but she seems to be losing it." He took one more turn about the room. "She also wishes me to pay the village children to go to school."

Garrett frowned. "She cannot be serious."

"She certainly is. She claims it will quell their anger over losing their jobs at the mines."

"Ah yes, the mines." Garrett stretched his legs out, forcing James to step over them to continue pacing. "How is the peasantry feeling these days? I understand there was a nasty scene the other day involving Margaret."

James stopped moving to stare at Garrett. "How did you hear about that?"

The younger man shrugged and picked up his quizzing glass, only to toy with the ribbon. "It is only natural that I should keep a close eye on the land I shall one day inherit."

James set his sherry on the mantel with a click, his irritation getting the better of him. "I have not cocked up my toes yet, my boy," he snapped.

Garrett was quick to reassure him, his smile conciliatory. "Of course not. And, with luck, you shall live a long and happy life. I am only taking an interest in my inheritance. Nothing more." He glanced up significantly. "Tell me more about this woman."

James frowned and turned away. "There is little more to say, except that she is determined to find me a wife."

"What presumption!"

"Quite so." He neatly snatched up his sherry and drained the glass. "She wishes to throw me a ball and invite all the eligible women in the area."

Garrett leaned forward, his opinion plain. "Good God, man, you cannot seriously consider it."

"Of course not!" James turned again, only to stare holes in the thick rug. "You know I do not wish leg-shackles. What I want is . . ." His voice trailed away. "I want . . ."

"*Her*." Garrett's voice was heavy with dread.

"What?"

"Good lord, you want *her*." Outrage pinched the man's face. Even his red hair seemed to curl in on itself, and his freckles suddenly appeared dark in his pale face. "This madwoman from the Colonies has turned your life upside down, and yet you want her!"

"Do not be ridiculous," James snapped.

"Bed her, man, and be done with it. But for God's sake, do not rivet yourself to her."

"I never said anything about marriage," James exclaimed, as he once again stomped across the room. "I do not even know the woman's family name. I know nothing about her."

"She is clearly not fit to be a countess."

James stopped dead, his body suddenly tense with affront. "Do not be impertinent. You have not even met the woman. She has a fire and a dignity that would make a king proud."

Garrett's response was to bow his head slightly, but his expression was anything but contrite. James cursed silently.

"Perhaps," Garrett began, "I should meet this strange woman of yours."

James shook his head. "She and Margaret are out hunting insects again."

Garrett raised a hand in a foppish gesture of disdain. "Insects? Is that an appropriate pastime for a young girl?"

James shrugged, ignoring his cousin's town mannerisms. "Carolly thinks so, and in truth the girl seems much happier of late. Why, she even laughed at table yesterday."

Garrett's hand dropped to his knee. "Table? Why James, never say you are eating in the nursery."

James looked up from a deep contemplation of his empty

glass. "Hmmm? No. We all dine *en famille* now. Even Miss Hornswallow. Carolly finds it cozier."

"I see."

James glanced at his heir, noting the wealth of meaning instilled in those two words. "You believe she has too much influence in my household." His words were dry, but they had the ring of challenge to them.

"I?" cried Garrett, his expression too innocent. "I can hardly say. I have only just arrived." He smiled as he ran his fingers over his silk waistcoat. "But you seem to believe she does. Why else would you mention it?"

James frowned at the mantel, unsure what he felt or believed. He never seemed capable of straight thinking when it came to Carolly, which is why he'd begun this discussion in the first place. He needed an objective viewpoint. Coming to a quick decision, he turned to his cousin with rare eagerness. "Garrett, do say you shall stay for a few days and meet Carolly."

His heir smiled quickly, the expression warm and genuine. "Why, James, it would be my greatest honor."

Carolly felt happy. She wasn't exactly sure why; nothing seemed to be going as it ought. James and Miss Hornswallow were showing absolutely no interest in each other. James still refused to even consider a ball or rabbits or pigs, though she was making some progress toward convincing his steward. She felt practically jailed on the near lands, unable to go anywhere alone, and she couldn't yet start plans for a school.

But at least she and Margaret were getting along. James let them go on excursions whenever they wished, as long as they stayed on the near fields. Margaret laughed much more and together, they had tossed out Miss Hornswallow's idea of an appropriate wardrobe. New clothes arrived daily from the local seamstress. They'd even talked a little about woman things, about marriage and men and the future. But other topics, most notably Mags's parents, were still strictly forbidden. Whenever

Carolly even touched on that area, Margaret clammed up, disappearing into a stony silence that reminded Carolly of James in high dudgeon.

In short, nothing was working according to plan. And yet, Carolly felt immensely happy. So happy, in fact, that she and Margaret were singing. Too bad neither of them could carry a tune.

They were halfway through their own peculiar version of "Greensleeves," renamed to "Green slop," when they burst in the back door, almost bowling over a frowning James. His presence was so unexpected Carolly nearly choked on the word "gangrene" while Margaret blushed a fiery red and tried to shrink into the background.

James simply checked his watch, his expression stern. "You are late."

"Late? For a very important date," Carolly quipped, feeling too good to be cowed by his dark countenance.

His frown deepened. "Madame—"

"Guess what. I remembered my last name today."

He stopped, his mouth half open. "Truly? What is it?"

She grinned. "It's Hans . . ." She frowned. "It's Han . . ."

"Hands?"

"No, no. Two syllables. I just had it. Criminy," she said, stomping her foot in irritation. "I can't believe it's gone again."

"Hanson," piped up Margaret from beside her. "Remember? We were talking about the carriages in London."

"Hansom?" James asked.

Margaret shook her head. "H-a-n-s-o-n. She spelled it for me."

Carolly frowned, frustrated beyond words. Why couldn't she remember the simplest thing?

"Ah," said someone from further down the hallway. "I thought I heard voices."

"I believe they thought they were singing," joked James.

"And such lovely songbirds they are," returned a tall red-haired man as he sauntered amiably over to join them.

"Cousin Garrett," breathed Margaret, shy awe infusing her voice.

Carolly turned slightly, her thoughts distracted as she heard the clear note of hero worship. Sure enough, Mags's eyes were wide with that desperate adoration peculiar to young girls on the verge of their first puppy love, and Carolly smiled fondly at the sight.

Then she shifted her attention to the object of Margaret's affections. Cousin Garrett was tall and angular, with the stub nose and freckles James had once mentioned. Fortunately for his looks, his face was already softening with the fat of good living. It gave him a boyish appeal that women of all centuries would appreciate—especially impressionable young girls. No wonder Margaret was practically swooning.

"Good evening, sir," Carolly said, giving the gentleman her best curtsy. "I hope our merriment did not disturb you."

"Of course not," Garrett responded, his hazel eyes twinkling. "The sound of a woman's laughter can never offend."

"You are most kind," Carolly responded with a demure nod. But as she moved, she noticed James's stunned expression. He obviously had not thought she could act so mannerly. Come to think of it, she hadn't realized she could either. Still, she was unable to resist teasing just a little. She turned and gave him an impudent wink. "I cannot be crass and boorish all the time, my lord. And certainly not around such a charming guest."

James stiffened slightly, and Carolly could see the beginnings of a frown, but Garrett was speaking, demanding her attention.

"As no one here seems willing to do so, I fear I must introduce myself. I cannot wait a moment longer to greet you. Garrett Northram, ma'am." The man executed a dashing bow, then lifted her hand to his lips.

Carolly flushed as his fingers caressed her palm, flustered by such elegance. "I'm Carolly H-something," she returned, forgetting to retrieve her hand. "And you, sir, are a flirt."

"Ah, you have found me out." His gaze was warm as he studied her face. "But I can hardly resist when presented with such a vision of loveliness."

Carolly laughed. She couldn't help it. His compliments were so effusive, so blatant, he reminded her of an old movie of the king's court where gentlemen were the epitome of charm and elegance even as they hatched nefarious plots. Still, she found him hard to resist when he made her the focus of such overwhelming attention. She responded in kind, taking his arm as he escorted her into the front salon, chatting away as if they were old friends.

"Tell me, Mr. Northram, are you staying for a visit, or do you return to the city?"

They crossed into the salon, and he escorted her to the settee. "I had planned to return, but suddenly London seems to have lost its allure."

"Truly?" Flirting came as second nature to Carolly, and she found all her old mannerisms returning: the coy glance, the shy smile, the teasing, half-suggestive comments. It had been forever since she had allowed herself such harmless fun, and even longer since she'd enjoyed playing with such an experienced partner. "I cannot image a man such as yourself wishing to seclude himself in the wilds of Staffordshire."

"Ah, dear lady, sometimes the wild rose is more appealing than the cultivated orchid."

"And so much more hardy." She laughed, knowing that she was acting very silly, but it made her feel young and alive. She glanced around the room, hoping to share her joy with the others, only to find them completely unreceptive. Margaret had disappeared, running off without even saying goodbye. And as for James, he stood by the door, arms crossed over his chest, glowering.

She sobered immediately. Good lord, she must be doing something totally inept to put him in such a foul mood. Carolly sighed. She had been so happy just a few minutes ago, and now everything was upset again.

"Will you join us for dinner then?" she asked, not knowing what response to hope for.

"Actually," returned Garrett, "James has prevailed upon me to remain several days. I hope I shall have the pleasure of your company for at least a few moments of that time."

"Why, of course," she responded politely, her thoughts awhirl. A few days? A few days when she would have to be excruciatingly correct, probably even wear a corset? A few days of tiptoeing around James, making sure she didn't eat with the wrong fork or perform some wretchedly vulgar act in front of Cousin Garrett's valet. Goodness knew, with the elaborate servants' network, her every crass comment would probably be broadcast throughout the London *ton*, embarrassing James to no end.

Carolly almost groaned aloud. Why did this man have to show up now? Didn't she have enough on her plate? But then Garrett settled down on the settee next to her and began sharing London gossip filled with dukes and princes, this marquis and that countess. It was dizzying keeping up with the names, but so tempting to slip into the rhythm of his easy charm. In the end, she gave up fighting his presence. If she had to have another man in the house mucking up the waters, she was grateful he was at least charming and dashing and funny.

At least Garrett knew how to smile.

At dinner, James stared morosely down the table at Carolly. She was amazing. He'd known she was lively. In fact, she nearly defined the word "sparkling." But never before had she shone as she did now.

Under the attentive focus of his cousin Garrett.

She laughed. She glowed. Her entire body seemed suffused with a radiance that stunned him. And all because of some *on-dits* from Garret. In fact, Carolly dazzled like a woman born to parties and gaiety.

Garrett was clearly mesmerized.

James toyed with Cook's special lamb creation, his gaze traveling reluctantly away from Carolly to his cousin and heir. A town exquisite, Garrett knew how to amuse a lady. He knew how to charm and flirt and compliment a woman until even the most sour dowd would simper and giggle as a girl in the first blush of youth.

Compared to Garret, James practically defined lackluster. Secure in his isolated country home, the reigning peer of the county, James had been content with his books and his niece. Now he realized how much he lacked as a gentleman. And just how much Garrett possessed.

The thought made him squirm. But there was nothing he could do. He would not blight Carolly's happiness. If she enjoyed Garrett's company more than his, then so be it. He would play the courteous host to the best of his ability.

His gaze shifted to the other occupants of the table. Miss Hornswallow sat as polite and correct as ever. Her gown—a demure, high-necked gray thing—reflected her somber attitude. She chanced to look up at him. Their gazes met, and she smiled. Her expression was filled with compassion, and James was momentarily startled by the understanding he read in her dark brown eyes. Surely his thoughts had not been so obvious. But of course Miss Hornswallow would understand them, he realized. Forced by circumstances to become a drab creature at best, the austere governess would easily comprehend the feelings of someone relegated to the shadows.

He smiled warmly at her and felt a rush of pleasure when she blushed a becoming shade of rose. Perhaps Carolly had spoken the truth. Content in his pleasant cocoon, James had missed the possibilities right under his nose.

After that, the meal progressed almost pleasantly. Unable to compete with Garrett, James turned his attention to his niece. She sat slouched in her chair, casting hopelessly lovelorn glances at Garrett. For the first time ever, she reminded James of himself as a child. He could recall dinners spent slumped in his chair, staring with desperate shyness at some pretty maid while his older brother teased and cajoled the girl into a kiss.

Now his niece lived through that same horror. James leaned forward and touched the girl on her arm. She jerked slightly, then gave him a surprised look.

"I understand you and Carolly went hunting for insects today. Did you find anything of consequence?" he asked.

"No." The word was flat with resentment.

"Nothing at all?"

"No."

He frowned, wondering what he should do next. He glanced up, noting that Garrett and Carolly had fallen silent, and poor Margaret had taken center stage. Unfortunately, that was the last place the girl wanted to be, so she shrank even lower into her seat.

James glanced at Miss Hornswallow, hoping she could help, but she was busy frowning at Margaret, clearly disappointed at the girl's poor showing. Garrett was simply amused, his loud sigh of resignation easily heard by all in the room. Finally, James sent a desperate look at Carolly, who merely smiled encouragingly. She clearly wanted him to continue, except he had no idea what to say.

"Let me see," he began, counting off the facts as a way to stall for time. "You went out early this afternoon, returning only just before supper in exceedingly high spirits. Yet you say you caught nothing of consequence." He let his gaze linger thoughtfully on his wine glass. "It must be, then, that you were doing something different than catching insects."

"Oh, no," Margaret cried, clearly insulted. "We were looking . . ." Her voice trailed away as she looked around the room, clearly focusing on Garrett's bored expression. "It was nothing," she said in a stifled whisper.

"Or perhaps," James tried again, "you were chatting more

GET TWO FREE* BOOKS!

SIGN UP FOR THE LOVE SPELL ROMANCE BOOK CLUB TODAY.

LOWEST PRICES EVER!

Every month, you will receive two of the newest Love Spell titles for the low price of $8.50,* **a $4.50 savings!**

As a book club member, not only do you save **35% off the retail price**, you will receive the following special benefits:

- **30% off** all orders through our website and telecenter (plus, you still get 1 book FREE for every 5 books you buy!)

- Exclusive access to dollar sales, special discounts, and offers you won't be able to find anywhere else.

- Information about contests, author signings, and more!

- Convenient home delivery of your favorite books every month.

- A 10-day examination period. If you aren't satisfied, just return any books you don't want to keep.

There is no minimum number of books to buy, and you may cancel membership at any time.

* Please include $2.00 for shipping and handling.

NAME: _____

ADDRESS: _____

_____

_____

TELEPHONE: _____

E-MAIL: _____

_____ I want to pay by credit card.

__ Visa   __ MasterCard   __ Discover

Account Number: _____

Expiration date: _____

SIGNATURE: _____

Send this form, along with $2.00 shipping and handling for your FREE books, to:

Love Spell Romance Book Club
20 Academy Street
Norwalk, CT 06850-4032

Or fax (must include credit card information!) to: 610.995.9274.
You can also sign up on the Web at www.dorchesterpub.com.

Offer open to residents of the U.S. and Canada only. Canadian residents, please call 1.800.481.9191 for pricing information.

If under 18, a parent or guardian must sign. Terms, prices and conditions subject to change. Subscription subject to acceptance. Dorchester Publishing reserves the right to reject any order or cancel any subscription.

than looking?" He watched his niece blush a fiery red. There had to be some way to cajole her out of her shyness. What had his brother done, what did Carolly do, he wondered, when faced with a shy girl?

Suddenly, he remembered. They descended into utter mischief, speaking outrageously about nonsense. Perhaps he could give it a try.

Pretending to ponder the question of what had so occupied Carolly and Margaret, he tapped his finger against his mouth, then suddenly brightened. "I have it! You were doing one of those secret rites for females."

Margaret blinked. "What?"

"Of course you were. It is what females do all the time in their boudoirs and late at night when they giggle under their bedcovers." He leaned in close to his stunned niece. "Tell me the truth," he whispered, "what do you really do? Do you dress up in odd clothes and whisper in a secret language?"

"My lord!" exclaimed Miss Hornswallow, clearly shocked. "You must know—"

"Don't tell him, Mags!" interrupted Carolly in dramatic accents. "Men must never find out."

Margaret's gaze hopped between her uncle, Carolly, and a frowning Miss Hornswallow. In the end, she landed with mischievous intent on James as he smiled encouragingly, inviting her to share in his outrageousness. "I shall tell you, uncle," she finally whispered.

"Oh, no, our secret is out!" wailed Carolly, pressing her hand to her chest in feigned horror.

"We . . . We . . ." Margaret was obviously trying to think of something preposterous, and James waited with breathless anticipation to find out what she would say. "We sneak food from the pantry and . . . and talk about underclothes and hair pieces!"

"Margaret!" That came from Miss Hornswallow, but James ignored her, putting on an expression of shocked amazement.

"Truly?" he said breathlessly. "I have always wondered." He

leaned back and frowned as he picked up his fork. "That is most interesting, Margaret. Did you know that is almost exactly like the male secret ritual?"

Margaret sat up in her seat, her eyes bright. "Truly?"

"Oh, absolutely. Hairpieces and underclothing. Although we discuss horses as well."

Margaret wrinkled her nose in disgust. "Well, I already knew about that."

James shifted, slightly surprised. "I thought you liked horses."

"Oh, they are fine for riding, but they are not nearly as interesting as insects. Why Baron Lansford says there is little variety in horses compared to the insect world. And they are not nearly as smart."

Across the table, James could hear Carolly nearly choking on merriment. But it was Garrett who spoke up, his words cutting and cruel. "What a deuced odd thing to say!"

James did not need to look to see the animation leave his niece. The object of her adoration had just called her odd in the most insulting of ways. He actually heard Margaret sink deeper into her chair, fading back into the formless lump she had been not more than five minutes ago. Across the table, he saw Carolly's eyes flash as she girded herself for battle. She was obviously prepared to set to Garrett with all the fire in her passionate soul. Except James could not allow it. A scene would only increase Margaret's mortification and cause as much damage as Garrett's thoughtless comment.

Carolly opened her mouth. "How—"

"Odd?" he interrupted smoothly. "Perhaps, but it was also quite correct." He glanced down at his niece. "And I will take a truthful oddity over fashionable nonsense any day."

He saw Carolly shut her mouth with a snap, surprised. He merely smiled.

"You are obviously well-versed regarding insects," James continued to his niece. "Does Baron Lansford tell you all these things?"

"Yes," Margaret began slowly. James nodded encouragingly, and the girl continued, her voice growing stronger with each word. "He has the most amazing collection. Miss Hornswallow and I go there often. We spent the entire afternoon there only yesterday."

"Is that so?" James said, noting Miss Hornswallow's bright pink cheeks.

The prim governess shifted uneasily. "I have always found it beneficial to encourage a child's interests."

"Of course." James nodded sagely. "But I must insist that horses be given equal time." He looked back at Margaret. "How would you like to go riding with me tomorrow? Perhaps Shadow and I can teach you to appreciate the finer aspects of horseflesh."

Margaret nearly hopped up and down in her seat. "I can go with you tomorrow?"

"Absolutely." How could he resist such honest enthusiasm? Especially since it was the first such excitement he had ever seen in his ward. That it was directed at him was more rewarding than he could have thought possible. That Carolly's eyes shone with a misty delight only added to the sweetness. "Provided, of course," he admonished, "that you dress appropriately. In your riding habit."

"But I don't like my habit!" she wailed. "It's hot. And it pinches."

James shook his head. "I will not allow you to join me improperly attired. I know it is hot, but lighter dresses will not protect you from scratchy branches. And if it rains, you will stay warm. Besides," he added with a wink, "I think you may find that it isn't tight anymore."

"Really?" asked Margaret, her eyes shining with surprise and pleasure.

"Really," answered James.

From across the table, Carolly knew it was true. Happiness and good exercise had helped Mags slim down. And, she thought with an embarrassed grimace, she now knew why

James had walked away from his niece that first morning. He hadn't allowed Margaret to be anything less than appropriately dressed. For her own welfare. Not to mention that, with the villagers already against her, the girl had to show well, had to be excruciatingly correct. Even if that meant wearing a riding habit she hated.

As Margaret and James began to discuss where they would go in the morning, Carolly leaned back in her chair and felt a grin spread across her cheeks. Finally, uncle and niece were moving toward each other. The rapport was tentative at best, but Carolly had no doubt it would grow quickly. After all, whether they realized it or not, they yearned for affection from each other. If Carolly just kept herself and everyone else out of the way, James and Mags would develop a strong bond.

She glanced at Miss Hornswallow. She was no problem. The woman excelled at dissolving into the shadows. Besides, she appeared thrilled at the growing relationship between James and Mags. Beneath that starched and prickly exterior beat the heart of a very compassionate woman who cared deeply for her charge. Miss Hornswallow would not interfere.

Garrett, on the other hand, could be difficult. Poor man, she thought with a sigh. He had no idea how poor an appearance he made next to James. He had been clearly aware of Margaret's puppy love, but had done nothing to ease it or direct it elsewhere. He'd simply ignored the girl in favor of more adult entertainments. And now that Mags's childish infatuation seemed to be shifting, he acted insulted, taking solace in his wine glass and nastiness.

Was this what James had meant when he said his cousin was bred for the city? True, Garrett was handsome and elegant with an almost overwhelming charm. But beneath his debonair exterior, the man lacked the solid core Carolly found so appealing in James. Though she might flirt more easily with Garrett, she could rely on James. And although Garrett worked at being a delightful companion, James was the honest and worthy one.

Still, in this case, she would have to forgo the better man in favor of the lesser. James needed time to get to know Margaret, and that meant Carolly would have to vigilantly keep Garrett out of the way. She reached for her glass, listening with half an ear as the child regaled her uncle with the mysteries of the insect world. Then her gaze drifted to Garrett, who suddenly winked at her.

Out of habit, Carolly winked back. She smiled. She supposed there were worse things than being forced into the company of a charming man. Still, her heart was heavy as her attention wandered back to her host. All in all, she'd much rather discuss the wonders of insect larvae with James and Margaret.

James stared at his book. He tried to focus on Homer's epic poem, but instead he saw the smile Carolly gave Garrett just before they had left for their stroll—nearly three hours ago. He had been occupied with Margaret at the time, but he could hardly miss their silent exchange.

Now Margaret and Miss Hornswallow had left for bed, and he had no other soul with whom to while away the time. He looked at his book. Just over his right shoulder, on the parlor mantel, an elegant ormolu clock ticked away the seconds. He turned the page, but the image of Carolly strolling intimately with Garrett remained in his mind's eye.

The candle sputtered and died. It was several moments before he noticed.

Standing quietly, he crossed to an end table and pulled open the drawer. Retrieving a fresh candle, he returned to his seat, carefully replacing the spent taper. As he moved, his cassimere pantaloons shifted with a slight sigh of fabric, and the sound seemed overly large in the empty parlor. Once the new candle caught fire, James reopened his book. The clock ticked. The house remained silent.

In his mind's eye, Carolly and Garrett exchanged more than *on-dits*.

James had turned two more meaningless pages before a new sound broke the stillness. It was Carolly, her low laughter stirring his senses as it floated on the night air. Soon it was followed by soft footsteps and male tones, and then, eventually, finally, the French windows burst open and she and Garrett sauntered in.

James did not have to move to see their entrance. His seat gave the perfect position from which to observe.

"Oh, James!" Carolly exclaimed as she crossed the threshold. "I had not realized you would still be awake. I hope we are not disturbing your reading."

James rose from his seat, closing his book and setting it aside as he did. "Homer is ever dull after midnight."

"Before midnight too, if you ask me," suggested his cousin.

Carolly merely smiled and lit a nearby candelabra. "Goodness, James, doesn't it bother your eyes to read in the dark?"

James did not respond. He spent his energies studying his two companions. Garrett had loosened his cravat, his hair was windswept, and his clothing appeared in noticeable disarray. He wore the cheeky grin of a man satisfied with an evening's work and the smug expression of a libertine waiting to brag of his next conquest.

Carolly, too, looked mussed. Her short hair, though coiled at the nape of her neck, seemed to tumble over the ribbon that tried to restrain it. Her eyes were bright, her smile easy and sweet. She did not appear overly shy nor excessively nervous, in the way of women playing the coquette, but then she did not need to play at anything to be appealing. Indeed, in the candlelight, even her skin seemed to glow with golden beauty.

Was this the face of a woman who had engaged in a tryst? With most women, he would have known immediately, but with Carolly, he could not judge her reactions. Her clothing appeared slightly disheveled, and her skirt sported dirt and leaves. If he were not mistaken, she had torn the hem. But, for all he knew, she could have done that climbing trees this afternoon with Margaret.

"James? Are you quite all right? You're staring."

He blinked, feeling his face warm with embarrassment. "My apologies. My mind was wandering."

"Hmmm," commented Garrett dryly, his eyes twinkling. "Must be careful, old boy. Happens with age, you know."

James felt his spine stiffen and wondered at his prickly reaction. He was what he was. His age neither enhanced nor detracted from his abilities, and he was not ashamed to have recently found his first gray hair no matter what his younger, more dashing cousin implied. Or so he told himself.

"Yes," he responded dryly. "I fear advanced senility is ever nipping at my heels. Therefore, I bid you both good-night. I find the total obliteration of sleep much more soothing than the piecemeal subtractions of advancing years."

He had started to walk away when Carolly's laugh stopped him. It was the laugh he so loved to hear, brimming with unfettered good will, filling the air with a sweetness like chimes. He turned to her, unable to resist.

"Oh yes, James," she teased. "I can see we shall be calling on the doctor to cup you regularly against the ague. All too soon, Shadow shall be put to pasture for lack of a rider."

He met her smile with one of his own, his humor returning as he gazed into her sparkling eyes. "Perhaps," he proposed, with an intentionally quavering voice, "as I am so near my dotage, you would oblige me by assisting me up the stairs."

"La, my lord, I could do no less for one in such a weakened condition." She stepped forward, placing her right hand lightly on his forearm while her left pretended to support his elbow.

He felt the warmth of her body so close to his, the weight of her hand on his arm. It all was somehow *right*. He pulled her closer, drawing her ever nearer, and she came willingly, her laughter softening into an intimate smile.

"Well, I can see I am *de trop*," commented Garrett from somewhere behind them. His voice was hard, and James felt

Carolly stiffen beside him. She turned, and James was forced to follow, however reluctantly.

"Garrett?" she asked, confusion coloring her voice.

James watched in silent jealousy as his cousin shifted into his charming persona once again. Garrett gently detached one of Carolly's hands from James's arm, and lifted her fingertips to his lips for a long, lingering kiss.

"Forgive my ill humor. It is hard to see such a charming lady on another man's arm."

Carolly blushed. But what James most noted was how her remaining hand began to slip from his arm. He was quick to cover it with his own, anchoring her against his side. This left her somewhat stretched, one hand fixed to James's arm, the other pulled toward Garrett. It should have been an awkward position for her, but she seemed oblivious to it, her attention centered on his cousin.

"You are too kind, sir," she said softly to Garrett, and James frowned at her intimate tone. "Perhaps we can talk more in the morning while James rides with Margaret."

"Or you could join us," James offered quickly.

Carolly hesitated, worrying her lip in consternation. "I don't know. Perhaps." But it was clear from her expression she did not intend to join him.

"Excellent," said Garrett, his teeth pearly white in the gloom. "Then I shall await your pleasure." He still held her hand, and James could see the subtle shifts in his arm muscles as the man stroked her palm just below sight.

Carolly did not withdraw her hand.

James did not grind his teeth in frustration. That would be the action of a less controlled man. He kept his emotions tightly reined, his irritation masked by an urbane manner. But his gaze was steady and his regard cold as he stared at his cousin.

He would not allow an illicit affair between Carolly and his heir. Carolly was too good and too vulnerable to handle Garrett's typical liaison. She was not a demi-rep or a widow available for his pleasure. As he would make clear to his lascivious heir.

He did not have to wait long to make his point. Garrett lifted his gaze from Carolly's face, and as he did, he encountered James's hard stare. His cousin's reaction was quickly covered, but James saw it nonetheless. There was a momentary challenge that flashed in the younger man's eyes, manifesting in an arrogant lift of his eyebrow. But then it abruptly disappeared. Garrett stepped backward, releasing Carolly's hand as he gave a slight bow.

Garrett would not seduce Carolly. Or so his movement suggested.

Yet, for the first time ever, James did not believe his heir.

How odd. James had known the boy from the cradle, seen the soft child grow into a dashing man. And yet, James suddenly was racked with suspicions and doubts regarding him. He had thought he understood Garett's strengths and weaknesses, viewed him clearly, albeit with the fondness expected from family. And yet, now he wondered just how well he knew his heir. What had the boy been doing all this time in London—beyond wenching and card playing?

He didn't know, and that very ignorance annoyed him. Or perhaps he simply refused to take chances with Carolly's heart. In either event, the emotions felt most uncharacteristic. Yet he could not ignore his misgivings.

James tightened his grip on Carolly's hand and drew her toward the door. "Good evening, Garrett."

"Good evening, Cousin. Miss Hanson."

Beside him, Carolly nodded goodnight with a smile. "And please, call me Caroline," she added.

James was startled. Had she said Caroline? But his thoughts were forestalled as Garrett once again bowed over her hand.

"Good night, Caroline."

James pulled her away, escorting her firmly to her bedroom. Just outside her room, he paused, reluctant to release her just yet. "Why did you ask him to call you Caroline?" he asked.

She looked up at him, her blue eyes sparkling in the light from candles left in the hallway. "We all use our Christian names here. Surely you cannot wish me to stand on formality."

He shook his head. "Why should he call you Caroline and not Carolly?"

He watched as her brows drew together and her eyes clouded with confusion. "Whyever would he call me Carolly? My name is Caroline Handren."

An icy hand fisted in his belly. "You told me your name was Hanson."

Her gaze skittered away, and he tightened his hold on her hand, if only to keep her close.

"Hanson?" she said. "Hanson. Handren. Hanson." She said the words as if trying them on, repeating one after the other while her fingers tightened on his arm. "Carolly Hanson." Her voice took on more strength. "I'm Carolly Hanson." Then she looked at up him, and he read panic in her gaze. "But then who is Caroline Handren? And why do I remember her life?" Her breathing was rapidly becoming erratic, and he feared she would become ill. "James," she cried, "who am I?"

Coming to a swift decision, he pushed open her bedroom door, quickly kicking it closed behind him. He supported her to the bed. She trembled in his arms, her entire body shaking as she clutched his arm.

"James?"

"Shhh. Do not worry. We shall figure this out. I promise."

Without thought, he joined her on the bed, sitting with his back to the headboard as he drew her into his arms. She resisted at first, but eventually he succeeded in pulling her close and placing her head against his chest. Her right hand grabbed the lapel of his coat, holding on as though he were her only anchor in the world. Her left hand fisted tightly between them, curled against her chest. It was a hard reminder of her fears as he let her rest against him.

Outside the world was peaceful, the night filled with the gentle sounds of owls and toads. Inside, a tense silence reigned, and the thready whisper of her unsteady breathing.

He had to say something. He needed to ease her pain, but he was not sure what to say. He let his cheek drop to the top of her head. He smelled the clean scent of lemon and felt the silken brush of her hair. "Tell me what you remember," he coaxed.

Her body clenched, but he was prepared. He stroked her shoulders and back, easing her muscles with gentle caresses.

"Just tell me what you are thinking."

Her voice was small against his chest. "It makes no sense whatsoever."

"That does not matter. Perhaps we can find the sense of it together."

She took a shuddering breath, then released it, letting her body coil tighter against him. Then, slowly, as if working a rusty hinge, she began speaking.

"I'm Carolly Hanson," she said. "I was born in 1978. I died in a car crash that was my own stupid fault."

She took another deep breath, her voice growing stronger as she spoke. "Next came early New York. And there was this man." She stopped.

He lifted his head, shifting enough so he could watch her face as she continued.

"Or was that later? I was so focused on trying to get back to my real life. No, his name was Thomas and he diagnosed me as a paranoid schizophrenic, and I was put away." She fell silent.

James held her close, using her silence to order his own thoughts. He had wanted her to explain her so-called former lives, wanted to show her they were not real. He had no idea she would spin fantasies so elaborate they included doctors in the colonies. And she used words he could not fathom.

"Carolly . . ."

But she was not listening to him. Her mind was far away as she seemed to pull out details with painful slowness. He might have thought she invented the stories as she spoke, but she had the air of one fighting with a memory, not searching for new ideas.

"A farm in Wales."

"What?"

"Long ago. Medieval. An old woman who grew herbs and talked to faeries." Her voice grew softer, and he thought he detected a slight Welsh lilt to her words. "She told me I was learning to be an angel."

James tried to tamp down his frustration. How could he tell the truth from fiction when they were so inextricably entwined in her mind?

She shifted against him, and for a moment he was distracted by the play of her body against his. Lust infiltrated his system, robbing him of breath. In his arms, she felt so very womanly against him—warm and yielding, and so very beautiful even in her distress.

She was still speaking, oblivious to the painful throb of desire she awoke within him. And he worked hard to focus on her words, listening to her disordered mind while his body clamored for more.

"That old woman read cards, James, and she talked to me about the stages of the soul. She believed in angels and all sorts of divine assistance to us mortals. And she told me that every one of us has something to learn before his soul can progress."

He frowned, trying to sort through her unorthodox theology. "Progress how?"

"To become an angel."

He shook his head, needing to point out the inconsistencies in her story. "I thought you were paying for your sins in your first life."

She nodded. "Yes, I am. I was very selfish in that first life. I must learn to be selfless. I must learn to give for the benefit of others without thinking of myself." Her voice grew firm, almost like a schoolmaster might sound as he passed out punishment to a recalcitrant student. "I was so self-centered the first time, and now I must learn to be angelic."

James fell silent. Why was her madness beginning to make sense to him? Then suddenly she bolted upright in his arms.

"Jeanne!"

"What?"

"Jeanne. I had to save Jeanne. I had to do it."

"Was she the old woman?"

Carolly denied it with a quick shake of her head. "The old woman died. Burned as a witch. I tried to help, but I failed."

"Carolly, try to focus . . ." But she did not seem to hear him. She was so caught up in her story he could not tell if she spoke for his benefit or her own.

"He killed me. Her father. But I made sure there was a witness."

"Who killed who?"

She shook her head. "I don't remember. It's all a jumble in my mind."

He sighed and let his head drop back against the headboard. Her logic was based on things incomprehensible to him. Angels living among men. Traveling through time as easily as if she were catching a coach to London. Souls that grew and changed and became angels. It was all beyond him. And yet it made a bizarre kind of sense.

Perhaps this was a danger when associating with the mentally ill. One risked joining them in their delusions.

He looked at her. She had drawn away from him, wrapping her arms around her midsection as if protecting herself from blows. Then she turned to him, her eyes pleading with him despite her words.

"You don't believe any of this, do you?"

He had to answer truthfully. She would know the truth even if he tried to lie. "I see that you believe it, and . . ." He paused, wondering what he intended to say. "And I can accept your beliefs without agreeing with them."

She sighed. "I suppose that's something."

He needed to touch her, so he sat up, reaching out to stroke her arm. And with that caress, she relaxed, drawing closer to him until he held her once again.

Somewhere in the back of his mind, a voice spoke of propriety. But for the first time in a very long time, he wanted to ignore the tedious reminders of civilization, the restrictions and rules that kept him from her.

Yet somewhere else, somewhere very close to the surface of his consciousness, was a knowledge that the longer he stayed in her room, the more he touched Carolly, the more he smelled the sweet scent of her skin and exchanged quiet confidences with her, the closer he came to wanting it all. Bit by bit, he had gained access to her mind. How long before his lust slipped past his restraints and took her body as well?

But for all he acknowledged the warnings and his fears, he still would not leave her bedroom or let her leave the comfort of his arms. So he pulled her tighter against him and breathed deeply of the soft scent of lemons that lingered on her skin.

"Are you sure it was Jeanne?" he whispered against her temple, letting his lips brush against the curve of her brow. "Perhaps you meant Janice."

"J—the girl. The little girl."

Clearly there had only been one girl, one sister. And a man. Was she thinking of him and Margaret? Had she taken his situation and spun out an elaborate fantasy? He looked up at her, trying to read her face, but saw nothing but an innocent mind lost in confusion. "Are you afraid I will hurt you?"

She started, her eyes pulling wide. "What?"

He set her aside, distancing himself from her to clear his thoughts. Then he pushed to his feet, pacing before her as he constructed a coherent hypothesis. "You are confusing Janice and Margaret and somehow coming up with Jeanne—"

"No!" She watched him with wide, frightened eyes.

"And the man who 'killed' you, perhaps he is the one who beat you before you came here—"

"He was . . ." Her voice trailed away.

"Was he your husband?"

"No!"

He spun her around, gripping her shoulders as he tried to make her see reason. "Can you not see it, Carolly? What you describe cannot happen. It is not possible."

She shifted to her knees on the bed, her eyes blazing in indignation. "Why isn't it possible? Because you don't believe? Must everything make sense to you before it can exist?"

"Think, Carolly! Angels wandering among us as people? It just cannot happen!"

"It can!"

"Then who is Caroline Handren? What do you know of *her* life?"

She paled abruptly, and he shifted his grip to catch her if she fell. But she did not. She simply remained as she was, kneeling on the bed, her eyes downcast and her shoulders suddenly slumped.

"Tell me," he urged. "Who is Caroline?"

She bit her lip, and he touched her under her chin, lifting her face until she once again looked into his eyes. "She was born in 1786, the only daughter of a minister in Norfolk. Her parents died in a fire ten years ago, and the trauma so unbalanced her mind that she was . . . she was . . ." Her lips trembled, and he returned to his place on the bed, drawing her back against him.

"Tell me all of it," he urged gently.

"Her uncle put her in a private asylum for the mentally ill. It is an evil place, located near here in Derby. She was beaten frequently and . . ." Her voice trailed away again.

"And?"

"And she escaped a few weeks ago. I think . . . I think she died. Then I must have . . . taken over her body." Her voice was empty now. There was no fight left in her, no fire to sustain her as she went limp in his arms.

He cradled her, tucking her against him as if he alone could keep her safe from harm while she finally gave him the answers he sought. Caroline Handren, escaped patient from the Boor-

stin Asylum in Derby. The beatings, the fire—it had all become confused in her mind.

"I am not her," she whispered, as if responding to his
thoughts. "I'm not."

"Shhh." He wiped away a tear as it trailed past her cheek.
He had the answers now. He could take steps to help her.

"James," she cried in a small voice. "Hold me. Please, just
hold me."

She already rested in his arms, but he tightened his grip.
His head was tilted so he could look into her eyes, and the
defeat he saw there cut him so deeply he winced. Her fantasies
had been exposed, and somewhere deep in her disordered
mind, she knew it. She was Caroline, the unbalanced daughter
of a minister. And as he watched, all the best of Carolly
slipped away. The fire and confidence so much a part of her
slipped into nothingness, leaving behind a shaking, terrified
woman.

It broke his heart to see her so robbed.

He leaned down and kissed her hair. "It will be all right,"
he whispered. "I believe you." He was lying, but he did not
regret it. He felt her steady, her body still.

"You believe what?" she challenged softly.

"That you will find your answers, and they will be the right
ones, even if I do not understand them."

He felt her smile, her lips curving against his chest. She
had not meant it as a sensual invitation, but it was powerful
nonetheless. He pulled her back, exposing her face just
enough for him to kiss her forehead, touching it lightly, gently,
to comfort her. But once begun, he could not stop. His mouth
trailed down her wet lashes and eased over the strong curve
of her cheekbones until he finally found her lips.

She opened willingly beneath him, her response slow and
sweet. Still, he hesitated. He did not want to push her further
into madness. And yet, how could he stop? Especially as she
drew him down toward her, teasing him with her responses,
urging him to deepen his caress.

He kissed her deeply and passionately. Her arms wrapped around him, kneading the tight muscles of his back and shoulders. She moaned softly, and James's blood began to beat with a hunger that stole his breath.

She was still dressed in her high-necked gray gown, but he found the fastenings, releasing them with deft movements. She sighed at the sudden relaxation of her clothing as he pushed the fabric down and away. She wore no corset. Merely a shift that was easily pushed up and away.

He kissed a moan from her lips when his hands at last slipped across her exposed, glowing skin. Ever since that first evening, he had wanted to do this. He held her breasts, molding them to his hands, teasing their erect peaks with his thumbs.

She arched beneath him, and he struggled against the last of his reason. He could not take her, and yet he could not refuse her. He trembled with indecision and desire. He kissed the curve of her neck, tasting the salt of her tears. He licked the sweet valley over her heart, then, at last, he kissed one dusky, pink nipple.

He stayed there a long while, teasing her with small, light nips.

He wanted her. He wanted to taste the fire that was Carolly, wanted to show her the ways of love. But most of all, James wanted to share with her the joy and delight of lovemaking as he never had with any woman. With her it would be wonderful.

But he could not. Not if she did not understand the consequences of their actions, not when she was a guest in his home, and certainly not when she was so vulnerable. He was a gentleman. He would not violate a guest.

He allowed himself one last, lingering kiss. Then he pulled away.

"James?"

"We cannot do this."

"Don't leave, James. Not now." She spoke in a throaty whisper that seemed to echo in his mind.

"I . . . I must." But he was weakening. He had to leave soon.

He stood, but she had hold of his hand. His movement pulled her upright on the bed, and her hair spilled around her in glorious disarray. Then, in one quick movement, she pulled off her shift, tossing it aside as her breasts bounced before him. They were firm and rosy, their blush beautiful in the delicate moonlight.

"James. It's all right. I . . . I want you to stay. If I'm not an angel, then at least let me be a woman."

He shook his head, his body at war with his mind. But he did not resist as she pulled him forward, drawing his hand back to the soft curve of her breast. "You do not know what you are asking," he whispered.

"I'm asking you to make love with me."

"You do not know what that means."

"Yes," she whispered. "I do." She lifted herself to her knees, offering her lips to him.

But he stayed away, his every muscle screaming with the strain. "It is immoral, unholy. Wrong."

"To make love?"

"To take advantage of you."

"You are not taking advantage of me, my lord," she murmured. "I am taking advantage of you." Then she tugged him ever closer to her, gasping as his hand trembled where it lay against her breast.

But then he gazed down into her eyes. He saw passion there, knowing it was mirrored in his own heated gaze. But he also saw desperation and fear. She was alone and vulnerable, seeking solace from him.

The sight pulled at his soul. He saw her pain and needed to assuage it, but he could not do so when she would hate herself and him as soon as her good sense returned. He could not do it.

She drew him down to her, and he was powerless to resist.

*   *   *

Carolly did not want to think; she only wanted to feel. What James did, how he touched her, how he kissed her—as if he feared to hurt her, and yet could not resist their mutual attraction—filled her heart and soul with wonder. Nothing had ever felt so right. True the part of her named Caroline was horrified at her wantonness, but Carolly was stronger, and she reveled in the pure joy of it all.

Except, it wasn't entirely perfect. Everything James did, every kiss, every touch, was sheer heaven, but he would not allow her to reciprocate. When she moved toward him, when she tried to touch him as he touched her, he shied away, distracting and preventing her.

James was making love *to* her, not *with* her.

"James?"

"Shhh."

"But—"

"Shhhh." He kissed away her protests until once again she was lost in a whirlpool of sensation. His hands moved lower on her body, stripping away her heavy clothing until she was naked beside him. She heard him suck in his breath, his expression awed. "My God, you are perfect."

She turned, embarrassment heating her face. "You were expecting some deformity?"

He shook his head, and she caught the hunger in his eyes. "I could not imagine a more perfect woman." He lifted his gaze to hers. "Oh, Caroline," he whispered, as his hands continued to stroke her in the most worshipful of caresses. "Let me show you what it is to be a woman."

She wanted him to. But she wanted more as well. She wanted to share this time with him, to be with him as a man with a woman. Not a man with a madwoman. "My name is Carolly."

He shrugged. "Caro, then."

She sighed, her passion growing cool, the mood shattered.

"Caro. Fine." Except it wasn't fine. This whole situation was far from fine. It was horrible.

How could she make love with a man who didn't believe what she'd told him? Who she was? Too depressed for words, she curled away from him, turning her back to him and rolling onto her side. He didn't stop her, but continued to caress her, his strokes long and sensuous. And apologetic.

"I did not mean to offend you . . ."

"No. You are correct. I am confused and lost. One cannot make love in such a state."

"But—"

"No."

He was quiet a long time, his only communication through long strokes of his fingertips. His hand slid from her shoulder, down past her elbow, grazing her hip and swirling lightly over her thigh. Then he reversed direction, tracing a path up her body once more. Carolly lay there in silence, focusing on nothing but the feel of his fingers as they soothed her troubled spirit.

"I can help you forget," he offered softly. "For a while at least. We can complete what we began."

She softened, and she felt a delicious sense of warmth grow in her belly. "Finish making love?"

"No." He paused, and his hand stilled against her hip. "Not that. But there are ways, ways to bring a woman pleasure without taking her virginity."

It was like being dropped in a pool of ice. Now she understood why he had earlier refused her touch. Why, in fact, he was still clothed while she lay naked beside him. "You never intended to make love with me."

"Caro . . ." His voice was choked.

"*Carolly*," she snapped, tears suddenly blurring her vision. She didn't truly know why this all hurt so much, but it did. She had thought they would touch each other in a very special way—*together*. But all he'd intended was to give to her, to hold himself apart as before. He would be the giver, she the receiver. They would never be equals. Didn't he want her as much as she wanted him? Obviously not, if he could still be so restrained.

"I think you had better leave."

He stiffened in surprise. "But—"

"But nothing." She sat up, dragging the sheet with her as she moved. "I don't want your pity, James. I wanted to share something special with you. But you couldn't let us do that, could you? The great Earl of Traynern couldn't possibly stoop to loving a minister's mad daughter, could he? Maybe I ought to have tried Garrett."

His eyes suddenly narrowed in fury, and she knew she'd struck home.

"At least with him," she continued relentlessly, "I know where I stand. With you and your honorable intentions, you fooled me into thinking we had something. But true feelings are something you can't or won't give."

"I was simply trying to preserve your reputation," he explained, once again sounding stuffy to Carolly's ears. "But I can see you have no sense of morality. I cannot understand why I was even concerned." He sounded bitter.

"What you were preserving was your own isolation," she snapped. "I don't know who hurt you, James, but it must have been something horrible for you to spend the rest of your life locked inside yourself. Good lord, you haven't even taken off your coat!"

James pushed away, standing up beside the bed with his jaw clenched and his hands tightened into fists. "I believe I shall bid you good night."

"That's right, James. Run away. Lord knows, if you stayed you might be tempted to *feel* something!"

He didn't deign to respond. He simply bowed with chilling correctness, then spun on one heel and left her room. He didn't slam the door, but closed it with a quiet click that seemed to reverberate through the room. She almost wished he'd torn it off its hinges. At least then she'd know he felt something, even if it was anger.

But he didn't, and all Carolly could do was stare at the back of the door and cry, her tears silently tracking down her face.

Chapter Eleven

"You are sending Carolly away, aren't you?"

James looked up from his desk at his niece. She actually looked pretty this morning, he realized with a slight start. She wore her trim riding habit of rich burgundy—which did indeed now fit her perfectly—and her hair was neatly pulled away from her face with a bright ribbon. But it was not her clothing that had caused the transformation. He had, in fact, seen her in exactly that same outfit earlier this morning when he, she, and Garrett had gone riding.

So what was it?

"Uncle, do not send her away. I like her here."

James felt his eyes widen in shock. She was standing up to him. This child, his usually sullen lump of a niece, stood erect before him, challenging him with every fiber of her being.

He did not know what to say, so he ducked the question. "Hello again, Margaret. I very much enjoyed our ride this morning. Shall we discuss where to go on our next trip? Garrett doesn't want to go, but—"

"No," she said, crossing her arms. "I want to discuss Carolly. Why are you sending her away?"

He frowned. "What makes you think I am?"

She jutted her chin toward the letter on top of his desk. "You are writing to the Boorstin Asylum in Derby asking if they have lost a patient named Caroline Handren." She paused, momentarily distracted. "Is that her real name?"

James leaned back in his chair and regarded his niece. When had her gaze become so focused, the set of her jaw so very firm? My God, he thought with a start, the child was positively military in her bearing. He stared at her, his expression purposely hard, but the child did not waver. In fact, she regarded him with exactly the same expression as he'd seen on Caro. It looked extremely dark and forbidding.

"Did you learn this from her?" he asked.

Margaret frowned. "Learn what?"

"How to stare at someone like that."

Margaret's frown deepened. "I learned it from you. Carolly told me the best way to handle you was to behave just as stubbornly as you. We even practiced."

James released a sigh. "That, young lady, is exactly why I am sending her away."

"No!" she returned, her voice as firm and final as his own.

He shook his head. It was unnerving to see how much change Carolly had wrought in the child in barely over a month. And he was not entirely sure he liked all the changes.

"Margaret, this is not something one discusses with a child."

The girl simply raised one eyebrow and settled in the chair opposite his desk, her posture as deceptively casual as his own. "I will not allow you send her away, Uncle. I like her. And you like her. Even the servants like her. She must stay."

Now James was sure. He definitely did not like this change. He liked that she was happier, but for his niece to demand he answer the very questions that had plagued him the night through . . . Leaning forward in his chair, he placed his elbows on his desk and peered at Margaret in what he hoped was a sincere manner.

"You must see that Caro is very ill. Neither you nor I can help her here. She must be under a doctor's care." That had been his conclusion early this morning. He had failed to help her. Indeed, he very much feared his interference had made her condition worse. And rather than see her delusions destroy her as they had destroyed Danny, he finally admitted that he must send her away. She must be under the care of a qualified physician, one who understood how to handle a disordered mind.

"I do not believe you," Margaret responded, her voice challenging. "She is not ill."

James frowned. "I assure you, I am not lying. Caroline—"

"You are, too. Her name is Carolly, and she is not sick. She is just different. You want her to be sick, so you can send her away." James was beginning to see the unhappy child appear again, the mulish, recalcitrant, miserable one. "I hate you!" she screamed. "I do not want Carolly to leave, and if you send her away, I will go with her!"

"You most certainly will not."

Margaret jumped to her feet. "I will! I swear it, I will!"

James stood, too, leaning forward on his desk to emphasize his words. "You will go to your room—"

"My father is dead. You took away my mother, and all I get is pasty-faced governesses who cannot even smile! I will not let you take Carolly away, too!" She spun on her heel and dashed out of the room, emitting loud, gulping sobs as she ran.

James could do nothing but stare after her, his hands clenched into fists.

"My, my. She was certainly upset."

James twisted, a sigh escaping his lips at the sight of Caro. She was dressed demurely in another one of her gray gowns, but all he could see was how she had looked last night, her beautiful body stretched out in glorious abandon on the bed, her skin the color of dusky pearls, her body alive and welcoming in the soft candlelight.

"Good morning, Caro," he said, but his voice sounded rough even to his own ears.

"What did she mean about you taking away her mother?"

"Have you taken to listening at keyholes?"

She shrugged. "Mags gets away with it."

He retreated to the secure comfort of his desk chair, feeling a headache building at his temples. "I begin to believe you two have entirely too much influence on each other."

"Is that why you intend to send me back to Boorstin?"

He looked down at the letter on his desk. He had not even sent the missive as yet.

"No," she answered for him, gliding forward until she could look down at his letter. "No, it has nothing to do with Margaret. It is because of last night."

He looked up, feeling besieged. "It has nothing to do with—"

"Of course it does. I make you uncomfortable. I challenge your understanding of the world." She leaned forward. "You can send me away, James, but it's too late. Your life has already changed. Mags knows how to confront you, and she won't be easily cowed again."

He groaned, knowing it was true. "Caro—"

"Did you truly take away her mother?"

"Of course not!" He nearly exploded, but all she did was settle quietly into the chair Margaret had vacated and fold her hands across her lap.

Lord, this woman was infuriating. When he glared at her, she smiled. When he screamed, she became serene. It was as if she had appeared in his life for the express purpose of contradicting him.

And yet, he thought with a sigh, he wanted to confide the truth of his niece to her. No one else seemed to understand Margaret as Carolly did. Perhaps she could give him the answers he needed.

He collapsed into his chair. "I received news of Bradley's death months after the fact. It took time to sell out my commission. One week after returning to London, I woke to the sound of screeching. I came downstairs to find a woman, an actress, with a bawling toddler squirming in her arms."

"Margaret's mother."

"She called herself Mags. It was her stage name."

Caro smiled. "No wonder you hate the nickname. And now Margaret uses it to torment you."

He swallowed, not wanting to admit how painful the name was to him. Every time he heard it, he was reminded of how much his niece had lost, and how much she blamed him for it.

"So, what happened?" Caro prompted.

James shrugged, trying to continue in a casual tone. "We left the girl with Cook, who plied her with milk and cookies. And then Mags and I retired to . . . negotiate."

Caro tilted her head. "Negotiate?"

James squirmed in his seat. How could he phrase this delicately enough? "She, uh, claimed to be Bradley's widow. She even produced a marriage license."

"You believe it was false?"

He shrugged. "I had no idea. It appeared legal, and Bradley was certainly wild enough. It was possible."

Caro leaned forward, her expression pinched with disgust. "You paid her off. You bought her kid and paid her to go away."

"I did not buy anything!" he returned hotly, pushing out of his chair to pace. "Except maybe her silence. She refused to leave the theater. She wanted me to keep Margaret. She told me the child had a right to a better life." He ran his hand through his hair. "I agreed. I provided Mags with a suitable income until she died a year later of the pox."

Caro remained silent, and so he turned around, needing to see her expression. He was shocked by what he saw. Her face had softened to a compassionate sadness. There were no recriminations, was no condescending hauteur, just kindhearted sympathy.

"James, you have got to talk to her. Margaret thinks you sent her mother away."

He leaned back against the mantel, feeling hopelessness well up in his soul. "It doesn't matter what I say. The more I talk, the less she will listen."

Caro stood up, advancing to touch his arm. "You're her uncle, James. She's your ward. You have lived together for four years. She must believe you on some level."

He gazed down at the thick library rug, knowing there was a beautiful pattern of rich colors just beneath his feet, but able to see only Margaret's tear-streaked face. "I do not know how to speak to her of this."

Caro's hand tightened on his arm. "You have to try. Otherwise, you'll just be throwing her away, and you need each other too much for that. To avoid a problem just because you don't know how to deal with it . . ."

James looked up. Had he been throwing Margaret away? And Caro, too? She had not said such, but the reasoning seemed clear. He reached out and brushed a finger across her face, feeling the downy softness of her cheek. "Is that what you think I am doing to you? Discarding you like yesterday's cravat?"

Her eyes flickered, and for a moment he thought she would lean in for a kiss. Then she stiffened and turned away so all he could see was her rigid spine. "You cannot throw away what you never had, James. I . . . I care for you. And Margaret. But you know I never intended to stay here forever." Her voice was high and brittle, and he knew she had forced herself to say those painful words.

He reached for her, needing to touch her, but she pushed out of her chair, twisting to face him with a determined expression. "I intend to right what is wrong here, James. I intend to help you and Margaret reconcile, and to find you a woman to love, and then I will leave." She smiled. "I *will* earn my wings, James. And then I will be happy, too."

He stared at her and slowly lowered his hand to his side. She was sincere. He saw that now, clearly. After all they had discussed, despite the fact that they now knew her true name and circumstances, she still persisted in her delusions. It was as he'd thought that morning. A cold fist settled in his stomach. He could not help her.

It brought him a different knowledge, too. He could not have helped Danny, either. He saw that now, as he witnessed how deep Caro had descended into her own madness. The last of his guilt over Danny slipped away. He now understood that mental illnesses were beyond his abilities to heal. Daniel and Caroline both needed a doctor. Danny had never had the chance. But James had the opportunity to help Caroline, to find her the treatment she required.

He *had* to return her to Boorstin Asylum.

His gaze strayed to the letter lying like an accusation on his desk. He had intended to merely inquire if they had lost a patient. He still wished to inspect the quality of the care they offered. But now he knew those had been mere tactics, ways of convincing himself he searched for her true identity when in fact he had been delaying the inevitable, trying to keep her with him for a few days more.

Except he could not. He now saw how selfish that thought had been. She needed help. Help that neither he nor Margaret could offer.

"You intend to send me back to Boorstin, don't you?" Her voice was soft, like a whisper on a breeze, but he felt her words like physical blows. "James?"

He could not lie to her. "Yes. I must send you back."

She nodded, as if she had expected no less.

He looked up at her, panic squeezing his chest. "I . . . I do not mean for you to go today. In fact, I thought we could have a party first. Perhaps a . . . a ball?"

She smiled at him, her expression a trifle strained, but a

touch of her humor returned. "A ball, James? To celebrate your release from a lunatic?"

He shook his head. "Celebrating a new friendship. One that will continue despite a minor separation." He took a step forward. "We will visit you, you know. Margaret and I. We can come every week." For perhaps the hundredth time this morning—in his thoughts if not in reality—he reached out to touch her, but as at the end of last night she shied away, her expression panicked.

"Oh, my," she said, looking anywhere but at him. "There is so much to do if you are to have a ball! I must plan—"

"A simple dinner party," he warned. "Perhaps some dancing. Nothing more." He glanced at her with concern. "I do not wish you to strain yourself."

"Strain myself? It's a party, James, not a military campaign." Then she frowned. "Military campaign. Military campaign . . . Waterloo! Napoleon! Of course. How could I have forgotten?" She suddenly grinned. "Now, if only I could remember the ingredients of Beef Wellington . . ." Her voice trailed away as she moved toward the door.

But James was there before her, trying to reassure himself that all was well between them. "Caro!"

She did not answer, and he had to grab her. "Carolly!"

She looked up.

He swallowed. Why did she have to look so beautiful? It was not her clothing or her hair or even her eyes this time, but the simple beauty of understanding. Of peace. There was no anger in her face at her ultimate removal to Boorstin, just a calm acceptance of her fate. He envied that serenity. Especially since he felt torn by conflicting desires and a guilty conscience.

"I do not *wish* you to leave," he said softly. "You know that, do you not? But it is for your own good. You need help that I cannot give you. It has taken me a long time to accept that. But as much as I want to, I do not know how to help."

She smiled sweetly at him. Then she raised her hand and

trailed a finger over his lips. "You are helping, James. You are going to reconcile with Margaret. You are throwing a ball so I can find you a wife. And your steward is importing rabbits to help your disgruntled ex-miners."

"Carolly—"

"And when that is all done, I shall leave. But not for Boorstin. I am going to be an angel."

He reached out for her, gripping her hands to try and make her understand. "Think, Caroline. For a moment, see what is real." He did not understand why it was so important to him that she accept the persona of Caroline Handren. Only that if she were rational, fully rational, even for a few moments, then he had a prayer that she understood what he did was best for her. "I do not want to hurt you, Caroline."

He searched her eyes, seeing them widen with panic as she struggled with her identity. He held tightly on to her fingers, praying she would emerge on the other side of her fantasies, her mind whole.

He waited, holding his breath.

Then, suddenly, the confusion seemed to disappear. It was as if she had purposely pushed any disturbing thoughts aside. She smiled at him, her face serene.

"I understand. Better than you do." Then she stretched up on her toes to give him a quick kiss before dancing away.

Chapter Twelve

Carolly wandered out toward the dawn. The morning dew soaked her slippers, chilling her toes, but nothing could diminish the simple joy of watching the sun rise. She liked the dawn. It symbolized new beginnings to her, something she desperately needed right now.

Everything was going great. The preparations for the festivities were running as smoothly as could be hoped, given that James had not hosted gathering of any sort in the last five years. Mrs. Potherby was a wonder, teaching Carolly everything she needed to know about fashionable entertainment and also a good many things she wasn't sure she was supposed to know. Things like what to do when the blacksmith elopes with the minister's daughter in the middle of a quadrille. Apparently that had happened, according to local folklore.

The party had been set for June 18. Carolly had added up the days for Napoleon's hundred-day campaign in France. The count began on the day he landed in France, with Waterloo occurring on the hundredth day. Unfortunately, the date of

Napoleon's arrival in France was not very clear. From what she could ascertain from the newspaper, she'd guessed the Little Emperor began his drive through France around March 1. That put Waterloo on June 9. Carolly had added another week, allowing for the guests' travel time and general excitement, and set the party for June 16. But then Mrs. Potherby had said the evening should be held on a full moon, so she delayed the ball two more days.

Mrs. Potherby assured her that everything would be in order by then.

As for James, he was most cooperative, giving her a free hand in the celebration, just so long as he did not have to actually assist in the details. He wanted his time free to spend with his niece.

After Carolly's talk with him in his library, James had finally joined Margaret in her bedroom and the two spoke at length. Carolly was not privy to the conversation, but they had emerged three hours later all smiles, suddenly the best of friends. Now they went on picnics and insect hunts every afternoon, rain or shine, reserving the wet days to hunt in the cellar or gardener's shed.

The two had truly bonded, and Carolly was positive she was well on her way to her wings. Yes, everything was going great. And if it were not for one minor detail, she would be the happiest pre-angel alive.

She'd fallen in love with James.

She hadn't a clue how it happened. Lord knew, he wasn't the most loveable man alive. But he was honorable, gentle, kind, and incredibly sexy. Carolly kicked a stray stone and groaned. Perhaps he *was* the most loveable man alive—for her. And she had fallen for him hard.

She didn't know when it had happened, either. The feelings had crept up on her quietly. All she knew was one day she had seen him laughing with Margaret, and her heart swelled. But then the pair of them walked away, leaving her alone, reminding her all too clearly that she was not part of their family. She was an outsider, and she would never be part of their circle.

The pain was so intense it caused a physical ache. That was when she'd realized she loved them. Yet soon she would have to give them up.

She heard hoofbeats in the distance and turned from the rosy morning light to see a dark silhouette of a horse and his rider stark on the horizon. They galloped past without pause, man and beast moving as one.

James and Shadow. Was there ever a more beautiful sight?

"He will never marry you."

Carolly started at the rough voice, spinning around to see Garrett, his face ruddy in the morning light. "Good morning, Garrett. I had no idea you ever got up this early."

He gave her a cheeky grin, and she smiled in return.

"You haven't been to bed, have you?"

"To bed, yes. To sleep . . ." He shrugged and rubbed his face. "I was just returning when I saw you standing here, and I could not resist the lure of your loveliness."

"Oh, my!" she responded in a sing-song voice, pretending to be all aflutter at his compliment. His only response was to offer her his arm. Carolly took it without hesitation. He was a poor second to James, but at least he rarely failed to make her smile.

His word, were not so welcome, though. "There can be no future for the two of you. You know that, do you not?"

Carolly let her gaze wander away, not liking that he had spoken her thoughts aloud.

"Caroline?"

"I know," she said quietly.

"He is an earl," Garrett continued. "Even if James had a heart to give you, his duty to the title would not allow him to stoop so low."

Carolly stopped dead in her tracks, annoyed at his harsh words. "You have too low an opinion of your cousin."

"I have known him much longer than you," he returned.

"But obviously not as well." She started to pull away, but he stopped her, keeping hold of her wrist when she would have withdrawn.

"Please, I have no wish to quarrel with you," he said.

"Then you should not say such hateful things." Carolly noted it was Caroline's prissiest tone that she used. She shook her head, wondering how long it would be before she could no longer distinguish between the part of her called Caroline and the part named Carolly. The two seemed to merge more every day, and her memories of her past lives sometimes slipped away almost completely.

"Caroline?"

Carolly jumped, feeling her face heat with embarrassment. "My apologies, Garrett. My thoughts were a hundred miles away." Or a hundred years.

He patted her hand. "That is not very flattering to my ego, Caroline, especially as I have come to offer you an alternative to your present situation."

Carolly frowned, turning away from the now brilliant sunshine. "My present situation?"

"I understand you do not wish to return to the asylum."

"I . . ." In truth, she had not worried too deeply about that possibility, assuming instead that when her work was done with James, she would suffer some sort of fatal accident as she always had before. But now his words brought the possibility firmly to mind. What if she failed? Or what if Heaven thought she'd failed? Would she stay here, trapped in this land and life?

Caroline's memories of Boorstin Asylum were very clear, and they did not paint an appealing picture. Abuses were rampant and conditions cruel. Patients were sometimes chained in their rooms, their clothing and bedding fouled. Beatings were common, as were daily visits by gawkers or, worse yet, those who assisted in the administration of the more violent "treatments."

Carolly took a deep breath, mentally pushing away her dark

thoughts. "Let us talk of something more pleasant. Shall you stay for the festival?"

Garrett hesitated mid-step, then turned toward her. "Festival? I thought it was a ball."

She grinned, feeling her good spirits return. "Yes, it was. But now it is a festival, too. A day off for the villagers to party and enjoy a good time on the earl."

Garrett's eyes narrowed to a thoughtful squint. "You are trying to turn their sentiments."

She shrugged. "They are hard-working people who deserve a break. If they have cause to thank James for that, all the better."

"I see." Garrett fell silent, clearly deep in thought as they continued to stroll through the near garden. But it was not too long before he gently disengaged Carolly's hand from his arm, pulling her around to face him directly. "Caroline, I know you do not wish to discuss the asylum, but we must."

She winced. She couldn't help it. "Garrett—"

"There are other options than Boorstin, you know." He raised his hand to trail his knuckles along her cheek. "I have thought of a way for you to find wealth, independence, and even happiness."

His touch was gentle, but the stroke was more practiced than heartfelt. She felt some surprise at what seemed obvious. "Garrett, are you proposing marriage?"

He hesitated. "Surely you know I cannot wed you, Caroline. You have been hospitalized for many years. You cannot hope for a respectable marriage. I am sorry, but it is true." He looked so genuinely sad that, for a moment, she believed him. For a moment.

"Then just what do you propose?"

"That you can live better than even I or James. You can have gentlemen, jewels, and a place in society."

She knew what he was suggesting, and her entire being rebelled at the thought. "As a demi-rep?"

"As a mistress. Your madness would be an asset then, a source of fascination to many men."

"I see," she said dryly.

He shook his head and his gaze traveled almost tangibly down her body. "No, I imagine you do not. But I could teach you." His voice was husky. "There are many pleasures of the flesh you can learn. Indeed, you *must* learn. I can teach you, and then I will introduce you to my friends. You are a beautiful woman, Caroline. Many men would pay a high price for you."

"I—"

"No," he whispered, drawing her closer. "Do not answer. Ponder your choices, my dear. Remember, your other option is Boorstin." Then, before she could stop him, he was kissing her with a passion cleverly orchestrated to inflame the senses of an innocent girl.

Too bad she was no innocent. Caroline was angry, not inflamed. But before she could react he slipped away, back into the house, leaving her to stare after him, silently fuming.

He was a pig. A skillful pig, but porcine nonetheless. Carolly sighed. His offer might actually hold some merit—at least, to the kind of naive, frightened girl he thought she was. If the choice truly was between Boorstin and becoming a high priced call-girl, Carolly might very well pick London. There she had the chance of living in luxury, and eventually earning enough money to win her freedom. Boorstin only offered degradation and brutality. Fortunately for her, she had other options.

Unless, of course, her thoughts of becoming an angel were fantasies. Carolly felt a chill invade her heart. Was it possible? It seemed so far-fetched. She frowned. Earning angel wings was the stuff of fiction and mov—m—moving pictures?

Her knees went weak, and Carolly stumbled to a bench, her mind in turmoil. Her name was Carol . . . Carol . . . Carolly. She was born in . . . in . . . She could not remember.

She struggled and fought and wrestled with her mind,

searching for the memories, but she could not find them.

Her litany was gone.

But she had remembered once. She remembered remembering. She had known once with unswerving faith that she was earning her wings to become an angel. That she had been self-centered and cruel, and now she was learning to be kind and selfless. That if she succeeded she would become an angel.

She remembered that.

She looked up and saw James on Shadow, poised on a rise, overlooking the garden. She started to stand, to walk toward him, but it was too late. He turned away. In her mind's eye, he was replaced by Garrett, offering her his own version of Eden, and then again by the elusive and fading dream of becoming an angel. Somewhere in the back of her mind, looming over the whole confusing mass, was the horrifying thought of Boorstin and the terrifying memory of flames.

She shook her head, trying to sort through it all, but Carolly saw only a swirl of faces she could neither identity nor understand.

She felt a sob catch in her throat, and she pressed her hand to her mouth. What was happening to her? Who was she? Lying down, she curled her knees to her chest and closed her eyes, one thought emerging above the rest. It was a simple truth, and one that rocked her to the core.

She knew, without a doubt, that she had finally gone mad.

"Uncle?"

James shifted his gaze from his foreman's report, grateful for the reprieve. The news from the mines was grim, citing worker unrest and general unease that was only an echo of the hatred brewing at the village. Unfortunately, there was little he could do about it except ride out the storm.

At least his home was more peaceful than ever, thanks to his new rapport with his niece.

"Good morning, Margaret," he said with a smile. "You look very pretty today."

Margaret wrinkled her nose at him. "You always say that."

"It is always true." In fact, it was more true every day. Margaret was standing taller, walking with the pride and confidence that should have been her birthright from the very beginning. He was pleased to see her spirit finally matching the bright clothing she now wore.

But despite all that, Margaret was still young, and he was never more aware of it than when she flopped down into a chair beside his desk, her ribbons flying every which way, her skirt billowing out around her.

"I want to talk with you, Uncle."

He tried not to laugh at her serious demeanor. "I can see that. What did you wish to say?"

"It is about Carolly. I am concerned about her."

James sobered. He, too, was concerned about Caro. They barely spoke anymore. He tried, making every excuse to see her, but she brushed him off, burying herself in preparations for her festival and would not discuss anything more than banalities. The only thing he could think to do for her was to continue to give her free rein with her ball, hoping that, at least, expressed his concern for her.

"Uncle, she weeps almost all the time."

He turned to his niece. "You have seen this?"

She shook her head. "She does it in her room, but I can hear her through the door."

"You should not listen at doors, Margaret." His reprimand came out of habit, and the child shrugged it off as usual.

"Have you seen her eyes?" Margaret persisted. "They are always puffy now."

Yes, James thought sadly. He had seen them, but how could he help when she always ran away? He leaned forward. "How do you think we can help her?" he asked, amazed at his own question. Two months ago, he would never have considered asking a child for advice. But since Caro's advent into his life, he had learned many things—one of which was that Margaret possessed an uncanny understanding of the inner thoughts of his staff. She managed them in a way he never believed possible. It was only logical that James turn to her for advice on Caro. "I am willing to consider any suggestion."

Margaret frowned, chewing on her lower lip, then turned her large brown eyes to him in entreaty. "Do not send her away."

"Any suggestion but that."

"But, Uncle—"

"Do not ask that, Margaret." His voice was firm, yet absolutely useless in the face of the child's clear determination. James sighed and dropped back in his chair. When had the girl become so strong? "Please try to understand, Margaret. Caro is sick. She needs a doctor's help."

"Then, bring a doctor here."

He grimaced. "She and Dr. Stoneham do not get on."

"Then send for a better one than that mean old man. Send for one from London."

He shook his head. "Caro will refuse to see any of them."

"You cannot send her back to that awful place!"

He sighed. "Boorstin? I do not intend to. I looked into the conditions, and they are awful. But look." He opened his desk drawer and pulled out the letter that had been in his thoughts ever since its arrival yesterday. "This is from Caro's uncle. He is coming for the festival."

Margaret jumped to her feet. "But *he* will send her back to Boorstin!"

James took the girl's hands, tugging her closer to him as he tried to reason with her. "I will discuss the matter with him, but you know I am not her guardian. Her uncle must decide what is to be done."

"But Carolly—"

"Is very confused right now," he interrupted. Then he pulled his niece the remaining distance until he held her in his arms, finally lifting her up onto his lap. "Can you not see how selfish it is to keep her with us? To encourage her in her illness? And refuse to give her family the right to decide what to do with her?"

Margaret did not respond except with a sullen pout, but she did lean into his body, curling against him as never before. He wrapped his arms around her, pulling her closer still, cherishing this new and special closeness with his brother's only child.

Then he spoke the words he knew might shatter her. "You know I am right, Margaret. As much as we might want her here, we cannot keep her."

As he feared, she struggled out of his arms, challenging him with every fiber of her being. "Truly, Uncle? Do you truly want her to remain here? Or are you just pretending?"

He frowned, uncomfortable with his niece's penetrating regard. "Margaret, I care very deeply for Caro. I wish her to be well."

"That is not the same thing as wanting her here."

James did not answer. His niece was a very perceptive child, and she had asked the questions he had been fighting ever since Caro threw him out of her bedroom. Did he want her here? Did he want her in his life at all?

He thought about her almost all the time. He remembered tiny things about her, such as the way she tugged at her hair when she thought hard, and the way she ate her food with such amazing verve and energy. Perhaps that was what most drew him to her: her vitality and confidence—as if she knew who and what she was, despite the fact that she sometimes forgot, and that her claims sounded so fanciful. No matter the folly, she still *believed* in herself.

Until lately.

Until he had forced her to remember Caroline Handren and Boorstin. Now she faded before his eyes, and he was not sure whether to be thankful for her return to reality or guilty that she was losing the best part of herself because of his stubbornness.

Did he want her in his life?

Yes. But as the old Carolly, not the new Caroline. And that thought made him the saddest of all.

He sighed. "I wish her health and happiness, Margaret. And I know she cannot find it here." He looked deep into his niece's dark eyes and hoped she would understand. "I have brought her nothing but pain. It does her no good to remain here."

"But—"

James stopped the objection with a raised hand. "Her uncle arrives in four days. Neither you nor I can change that now."

Stubborn to the core, Margaret continued to argue. "But if we convince him to let her stay, will you allow it?"

James hesitated, torn between his desire and what he knew was best for Caro. "I cannot see that it would be good for her," he said slowly.

"But will you let her stay?"

"Her reputation—"

Margaret shook her head and interrupted. "Was already beyond repair. What further harm can we do? Please, Uncle. For me, will you please let her stay?"

"I . . ."

"Please?"

He sighed, unable to say yes or no. He settled on the one word that had most frustrated him as a child. "Perhaps."

Margaret jumped forward and wrapped her arms around him. "Oh, thank you, thank you, uncle."

James received her hug, drawing her small body close. Two hugs in one day, he marveled. His life was indeed changing. Still, honesty compelled him to warn Margaret of the truth. "Caro's uncle will not let her stay."

She pulled away, her eyes bright with excitement. "Of course he will. We will convince him."

She made to spin off, but he grabbed her arm, holding her near. "In all your exuberance, try to remember Caro. We must try to get what is best for her. Remember that."

Margaret wrinkled her nose, making a childish face that said he was being a complete idiot. "Well, of course I shall remember her. And what is best for Carolly is to stay here with us."

James regarded his niece, holding her gaze to impress her with the gravity of the situation. "Have you asked her what she wants?"

Margaret's gaze shifted to her feet. "Not exactly."

"Well, you must ask—*exactly*—before we go speaking with her uncle."

Margaret's shoulders slumped, though the fire of determination still kindled in her eyes. "I will ask. I promise." Then she brightened. "But first I must plot my scheme to convince her uncle. He is probably stiff and stuffy like you. So all we need do is show him how to laugh, and he will come around."

James pulled back, startled by her perception. "I beg your pardon?"

"That is what Carolly did for you. She told me so. She said all we needed to do was make you laugh often enough, and then you would come around. You would be nicer. And you have! You are!"

James frowned. Was that true? Was that how Margaret saw him—stiff, stuffy, joyless? "Margaret, I laugh quite often."

She grinned at him. "Of course you do. Since Carolly came here." Then she dashed away.

Chapter Thirteen

When Baron George Handren arrived, Caroline was busy overseeing the airing of the guest rooms. Her uncle was only the first of many guests from London come for what had now become an extended house party. The ball was set for a week hence, and she wanted to be sure everything was perfect. There would be no gossip about James's home or staff as long as she was in charge. She and Mrs. Potherby were of the same mind on this, and the two had spent many long hours reviewing even the tiniest details of the long event.

Mrs. Potherby also seemed to understand that Caroline required the mental distraction of detailed and thorough planning. The dear woman had stepped back, giving Caroline the freedom to interfere in things that would not usually be her concern.

But when Caroline heard the rattle of a carriage and saw a familiar and rather ostentatious vehicle tooling toward the front door, she knew her days of hiding were over.

Her uncle had arrived. She could no longer pretend.

Mrs. Potherby shot her a reassuring smile, then bustled away to see to the final details of Baron Handren's room. Caroline smoothed her skirt, tidied her hair, and then steeled herself to go downstairs to greet James's first guest.

Everything is fine, she told herself. The festival is all prepared, the menus are in order, the entertainment is in line. Even Margaret had been unusually delightful lately, taking every opportunity to make Caroline laugh. And if news of Waterloo had not yet arrived, it did not matter much, anyway. In fact, she began to wonder what she'd wanted to hear in the first place. Some battle she'd thought she recalled. She supposed it would happen if it happened.

It was time to greet her uncle.

Caroline walked slowly, if not totally serenely, down the stairs. She met James and Garrett on the front steps of the manor and watched with what she hoped was quiet dignity as the gilded carriage finally pulled to a stop.

She glanced to her left as Margaret joined them. The child, like the rest of them, seemed uncharacteristically silent. Even Miss Hornswallow, standing a discreet distance away, appeared more grim than usual. The affair was exceedingly somber, and Caroline could not help but wink at Margaret, thinking that at least the child should smile.

It did not help. The girl seemed almost militaristic in her bearing, her face set in the harsh lines of a soldier bent on a mission.

Then Caroline's attention was caught by the postboy who snapped open the carriage door. A familiar red velvet interior appeared, but the sight was quickly overshadowed as a large-bellied man in high fashion stepped into the afternoon sunlight.

He was quite a sight, and Caroline could not help but blink. From the tip of his beaver hat to the shine on his tasseled Hessians, he appeared a man of exquisite taste spoiled only by a ponderous waist. His cravat was intricately tied and his pantaloons a handsome dark satin, but his coat buttons drew the eye as they pulled and strained against his paunch. Still, as he stepped out of his carriage he smiled, practically bubbling over with effusive good cheer.

"My lord!" he called to James. "It is so good to have finally arrived. And my dear Caroline," he called, turning to her. "You look ravishing as always." Then he frowned, his expression confused. "You cut your hair."

She did not respond, but watched with a kind of horror as he mounted the steps and opened his arms to her. She did not move.

"What? No greeting for your doting uncle?" he boomed.

Caroline winced at the tone. He had always been loud, but never before had she realized how very vulgar. The man stepped closer to her, enveloping her in his familiar bear hug. Finally she was able to struggle free, but even then he stayed close by, holding her by the hand as one would a small child.

"Have you nothing to say, my dear?" he asked again.

She let her gaze slide away, feeling the last of her hopes die. She *had* been mad. Her memories of Carolly and her previous incarnations were fantasies. This was too real, the familiarity too strong for it not to be true.

"I . . ." She swallowed her tears. "I know you."

"Well, of course you do. I am your Uncle George." Then he patted her cheek with condescending affection. "Do not worry, my dear. I will take care of it all. I know this has been frightfully upsetting for you."

"No—"

"Hush, now," he interrupted. "Let me make my bows to the earl." He turned to James, executing his bow with all the creaks and groans of pulled fabric. "Baron George Handren, at your service, my lord."

James returned the greeting with his usual elegance. "A pleasure, sir. Allow me to introduce my cousin, Mr. Garrett Northram." Garrett made his bow, his expression bored. "And my niece and ward, Miss Margaret Northram."

Margaret stepped forward and executed her curtsy with stiff anger.

"Why, she is absolutely charming," exclaimed the baron, his face wreathed in smiles.

Margaret straightened and put her hands on her hips, her expression sour. "You are smiling," she accused.

Baron Handren pulled back. "Why, my dear, you do not like smiles?" He glanced over to James. "Children are such a delight." Then he laughed heartily, as if he had made the best of jokes.

"And you are laughing!" Margaret stomped her foot.

That only caused him to laugh harder until James intervened. "You must forgive my niece. She is under the impression that all uncles are as sour and forbidding as her own."

"Such nonsense!" Baron Handren chortled. "Simply delightful!" Then he continued chuckling all the way into the hall.

Caroline watched them go inside. Everyone left except Margaret, who stood loyally by her side, and Miss Hornswallow who remained near her charge. One by one every one disappeared into the manor. First James, then her uncle, then Garrett, and lastly a whole slew of footmen, postboys, and servants carrying more luggage than Caroline could ever remember seeing. And through it all, she herself stood on the sidelines, watching them scurry up and down the steps like frenzied ants.

"You don't want to go with him, do you?" Margaret asked, standing close by her side.

Caroline blinked and looked down. The child stared up at her, her liquid brown eyes earnest.

"You don't want to go with him," she repeated, but this time it was not a question.

Caroline looked away, her gaze straying to the northeast and Boorstin Asylum. "He is my uncle."

"Just tell Uncle James you don't want to go. Tell him that you want to stay here." Margaret was pleading with her, begging her to fight, but Caroline did not have any hope left in her. Not after having realized that this man was her uncle. She had obviously made everything up.

"I am very ill, Margaret. I think it is important I go."

"No!" The little girl stomped her foot for emphasis. "You are not sick. You are not confused. And you are *not* Caroline Handren."

Caroline sighed and settled down on the steps, half hiding herself behind a column. She drew Margaret along with her until they both sat comfortably in the shade. Miss Hornswallow hovered nearby. "Has there been any news?"

Margaret frowned. "You mean about . . . Waterloo?"

Caroline nodded.

Margaret sighed, "No. I am sorry. No news."

"I did not think so."

"It means nothing. It will happen. You said so."

Caroline let her gaze rise to the clear blue summer sky, letting her mind drift with the clouds on the horizon. "I said a great many things, Margaret. And most of it makes no sense."

"It does too! You are an angel. You are earning your wings, but you fell in love with Uncle."

Caroline cast her a sharp look. "Who told you that?"

Margaret kicked at a stone. "I reasoned it out."

"Well, I most certainly did not fall in love with your uncle!" returned Caroline sternly. "It would be most impertinent of me. He is an earl."

"Carolly! What has happened to you?" the child wailed. "You sound like Miss Hornswallow!"

In the distance, the governess stiffened, and Caroline spared her a smile. "There is nothing wrong with sounding like Miss Hornswallow. She is an excellent woman who is gravely underappreciated. I have always thought so."

"Carolly!" The word came out like a wail of despair, and yet there was nothing that could be done to ease the child's suffering. Caroline was what she was. Or had become.

Caroline frowned. What was she thinking? Nothing made any sense anymore.

In the end, she gathered up the child in her arms, needing Margaret's comfort as much as the girl seemed to need hers. They sat together on the steps, Margaret sobbing as though her heart had broken. Caroline held her, letting the child wail out in pain, but she herself did not cry. She simply let her gaze follow the lazy pattern of the clouds as they shifted and blew in their various directions.

Nothing made sense to her, but she found the heavens vaguely comforting.

Inside, James was enjoying a convivial guest and a hearty glass of brandy. He, Baron Handren, and Garrett had adjourned to the billiards room. It was not a room James used often, but it was the Baron's idea, and James thought it an appropriate enough place to become acquainted with Caro's only surviving relative.

"I cannot thank you enough for helping out my little niece," boomed the man heartily as he lit up a cigar. "Don't mind telling you the gel gave me quite a scare."

"I was only too happy to be of assistance."

"My only living relative," he confided in what was, for him, an undertone. "Sweet as can be, but not a thought in her brainbox. I will take her off your hands first thing in the morning. Best keep her in her room until then. Don't want her upsetting the staff."

James had been lining up his shot, but he lifted his head at the baron's remark. "Surely you intend to stay for the festival."

The baron took a long puff on his cigar, then turned. He wore a shocked expression. "My lord, you cannot mean to have her here during all that brouhaha. With all the people and the noise, no telling what might set her off."

James stood, a cold feeling building in the pit of his stomach. "She has been quite sane throughout her stay."

"Apart from thinking she is an angel," commented Garrett.

James shook his head. "But she has done most of the work for this celebration. You cannot take her away beforehand. It would be too cruel."

Handren waved his cigar in an expansive gesture. "Believe me, my lord, you do not want her destroying your entertainment. Your guests are members of the peerage. They will feel awkward in the presence of a madwoman."

"She is not mad," returned James, his annoyance building by the moment. The fact that he had called her mad earlier seemed irrelevant. These people didn't understand. "She is only . . . confused."

"Then you have been fortunate. Her fits are frightful to behold. I assure you—"

"And I assure you, there have been no fits while she has been here."

The old man sighed, his regard sad, as one who has seen too much. "Perhaps I could attend the festival. Then I will visit Caroline at Boorstin and give her all the details. She did so enjoy it when I used to tell her the news of London."

James carefully set aside his cue stick, turning his tone hard and implacable. "Baron, truly I must insist. Caro has worked too hard to not attend."

The man did not at first respond, so enthralled was he with his cigar. James waited patiently, his stance casual but his gaze fixed. Then the baron pulled back and looked directly at James. "I am only thinking of your guests."

"Do not concern yourself with them." James's voice was curt.

Both Garrett and the baron raised speculative eyebrows, but it was the latter who smiled. "You seem quite interested in my niece's welfare."

James shifted his attention back to the billiard table, his self-protective instincts surging to the fore. "She is a sweet woman. I would not see her hurt."

Handren stepped closer, under the guise of inspecting the table. "She has been here many weeks now. Unchaperoned."

James made his shot, the ball rolling far wide of his mark. But when he raised his eyes, he pinned the fat man with his stare. "Your insinuations do you no credit and her harm. I will not tolerate them."

"Insinuations!" The baron reared back, his laughter full and hearty. "My lord, I was merely concerned with sweet Caroline's reputation."

James stood, his hands tightening on the edge of the billiard table. "After putting her in Boorstin? It seems to me that you should be more concerned with Caro's welfare. When she arrived here, she had been beaten within an inch of her life."

Her uncle sighed, obviously disheartened, and began circling the table for his shot. "Ah, yes. I had a most lengthy discussion with the director regarding that very fact. It was a regrettable incident, he informed me. Two patients were fighting, and sweet Caroline, having more courage than sense, tried to intervene."

"She was incarcerated with male patients?"

"Sweet heavens, no!"

The baron came around to his side of the table, but James did not move. Instead, he folded his arms across his chest and watched the man fuss with his cue stick.

"A woman could not have inflicted those blows," he said softly.

The other man swung around, his fleshy face quivering with exaggerated horror. "My lord, you astound me."

"I merely state fact. How much do you know about Boorstin Asylum?"

The baron simply shrugged. "Only that it enjoys an excellent reputation, and Caroline was quite happy there."

"So happy, she was nearly beaten to death."

"I told you—"

"An unfortunate incident. Yes, I remember."

The two men regarded each other. Convivial the man might be, but he was clearly exaggerating his concern over his "sweet Caroline." Still, the man *was* her uncle. James knew he had no right to interfere, especially if an asylum was in fact the best place for her.

"Exactly what is your interest in Caroline, my lord?" asked the baron, his small eyes narrowing to tiny slits.

James paused, knowing his bluff had been called. Now was the time to either declare himself or back down. Glancing across the room, he saw Garrett straighten, his expression tight.

"My lord?" the baron prompted. "I am her guardian—"

"She is of the age of majority."

"She is insane. It is to me you must apply if you have interest regarding my niece."

James did not move, but his thoughts whirled. He did not know how to help Caroline, but he could not simply let her leave. And certainly could not let her go back to Boorstin. Not when he was still so unimpressed with the care she had received there.

His only choice was to stall for time.

"I do not wish her to leave before the festival." He smiled and turned to her uncle. "Surely it is not worth disappointing me over what is, after all, a trivial matter. My guests are my own, and I shall be responsible for Caroline's behavior. Do you not agree?"

The man nodded, his expression guarded. "If you insist."

"I do."

They stared at one another a moment longer, and though James had won this point, he knew his success had been costly. For all that Handren acted the clown, there was a core of shrewdness beneath the congenial exterior, and he didn't want Caroline to stay here. James had just made an enemy.

Yet Caro's happiness was worth any cost, so he simply nodded and watched as Handren quickly beat him at billiards.

"Another game, Traynern?" asked the Baron, his eyes twin points of challenge in his fat, grinning face.

James set aside his stick, his manner casual. "Not at this

time, thank you. But later." He turned back to the man, his look pointed. "Most assuredly, we will play again."

That night, James could not sleep. He was on edge as he had not been since leaving the army. This was how he felt before facing death, not a household full of guests.

Nevertheless, he was so on edge that not even the Greek poets could help.

Slamming his book shut, James tossed it aside and went to his bedroom window. It was a beautiful night and the shutters were thrown wide to the breeze. Leaning out onto the sill, he allowed his senses to roam freely, absorbing the smell of a rich summer and the gentle whisper of the night creatures. His eyes adjusted quickly to the dim light. The moon was nearly full, its delicate glow illuminating leaf and stone alike, but his gaze was caught by the sensuous curve of a woman.

Caro?

She was alone, her back against a tree, her eyes focused on the manor. Not his room, or even Garrett's, but her bedroom and the nursery.

He should leave her to her thoughts, he told himself. She was a woman tormented by confusion. Peaceful contemplation could only help ease the chaos in her mind. Clearly, if she had wanted to speak with someone, she would have sought him out.

She must want to be alone.

Yet he could not resist. It took less than five minutes for him to dress and join her by the tree.

"Good evening, Caro," he said, feeling awkward for intruding upon her solitude.

She did not move, but continued to gaze at the manor wall. "Good evening, my lord. You are out late."

He stepped closer, wanting to touch her but feeling her reserve push him away. "I came to speak with you."

She nodded, a near silent sigh escaping her lips. "Yes, my lord. How may I be of service?"

He hesitated. "You used to call me James."

Her gaze slid lower, dropping to his feet in a deferential gesture. "I know, and I must apologize for the impertinence."

It was too much. He needed to see her eyes. He touched her, lifting her chin with the slightest pressure of his forefinger. "Caro? What is the matter?"

"Nothing, my lord." She made to move away, but he would not release her, holding her face steady as he gently rubbed her cheek with his thumb.

"Is it the festival? Everything will be fine. You are a master organizer."

She shook her head, effectively pulling away from his touch. "Mrs. Potherby is the organizer. I merely gave her the room to run."

"Then, is it your uncle? He is . . ." He struggled with his words, wondering how best to describe the man who controlled her life.

"He is a boor, I know. But there are moments when he can be kind."

James stepped closer, joining her against the tree so their shoulders touched and he no longer need see the way her eyes slid from his. She had always been so direct, her boldness one of her most charming attributes. But now she seemed to skitter away from him, if not in body, then in conversation. Always before she had announced her thoughts with every power at her command. Now he felt as though he had to draw them out of her, practically forcing her to speak with him.

And conversation had never been one of his strong suits. He looked at the starry sky and searched for something to say.

"Your uncle wished to take you to Boorstin tomorrow." He felt her stiffen beside him and was quick to reassure her. "I convinced him to let you remain at least through the festival."

"Thank you."

He waited for her to relax, but she did not. Her stance beside him was as rigid as the tree they leaned against. He turned to face her, trying in vain to see her eyes.

"Tell me about Boorstin. How were you hurt?"

She began to move away from him, but he caught her hand, keeping her nearby, if not close to him. He thought at first she would fight, but instead she held on to him, her palm cold and slick with sweat despite her calm words.

"It is not so evil a place. The patients are a sad and frightened lot. I give what guidance I can."

"How were you hurt?"

Her hand clenched, and he returned the pressure, trying to tell her without words that he would do everything in his power to help. "There is a man there," she said, shuddering. "A doctor or so he claims. He delights in giving pain."

"He beat you?"

She nodded. "When I would not do other . . . things." Shyly, she turned to him, her eyes imploring him. "With your help, we could make him leave. What he does is unthinkable, and yet as patients, we are powerless to stop him. If you—"

"Done."

She stared at him. "My lord?"

"Give me his name, and he will be gone. Think no more of him."

He saw the relief wash through her and was startled to realize she had been concerned about asking for so small a favor. "Thank you, my lord," she breathed.

"James. My name is James."

She smiled tremulously, and he ached to see such uncertainty in her. But she gave him the so-called doctor's name, and he silently resolved to see the man out of England, his medical credentials stripped away.

With that done, he expected at least some of her reserve to melt. But she remained aloof and the silence stretched between them once again.

"Caro," he said softly.

She flinched slightly and he turned, wondering what made her so skittish.

She swallowed. "My lord?"

"You need not go back to Boorstin at all, if you choose not to. There are . . . other options. I have money. You could go to the colonies. . . ." His gut clenched at the thought of her moving so far away. "Perhaps you could find a cottage nearby. Not in the village, of course, but there is land available."

His mind was already mapping out the surrounding area, choosing a location near enough to him, but safe from the prejudice and hatred brewing in the village. But she was shaking her head, her voice firm.

"No. I will go to Boorstin."

"But—"

"At least there I can be of service to those in pain."

"Caro," he said gently, "that is for the doctors to do."

Her hand tightened against his. "You do not understand what it is like in there. I am important there. I am a minister's daughter, and I provide spiritual guidance in a way the doctors do not."

"Spiritual guidance? Caro, you are there to get well."

"No. Yes." She shook her head. "Perhaps. I only know I belong there. I am one of them, and I help them."

"You could visit them," he offered. "Daily, if necessary. You need not reside there."

"It is the only place I belong."

James fell silent, seeing the determination in her face. Still, he had to ask, he had to have her say the words. "You are decided?"

"Yes."

He sighed, feeling frustration drag at him. She had apparently found a purpose to her life, a meaning that still sometimes eluded him. He should be happy for her, and yet he could not feel anything but a great sense of loss. He reached out to touch her, to feel her skin against his palm, but she twitched away, her expression pained.

"Caro? What is it?"

"Nothing, my lord."

Suddenly, he was angry. He did not know where the emotion came from, he only knew it surged through him, filling him with a near violent energy he did not know how to disperse. It boiled within him, and he slammed his fist so hard against the trunk that the tree shuddered above them, spilling leaves and twigs.

"My lord?" Caro's voice was a mere whisper, but he could tell she was frightened, and that only infuriated him more. This was a woman who had faced down a mob, who had teased and tormented him in his own household, and yet she stood before him, "my lording" him to death, flinching at his merest touch.

"What has happened to you, Caro?" he cried, his voice fraught with emotion. "I have lost you, and I do not know how or why."

She touched him. Her fingers were shaky as they feathered across his cheek, but it was the first time she had reached out to him in days, and he felt it to his core. He stopped moving. He stopped breathing. He stopped doing anything for fear she would withdraw. But she did not, and he closed his eyes to better feel her trembling caress.

"Caro." The word was half groan, half entreaty.

"I have lost myself, James. The woman you knew, the woman who entered your house those weeks ago is gone. I think back on what she did, and it is like seeing another person." She twisted away and pointed at the wall. "Do you know I have come here every night for the last four days to stare at the side of your house? Do you know why?"

He shook his head, his throat too tight to allow words.

"Because I remember walking along the ledge there. I remember it, but I do not know why I did it. What purpose did it serve? I stare and I stare, and I cannot imagine myself doing such a thing."

"But surely you remember—"

"I cannot conceive it."

"But—"

"No!" She rounded on him, anger flashing through her eyes

as James had not seen in days. "Even you know I am different. You might as well call me Caroline, because I am that timid, frightened, beaten woman now. Carolly is lost to me. I cannot find her within me anywhere."

"But she is a part of you. You are the same person. You must remember her."

Her hands tightened into fists, and he watched in alarm as tears slipped down her cheeks. "I remember nothing of her. I have tried and tried, but she is gone. You know she is gone. Even Margaret knows it."

James stared at her, seeing not her tearstained cheeks or the trembling desperation of her lips, but the anger beating just below. Carolly was within her. She was simply submerged, lost beneath the return of Caroline. The return of the sane woman, Caroline. Or—had he been mistaken all along?

He gripped her arms. "Margaret is wrong. I was wrong. And yes, even you, Caroline, are wrong. Because Carolly is within you. She is part of you. And we will bring her back."

Caroline gazed at him, and he felt her trembling ease. Her mind latched onto his determination. "How? How will we find her again?"

He gentled his hold on her, releasing one of her arms to stroke back the hair that had fallen into her eyes. "Perhaps we should begin with the ledge."

She raised her gaze to his, her brow creasing as she tried to understand. "I told you, I have thought and thought on it and have found nothing."

"Then," he said, feeling a smile curve his lips, "it is time we did more than think."

Chapter Fourteen

"You cannot be serious." Caroline looked out her bedroom window at the seemingly mountainous drop to the ground. The very thought of stepping out on the ledge terrified her. But James was relentless as he pulled her out to join him on the ledge.

"Come on. I am right here. It is perfectly safe." He shrugged. "It is much wider than it seems."

She shook her head, clutching the sill. "But I shall fall."

"I will not let you go. Do not be afraid." She felt him gently detach her left hand from the sill, wrapping her fingers around his sturdy ones. "We must walk this ledge, experience everything. Then perhaps you will remember Carolly."

She nodded, understanding his logic. "I—I am not afraid," she stammered.

"Good."

"I am terrified."

He smiled encouragingly at her. "Not as good."

"But—"

"Come. Or I shall be forced to carry you, and you know my leg will not withstand your weight."

His meaning took a moment to penetrate her fears, but when it did, she frowned up at him. "Just what do you imply, my lord?"

He grinned at her. "Only that you are as solid as you are beautiful."

"Harrumph."

"Quit stalling. Climb."

She took a deep breath then blew it out, wishing she could as easily blow out her fears. She could not, of course, and so she intended to tell his imperious lordship. But when she looked into his eyes, she saw him preparing to lift her up into his arms. And while the thought of that made her knees go weak, she knew it would be disastrous for his leg. Without another word, she scrambled out onto the ledge.

She immediately flattened herself against the wall, feeling the rough-cut stone against her palms. But as she settled there, she felt James, warm and comforting beside her. The tension around her throat eased, and she began to breathe easier.

"Smell the air. Isn't it wonderful?" James's voice was soft against her ear, and she smiled at him as she closed her eyes.

She could taste the summer on the breeze up here. The steamy heat was gone, leaving a soft whisper of wind that brought the tangy mixture of grass and pollen to her lips. She wondered if there were an apple orchard nearby, and her thoughts spilled to that burst of delight she experienced whenever she bit into the first apple of summer.

Her thoughts did not seem odd to her. She knew these were Caroline's memories, and she cherished them. Simple joys were a special part of who she was now, and she would hate to lose them as much as she regretting losing Carolly.

It was all so confusing.

"Do you remember the last time you were up here?" She felt James's hand draw her closer to him. She felt his clothing, brushing lightly against her bare arm.

"I remember being here, of course. But—"

"But not why?"

She nodded. It was like looking through a window at another person. She could see what was happening, but she could not comprehend it.

"I believe," commented James, his eyes twinkling with boyish delight, "that it had something to do with a toad." Then he lifted a green, slimy creature out of his pocket.

"Oh, James, put that thing away!"

"I will not." Faster than she could react, he snared her wrist and gently placed the disgusting creature in her hand. "We must duplicate the circumstances exactly."

"Then you should go away, for you were not with me the first time."

"Ah, but if I did that, I think you would throw the hapless toad to his death and run inside. I cannot allow that."

She twisted on the ledge, trying to not to squeeze the unhappy creature too tightly. "You are enjoying this!" she accused hotly.

"Yes," he said, sounding somewhat surprised. "I believe I am."

"James—"

"Come along," he interrupted. "Start walking."

"But . . ." He crowded close to her, and she took a step out of necessity. "I am out on this ledge. Why must I walk?"

He leaned close to her, tickling her ribs as he urged her forward. "Because you are returning the toad to Margaret."

Carolly squirmed away, moving another couple steps as she evaded James's mischievous fingers. "Margaret's bedroom is on the other side of the wing," she said, her voice trembling with laughter.

He grinned. "Yes, but you did not know that."

"I do now."

"It does not matter."

"James—"

"Go!"

So she walked, and he followed. In truth, the ledge was quite wide. There was even room to lie down if need be, but all she could think about was the cobblestones of the walkway below. If they fell, they would both be quite hurt.

Yet somehow she felt safe. James was with her, still holding on to her left hand. In her right, she kept the toad quiet, if not exactly content.

Suddenly she stopped, realizing this trip was much too easy. "Where is the ivy?" She heard James's chuckle and turned to look at him. "You had it cleaned off!"

"Well, you never actually promised not to walk along here again. I could not have you breaking your neck simply because I neglected a simple gardening task. Now there is plenty of room."

She tried to frown at him, but her sense of humor was returning. "You said it would serve me right if I plummeted to my death."

"And so it would," he cheerfully agreed. "But that does not mean I shall allow anything of the kind."

Finally she smiled at him, her heart warming with his words. He would not let anything happen to her. He'd been looking out for her all along. "And the nursery window?" she asked.

"Unlatched."

She grinned. "You have thought of everything."

His smile faded, and his face fell into shadow. "What about you, Carolly? Have you thought of anything? Have you remembered?"

Caroline frowned, trying to assess herself in a vague, unfocused way. She felt the same as always, but was she Carolly or Caroline? "I don't know."

"Relax. Enjoy the beautiful night."

"But . . ."

"Hush."

She frowned. "James . . ."

He silenced her by placing his forefinger on her lips. "Do you remember that other night?" he asked, sending a shiver of delight down her spine at his husky whisper.

"I—"

"Shhhh."

She could not disobey him, not when his eyes were so commanding, so deeply mesmerizing that they seemed to hold her still even after he removed his finger from her lips.

"Close your eyes."

She did.

"What do you remember of that night?"

"I remember inching along the ledge, that poor toad wiggling in my pocket."

She felt his fingers, long and sensuous, slide around her hand and the hapless amphibian. She relaxed her hold, thinking he would take the toad, but he didn't. Instead, he guided her arm downward and together they placed the creature into her pocket.

It was a simple movement, but her eyes were closed, her senses inflamed. She felt the long stroke of his thumb along her wrist and the slight pressure of his knuckles against her thigh as they maneuvered the creature. She gasped in reaction, especially when he lingered there, one hand against hers, the other pressed intimately high on her leg.

She felt her nipples contract and a fire begin low in her belly, but she couldn't move, not even when he withdrew his touch with deliberate slowness, taking the time to stroke her body gently, erotically.

"James . . ." she whispered.

"What else do you remember?"

She opened her eyes. "I remember seeing you in the moonlight." She reached up and touched his hair, ruffling it so it fell over his forehead. "You looked so dashing that night with the silver moonlight in your hair. I imagined you my own personal pirate come to whisk me away."

He didn't move, and Caroline wasn't even sure he breathed, but she didn't stop. Suddenly, she seemed fascinated by the smallest details of his face. She traced the harsh angles of his cheeks, eased the worry lines creasing his forehead, and even trailed along to the tip of his aristocratic nose.

"I thought I had never seen anyone so handsome."

Her fingers found his lips, caressing the edges until he opened his mouth ever so slightly and she could feel his heated breath.

"I think I first fell in love with you then."

She felt his breath catch, and she knew she had surprised him.

"Do not be alarmed," she whispered, lifting her other hand to join the first. "I know you cannot marry me—a minister's mad daughter. But I wanted to say it. Just once."

He raised his fingers to hers, touching her hands with the same care she lavished on him. "That is not true . . ."

This time she stopped his words with her forefinger. "Shhh. Don't say what we both know will never be."

"Carolly—"

"You are an earl. You cannot stoop so low as—"

"I care nothing about biddies. Tongues will wag whatever I do." His tone was forceful, almost angry, but she did not draw away.

"Yes, I suppose they will. And you would never let that sway you. But what about our children?"

He frowned, but there was a dreamy look misting his eyes. "Our children," he echoed.

"How long before you would look for madness in them?"

He stilled, and she knew she was right. "You would be forever looking at your children, your sons especially, afraid that the slightest play, the most harmless prank, was a symptom of my madness. It would be horrible for the child, and it would rip you apart."

"No." His voice was thick with denial, but she saw the panic in his eyes.

"It would destroy us and our children."

"I would love them."

"Yes, but you would doubt them, too. What child can live with that?"

"I . . . I cannot lose you Carolly." His voice was a soft cry for help.

She lifted his face, kissing him tenderly. "You can't lose what you never had. I am to be an angel, James. I am not meant to live here on Earth."

He searched her eyes, his expression dazed. "What?"

Suddenly it all came flooding back, rushing into her mind with the force of a whirlwind. Carolly had returned. Carolly the wild, impetuous, vibrantly wonderful pre-angel soul became part of her again. And she laughed out loud with the sheer joy of it. "I remember!" she cried. "I remember all of it!" She spread her arms wide, lifting her face to the shimmering glory of the full moon on a clear summer night.

"Carolly!" He grabbed her, pulling her back against the wall. "You will fall."

She turned in his arms, feeling happiness fill her soul. "I am whole again, James." She grinned at him, leaning close to his face. "Thank you," she whispered.

Then she kissed him.

It was meant to be a chaste kiss. A touching of lips to share joy and to show appreciation. But as she lifted her mouth to his, as she inhaled the rich masculine scent of him and felt the hard muscles of his arms tighten around her, her body began to respond in ways that had nothing to do with angels or God. Her body reacted as a woman desperately in love.

She initiated the kiss, and as their mouths touched she surrendered. His mouth slanted over hers in bold demand, and she released a small sound of surprise. It was as though he captured that sound, taking it and her within him as he pulled her deep into his embrace.

Her head fell back as he kissed her. He pushed her against the wall, flattening her between stone and his lean form, and she reveled in the hard press of his body. Her hands traveled up his chest, feeling the ripple of muscle beneath her fingertips as he abruptly pulled off his coat and tossed it aside.

"James—"

But even that soft word was not allowed to escape. He would not release her mouth, would not withdraw his kiss, and all too soon she found her own hunger matching his. She stretched upward, letting her hands roam through his hair, drawing him to her. She arched into him as he ground his pelvis against her.

His hands left her face to stroke her neck, slipping apart the buttons on the front of her gown until he could plunge a hand into the vee he created. Her shift stretched taut, and she was grateful when it finally ripped open.

She was exposed then from the waist up, and James was free to let his fingers roam over her breasts. His hands were large and strong, their caress rough as they chafed her delicate skin, but the sensation was beyond erotic, sending bursts of fire coursing through her blood.

He pinched her nipples, rolling them with his thumbs, and she cried out in ecstasy. She felt more of her buttons slip free as her gown slipped past her shoulders, pinning her arms down by her sides. She couldn't move. She could only drop her head backward, silently begging him for more.

His mouth left hers, trailing down her neck to kiss the fluttering pulse at the base of her throat. His hands cupped her breasts, lifting them higher as his mouth found one pebbled tip. He drew it into his mouth, teasing it with his tongue before abruptly shifting to the other. The sensation of his kiss on one side while cool air brushed across the other left her moaning with hunger.

Her knees weakened, and he thrust his thigh between her legs, crushing her in a way that forced all reason from her mind. She spun in a maelstrom of sensation, her only thought to continue.

She began kissing him as she could, whatever she could touch. She shrugged off the restraining sleeves of her gown to finally touch him. She pulled at his shirt, slipping her hands inside to run through the dusting of curls across his chest. Her nails found the flat disks of his nipples, scratching lightly as he gasped her name.

His touch slipped to her waist, tugging at the gown, inching his fingers lower, toward her womanly core. She moaned in response, already opening for him.

Then he stopped, his muscles tightening beneath her fingertips as he took a small step back.

"James?" Her voice was a whispered plea, but he shook his head.

"We cannot do this here." He glanced behind him, and she slowly recalled their location on the ledge. Below them, the garden remained bathed in moonlight, above them tiny wisps of clouds played hide-and-seek through the stars.

It was a beautiful sight. A night made for lovers. But they were on a ledge, and she was naked to the waist in full view of God and man.

"I . . ." She took a deep breath, the air suddenly too cold on her skin. "I . . ."

"*Croak!*" From somewhere deep in her pocket, the toad chose to raise its own objections.

Both Carolly and James jumped, startled by the sound.

The noise had been God-sent. Carolly was sure of it. She was supposed to become an angel. She could not afford to be swept away by the tides of passion. It simply wasn't what angels did.

Yet when she looked at the dazed hunger in James's eyes, her breath echoed the ragged edge she heard in his groan. "Inside," he urged.

She wanted to make love to him. Lord, she wanted nothing more than to do as he bade her, to open herself to him in every way a woman could. But then they might have children. Even if she did not leave as she always did, their union would only cause them both pain. He would not marry her, and she could not be happy as his mistress. And if their passion produced children . . .

"Think of the children," she whispered. "We can't. Oh God, James, I want to, but . . ." She tugged at her gown, trying to cover herself, and he looked down in surprise.

"Oh." He pulled back, and she gasped. He meant to catch her up again, but she stopped him, drawing quickly away before he could touch her.

"Carolly . . ." His word was strangled, and she made the mistake of looking into his eyes. They were like dark windows to a tormented soul.

Yet there was nothing she could do. There was no way to ease either of their pain. So she turned away, pulling on her gown as well as she could, fumbling with the buttons, her fingers shaking. He reached out to help her, but she stepped away, stopping him without touching him.

"I . . . I think you ought to return this poor creature to his pond." Before he could object, she lifted the toad from her pocket and placed it in his hand.

"Carolly." It seemed to be the only word he could say, and it pulled at her, tempting her to return to the madness of only a few moments ago.

"Please, James. This cannot help either of us." She didn't stay to speak with him. Her senses were still too inflamed, her will too fragile to withstand more. She slipped away, moving quickly along the ledge until she ducked into her bedroom window, closing it firmly behind her.

James watched Carolly leave and felt a sense of loss greater than anything he had ever before experienced. She'd left him. And worse, he'd let her go.

She had been warm and giving in his arms. Making love to her was as perfect a feeling as he had ever known. And yet, he had stopped. Yes, the location was indecent. But it would have been the work of a moment to carry her into the empty bedchamber where they had first kissed so many nights ago. He could have done it. Even with his injured leg, he could have brought her to the bed and shared ecstasy with her.

But he'd stopped. He'd withdrawn his hands and let her compose herself. Then she'd dashed away as if Satan himself pursued her.

And perhaps that was true. He was supposed to be her friend, yet he encouraged her madness. He didn't know whether he wanted the sane, sedate Caroline or the mad, vibrantly alive Carolly. He'd brought her to the ledge, forcing her to grab hold of her fantasies just after she'd recovered some sense of reality.

That was not the work of God, but of the Devil.

And when she'd meant to thank him, he'd taken advantage of her, using her body against her, reminding her of the pleasure that flesh alone could give. Her mind was aimed toward Heaven, and he'd forcibly brought her back to the flesh.

He looked over to her window, shut fast against him. His body still ached for her, eagerly urging him to go to her, to find some way into her bedroom. But he would not.

He was not her friend. The sooner she left his home, the better for her.

Yet the thought of spending the rest of his life without her was too painful to contemplate. He tightened his fists, hating himself for his sins, for his hunger for a madwoman.

"Croak!"

Startled, he looked down at the hapless toad struggling in his hand, and he abruptly eased his grip. What in Heaven's name induced him to bring this poor thing along?

God, he decided. God had planted the idea. Because without its hapless interruption, he and Carolly would now be wrapped in each other's arms. The thought was so believable, he nearly tossed the toad away and let it plummet to its death, but something stayed his hand.

After their lovemaking, there surely would have come a morning of recriminations, confusion, and heartbreak. He would feel obliged to marry her, and he would spend the rest of his life doubting her, questioning her, wondering about her sanity. She would be a countess with responsibilities and a place in society. What would he do if she spoke publicly about being a "pre-angel?" The local families would never accept her, the members of the *ton* would ostracize her, and her husband would be ashamed of her.

No, she deserved someone who could accept her—madness and all. Who loved her without reservation, and who would adore their children without fear of some taint.

Carolly was right. He could not marry her. Not because she was socially beneath him, but because she deserved a man, not a coward.

With a heavy heart, James crossed the last bit of ledge to the empty bedroom next to the nursery, maneuvering himself inside. Minutes later he was down beside the pond, releasing the toad back to its lily pad.

He stood by the water a long time, his thoughts a whirling sea of self-recrimination. Then, finally, he lifted his eyes to Heaven, praying for the first time in many long years of lonely isolation.

"Please God," he whispered, "make me worthy of her."

Chapter Fifteen

"Are you sure you want to go? And with Miss Margaret? I'd be happy to go for you."

Carolly smiled at Mrs. Potherby and tried to find the words to reassure the woman. Especially since she wasn't feeling all that confident herself.

But it had to be done. There were a thousand things yet to be purchased for tomorrow's festival, and now was the time to do it. Hopefully, spending all that money in the village would diffuse some of the anger still simmering there.

Thank God James had given her free rein when it came to expenses. She carried a purse loaded with coins and bills. If she couldn't spend all of it by this evening, then she wasn't worthy of her gender.

Carolly patted the housekeeper's arm. "At least I've learned how to drive a gig. We won't get ditched this time."

"Let me have Bob drive you—"

"No, truly, Mrs. Potherby. We will be fine." Then she leaned forward, whispering into the good woman's ear: "I shall be a model of propriety, no matter what happens. I'm even wearing a corset."

The older woman frowned. "It is not *your* manners I worry about."

Carolly smiled and turned away, refusing to be cowed. She would meet the villagers on their own ground. And then she'd spend her last crown trying to bribe them into better humor. Or rather, Margaret would. All Carolly would do was smile and look motherly.

Mags met Carolly at the front door. She wore a pretty frock of bright yellow, and matching ribbons peeked through her dark curls. But even that gay ensemble could not disguise the nervous way she pleated and repleated her skirt.

"Carolly, you cannot truly wish to go back there."

"Hush. Do you want to be a prisoner all your life? We must face them."

"But must it be today? And alone? I am sure Uncle would not like it."

Carolly felt her misgivings sour her stomach. "He would only want to come along, Margaret, but this is something we must do without him. Do you understand that?"

The girl pushed out her lower lip. "But you promised him you would not go without speaking to him."

"And I have." Just not explicitly. She'd told him that provisions still needed to be brought up from the village today. She hadn't mentioned a thing about who would get them. "Besides, Mrs. Potherby knows where we are headed. If you don't want to come along, so be it. But I am going." So saying, she stepped firmly out the door, her face lifted toward the sun, her heart in her throat for fear the girl would call her bluff.

Fortunately, Margaret wasn't one to refuse a challenge. Not anymore. Very soon, Carolly heard the girl's angry stomp behind her. Ten minutes later, they were in the gig and tooling down the lane at a slow, steady pace.

"Could we please go faster?" the girl complained.

Carolly twisted slightly, unable to resist teasing her. "A few moments ago you acted like you'd rather die than go. Now you complain I'm driving too slow."

"Since I am to die, I want to do it quickly and get it over with." The girl sounded truly nervous.

Carolly reined in the horses, stopping them cold in the middle of the road. "Do you really think they will kill us?"

Mags folded her arms and pouted. "They tried to last time, didn't they?" she said.

"Well, sort of." Carolly tried a different tack. "Do you understand why the villagers are so angry?"

"Because Uncle James will not hire them in the mines."

"Yes. Sort of. It is because they are starving. Do you think they would be so upset about losing their jobs if they had other ones to go to? Other ways to make money?"

Margaret chewed on her bottom lip. "I guess not." Then she looked up, her eyes wide and vulnerable. "But why do they hate *me*? None of this is my fault."

Carolly sighed. "I know. That's why I wanted you to come along."

"But—"

"Just listen to me. They hate you because you're a lot easier to hate than James. After all, he still supports most of their jobs. They also don't know anything about you. So we're going to let them get to know how generous and sweet and totally innocent you are."

Margaret tugged at her hair, her face puckered in a worried frown. "But how will we do that?"

Carolly pulled her large purse out of her pocket and dropped it in the girl's lap. "You're going to spend that."

"All of it?" Margaret asked, her eyes wide as she hefted the heavy bag.

"All of it. You're not going to give it away, mind you. You will buy things. Lots of things. We will get presents for all the staff, and we're going to tip little boys and girls to carry out packages to the gig. We're going to admire the craftsmanship of everything and everyone, and we're going to be cheerful and happy and gay."

Margaret appeared to mull that over. "But what if they start saying awful things?"

"Then you will smile like you haven't a brain in your head and stare at them vacantly."

"But—"

"You're a little kid, remember? Young. Innocent. You don't understand how nasty they're being."

Margaret puckered her face, clearly uncomfortable with the characterization. "But I do understand."

Carolly sighed. Truly, the girl had lived with James too long. She was simply too honest. "They don't have to know that, do they?"

"You want me to pretend I'm stupid?" Margaret's frown turned into clear outrage.

"I want you to show them how wonderful you can be."

Margaret shook her head, still not willing to act stupid, even for safety's sake.

Carolly bit her lip, trying to come up with other options. "All right. How about when they say something mean, you smile indulgently at them? As if you had a great secret no one else understands."

"But—"

"Mags, the trick is to meet their hostility with mystery or innocence. Or compliments—those are always good. Just so long as it isn't anger or the sulks." She leaned forward, trying to get Margaret to see. "Pick an attitude. Make it part of you and use it whenever someone tries to hurt you. If you can react differently than they expect, you've won half the battle because you've kept control." She reached for the girl's hand and squeezed it tight. "Do you understand any of this?"

Margaret nodded, but the movement was slow and slightly forced. "So, what should I do?"

"What do you want to do?"

She was quiet a long time, but when she spoke it was with

conviction. "I think I'll tell them about my mother. Show them how happy I am to be the daughter of a commoner. That's what Uncle James said to do, and it will be easy for me because I really am glad she was my mother."

"Well," said Carolly, her insides melting with love, "I think your Uncle James is a very smart man. And I think if your mother were here, she'd be very proud of you. I know I am."

Margaret looked up, her eyes filled with a cautious uncertainty. "Do you really think so? That she would be proud of me?"

"Most definitely."

Then the two grinned at each other, suddenly very much in accord.

"Okay, Mags," Carolly teased, "are you ready to spend an unseemly amount of money?"

Margaret nodded, her eyes shining bright in the morning sunlight.

"Then let's get to it!" Carolly flicked the reins, and they were off again, tooling down the lane in high spirits.

Twenty minutes later they strolled into the general store. It wasn't easy. There were some gasps and stares and a lot of grumbling. But all that negativity quickly ended with the flash of gold.

Carolly started out simply, paying for the things they ordered while Margaret tipped generously wherever they went. It didn't take long for Carolly to realize that power shopping was the same whatever the century, and soon she and Mags were having a marvelous time.

It wasn't until the fat woman from the inn came into the bookstore that their first truly awkward moment occurred. The two of them had been giggling over some scandalous political cartoons when the woman entered and gasped in horror.

"Whatever were you thinking, Silvia?" the woman exclaimed to the shopkeeper's wife, "to allow *her* within your doors?" She looked down her nose at Margaret as if the girl were some sort of disgusting bug.

It was on the tip of Carolly's tongue to tell the woman exactly what she could do with her high, pointy nose, but this wasn't her battle. All she could do was nod encouragingly at Mags and keep her mouth shut.

The girl stepped forward, her face open and sweet. "My mother had hair like yours," she said, her tone openly admiring. "I used to watch her dye it. It would make her arms all brown, but you must come by yours naturally."

The woman gasped. "What contemptible taradiddle! Comparing me to that strumpet."

Margaret only smiled. "But my mother was the most beautiful woman alive. Except she didn't have your hair, so she had to dye it. And that made her arms dark. That's why she wore gloves all the time."

The woman stood there gaping while Margaret sailed sweetly past. Carolly followed quietly behind, trying desperately not to laugh. She settled for a fond grin, knowing that Mags would be fine. Even if Carolly left tomorrow, the girl had discovered a confidence that would carry her through life beautifully.

They moved on to other stores.

Everything went splendidly until the moment they saw Garrett on the road. He was surrounded by a circle of women and a few older men. Carolly wasn't sure why the sight bothered her, she only knew that it did. She paused, narrowing her eyes to pick out more detail.

As usual, Garrett cut a figure of distinction. His clothing was elegant, though understated; the cut fine, but dark. In fact, his short nose and freckles were the perfect touch, making him seem more approachable and honest than James with his austere features. And, as usual, Garrett was oozing charm.

"Stay here a minute, Mags," Carolly said softly. "I want to hear what he's saying."

Carolly walked slowly toward him. Garrett was speaking passionately to a couple of young women, and the others had simply stopped to overhear. In fact, Garrett seemed almost uncomfortable with all the attention—not that that stopped him.

From the distance, Carolly couldn't hear what he said, could only pick out his mannerisms. He seemed compassionate and sincere, as a minister or politician might be. And whatever he was saying, he certainly had popular opinion on his side. Carolly heard more than a few mutters of " 'E's right" and "Wish 'e weren't the nestle-bird," whatever that meant.

One old geezer shook his head at her and wandered off muttering something about "stubbing the nest." It made no sense to her, but Carolly didn't have time to learn more. She heard the pounding of a horse at full gallop coming fast up behind her.

She spun around, nearly tripping over Margaret who had followed despite Carolly's warning, only to have James and Shadow nearly run them both down.

"James!" she exclaimed, as he reined in his stallion. "What are you doing?"

"Are you all right?" She watched him scan the scene, his gaze taking in everything from her muddied hem to the shocked and disgruntled expressions of the people around them.

"We're fine," she said smoothly. "We were just picking up provisions for the festival." Carolly stepped forward, pressing her hand against Shadow's sweat-streaked neck as she looked up into James's worried face. "Aren't you supposed to be at home greeting your guests?"

He frowned down at her, and when he spoke, the words were forced through his clenched teeth. "You promised you would not leave without speaking to me first."

"James," she began, but Garrett interrupted her.

"Come now, dear cousin. Caroline is not your prisoner," he said.

Carolly frowned at Garrett as he took her hand and began escorting her and Margaret back toward the gig. She would have thought him concerned only for her welfare, except that he kept his voice loud. It carried easily to the people still milling about the street.

"Try not to be so cruel, James," Garrett continued. "She was only trying to spread a little good cheer."

The villagers nodded and muttered while Carolly beat her brain for some way to redeem the situation. All around them people sent her and Margaret looks filled with sympathy, saving their acid gazes for James. Somehow, in the space of a few moments, Garrett had managed to turn public hatred toward James while reserving the roles of helpless victim for herself and Mags. And by glaring right back at them, his posture defensive, James was playing right into Garrett's scenario.

"James," she began.

"Hush, Caroline," interrupted Garrett. "I know you have had a difficult day. Let us get home immediately so that you may rest."

"But—"

"Come along, Caroline. Margaret." That came from James, ordering them to fall in line in his most imperious manner.

Carolly sighed, knowing she wouldn't be able to fix things right now. James was too angry with her for disregarding her promise to him. He was staring daggers at everyone, herself included, which only reinforced his evil image. She'd have to try another day.

Giving in to the inevitable, Carolly allowed herself to be escorted back to the gig, now buried beneath their morning purchases. She had no choice but to sit demurely while Garrett drove them back to the manor, James and Shadow walking steadily beside them.

She might have sunk completely into the dismals if it hadn't been for Mags. Just before they started off toward the manor, the child sent her a look filled with commiseration. *Next time,* her expression seemed to say. *Between you and me, we'll set things right.*

*   *   *

"You deliberately went back on your word!"

Carolly sighed and plopped down in the chair across from James in the library. "This is old territory, James. Read me the riot act and let's be done with it."

He frowned at her. "What has the Riot Act have to do with this?"

She shook her head. "Nothing. Listen, James—"

"No, Carolly. It is time you listened. You gave me your solemn oath you would not leave the grounds without consulting me first."

"And I haven't!"

"You did today."

"I haven't until today."

"Is that supposed to make a difference?"

"Yes!" She leaned forward, setting her forearms on his desk as she tried to make him understand. "It was important that Mags and I go alone. If I had told you, you would have insisted on coming along."

"I certainly would have. Imagine my shock and fear when I learned that the two of you had gone out alone. Again!"

"But nothing happened!"

"That is entirely beside the point."

"No, James, that *is* the point." She pushed away from the desk, standing up to pace between two dark mahogany bookcases. "If I were you, I'd be more worried about what they'll do to *you* next time *you* show your face down there."

"I am the earl. They will do nothing to me."

Carolly swung back around to face him. "Don't count on it. Garrett was—"

"Garrett was simply trying to protect you. He was helping them see you in a different light."

Carolly threw up her hands in disgust. "Don't be so naive, James! He was turning them against you."

She hadn't realized the truth of her words until she spoke them aloud. Even though she hadn't heard Garrett's words, she now realized he had been skillfully manipulative, inciting the village against his cousin. How could he do that? And why?

She turned toward James, needing to see if he understood the horrible things his own heir was doing to him. But when she looked, she didn't see dawning comprehension, only a grim certainty.

"James?"

"I am not naive, Carolly."

She paused, licking her suddenly dry lips as she stepped toward James. "You mean you know what Garrett has been doing?"

James shrugged. To her surprise, she realized his anger had dissipated, replaced by a sad acceptance as he folded his hands precisely in front of him on the desk.

"But why?" Carolly asked, starting to pace again. "Why would Garrett do this to you?"

James did not answer until Carolly collapsed back into her chair, and then only because she glared at him until he spoke.

"Besides the inheritance, Garrett owns a sizable share in the mines and deeply misses his lost income. I believe he thinks if he can incite the villagers, I will be forced to rehire the women and children."

"Thereby returning the mine to its former production level and his previous level of income."

"Yes."

Carolly shook her head, unable to fathom that anyone could be so greedy. "How badly does he need the money?"

"Bad enough."

Carolly tilted her head, wondering what alternative to suggest. She decided to try being blunt. "Cannot you simply forward him the income?"

"Were he to ask for my assistance, I would gladly forward him the required amount. But he resents taking funds from me almost as much as I dislke his wastrel lifestyle."

Carolly frowned, disliking the note of censure in James's

voice. "You would punish him for his problems? I thought you were friends."

"We have our moments. But I would definitely take steps to prevent him from falling into such difficulties again, were I given the opportunity."

Carolly squirmed in her chair, disliking James's firm stance, but recognizing the sound of an entrenched position. James clearly did not like the life Garrett led, but he refused to help unless asked. And Garrett was clearly too proud to ask, but was becoming more desperate by the second. Whose pride would break first? And what damage would occur in the meantime?

"Have you tried speaking to him? Perhaps if you phrased it just the right way, he would feel more able to talk with you."

Carolly hadn't thought it possible, but James's expression became even more grim. "I am afraid not. None of my talks and lectures, or even my more subtle interventions, have sufficed."

Carolly bit her lip. "This has happened before?"

He nodded once, a quick slash of frustration.

She looked down, toying with the folds of her skirt. "Just how long have you been paying off his debts?"

"Since he was in leading strings."

Carolly sighed. "Perhaps if you helped him this last time and told him it was his very last chance. That you would not—"

"I did. *Last* time."

"Oh." Carolly bit her lip, racking her brain for a solution.

James looked at her, his eyes bleak. "I told him that the next time he approached me, I would put severe restrictions on his income, and I would also let it be known that I had disinherited him."

Carolly sat bolt upright in her chair. "Can you do that?"

He shrugged. "He'll receive the title and a modest income from the near lands no matter what, as long as I don't have a son." His gesture was expansive as he indicated the house and grounds. "The rest is mine to dispense as I wish."

She began to understand the depth of the problem. "Then, if Garrett is in debt again, he must be very worried."

James nodded. "Yes."

"But . . . why do you let him incite the villagers to riot?" She tried to read an answer in his expression, but his gaze was abstract, his manner resigned.

"I cannot stop him. Short of locking him up, he will find some way to speak with them."

Carolly frowned, trying to follow James's plan. "So you eventually intend to rehire the women and children?"

"No."

"But—"

James pushed to his feet, coming forward to gaze earnestly down at her. "You must trust what I say, Carolly. The villagers will not riot. I am very nearly the sole employer here. They will not move against me. Plus, this summer's crop looks good. Things will turn around soon."

She sighed, imagining he was right but unable to accept it. She had thought Garrett a feckless charmer. Now she saw him as a monster. One who actually plotted against James for money—and one whom James didn't seem to fear.

"What will you do?" she asked, her voice hushed.

"Pray for a good crop. Meanwhile, you will promise me again that you will not go into the village without speaking with me first." He leaned forward. "And do not think I shall be as forgiving next time. If there is a next time."

Carolly clenched her hands together, hating to again be on the receiving end of James's disapproval. She had a fleeting moment of sympathy for Garrett. But then she remembered what James's heir had done—was doing—and her charitable feelings fled.

"James . . ."

"You will obey me in this!"

Carolly closed her mouth, knowing that further discussion would be futile. The situation with Garrett was clearly far more complicated than she first thought. As for her broken promise, she was beginning to feel quite guilty about it. Although he hadn't said as much, James had been desperately worried about her. She could tell. She would no doubt go to her grave remembering the fear in his angular features as he came tearing into town—probably expecting her to be the object of another stoning.

"I'm sorry, James. I should have spoken with you first."

"Yes, you should have."

She looked up at him one last time, defiance surging through her. "I should have spoken with you, but I still would have gone."

He frowned at her. She remained composed, refusing to be cowed. He glared, and she raised an eyebrow. Then he cursed in an explosion of breath.

"I . . . worry about you all the time," he admitted, his words halting and stiff. He abruptly gripped the edge of his desk, his fingertips white with the strain. "You must be more careful."

Never before had she seen such torment in his eyes. Not even that first time when he'd rescued her from the mob. It was shocking, and she was beside him in a moment. "James, what is it?"

He took her face in his hands, searching her features as though memorizing every detail. "You need not go to Boorstin—"

She cut off his words quickly, hoping she could forestall the coming painful exchange. "James, we have discussed this."

"But you were beaten—"

"*James.*" She fell silent, feeling the heartache build again. She had almost convinced herself that she would go happily to Boorstin. Soon, after the festival. When her uncle forced her to. And she'd convinced herself she would not miss James or crave his touch. But now his words exposed her wound again, and she looked away, fighting the tears in her eyes. "Please don't—"

This time he stopped her words with a kiss so swift it startled her. His lips were bruising, hungry, demanding, and somehow frightened. She did not need to think about her response. His touch had always inflamed her senses, but even as her body matched his passion, she tried to soothe his fears. She stroked his arms and back, let her fingers find the tense muscles of his shoulders. Then he raised his head, gasping for breath even as he pulled her tightly against him. She rested her head against the hard wall of his chest, listened to his heart beat triple time. It took a long while, but eventually the beat steadied and she felt him calm.

"Carolly . . ."

His strangled word was interrupted by the rattle of a carriage outside. Another guest. Someone who needed to be greeted and escorted and settled into a room. Both Carolly and James groaned as one, knowing they would not have time to talk about this anguish they both felt.

But then, maybe it was for the best, Carolly thought sadly. "You should see to your guests," she said.

"I don't give a damn about my guests," he snapped.

"James!" she exclaimed, a part of her annoyed, wanting to push him away. "One of them may be your future wife! *Should* be your—"

Suddenly he caught her by the upper arms, his hands clenching as he drew her to him. "I do not want *them*. I do not want them in my house, or in my bed, or as my wife! Damn it, Carolly, can you not see what this does to me?"

She shook him off, forcefully shoving him away. "Just what is it doing to you?" She waited, staring into the swirling gray torment of his eyes, praying he would say something, anything, about *loving* her. If only he would say the words, ask her to come to him, maybe she would throw everything away just to be with him.

But he remained stubbornly silent.

Her anger built to flashpoint. "Quite a problem, isn't it, James?" she said, sarcasm lacing her voice. "You're too honorable to take me as a mistress and too proud to have me as a wife. But it's killing you to just let me leave." Tears blurred her vision, but she refused to cry. Not now and certainly not in front of him. "Good thing I'm not meant for this world," she reminded herself, "or this could really hurt."

She started to turn away, but he grabbed her, spinning her back to face him. "Leave this world? Carolly, you never arrived! You appeared at my door and told me you were here to help me. Help me? The truth is, all you wished was to play around in my life and then abandon me!"

"I'm going to be an angel!"

"You are going to be alone!" His hands felt like fiery manacles around her arms, and she saw the steady throb of anger in his temple as he continued. "I thought you were the boldest woman alive, but now I see you are truly a coward. You refuse to live your life, to take what is offered with both hands."

She pushed him away, stung by the echo of truth in his words. Could she truly be using her hope of becoming an angel as an excuse not to live the life she should? Carolly shook her head, denying it even as a part of her agreed. "I am not running away," she said as she glared at him. "I am running toward something. You just can't accept it."

"That you will be an angel?" He swung away from her, stomping toward the cold fire grate. "Is that your big dream?" He twisted around to confront her. His eyes pleaded with her to think. "Look at yourself, Carolly. Anyone can be good and holy and chaste. All you need do is spend your life saying no. The challenge is to say yes. To take the risk of living."

His words intensified the ache she'd fought all this time, but she stubbornly continued to refuse to acknowledge it. "I have taken that risk. I have fallen in love. *I-love-you.*" She punctuated her words with her fist, beating the air in front of her. "But apparently, James, you haven't. So I intend to bring you other women to love. I have reconciled you with a niece you barely even knew, and now I'm working on the villagers. I have taken risks, James. How about you?"

"Me?" He stepped forward. "Would you give up saying

you're going to be an angel for me? I thought I'd wanted this fanciful nature back; but not if it keeps us apart. Will you toss aside your madness, your fantasies, and your pretend games to be my wife?"

"They are not pretend!" she screamed.

"Then you do not love me as much as you say!"

They stared at each other. Barely a hand's breadth separated their bodies, but their souls seemed to glare at each other from across a huge expanse. James refused to believe in her rationality, and she couldn't cross over to his. She wouldn't give up everything she knew to be true just to make him comfortable. Heck, he'd even helped her regain it again—her past, her identity. . . .

Into the silence came a discreet knock.

And another.

And another.

"Yes?" James's word split the air like a knife.

The door opened, and James's rigidly formal butler entered, his face impassive even as his gaze hopped from Carolly to James. "Excuse the interruption, my lord, but the Viscount and Viscountess of Drebes have arrived with their two daughters. As have Lord and Lady Phillips. Three daughters, one son."

"Thank you, Wentworth," James ground out. "Please show them to their rooms. I shall be there directly."

The butler nodded and withdrew, his movements slow as he quietly closed the door behind him.

Carolly waited to speak until she heard Wentworth's measured footsteps fade away. "You should greet your guests," she commented softly.

James nodded, but the movement was forced. "Come along, then."

Carolly took a step backward and drew her arms around herself, shaking her head. "No, I don't think so."

"I beg your pardon." His tone was stiff.

"This is your party, James. I've taken on the role of Girl

Friday for you, but I cannot sit around to watch you marry someone else."

He stepped toward her. "But—"

She skittered backward. "I will be with Mrs. Potherby, James. Good day." And with that, Carolly spun around and fled.

James watched her leave, feeling as if his body had been battered from all sides. He could stop her, but he checked the impulse. Too many thoughts collided in his mind, too many feelings ripped at him. He had once prided himself on his strength, on his solidity even in the midst of turmoil.

Now he realized what he had called strength was merely isolation and stubbornness. Since Bradley's death, and maybe long before that, he had remained aloof, watching the world as he filled his hours with silence.

Then Carolly had appeared in his life with the force of a tornado. She'd ripped open his world, making him feel and experience and see for the first time. He'd never before experienced panic as he had today—a physical torment that racked him as he raced to the village, fearing that she or Margaret was hurt.

It was frightening. And yet, he had never felt so alive.

James shook his head. He needed time to reflect on these emotions. And more than that, he needed to think about her words. Was he truly too proud to marry her? He'd just offered, hadn't he? Was she truly running away as he claimed? Or was she rushing toward something so divine he could not comprehend it?

Most importantly, whichever the case, would he be able to let her go?

Chapter Sixteen

Carolly remained out of sight the rest of that day and most of the next. She refused to come to meals, choosing instead to spend her time with Mags. Both she and the child knew she would be leaving soon, and so each made a special effort to make the days memorable.

Unfortunately, a house full of titled guests was the most exciting thing ever to happen for Mags, so she and Carolly spent hours spying on the intruders, and even more time ruminating on James's potential wives. Fortunately for Carolly's battered ego, Margaret was able to find some fault with each of the beautiful women trying to catch themselves an earl.

But even with the constant distractions of last-minute details, menu plans, and Mags's excited chatter, Carolly found more than enough time to think. In fact, it seemed to her that all she could do was think, ponder, and wonder.

Did she focus too much on the future? On becoming an angel? Perhaps there was more for her to learn in this life. Was it possible the reason she'd failed in her previous lives was exactly what James said—she refused to live in the present and so, ultimately, was doomed to be ineffective? Was she so afraid of being hurt that she ran to the hereafter rather than face the present?

An uncomfortable thought. Unfortunately, it was true. She did run toward divinity rather than live in the present. She did hide herself from those she most wanted to help. James was right.

But what could she do about it? Even if she set aside her goal of becoming an angel, what would she do? James would not accept the "madness" of her past lives, and she would not pretend it an elaborate fantasy. That left them right back where they started: Apart.

Yet in love.

Yes, she finally realized, he loved her. There was too much pain in his eyes when he looked at her. He had to be feeling the same torment she did every night, every day, being so close together but not able to touch, to share, or even to say the words: *I love you.*

He would not allow himself to do more than long for her from a distance. He loved her, and yet he would not admit it, would not accept her as she was. And she would not give up everything she knew for anything less.

It was an impasse. Until she saw her ballgown.

The dress arrived the day of the actual ball. Carolly spent the morning supervising the preparations, the afternoon circulating at the festival, buying dinner there, and had only just returned to the house an hour before the music began. She felt hot, dirty, and exhausted.

Then she saw the gown, neatly draped over her bed.

Margaret's eyes shone as she smoothed out non-existent creases. "Have you ever seen anything so beautiful," the child breathed.

Carolly shook her head, her throat too tight to allow words.

The dress was stunning. Carolly stepped closer to the bed, unwilling to touch it for fear she would mar its beauty. Made of satin gauze, the gown had elegant puffed sleeves and a skirt trimmed with a deep flounce of lace. Tiny flowers mixed with seed pearls were sprinkled throughout the design.

Yes, it was lovely. But most of all, it was white—the color of purity and innocence. And of angels.

"Tut, tut," said Mrs. Potherby as she bustled into the room. "No need to dilly-dally about, staring. Into your bath. Quick now!"

Carolly barely had time to blink before she was stripped, bathed, and dried. Next came corset, underclothes, stockings, and slippers. Then she was shoved into a chair, her hair ruthlessly tugged and twisted by Commandant Potherby. It had grown out, and the woman ruthlessly styled it. And through the whole process, Carolly's mind was filled with the sight of her gown.

It was white—as were the gloves, the fan, and the flowers that Mrs. Potherby shoved in place in Carolly's locks.

Then came the time to put on the gown. But she could only stare at it, feeling somehow that it wasn't hers to wear. She hadn't earned the right to look so much like an angel. Not with what she'd—

"Tut, tut. In you go." Mrs. Potherby would not allow any lingering, and Carolly was forced to don the gown or risk ripping it as the stern woman pulled it up over her shoulders.

"Oh, Carolly," whispered Mags from her position at the foot of the bed. "You look heavenly."

"I—"

"You shall do me proud tonight," Mrs. Potherby said, her stern expression relaxing into a warm smile.

They all turned at a soft knock on the door. Given all the noise and commotion surrounding them, the sound could have been anything from a dropped corset to a pot boiling over in the kitchen.

But it wasn't. James stood on the other side of the door, and they all knew it.

Suddenly, Mrs. Potherby was hustling Margaret out the

door while James waited. Then, finally, he stepped inside, drawing the door shut behind him.

"Oh, James." Carolly couldn't help but gasp. She didn't think a man could look as handsome as he did. He wore a dark gray coat emphasized by a white silk cravat and a single pearl neckpin. It was barely more formal than the clothing Garrett had worn countless nights to dinner, and yet the elegance seemed to fit James better. Perhaps the clothing accented his aristocratic bearing and very masculine presence. Or perhaps she simply loved him and would think him stunning in sackcloth. All she really understood was that he stole her breath away.

It was some moments before she realized he gazed at her with as much hungry adoration as she had for him.

"Had I but known this would be the result, I would have thrown a ball much earlier."

She flushed, not at his compliment, but at the clear admiration in his eyes.

"I don't feel like I deserve to wear this," she said.

He frowned, clearly surprised. "But why ever not?"

"James, this is for an angel."

"As you are."

"Except that you don't believe it."

He shrugged, dismissing his earlier doubts as if brushing away a pesky fly. "You are already an angel to me."

She bit her lip, suddenly feeling awkward. "James, everyone believes me to be your mistress. How can I wear white?"

He smiled at her, lifting his hand to trail it along her cheek. "Because it is beautiful on you. Because I wish it. But mostly because I want to show the *ton* exactly what a treasure I have found."

"James—"

He silenced her, pressing his finger to her lips. "I have a gift for you."

She looked up, surprised. "But surely this gown is more than enough."

He shook his head, his eyes dancing with a joy she had not thought to see in him. "No. It is not enough, not nearly enough."

He placed a heavy jeweler's bag into her hand, his touch gentle as a caress. But Carolly didn't move to open it. It all felt so wrong. "James, I cannot. You have given me too much already."

"And, as you mentioned, you have reconciled me with my niece and given the villagers something to celebrate instead of grumble over. Surely that is worth a small token."

"But—"

"Here." Taking the bag from her he opened the top, letting a double strand of pearls spill into.her hand.

"Oh, James." She could only stare at the perfectly matched pearls, wondering at such extravagance. In all of her lives, she had never been given a gift of such wealth or beauty. "Are you trying to bribe me?" she asked, her voice quavering at her feeble attempt at humor.

"I am trying to say thank-you," he whispered. Then he turned her around so she faced the mirror as he slipped the pearls around her neck. "Perfect," he breathed, his breath coiling about her neck, as sensual as the caress of the cool stones. "I had thought to buy you diamonds, but somehow the pearls are more like you. They are warmer, and they seem to glow as you do."

She raised her gaze to his reflection, seeing him behind her, his darkness a perfect balance to her brightness. "I have misjudged you, James. I thought you were a cold man, trapped inside yourself and unable to love. But the truth is, you love better than I. You see things more clearly. You have allowed a madwoman into your life, given her shelter, clothing, food." She touched her necklace. "Even pearls. But most of all, you have given me the time to collect my thoughts."

She turned to him, meeting the dark gray of his eyes. "You were right yesterday. I have been running away. I hurt my family so badly the first time, I think I am afraid to try again, to live again."

He did not move, but she felt him change. It was a subtle shift of attitude. His eyes widened ever so slightly, and his breath seemed to catch, suspended in the air between them. Finally he spoke, but his voice was barely more than a whisper. "What does this mean?"

She looked away, unable to bear the intensity of his gaze. It would only take the slightest of movements for her to be in his arms, but she held back.

She took a deep breath. "It means I will try to be both human and . . . whatever. I still want to earn my wings"—she glanced back at him, her body aching to touch his—"but I have decided that living and loving here, as Caroline Handren, is just as important."

He touched her chin, gently bringing her gaze back to him. "Carolly, about your other lives . . . There has been no news of your battle."

"Waterloo."

He nodded. "You said it would occur ten days ago, and yet there has been no word."

"I know." At first it had worried her, making her question her belief in her own identity again. But lately she had relaxed, letting Caroline and Carolly merge without friction or distress. Carolly accepted that Waterloo would happen when it was time. Caroline was content to wait and see. Both knew this was not insanity.

"Carolly." The word was rough as James drew her toward him, but she held him back.

"Very soon, James, there will be a ballroom full of women all trying to snare your attention. Look at them, dance with them, be with them before you choose me. I will not change, James. What you call fantasies are my reality, and I will not release them. If, at the end of the night, you still want me . . ." She stretched up on her toes, dropping the lightest of kisses on his lips. "I will be here."

Then she left him, feeling as though she had just laid her heart and soul out for judgment. The world thought her a madwoman, and tonight James would feel the full force of public opinion as it reviled her. Could he turn his back on society? Could he be with her despite her oddities? He hadn't been able to so far, and there was no reason to expect tonight would change his mind. The possibility that he would choose elsewhere remained very real.

If he did, if he found another woman, how would she survive the rest of her life, much less all of eternity?

Telling James to dance with a flock of eligible women and actually watching him do it were two entirely different matters. Carolly didn't regret asking him to look his fill tonight, but she did have trouble remaining in the ballroom while he smiled and chatted and generally courted a few dozen beautiful girls, most of whom were half Caroline's age and twice as pretty.

Still, Carolly had never attended a party she did not find some way to enjoy. And if her dance card wasn't exactly filled, she didn't spend her time as a wallflower, either. Enough gentlemen spoke with her to make the evening lively. And she learned quickly enough to ignore the condescending or openly jealous comments of some of the ladies.

Her only true friend seemed to be Miss Hornswallow, who remained by her side, guiding her through the shifting social waters. Or rather, she stayed nearby until Baron Lansford arrived. The dear man greeted Carolly then swept Miss Hornswallow away, monopolizing the governess for the rest of the evening.

Fortunately, Carolly and Caroline had completely merged now, their disparate memories accessible without conflict. Carolly was able to use Caroline's knowledge of manners to acceptable effect. Even without Miss Hornswallow's presence, Carolly recalled intricate dance steps, knew which fork to use when, and was even able to address this matron and that lord without stumbling through faux pas after faux pas.

That is, when any of them deigned to speak with her at all.

Much to her surprise, the most exasperating aspect of the evening did not come from the guests at all, but from James. She could feel him watching her wherever she went, whatever she did. She was used to being conspicuous, she told herself. She'd practically made a career of it in her first life. But this time was different. This time *James* watched her. His attention felt like a tingle that simmered along her spine, focusing just between her shoulder blades. It electrified her senses, throwing tiny details into sharp relief, making her more conscious of him and of herself than ever before.

"You seem preoccupied tonight, Caroline."

Carolly turned, surprised Garrett had thought to join her where she stood, near enough to the dowagers for propriety, but far enough away to give the elderly ladies the illusion of privacy. She'd never thought Garrett would waste his time searching her out when he seemed so taken with the more fashionable, richer ladies of the *ton*. But here he was, bowing over her hand.

"Good evening, Garrett. You look very fine tonight." It was an automatic compliment. He always looked dashing. Unfortunately, his handsome appearance, smooth manners, and all she knew about him left her somewhat suspicious. She knew there was more to Garrett than met the eye, and even worse, his hidden depths were decidedly unpleasant.

"You are simply ravishing in that gown," he enthused as he stroked her palm in an intimate caress. He leaned forward, his voice low and intimate. "But you were made for more costly jewels, Caroline. Pearls do not do you justice."

"I like them quite well, thank you," she said coolly, withdrawing her hand from his.

"But in London you would have diamonds and rubies and—"

"I believe this is my dance."

Both turned at James's firm tones. Carolly felt her face heat.

She didn't have to look at her card to know James had not reserved this dance. She went to him anyway, knowing King George himself could not keep her from his arms—not when he looked at her with such intensity, his dark gaze mesmerizing and holding her as firmly as a net. She did not even say good-bye to Garrett as James led her onto the dance floor. Nor did she resist when he pulled her into his arms for a waltz.

"You are the most beautiful woman here tonight."

Carolly laughed, her heart soaring at this simplest of compliments. "Surely you can think of something a little more original, James. What about my eyes? Do they sparkle like diamonds? Or are they the eyes of a lunatic?" She smiled up at him, giving herself up to the music, letting the feel of his powerful thighs spin her into a universe all their own. Heaven could not feel more perfect, and she was grateful when he let her revel in the moment. But all too soon, he spoke again, his face lined with gentle concern.

"Has it been so very bad for you?"

She blinked, unwilling to be pulled back to reality. Especially not when he drew her deeper into his embrace, sliding his hand in a sensual caress along her waist.

"I could talk to him, if you wish," he offered.

She was confused. "Talk to who? Garrett? My uncle? Or do you mean every man who tries to take advantage of my madness—or perhaps every woman who is spiteful because I am moderately attractive?"

She felt James tighten his hold on her, as if he could protect her from every careless or intentional evil in the world. "All of them. I would speak for you against all of them." His words were a vow, and she treasured him for it. But there were some things even he could not change.

"I can handle Garrett," she said. "As for my uncle, he seems to delight in warning all my potential suitors that I am mad as a hatter. The others seem merely jealous because you bought me the most stunning gown in the room. Truly," she lied, "nothing pains me."

He spun her in a tight circle, letting his cheek rest, however briefly, on her temple before letting her slip back into the required distance between partners. "I meant I will speak with your uncle."

Carolly shrugged. "It will not help. He sent me away as soon as he assumed guardianship."

James frowned, his expression suddenly pensive. "Carolly, what do you know of . . . Caroline's inheritance?"

Carolly thought back, at ease with the question despite the awkward phrasing. "I don't know. My family had a pleasant home, nice clothing, plenty of books and . . ." Her voice trailed away. Caroline's father had been a minister of a poor parish. Not a chance that the collations could have sustained them, especially since her father gave away almost as much as the tithes brought in. There must have been money outside of his benefice. "I . . . I suppose my father must have had some sort of family money. An inheritance of some kind. Do you suppose I did, too?"

"You have no other relatives? Other than the baron?"

Carolly shook her head. "None."

"Then your uncle now controls everything." James's voice was flat, but she understood his implication.

"You think he has deliberately prevented me from marrying, even put me in the asylum, so he can keep my money?"

The dance was ending, and they were forced to stop. As Carolly pulled reluctantly out of his arms, her body still seemed to spin with the dance while her mind reeled from her thoughts.

"James—"

"Hush. I will speak with him."

She touched his arm. "Can I not come with you?"

He shook his head and led her back to her chair. "Not this time. You may confront him later. I promise." Then he touched her cheek, his eyes warm. "Rely on me."

She smiled, feeling unaccountably reassured. "I shall." She

watched with a surge of happiness as James bowed over her hand, whispering into her palm.

"We will speak more tonight," he said. Then he was gone, heading toward the card room where her uncle was no doubt gambling.

Carolly sighed, feeling bereft despite the joy that still lingered from their dance. But she barely had time to register her feelings before Garrett appeared by her side and pressed a glass of champagne into her hand.

She turned to him out of politeness, but her thoughts were still on James. "Thank you," she murmured. "But I think I would rather have lemonade."

"Nonsense, Caroline," he said, gently lifting the glass to her lips. "You must drink this." He leaned closer to her. "Then you must follow me outside."

The champagne tasted sweet as he forced it to her lips, the liquid spilling into her mouth as she tried to move away. "Garrett!" she exclaimed as some of the drink spilled down her dress.

But he ignored her protest, lifting her hand and trying to draw her to the open doors which led to the garden. "You must come."

"Garrett—"

Suddenly he was hissing anger as he bent to her ear. "Do you want to make a scene in front of James's guests? Come immediately."

"But—"

"Now!" Then he stood, releasing her hand before striding out the door.

Carolly looked around, noting more than one guest had watched their little altercation, and she smiled wanly in their direction. They already thought the worst of her, she knew, and was suddenly seized by a feeling of recklessness. Why not make the situation complete by following Garrett? He obviously had something important to tell her. No doubt there was some difficulty with the food or guests. Maybe a fight.

Any number of possibilities sprang to mind. The only way to find out was to go.

Or, she thought, her courage growing by the second, she might be able to lure him into confessing his infamous plans.

With an impudent smile aimed at any of the snobbish guests who dared to disapprove, she squared her shoulders and sauntered out into the garden.

James did not search long for Caroline's uncle. Baron Handren had previously announced his distaste for dancing, no doubt because of his size. His only other interests were eating and gambling, and given that the midnight buffet had already been consumed, the man would no doubt be in the card room.

He was. In fact, the baron sat at the center of a small group of gentlemen, smoking a cigar, regaling the company with a story of his niece's mad escape from the asylum.

It was enough to make James strip off his glove to challenge the boor. But reason soon asserted itself. A duel would not serve his purposes. He could not keep Carolly and flee the country at the same time. Reining in his temper, he called for a deck of cards and settled into a chair at the baron's table.

"Good evening, my lord," the man bellowed congenially. "Come to share some of your excellent brandy?" He lifted his glass and drained it.

James smiled, pleased to see his guest in such good spirits. He would take great delight in squashing them. "Actually, Baron, I have come to challenge you to a game of piquet. Care for a hand?"

The man frowned. "Piquet? Don't mind if I do. Shall we play a monkey a point?"

James smiled at the high stakes. Normally he disdained such play, but tonight he had an ulterior motive. "Done," he responded firmly. Then he passed the deck to the baron for the cut. Around them, gentlemen began to gather, intrigued by the sight of their host playing cards. James simply smiled at them, encouraging as much of an audience as possible. He began his campaign moments after dealing their hands.

"Caro is quite fond of you, you know. She tells me you have been exceedingly kind since her parents' deaths."

The baron puffed on his cigar, his ruddy face beaming with pleasure. "Such a dear gel. Pity she's such a queer noddy."

James felt his insides clench at the slight to Carolly, but forced himself to remain cool as he played a card. "Yes, well, she seems to think highly of you." He looked up, noting his opponent's shrewd cardplay for all that he sometimes acted the buffoon. "In fact, she said you have been quite a successful investor, and I must agree. Your small baronetcy cannot bring you much, and yet I hear you spend a large portion of your time in London, always dressed in the best, always generous with your funds."

The baron looked up, his large face registering surprise at James's compliments. "Well, I have the knack, you know." Then he grinned. He drank merrily from his now refilled brandy glass before confiding, "My father rarely had two sous to rub together. But I don't mind telling you I made three times what the old man gave me. Three times."

"Amazing!" James collected the cards for the next deal. The last hand had split evenly, but as he dealt again, he let his gaze wander over the gentlemen who either openly watched their play or lounged nearby. "I understand you manage a number of investment groups. Why, I would not wonder but some of your investors are here today."

"Four of them, actually." The man spoke loudly, preening even as he nodded to two of his clients.

James lifted his cards, making a pretense of studying them as he noted which of his neighbors had been taken in by this braggart. "Well, then I must consider myself the most fortunate of fellows."

Handren frowned as he played a card. "I don't follow you."

"I hesitate to mention it thus." James leaned forward as he spoke, and the baron was quick to follow suit, anxious for whatever news James might confide.

"I am the soul of discretion, I assure you," said the baron, his breath foul in James's face.

"Of course," James responded, drawing back the slightest bit. "I am sure I can count on you." He made sure to speak just loud enough for the nearest gentlemen to overhear. "Caro and I intended to approach you more properly, but I find myself unable to contain the news." He paused for dramatic effect. "She and I are betrothed."

The baron nearly choked on his own shock. "Betrothed? But she is mad!"

James leaned back, noting with pleasure the whispers already spreading the news throughout the room. "Mad?" he said. "Nonsense. She merely has an unorthodox sense of humor. Which was earlier misdiagnosed."

Handren clutched his cards, nearly crumpling them as he spoke. "But she has fits."

James played his card, his movements becoming slower and more casual as he relished the scene. "Fits? None that I have ever noticed."

"Terrible ones. Horrible to behold." The baron was shaking to the point that his flesh seemed to quiver all about him. "I am sure you would not want to be witness to such a thing. And think of your children."

James merely smiled. He *had* been thinking about children. Quite specifically and for a while now. "I have come to realize," he said, allowing a secret smile to curve his lips, "that Caro would make an excellent mother. She has, in fact, done wonders for Margaret. And I believe our children would benefit from a solid imagination and a lively sense of humor."

"Y-you cannot be serious!" sputtered the baron, echoing the murmurs of stunned surprise circling through the room at that statement. James ignored them.

"I recall," he continued to the room at large, "that I myself once pretended to be a bat for an entire month as a child. I caught insects and tried to sleep upside down. Nanny was most horrified," he remembered with a grin. That, of course, had been the best part. "And Thomas," he said, remembering one of his childhood friends, "wanted to be a polar bear. Went about roaring and capturing maids. Freddie wanted to be a horse, running circles in a field with his favorite colt. I believe he even slept in the barn that entire year." Then he raised his voice, making sure his words carried throughout the room. "I have never seen any signs of madness in Caroline," he said pointedly. "In fact, I would take it as a personal insult were anyone to suggest she was anything but the picture of health and sanity."

The baron blinked, his large face sallow. "But she thinks she is an angel. Your cousin Garrett said so himself."

James grinned. "And so she is. The angel of my heart."

"But—"

James collected his last tricks, noting his opponent's game had deteriorated most dramatically. "In any event, the banns shall be posted on Sunday."

Handren nearly bolted out of his seat. "What?"

James perused his cards. "Needless to say, she shall never see the inside of Boorstin again."

His opponent was no longer listening, was not even playing his cards. Apparently, the baron's mind was focused elsewhere. Perhaps he wondered where he might find the funds for Caro's dowry in three weeks' time.

"Baron? Are you quite well?"

The man came back to reality with a sick gasp. "What?"

"As I was saying, because of your financial skills, I believe myself the most fortunate of fellows to be joining your family." The man could only gape as James continued, taking great joy in pounding the last nail in the lout's coffin. "Caroline's dowry has no doubt tripled under your excellent management."

Handren never picked up his cards for the next hand. Instead, he poured himself some more brandy, his hand visibly shaking. "Well, as to her dowry," he muttered, "I am afraid I, um, did not, in fact, invest her funds . . ." His voice trailed away, and James happily took up the slack.

"Ah, kept it in a separate account? How prudent of you."

The man was sweating now, his shirt points wilting almost before their eyes. "Ah, well, as to that . . ." he said.

"No matter." James waited a moment. "I shall be quite content with her original dowry."

The baron straightened in his seat, seemingly intent on his cards as he latched on to James's idea. "Original dowry? Oh, but that was quite small. Almost nothing, you understand."

"Truly? How odd." Handren misplayed, and James picked up the next five tricks. "In fact, I had quite a different impression." He played his next card with an indifferent shrug. "No matter. I am sure Mr. Oltheten will have an exact estimation of her inheritance."

Handren's fingers were almost white as they gripped his last card. "Mr. Oltheten?"

"Why, yes. He is the solicitor who handled Caro's parents' estate, is he not?" James assumed it was the same man who'd responded to his previous inquiries.

The baron dropped his card and gulped the last of his brandy. "Oltheten. Yes, yes, of course."

"Excellent." James actually allowed himself to grin as he delivered the killing blow. "I have already posted a message to my solicitor in London. I am sure he will contact Mr. Oltheten immediately."

"Immediately?" Handren echoed weakly.

"I am sure of it." He stared hard into the baron's pig-like eyes, knowing now his fears were correct: Caroline's uncle had spent her dowry. He had no doubt locked her in Boorstin just to keep control of her money. But James would get every penny of her inheritance back if he had to ruin the fat fool to do it. Then he would gift her with it on their wedding day.

James leaned forward, unaccountably pleased to realize that though this card game was over, Handren's torment had just begun. With a final, cold smile, James played his final card. "Piquet," he said. "I believe you owe me five hundred pounds." Then he bowed politely to the pathetic man and left, not surprised to hear him already calling for his valet.

The baron would probably leave for London as soon as his carriage could be brought around. After all, he had to roust enough ready cash to pay Caro's dowry, and such financial maneuvering took time.

But James had no doubt Handren would find the money. It would be disastrous for a man in his position to be caught embezzling from his own niece. The thought made him grin. Carolly would at last be free from her uncle.

He wanted to find her and tell her his plan before she heard it from someone else. He could see news of his betrothal had already spread to the ballroom. More than one matron cast him a scathing glance while the young girls seemed to huddle together as if for comfort.

James shook his head at the vagaries of human nature. He knew how strongly women coveted his title, but they acted as if he had betrayed a state secret. He tried to dredge up some sympathy for them, but could find none. His mind was completely absorbed with finding Carolly and imagining the joy sparkling in her eyes when he told her they would wed.

But where was she?

Chapter Seventeen

Carolly took a deep breath of the cool night air. It felt good to get outside, away from the haughty stares in the ballroom. The garden lay hushed and still. Peaceful. And if she listened very closely, she could hear the quick tempo of the folk music playing at the village festival. She had arranged through Mrs. Potherby for local players and a dance on the near meadow. Listening now to their lighthearted music, she was tempted to forego the dubious pleasures of high society for the simple satisfaction of a true country romp. She would have gone if the villagers accepted her. But she knew they wanted her even less than the snobbish matrons inside.

Weeks ago, that realization would have depressed her. It still would, except for one thing: James. When she was with him, she didn't feel so out of place. She fit with him, and that made her happy. Or, at least, it made her as happy as she could be considering she was out in the garden following Garrett in the vague hope that he had something serious to tell her. Or was he looking for another way to ruin her reputation?

A month ago such nonsense as a "reputation" wouldn't have bothered her. But now that she had integrated with Caroline, she paid more attention to societal strictures. Which was why she intended to return to the ballroom if Garrett didn't reappear soon. The village musicians were finishing their last set. The guests were leaving, and Carolly wished to be close at hand when James blew out the last candle.

Perhaps then she would finally get her answer: Did he want her?

Now she would deal with Garrett's nonsense. And hopefully dissuade him from his ridiculous plans for the villagers.

She took one final turn about the garden, giving voice to her irritation in a whispered hiss. "Garrett! Where are you? I swear I'm leaving this instant if you don't—"

Two strong hands grabbed her around the waist and dragged her backward into a semi-dark area between two tall hedges. She didn't need to see to know it was Garrett. The spicy scent of Imperial water was too strong for it to be anyone else.

"Let go of—mumph!"

His mouth came down on her lips, bruising them as his hands found and squeezed her bodice. It was disgusting and frightening to be manhandled so easily, and Carolly redoubled her efforts to shake free.

"Garre—"

She should have known better than to open her mouth. He invaded her in a moment, pushing his tongue into her like a thick worm. As for his hands, she was having no luck in peeling them off her. No matter how she shifted, he tightened his hold, pressing her much too intimately against the evidence of his unwanted desire.

There was no choice. She had to end this attack now. Carolly bit down hard, tasting blood as Garrett suddenly reared back, his cry echoing through the garden. Then Carolly took advantage of his suddenly slackened hold and raised her knee. Hard. She was gratified to see him double over, his curses abruptly cut off as he gasped for air.

He dropped to the ground, and she stepped away, smoothing her skirts as she went. "Good heavens, Garrett—if this is how you try to pick up women, it's no wonder you're still a bachelor. Was this supposed to be romantic? Please!" she exclaimed with a shudder. "You're repulsive!"

Then she spun around and stomped back to the ballroom. At that moment, she didn't care anymore what his nefarious plans were. She and James together would find a way to best him. In the meantime, he had best stay out of her way!

Carolly made it back to the ball, remembering at the last minute to smooth out her clothing before entering. Once inside, she was relieved to see the room nearly empty. The musicians had stopped playing and were packing up their instruments. The last of the guests were taking their leave of James by the door. No one seemed to pay any attention to her. Except James. Even from across the room, she could see his eyebrows rise, and she turned away in guilty embarrassment.

The last thing she wanted was for James to see her right after her sordid encounter with Garrett.

Leaving James to his guests, Carolly began to wander around the ballroom. Except for a few footmen and maids, she had ordered all the other staff to depart after the midnight buffet was cleared. That left just her and Mrs. Potherby, since Wentworth was busy managing the carriages.

She dismissed Mrs. Potherby, sending the exhausted woman to bed. Then she checked the kitchens before meandering back to the ballroom, extinguishing candles along the way. Soon James would come to see her, and she would know how he felt.

Soon.

"Carolly."

His voice was a whisper, but it had the force of a lightning bolt. She stood, electrified, her hand raised toward a flickering candle.

"Carolly? You look . . . disturbed."

She turned slowly, forcing herself to meet his eyes. "I . . . I guess I'm a little nervous. I . . ." Her voice trailed away as he reached out and pulled a leaf from her hair.

"How odd," he said, his voice low. "I don't remember this here when we started the evening."

She felt her face heat with mortification, and she quickly ran her hand over her coiffeur, checking for any other remnants of her time outdoors.

"Carolly, have you been climbing trees in your ballgown?" Although his voice was light, she could hear a steely note of suspicion underneath.

She looked up at him and sighed. She wanted to know how he felt about her, not talk about Garrett. "It was nothing," she said. "An ill-conceived attempt at seduction—"

"I beg your pardon!" he exclaimed in stiff accents.

"But I handled it. It's over. Honest. Can we just forget it?"

He would have none of it. "You will explain yourself. Now." His tone was not angry. It was simply cold, detached, and very, very firm.

Carolly clenched her fists, wishing she could plant them in Garrett's face. Of all the times for them to be discussing this . . .

"Carolly," James said, his tone more a warning than a prompt.

She sighed. "I think Garrett is concerned about losing his inheritance."

James frowned. "What has that to do with—"

"He told me to come outside to talk about something vital. The next thing I knew, I was thrown into a bush, and Garrett was imitating an octopus."

She saw James's jaw clench, and she pressed forward, touching his arm. "James—"

"He goes too far."

"I told you, I handled it."

He looked down at her, his expression fierce. "How?"

She grinned at him, reliving the moment in her memory.

"I kicked him in the . . ." She bit her lip, searching for a delicate way to phrase it. "Last time I saw him, he was lying on the ground clutching his . . . uh . . ." She frowned. "I assure you, he won't try it again."

She saw a glimmer of appreciation light his dark eyes. "You did well."

"Thank you."

"I will speak with him tomorrow."

"But—"

"And as for you . . ." He frowned down at her. "Henceforth, you will not leave a ballroom without my escort."

"James!" she exclaimed, annoyed. "I told you, I handled it."

"Yes," he said, drawing her arm through his as he led her back to the ballroom. "But you cannot be sure of such effectiveness in the future."

"I assure you," she said dryly, "I can handle myself."

"Nevertheless."

"Oh, just stop it," she snapped. Her nerves were worn thin. Between wondering about his decision, making sure the ball and festival went off without a hitch, and fighting off Garrett, she had no patience for these chivalrous, overprotective instincts. She simply wanted his answer. Now. Immediately. "What have you decided?" she demanded.

He paused, stopping halfway up the stairs. "About what?"

She didn't know if he was teasing or just being dense. Either way, she would not stand for any more of it. She turned to him, trying not to let him see how anxious she was. "Don't do this to me. I have been racked with doubt all evening. James, what are you going to do?" A memory flashed through her mind of him dancing with a dark-haired beauty. The woman had poise, a title, loads of money, and looked extremely good on his arm. The biddies had been predicting a match between them within a fortnight. Carolly swallowed. "Will you offer for Lady Beatrice?"

She saw his eyes widen with shock, no doubt surprised she was so perceptive. She felt her chest squeeze tight as her worst fears were confirmed. Her hand clenched on his arm, and she made to withdraw, but he stopped her, trapping her hand beneath his.

"So impulsive," he said. "When will you learn to ask first and conclude later, at leisure and after much reflection?"

Carolly stilled, barely even daring to hope, after his face curved into a warm smile.

"I have already announced our betrothal," he said, his voice soft and intimate.

Carolly felt her world spin, and her throat felt thick. "Already? She has agreed already?"

"She?" His voice held a laughter she found both confusing and vaguely insulting. "Carolly, I am speaking of *our* betrothal. You and me. The banns will be posted on Sunday."

"The banns?" She had to scramble through Caroline's memory to understand his meaning. When she discovered it, she nearly collapsed under a fresh wave of panic. Marriage. He meant to marry her. In just over three weeks.

"Carolly!"

She hadn't even realized she was wobbling on her feet until he scooped her up in his arms and strode up the stairs.

"James, you must put me down. Think of your leg! James!"

He wasn't listening to her. His arms were firm and comfortingly strong as he carried her through the house. Her worries about his leg appeared groundless, since his stride was as confident as his expression. He did not stop until he laid her gently on her bed.

"You have had a long night," he began, his manner tender despite his correctness. "You should rest. There is plenty of time to plan the wedding tomorrow."

Carolly scrambled to her knees on the bed, pushing a stray lock of hair out of her eyes as she regarded him. "Wait! Don't I have a say in this?"

He stopped halfway through his bow, straightening slowly. "You may plan the wedding however you wish. Only tell me the date and time, and I shall be there with alacrity."

She shook her head, panic welling up again. "No, not the wedding. I mean the marriage! James, why do you want to marry me?"

He softened toward her then. His smile relaxed until it seemed to ease the strain in his whole body. He settled on the bed beside her, taking her hands into his, stroking them gently as he spoke.

"I have no skill with romantic words. I can only tell you I had no wish to be with those other women tonight. I could only think of you. Every time you laughed with another man, I grew insane with jealousy. As for the other women . . ." He shook his head. "I found fault with all of them. One was too tall, the other too dull. They never seemed to smile enough." He raised her hands to his lips, kissing her fingertips one by one. "I discovered tonight that I love you. And so I will marry you."

Carolly felt her heart swell. The precious gift of his love affected her more deeply than she'd ever imagined. To finally hear the words filled her soul to overflowing. He loved her. He wanted to marry her.

But she could not marry him.

Gently she withdrew her hands from his, struggling to find the words to explain, both to herself and him. She'd changed her mind about this so many times. "James," she tried, her voice raw. "I promised to be with you tonight if you wanted, and I will. But I cannot promise to marry you."

She felt him stiffen even though they were not touching. His entire body stilled, and the warmth left his eyes.

"Try to understand," she begged. "You are speaking of marriage. Of a future and commitment. I am . . . not in control of where I will go. What if—"

"*Carolly*." His voice was a low growl of warning, but she continued, ignoring him.

"Just listen to me. I cannot promise to live with you and love you when I might be called to Heaven." She pushed forward on the bed. "What if this isn't to be? James, angels don't get married, they don't have husbands, and they don't have children. That is for humans, for mortals. I don't know what will happen, who I am. How can I promise a future I don't know I have. Can you understand that at all?"

He didn't answer, but Carolly could feel the fury building in him. It crackled in the air between them, stiffening his shoulders and raising his chin until he transformed into the haughty aristocrat she once thought him.

"Tonight." His voice was cold, edged with a bitterness she could hear in each hard word. "You asked me for an answer. You were willing to come to me tonight. But not in marriage?"

"I've spent four lifetimes trying to be an angel. Don't ask me to ignore that possibility." She leaned forward and tried to touch his hand, but he jerked backward.

"Ignore that possibility? What possibility?" He stood up, then turned so he towered over her, glaring down. "I have already announced our betrothal. I have committed my honor to the fact that you are sane. You cannot go around even *talking* about becoming an angel. It is all merely your imagination!"

She pushed to her feet, the movement slow and painful as she reminded herself over and over to stay calm. She had to fight this attack with an icy politeness all her own. She didn't speak until she stood and lifted her chin to glare right back at him.

"I don't need to talk about it, James. All I need is to know it. In here." She tapped her chest over her heart. "I don't care what you've committed your honor to." She practically spat the words. "You never asked me—"

"I am asking you now."

"No. You're ordering me."

He took a deep breath, the sound loud in the room. "Is that what you want?" He dropped to one knee and clasped her hand in a bruising grip. "Caroline Handren—"

"No!" She tried to jerk away, but he held her too tightly.

"—will you do me the honor—"

"This is not what I want!"

"—of marrying me?"

"No!"

His grip clenched tighter, and she dropped to her knees before him, frustration making her words clipped and hard.

"Don't you think I want this, too? I said it already. I have loved you from that first moment when you waited for me to escape from my sickbed. But, James, you are asking me to promise the impossible."

"No, Caro, I am asking you to give up your fantasies. Look at yourself." He hauled her upward and dragged her to the mirror. "Look. You are alive." He lifted her arm, pressing his hand into her wrist. "You have a pulse. You are Caroline Handren."

"No—"

"Your uncle has kept you in Boorstin so he could control your inheritance. You are not insane, and you are not going to be an angel!"

"You don't know that!" She whirled around, losing her calm as she defended against her worst fears. "And we can't change it just by wishing it weren't so."

"Wishing? Shall we speak of wishing?" He folded his arms across his chest, matching her anger with cool fact. "Has there been some great battle against Napoleon? Where is this Waterloo?"

She squared her shoulders, trying to appear as confident as he. "It will happen. I just miscalculated the dates."

"No, Caro." He stepped forward, gentling his voice even as he gripped her arms. "It will not happen because you do *not* know the future. You are Caroline Handren, and . . . and I love you."

She closed her eyes. Why did those words cause so much pain? He loved her. And yet, how could he? He did not believe anything about her. "James. . . ." Her voice was a soft plea for understanding.

He drew her into his arms, speaking softly as if crooning to a child. "I love your imagination. I love your fantasies and your laughter and your odd way of speaking. I love who you are, Caro, but you must not give up a future with me because of a silly dream."

"A dream?" She was torn, her body tight and angry in his arms. Half of her begged for his understanding, needing his love, while the other half stubbornly demanded his trust. "I will be an angel."

"No, Caro. I am sorry, but it will not be. And, as my countess, you cannot keep speaking as if it will."

She felt her defeat as a heavy weight, pulling down her shoulders, dragging her away from him. "You have never believed me." She lifted her head, hoping to see the tiniest bit of doubt in his eyes. Hoping to see that he didn't believe himself in love with a lying little fool.

He sighed, his gaze steady and confident. "No, I never have."

She searched his face, pushing him to say it again and again. "Even on the ledge with the toad. You brought my memories back."

"Yes."

"But even then you didn't believe them?"

He shrugged, as if trying to explain something he didn't comprehend. "Those memories give you strength. They are part of you. I do not pretend to understand it, but you are at your best when you are both Carolly and Caroline. Both sides of your personality are important to me. All of it."

"So you helped me remember, even though you think they are sheer invention."

"Yes."

She shook her head, amazed at her own gullibility. "I thought . . . I'd hoped this was different. At last someone believed me, someone respected what I was doing and believed."

He lightly grazed her cheek with the edge of one thumb. "I am different. *I love you as you are.* I will allow your games and your pretense. But I cannot allow them to stand in the way of our marriage."

"James, they are not games."

He opened his hand, twisting his fingers as he cupped her cheek. "All right. They are very important to you. I realize that."

She shook her head.

He brought up his other hand, stepping closer to her, lifting her face for his kiss. "I want to marry you. Please, Caro, please marry me."

The heat of his breath warmed her lips. Her face tingled with anticipation, and her body already arched toward him, aching for the sweet heaven of his touch.

"I will never be your equal," she persisted. "You think me unbalanced."

He let his lips trail over hers with the tiniest brush of sensation. "I think you are amazing," he whispered. "I will care for you, protect you, and love you forever. I swear it will be wonderful between us. Give in, Carolly. Listen to your heart. And mine."

This was seduction at its very best. His body and his touch were only part of the appeal. He offered her everything she had once dreamed of: a man to love and cherish her; a home, wealth, and even social power to affect the world in ways she could only dream of in her first life. The price he asked seemed so small. Marriage. Commitment. And the denial of the one thing she had believed for four lifetimes. "James—"

"Marry me."

She hesitated, her heart beating painfully in her throat. "I can't."

He did not release her. His hands dropped lower on her body, moving in leisurely strokes that tormented her even as she pressed against him, silently begging for more.

"You said you love me," he whispered, his voice husky.

"I do."

"Then be with me. Forever." His hands dropped to her hips,

pulling her closer, harder against him, urging her to accept him in ways that were only in the here and now, the earthbound present. "Come to me."

She couldn't refuse him. Even if meant giving up everything she ever wanted, he was here with her now, his heart and his mind focused on loving her. She couldn't think of the future or even of Heaven. She let her hands slide up his body and she melted into him.

"I love you, Caro."

"And I love you," she whispered.

His kiss was slow, leisurely. Always before there had been an urgency to their touch, a reluctance overcome by passion. But she knew he was taking no chances this time. There would be no interruption to their lovemaking, no running away or distractions. He meant to have her. Tonight. And with every kiss, every shared intimacy, he bound her to him more closely than marriage vows.

It was as if she could read his mind. She knew so clearly what he was doing. Once she shared his bed, made love, then she would be unable to leave him. Especially if she was with child.

The thought was as compelling as it was frightening. She knew his plans, knew she should refuse, but the idea of carrying his child woke a fierce longing within her. Then his hands trailed down her spine, releasing the line of tiny pearl buttons that bound her dress, and her judgment faded away.

She could not fight the needs he awoke in her. How could Heaven be so unfair?

Arching against him, she let his tongue invade her mouth as never before. She met him in the same moment: reacting to his passion, letting it stoke her own, letting it blind her to all else. His hands were deft along her back, releasing her corset and pulling a shoulder of her gown down and away, exposing one breast to his gaze.

Cool air touched her skin in a shivery caress, and she gasped as his dark gaze caught and held her. He shrugged off his coat, and she didn't move, feeling mesmerized by the look that filled his eyes.

"I will not give you up," he whispered, and his need sunk into her bones more firmly than any vows. She saw the force of his determination even as he stripped away his waistcoat, cravat, and shirt.

Her gaze slipped to his body, drawn by the sight of his naked torso. She had touched him before, but never had she seen the dark whispers of hair on his chest. His breathing was unsteady, and his breath caught as she reached out and trailed her fingertips across him. She was fascinated by the ripple of muscle that followed her touch, and she edged her other hand along the hard planes of his body.

His only response was a soft sigh of delight. She smiled, intrigued beyond reason by the feel of him. And while she touched and tasted him, he carefully removed the pins that held her coiffeur until her hair flowed freely over his hands.

But her clothing still restricted her movement, and almost without realizing it, she shrugged it away, stepping out of the puddle of fabric to walk into his heated embrace, her stockings and slippers her only attire.

He tilted his head, intending to claim her mouth, but she would not kiss him. She whispered her plea. "I will be your mistress, James. Must you force me to give up what I know?"

He cupped her face, holding her steady as he gazed into her eyes. "You were the one who burst into my life. You forced me to open my heart. I am in love now, Caro. I will not lose you."

"But everything I have—"

"Keep your dreams, your fantasies, my love. Only marry me. Commit to me." As he claimed her lips, he whispered his final request. "*Love* me."

How could she not? What was eternity when compared to James? She didn't want to answer her own question, and so she let him kiss her until her senses reeled and her mind went blank. His hands found her breasts, and he teased them with consummate skill. When she moaned with desire, he swept her into his arms, carrying her to the bed.

She did not resist, her mind long since numbed by his sensual assault. She did not even react when he refused to follow her down to the bed. She merely gazed at him, wondering at his intentions until he lifted her leg and began inching down her stocking.

His movements were erotic, his gaze hungry as it roamed over her, arousing her with only the intensity of his eyes. She moaned softly as he kissed the arch of her left foot. She seemed caught in a whirlwind of sensations, her body keenly aware of the slightest passage of air and the most delicate of touches. James took advantage of it all, nibbling along the inside of her legs, brushing his tongue behind her knee, exploring and opening her with his hands as no one had ever done before.

She gasped, pulling away as she tried to regain some of her reason, but he would not release her. He pressed his mouth against her, using his tongue to explore parts of her already slick with desire. She arched against him, crying out in surrender.

She wanted him. She loved him. She would give him anything.

She pulsed with an ecstasy that overwhelmed her. And still he continued. Until, at last, her world exploded.

"James!"

He pulled back, letting her catch her breath, letting her body rest while he kissed her hips, her waist, her belly.

"James." It was a whisper. A prayer. And she felt him smile against the underside of her breast.

Then he lifted his head, his eyes dark and intense. "You are mine," he said.

"Yes."

She had not realized he was naked until she felt his legs, strong and powerful, pressing against the inside of her thighs. Then his mouth found her breast, suckling first at one, then the other, murmuring endearments as she writhed beneath him.

She had not believed her passion could be aroused again so soon, but the rough brush of his tongue pulled at her, shooting currents of fire from her nipples to her core. Her mind reeled, surrendering again as he kneaded and teased her body.

All too soon she wanted more. Running her hands along his sweat-slick body, she traced the shape of his chest, his tense muscles, his narrow waist, and the bony crest of his hips. Then she found the hard evidence of his desire.

As he gasped in surprise, she used her hands to tease him as he had tormented her. She used her nails to scrape along the sensitive underside while her thumb spread the tiny bead of moisture at his tip in ever increasing circles. Then she squeezed him, ever so slightly, and he moaned against her neck.

"Caro. My Caro . . ." His legs trembled along her thighs, even as he remained apart from her.

She raised her legs, edging her heels along the rough texture of his calves until she gripped him, urging him to a deeper union.

But still he held back, though the restraint made his breathing ragged. "Be sure of being mine," he said, his voice thick with desire. "Once done, I will not release you to God Himself."

She smiled, letting her fingers glide upward to his narrow hips, guiding him as she drew him closer. "I am yours."

Then he thrust into her, and she cried out in sudden pain.

He held himself still, deeply imbedded within her as she bit her lip, confused and startled.

She was a virgin?

"The worst is over, my love," he whispered. "Trust me."

"I do," she answered. And as they lay still, completely entwined, the pain receded, buried under a delicious feeling of fullness.

"Caro," he breathed.

She smiled, loving the sound her of name on his lips. "I love you," she whispered.

Then he began to move, his rhythm slow at first, careful not to hurt her. But all too soon, she urged him to increase his motions. His thrusts became faster and harder. She met his force with her own power, accepting it, yielding to it, multiplying it.

Nothing had ever felt so right.

He was hers.

She was his.

"Yes!"

They shattered together, their world exploding outward into the infinite. They danced among the stars. They were everything and everywhere. And when the rush receded, their consciousness returned to earth and reformed as one.

They were one. Vows and ceremonies meant nothing. In every way that mattered, they were married.

James collapsed beside her, his face the picture of ecstasy, of exhaustion. And of victory.

She settled into his arms, curled into his side as she listened to the steady beat of his heart mingling with hers. They were alive. Together. And she would never become an angel. The dream of four lifetimes had been swept away. It must be. There was no way Heaven could take her now. Was there?

He pulled her close to him, kissing her deeply. She fitted herself to him, finding more than delight at his side. She found joy.

Chapter Eighteen

Carolly woke when he left her early the next morning. James was ever cautious of her reputation, even when the rest of the world already thought her his mad mistress. She only smiled and watched him dress, desire sparking within her again. If it had been up to her, he would have remained with her in her bed for the rest of the morning and probably the rest of the day, if not the week. But he was steadfast. He gave her one last, lingering kiss, then slipped away.

She remained in bed, her daydreams filled with gorgeous gowns and wedding plans. But before long, her pleasant thoughts were interrupted by bells. Church bells ringing and ringing and ringing.

Something momentous had happened.

Hope, excitement, and a quivering fear trembled within her. Could it be? Was it? Waterloo? Anxious to discover the truth, Carolly dressed quickly, running downstairs at an unseemly pace. She found James seated in the breakfast room, frowning at bright day just outside the window.

"What has happened?" she asked.

"I cannot imagine," he answered, but his frown deepened.

She tried to catch his eyes, but his thoughts were obviously on the bells which continued to ring. They were too far from the church for the sound to be irritating. For Carolly, it was a fitting sound for the happiness that continued to bubble inside her.

"It is rather merry, don't you think?" she asked. "Sort of like chimes, only clearer." She found it surprisingly easy to control her curiosity. After all, she had made her choice last night. She would stay with James. Heaven could wait. Waterloo or not, she was too happy to be distracted by bells.

James, on the other hand, seemed profoundly disturbed. He stood up, crossed to the window, and stared out toward the village.

Carolly sighed. There was nothing for her to do but settle down for breakfast. She knew how anything mysterious obsessed James almost to the exclusion of all else. This was just one of those times, and she resigned herself to waiting out the course of events in silence. James's remaining guests had not yet stirred from their beds, so she was not likely to have any other conversation until James decided to return to the present.

It would be part of being married, she decided with a grin. No doubt she had her own peccadilloes he would have to suffer in silence as well.

Yet Carolly had no more than stepped to the sideboard when Margaret burst through the door. "Have you heard? Isn't it wonderful?" The girl launched herself at Carolly, wrapping her arms tight around Carolly's waist. "I knew you were right. I just knew it!"

"Mags—"

"Margaret!" James's voice cut harshly through the child's enthusiasm. "Please, have some sense of decorum. You are a young lady."

But Margaret remained undeterred by her uncle's sharpness.

She merely spun around, taking Carolly with her as she jumped toward her uncle. "It is truly wonderful! Carolly was right!"

"Do not imagine things that cannot be true," James responded repressively. "Just because of bells, doesn't mean—"

"You are just sour because you did not believe her," said Margaret. Then she twirled around again and faced Carolly. "But I did. I believed you the whole time!"

"Wait, wait!" cried Carolly, laughing despite James's darkening features. "What has happened?"

"Waterloo!"

Carolly gasped and clapped her hands. "Truly? Oh, I am so pleased. Now all those soldiers may come home at last." Then she clasped Margaret's hands and pulled her to a seat at the table. "Come. Tell me all the details."

"There are no details," said James, his voice hard and cold. "Margaret only guesses." Then he lifted his teacup—as if that ended the discussion.

"I am not guessing!" retorted the child, turning back to Carolly when her uncle refused to acknowledge her. "Cook heard it from her niece who came in from town this morning. I heard her tell Mrs. Potherby and Wentworth."

James set down his cup with a click that clearly voiced his disapproval. "It is all nonsense, Margaret. You were confused. Carolly's Waterloo is only a fantasy."

"It is not!" returned Margaret, her words angry. "Tell him, Carolly. Tell him it is true."

Carolly hesitated. James had made his position clear last night. He did not want her making her "delusions" public. And, as his wife, she needed to accommodate him—especially with a household full of guests ready to spread the tale to London. Still, she could not deny that Waterloo probably had happened. She could think of nothing else to account for the bells and Cook's niece's news from town.

"I . . ." she began, glancing at James's angry countenance. "I think we should wait for the paper." She turned to James.

"Perhaps we should send for the London newspaper. I am sure it will explain all the commotion." And prove once and for all she wasn't delusional, she thought with a grin.

"Uncle James has already sent for it," Margaret piped in. "He always does."

Carolly nodded, giving Mags a warm smile. "Well, then, all we need do is wait."

She resolutely turned toward her breakfast. Margaret chattered away at her side: The girl was thrilled that Carolly and James were to be married. She had heard it first thing this morning, of course. But she'd known it would happen ages ago. And wasn't the ball fabulous? She had peeked through the window for almost an hour. Cook had outdone herself with the food. And the gowns were gorgeous. None like Carolly's, of course, but Margaret couldn't wait until . . .

Suddenly, Carolly was laughing. "Heavens, Mags. Take a breath."

"Oh, but I am so excited! Miss Hornswallow is to be married as well!"

Carolly stopped, her fork halfway to her mouth. "What?"

"Baron Lansford proposed to her last night, and she accepted."

"Are you certain?" Carolly asked.

"Absolutely. I overheard them in the garden." Margaret grinned until her uncle cut in, his voice stern and repressive.

"And what were you doing in the garden, miss?"

The child flushed a dusky purple, flashed Carolly a grin, then scrambled out of her seat. "Well, I best be getting back to my lessons. I will see you later, shan't I?"

Carolly grinned, amazed at Mags's bright spirit. It was hard to believe this was the same girl who had been little more than a sulking lump two months ago.

"Carolly?" Mags prompted.

"Of course I'll be here, sweetheart. I guess I'm going to be your mother now."

"Oh, it will be wonderful!" enthused the girl. "I shall be

your bridesmaid, and we shall have the most beautiful gowns. And Uncle will be the most handsome man alive, and—"

"I believe you mentioned studies," interrupted James.

Margaret grimaced, then dropped a quick kiss on Carolly's cheek before she dashed away.

Carolly laughed, her spirits fully restored despite James's glower. "She's going to be a handful in a few years," she commented, inordinately pleased at the thought.

"She is a handful now."

Carolly turned to James, wondering at his foul mood. Surely he didn't regret last night, did he? She took worried bites of her toast, then finally dredged up the courage to ask, "James, do you wish perhaps to withdraw your offer? I understand if you've changed your mind about marrying me." She wouldn't, of course, but she had learned there were some things one had to accept gracefully.

She waited in silence, closing her eyes when the moment stretched to minutes. Her heart beat faster and faster within her; then she jumped as she felt a hand gently lift her chin. She opened her eyes to see James poised above her, pulling her upward into his embrace.

"James?" Her voice trembled as she stood.

"Nothing between us has changed. And I could never regret last night. Ever." He sealed his statement with a kiss. It was powerful, intense, urgent, and Carolly responded with the same fire James always seemed to ignite within her.

Then he pulled away.

"It is just these damned bells." He wandered to the window, his frown back in place.

Carolly watched him for a moment, seeing the rigid set to his shoulders, the concentrated stare as he scanned the lawn for some clue, and she felt the first tiny shiver of misgiving. "Are you afraid that it truly is Waterloo?" she asked.

"Do not be ridiculous."

She stepped forward, searching his face for some hint that she was wrong. But all she could see was his clenched jaw and the determined focus of his eyes. It was as if he tried to force the truth away by the power of his will alone. "You are afraid," she breathed. "You have had it in your mind that I am delusional—"

"What?"

"That I make up stories, and they become too real to me. But now it may be that I am right. That everything I have told you is correct, and you can't handle it."

He shifted, moving his body so he faced her more fully. His gaze remained steady and firm, almost as if he intended to force her to agree with him. "You cannot see the future, Carolly. I thought we established that last night."

She shook her head, fear rising in her throat. "No. You established that. I . . . I merely went along with it."

He grabbed her, gripping her arms almost desperately. "Carolly—"

"Your newspaper, my lord."

James's reaction was immediate. He dropped Carolly's arms as if she were poisonous, his entire attention drawn to the paper that Wentworth placed facedown on the table. "Thank you, Wentworth. You may go."

The butler's gaze flicked rapidly between her and James, no doubt memorizing the scene before he bowed and withdrew. Carolly didn't move.

"Don't touch it, James," she warned, her voice flat and hard. "Not unless you can accept that I was not wrong."

He ignored her, as she knew he would. Carolly watched him, her world suddenly moving in slow motion. He walked around the table and reached for the paper. Then he opened it. She heard the sharp intake of his breath as his eyes slowly widened and he began to read. She even saw the slight tremor in his arms as his hands began to shake.

She didn't have to see the words to know. Waterloo had occurred. Napoleon was vanquished. Wellington was a hero.

She was totally sane.

What a morning after, she thought with rising hysteria. No

flowers. No good-morning kisses. Just the firm belief that she was daft despite mounting evidence to the contrary. What kind of man wished for his wife to be crazy?

"How did you know this?" His voice was harsh and uncompromising.

"I have already told you that."

He whirled toward her, his face contorted. His confusion made him angry. "Are you some sort of spy?"

She gaped at him. "A spy?" Her voice dripped with sarcasm as she said, "That's right, James. I'm a French spy sneaking about in Staffordshire predicting Napoleon's humiliating defeat. Too bad my carrier pigeon died, otherwise the grand emperor would have known to go to Spain."

James's hands clenched, crumpling the newspaper. "How could you have known this?"

"How could you not know it?" She bit her lip, fighting back tears. "You say you love me, and yet you could not accept the truth I spoke all along."

"You are not what you said!" he roared.

She nodded, her tears flowing freely despite her efforts to restrain them. "Yes, I am." She angrily wiped her tears away, her hands shaking with emotion. She loved him. She had given up everything for him, and yet, despite all they had between them, he couldn't accept who she was.

"You'd think I'd have learned by now," she said bitterly. "After so many lives I should know people can't accept anything outside of their little realities."

He looked away from her as if shielding himself from the sight. "I cannot discuss this right now. I need to think."

"Think? You need to think?" She stepped forward, her hands clenched. She beat the table between them. "How are you going to explain this, James? What other logical explanation will you find for this? For me?"

He shook his head, still turned away from her. "I do not know, but I will find it."

She stared at him, seeing his averted face, hearing the ragged edge to his voice as he fought with her reality. She didn't even wait to see the end. She knew she would lose.

"Fine, James," she finally said, each word hard. "You go think. Go reason and plan and find some way to fit me into your little world." She whirled around, heading for the door.

"Where are you going?" His voice was as harsh as hers had been.

She spun back, glaring at him. "I'm going to church, James. I'm going there to pray for my sins. And then," she said, taking one step closer to him, "I'm going to decide if I ever want to come back to you."

She left, whipping past Wentworth to storm out the front door. Her steps didn't slow until she sailed past the circular drive and was firmly headed toward the church bells. Her feet pounded the ground, beating out a rapid tempo of hurt and frustration.

He had turned away from her! He couldn't even look at her.

She clutched at her chest and tried to suppress a sob. Then she gave up the struggle, letting her tears flow freely as she stormed her way toward town.

It wasn't until she was half a mile down the road that she realized she had been a fool. Not about James, but about her departure. She had left so impetuously, she hadn't stopped to think. She had no money, no transportation, and she hadn't even changed her slippers to boots. Each pebble, each tiny rut in the road ate away at her thin footwear until very soon she would have nothing but her bare and bleeding feet.

She sighed, feeling the weight of her existence as never before. Would she ever be able to toss it aside in favor of angel wings? Would she forever be doomed to fighting human misconceptions, and her own rash stupidity?

Kicking a stone out of her path, she winced at the pain it brought. At least the day was warm. And she was fully dressed, except for her absent corset. The villagers would not harm her, especially since they were probably in a good mood after her festival.

She resumed her dogged path toward the church, wondering what she would do now. She doubted she could still become an angel. Despite James's reaction this morning, she still felt bound to him. She loved him. Despite his rigid nineteenth century mindset, despite his arrogance and his formality, despite everything, she still loved him.

And she was still irrevocably tied to him. She had been willing to give up everything for him.

Besides, her lascivious actions last night clearly demonstrated she was not quite ready to become a chaste heavenly creature.

So, what did she do now? Their marriage was apparently in her mind only. She doubted he would go through with the formalities of making it legal, especially when he couldn't even bear to look at her.

Carolly kicked another stone. As far as she was concerned, her only hope now lay in divine intervention. She prayed for it. She wished for it. She even begged for it, but she didn't truly believe she would receive it. If God were in the habit of explaining Himself, she would have had a number of conversations with Him over her last few lives.

Thus she experienced considerable shock when, moments later, a rescuer did appear. Especially since it was Garrett on his brown thoroughbred stallion.

"Caroline! Have you lost your wits?"

"That isn't funny," she commented dryly, continuing her steady pace toward the bells.

"You cannot walk to town alone. At least ride with me. I can carry you wherever you wish to go."

Carolly winced as she trod upon another sharp stone. His offer truly appealed, even though he'd been such a cad. Her feet were already sore, and she had a good distance to go. "I don't know, Garrett," she said slowly. Then she stopped and put her hands on her hips as she squinted past the sun at his eyes. "Are you going to try another seduction?"

She was gratified to see his face flush, turning even his ears a dusky red. "No," he said in a cold voice. "I shall not touch you other than is absolutely necessary."

Carolly nodded, greatly relieved. "Then I accept your most gracious offer."

His face broke into a boyish grin. She merely sighed, remembering her ride on Shadow, her arms wrapped around an entirely different man.

Still, Garrett was being most gracious, and she should treat him accordingly. Putting on her best smile, she grabbed hold of the saddle and lifted herself up. With Garrett's help, she soon sat in front of him, awkwardly perched half on his thighs, half on the saddle. It was incredibly uncomfortable, and she silently prayed the ride would go quickly.

Garrett started with a sedate walk as she anchored herself against him.

"Are you secure?" he asked, his mouth close enough to her nose that she could detect the brandy lacing his breath.

"As secure as possible."

"Good." Then, with a sudden laugh, he turned his horse off the main road and kicked it into a gallop. Carolly screamed, throwing her arms around him to keep from flying off her awkward perch.

"What are you doing?" she screamed. But he merely laughed louder, hauling her tighter against him as he pushed his horse to greater speeds.

Carolly groaned. She felt every pounding hoof as if it were beating itself into her rear. She thought briefly of releasing Garrett and just allowing herself to be bounced right off the saddle, but one look at the speeding landscape convinced her otherwise. They were riding too fast, too hard. She would be lucky to survive a fall at this speed.

Perhaps this was the divine intervention she had asked for, she thought with a weird sort of disconnection. She could easily end this incarnation now. She would fall backward, probably break her neck, and then she would start over. Another life, another chance to get it right. That was what she was being given.

But she couldn't do it. Last night, she had committed herself to James. She had promised to live out her life with him, for better or for worse. She couldn't abandon him or her life just because things were horrible right now.

She couldn't.

So she clutched Garrett, cursing him with every breath, while a partially planted field sped by.

"Slow down, Garrett!" she screamed. "Are you trying to kill me?"

"Not yet, my dear," he bellowed back, his voice exultant. "Not just yet."

"What?" His words made no sense.

They rode on, over meadows, through fields, skirting the woods but remaining close to their tall, dark presence. She could no longer hear the bells ringing over the heavy beat of his horse. "I was going to church," she yelled at him.

"Things change."

"But—"

"Silence!"

She looked back at him then. She twisted as far as she dared and stared at his face. He was different, and yet more true than ever before. His expression was fierce, ecstatic, and purposeful, all at once—a far cry from his usual vague charm. He looked down at her, and she felt a shiver travel up her spine.

"Garrett?"

He merely grinned at her, and suddenly she reconsidered falling off the horse. But he tightened his grip, and she was locked in place as firmly as if she were chained. Despite Garrett's dandy exterior, he possessed alarming strength.

Glancing about her at the shifting landscape, she felt the pieces fall into place. She assembled motive, opportunity, and means, and the concept left her more frightened than ever before. "Where are you taking me?" she demanded.

He lifted his chin, jerking ahead at a dark, bare strip of land.

The mines.

"Someone will see you."

He shook his head. "You had James close it down completely for the week, remember? Because of the festival. Paid wages for the miners, too."

She swallowed, knowing he was right. And with everyone celebrating Waterloo, no one would think to look for one madwoman who had stormed out of the earl's house.

"Garrett, think about what you're doing. There has to be another way."

He shook his head, but his eyes gleamed. "I have been thinking." He grinned at her. "And this is the only way."

He reined in his horse just outside a black reinforced hole in the side of a hill: the mine entrance. Carolly was braced to run the moment his horse stopped, but she was too bruised, her muscles too slow. Garrett was on his feet, a pistol in his hand, as she fell to the ground.

"Get up," he ordered.

"I can't," she lied, pretending her legs were too stiff, too hurt. Maybe if he got close enough she could punch him or something. But he had known her too long to be deceived. He lifted his pistol and aimed.

"Get up now or I will shoot you here and drag your lifeless body into the mines. It matters not to me."

But it did matter to Carolly, and so she stood, her battered muscles protesting every inch of the way. "Why kill me, Garrett? I have done nothing to you."

He laughed mercilessly as he waved her into the black hole. "You are going to marry James."

"I wouldn't be too sure about that," she said glumly. Good Lord, she realized with shock; her last conversation with James had been an argument. If Garrett killed her now, James would think she had run off and abandoned him.

"Walk!"

Carolly bit her lip, choking back a panicked scream. She never had liked dark, ominous-looking holes. She liked them even less when a man stood behind her aiming a pistol at her back.

"What if I promised not to marry him?" she offered. Given the way they'd parted, she thought that extremely likely.

Garrett's only response was a merciless laugh.

Carolly started walking. It was amazing what she noticed as she took those first few steps into the mine. She didn't see the darkness, didn't truly feel the cold, damp air that seemed to surround her. Instead, she noticed a single leaf. Some weed, actually—straggly, pathetic, and not very green. But she knew she would remember it forever as she wondered if it would be the last living thing besides Garrett she would see in this lifetime.

This lifetime. The word echoed in her mind as she turned to Garrett. "You can't really kill me," she said, latching on to the thought. "I'm already dead. See, I'm sort of a pre—" He shoved her forward, and she stumbled onto her knees in the dirt.

"Keep walking," he growled.

So much for that idea, she thought glumly. She rose slowly to her feet, then took only two tiny steps forward, resorting to the oldest line in the book: "You won't get away with this, you know. You'll be locked up. Jailed. But if you let me go now, I swear I won't have you arrested."

Garrett ignored her, his attention centered on lighting the candle perched on the top of a nineteenth-century equivalent of a hardhat. She considered running, but her only choices were to try and get past him—not a very likely scenario—or to run blindly into the black hole of the mine where she would certainly get lost. She opted to remain where she was, at least for the moment. Maybe she could still reach Garrett.

"I bet," she said conversationally, "that if we really thought about it, I'm sure we could work something out. What exactly do you want?"

He held the hat and candle before him, its light making his eyes almost maniacal in the surrounding darkness. His eyes were quite a beautiful blue, she realized, and yet she saw no soul there that she could touch. No remorse, no regret. Only a hunger for something that did not belong to him.

"What do I want?" he asked softly. "I want my inheritance. I want all of this . . ." His expansive gesture encompassed not only the mine, but the surrounding lands and more.

"But killing me won't get you that. James . . ." She cut off her words, but she could not stop the thought, and he must have read the horror on her face.

"That is right. It all belongs to James. But not for long." Then he put on his hat and gestured with his pistol, pushing her forward. She hesitated, but she knew she would only remain alive as long as it was convenient for him. The moment she began causing too much trouble, he would quickly kill her.

She began walking. "Garrett, I'm sure James would not leave you penniless."

"Penniless? No. He will drop me some pittance as long as he is alive."

She pulled at her lower lip, thinking aloud. "But you want more than that?"

"I deserve more," he said softly.

She didn't have time to inquire exactly why he thought he was owed a living. He pointed her down a ladder braced against what looked to her like a hole into total darkness. But she didn't have a choice, and so she went, her every footstep as slow and cautious as she dared. And while she moved, he knelt over the hole, a bright spot of light gleaming off of a dull grey pistol, speaking casually to her as if they were sharing tea.

"I was perfectly content, you know, working behind the scenes, occasionally stirring up the villagers. I had them on the verge of rebellion. One of them was going to kill him. I understand young Billy even tried one night when you were out walking in the woods."

Carolly remembered the gunshot on their midnight stroll through the near woods. She had never believed it was a poacher.

"If that was your assassin," she remarked dryly, "then he was remarkably inept." She had to keep him talking. As long as he spoke to her, he wouldn't kill her. It was a tactic meant to help her take control of the situation.

But it didn't work. Her voice echoed weirdly in the tunnel, coming back to her in the oddest of whispers and hisses. For a moment, she had the horrible impression she descended into a pit of monsters—slimy creatures breathing just below her. The feeling nearly overwhelmed her, and she stood frozen in place on the ladder. Then Garrett began speaking again, his casual voice restoring her sanity.

"Yes, Billy was most inept. He apparently got terrified the moment he realized he missed. Stupid boy. Then you had to come and throw that damned festival."

Carolly took a deep breath, trying to focus her thoughts. The only monster here was Garrett, she reminded herself. And she could see him.

"Listen, Garrett," she began, still paused on the ladder. "About London. I've reconsidered," she lied. "I'd love to go there with you. I'm sure I could learn a lot from you."

"Do not try to trick me, my girl," he said dryly. "You are not capable."

She cursed the arrogant toad under her breath, wishing she could wipe that condescending smile off his face. But there was little she could do while he stood above her aiming a pistol at her head.

"Now, hurry up," he ordered. She began her descent once again, stopping only when she reached the bottom. "Good," he continued. "Now step back. Farther. More."

Carolly did as he bade her. At his command, she stepped

backward, a little farther and farther, sliding into the blackness until she couldn't see her own hand.

As she did, she started feeling around for a weapon. She had to work fast. Garrett was coming down the ladder with remarkable speed. This would be her only chance of escape.

Her hand closed over a rock. It was a little large for her hand, but it had sharp points and was heavy enough to, hopefully, knock her captor unconscious.

She tensed, feeling her way through the shadows to get to a better angle.

"Where are you?" bellowed Garrett when he was halfway down the ladder. "Come back into the light." He was getting anxious, twisting around on his perch. Very soon he would spot her, and he was too high for her to reach effectively.

Adrenaline surged through her as she realized she was running out of time. She tensed, gripping the rock in her hand.

"Come here this instant!" he bellowed.

She jumped for him, swinging the rock hard toward his head. She hit him, aiming for his temple. The impact jarred her up to her shoulder, and she felt blood spurt warm and slick over her hand. With luck, he would drop like a stone.

The light twisted crazily. Carolly scrambled to regain her footing while Garrett roared and reared back, swinging at her wildly. She had missed his temple, succeeding only in cutting his cheek.

Carolly ducked away, waiting for a moment to come at him again. She had no illusions about her strength in hand to hand combat. He could easily overpower her. She'd get one more blow if she was lucky.

He jumped to the ground just as she moved in for another strike. The light was wild flashes, almost like a strobe. She saw his bloodied face, rage warping his features into a hideous caricature of a face.

"You little bitch!" he screamed.

She struck, but this time he was ready for her. He ducked

and the blow glanced off of his shoulder. She had only a split second to see his fist coming down.

Thud.

He connected with her temple. She had expected the blow, bracing for the pain and accepting it. What caught her by surprise was the impact, the force that threw her backward off her feet. She stumbled. Fell. Then her thoughts exploded into starbursts of pain radiating out from the side of her head.

Her world went dark.

Chapter Nineteen

"I find it most odd. Do you find it odd, Mary Ann?"

"Absolutely. Most odd"

James leaned against the mantel and tried to maintain a polite facade as Lady Merrill discussed Baron Handren's departure ad infinitum. To them, news of Waterloo and Napoleon seemed secondary to the state of his betrothal to Carolly.

"One would think he would remain to celebrate his niece's match," said Lady Merrill.

"Absolutely," agreed her daughter. "One would think he would. Perhaps he was not too pleased with the match."

"Oh, I cannot imagine that," said Lady Merrill. She slanted James a coy look. "After all, the earl is a wonderful specimen of a man. Why, anyone would be thrilled to have him in their family."

"Anyone," echoed her daughter.

James took refuge in his brandy glass.

"In fact," continued the mother, "if for some reason someone found a match not to his liking, I would think that he would be anxious for a family who would embrace him whole-heartedly."

"Wholeheartedly."

James looked up to see both mother and daughter regarding him with sheeplike adoration. It was all fake, he knew. These two were the most calculating females it had ever been his misfortune to meet. They had been trying to snare him since their appearance at the breakfast table only moments after Carolly's departure. And he was cursed by good breeding that forced him to entertain them. Whatever had induced Carolly to invite such title-grubbing females into his home? Or him to allow her?

"What do you think, my lord?" asked the daughter, batting her eyelashes at him until she looked as if she had a twitch.

James groaned, throwing good manners to the wind. "I think," he said, pushing away from the fireplace, "that I must go for a ride."

Mary Ann hopped up. "What an excellent idea. I would simply adore a ride."

James nodded, his expression as polite as he could make it. "My stables are, of course, at your disposal." Then he turned on his heel and left, having absolutely no intention of waiting around for her.

As he had told Carolly not more than an hour ago, he needed time and space to think.

Yet his ride did nothing to ease the confusion in his mind. His mind seemed to echo one word: *Waterloo*. And while the rest of England was celebrating the event, it merely gave him pain.

Everything Carolly had predicted had come true. Which meant she was not insane. Which meant she just might be an angel. Or at least a pre-angel. Or whatever she said.

And at that his mind completely rebelled.

He was not entirely sure why the concept tormented him so. Most men would be thrilled to discover their betrothed was rational. Except her claims were *not* rational, and he could not find a way to reconcile the two.

And if that were not enough, one other thought rose to torture him, presenting itself to him in unadorned logic, despite the illogical situation: If everything Carolly had said was true, then she had indeed decided to try to circumvent the will of Heaven; had given up her directive to become an angel to stay on Earth as his wife. The thought was humbling. She had given up *everything* for him. And all he had done was laugh at her pain, calling her plans fantasies.

He had been insufferably arrogant, secure in his own egotism in the most appalling fashion. And yet, still his mind rebelled, still he fought what she claimed was simple reality. How could she possibly be an angel? She could not. But then, how had she known about Waterloo?

The circle began again, spinning about in his mind in a neverending dance of nonsense. Except it was not nonsense. It was all very, very real.

James reined in Shadow, slowing his horse to a steady walk as he reluctantly turned toward home. He had accepted Carolly when he thought her mad. Could he not accept her as she truly was?

But how did one lie with an angel, or a pre-angel, or whatever she was? How could he touch her without thinking of Heaven and God and all the things she'd been meant to do? How could he look at her every day and see the woman, not the creature out of time and reason?

He could not. And yet, could he give her back to God after having touched her, having loved her, and most of all, having brought her inextricably into his life?

He entered the stable yard, refusing the stable boy's assistance. He wished to care for Shadow himself, buying himself more time away from his guests. He had barely begun the rubdown when Garrett found him.

"It is about time! I have been waiting an age for you."

James straightened, eyeing his heir over Shadow's back. "Good God, man. What happened to you?"

Garrett's hair was matted with sweat and a dark gash disfigured his left cheek. His clothing was smeared with grime, and his eyes burned bright, almost eerily intense. James had never seen such absolute purpose in his cousin.

"What has occurred?" he asked, alarm surging through him.

Garrett shook his head. "I tried to stop them." He spread his arms wide. "You can see that I did."

James stepped past his horse, wishing his cousin would come out of the shadows. The stable was dark enough without having Garrett pressed against the corner of the stall. "What happened?" he repeated.

"It is the villagers. They have taken Carolly to the mines."

"What!"

"I do not know that they intend to harm her. They merely wished to speak with you and are using her to lure you there."

James turned quickly, fitting his saddle back onto Shadow while panic squeezed his chest tight. "How many are there?"

"Four, maybe five. They simply wish to speak with you." Garrett seemed breathless and excited. His words stumbled over one another until he almost babbled. "She is in the mines."

James quickly mounted, but his cousin held Shadow's head, steadying the horse while he continued in earnest undertones: "Go in the entrance, down the first ladder . . ." He then gave directions that James committed to memory. "I shall get Wentworth and some of the footmen," Garrett promised. "We shall be moments behind you."

James paused, despite the pounding of his heart, using all his personal power to impress his feckless heir. "I am relying on you, Garrett. Do not fail me."

"I shall not." Then Garrett smiled, the expression both reassuring and odd at the same time. But James did not have the time to ponder. His entire body clenched in fear for Carolly, and his mind flashed hideous pictures of what might now be happening to her.

She was alone with possibly angry, violent miners. James backed Shadow out of the stall, then turned quickly, intending to ride out of the stable. He nearly missed the small figure opening the door until he heard her soft call.

"Uncle?"

He reined back to avoid trampling her. "Margaret! Get out of the way!"

She jumped backward, her eyes large, dark spots in the gloom. "Uncle! Are you going to see Carolly?"

"Yes. Stay inside and wait for my return."

"But—"

"For God's sake, child, listen to me just this once!" Then he rode off, damning himself for winding Shadow earlier. What would he do if he arrived too late?

Carolly awoke to blackness. At first she thought she had not opened her eyes, and she blinked them several times to make sure. It was moments later that she came to the inescapable conclusion that she had gone blind.

It wasn't until she tried to move that she realized something else was dreadfully wrong. Her hands were bound behind her back. Her feet were also tied.

Other sensations began pouring into her befuddled brain. The side of her head throbbed painfully. She lay on a cold hard surface, and her clothing was damp. A rock stuck painfully into her upper arm.

She tried to shift position, crying out in alarm as she rolled slightly, dropping her face into a small puddle of slimy water. She gasped, rearing backward, shifting position once again until she was away from the liquid. Another rock cut into her hip this time, but at least she wasn't drowning.

It was then she realized that her cry had sounded odd. She tried again, speaking in her normal voice. "Hello?"

Hello . . . hello . . . hello. Her word echoed eerily.

"Hello?" she called, louder this time. Then she took a deep breath, screaming for all she was worth. "Help!"

The sound of her voice came back to her, the echo muffled and garbled. Carolly closed her eyes, fighting the panic that rose within her as her memory came flooding back. And with it, Garrett's plan in all its hideous glory.

She was in the mine. Garrett had brought her here as bait. Soon James would arrive, and Garrett would kill them both for the inheritance. But why had he left her alive in the first place? She did not know.

Carolly blinked her eyes, though that did little to ease her mind. She was still surrounded by total darkness, the silence absolute except for her breathing. Unsurprisingly, Garrett had not left her any light.

Desperately, she grappled with her panic, forcing it into submission as she tried to assess her situation. It was completely dark. And totally silent. And while that lack of sensation ate at her sanity, it also told her she was alone. It meant James hadn't arrived yet, and so there was still time for her to escape and warn him.

She turned her head, reassured now that she had decided on a course of action. First thing she had to do was find a way to cut the cords that bound her hands and feet.

She tested her bonds, disappointed to find Garrett had used a thick rope, tying the knots painfully tight. It would take her forever to work free. Still, she had nothing better to do, and excellent reasons to work quickly.

She struggled to sit up and finally managed it, although she scraped her elbow raw in the process. Then she began working on freeing her hands. The bonds were too tight for her to slip free, so she maneuvered around until she found a pointy rock. She shifted until she pressed her wrists against the sharpest edge and began to rub the rope against it. After ten minutes, she curled her fingers, trying to feel for some sort of progress.

"Great," she said aloud just to hear some sound. "At this rate I'll be free sometime next month."

But still she kept doggedly on, unable to bear the thought of remaining trapped here, helpless, while Garrett murdered her beloved.

"I won't fail you, James. I swear."

James approached the mine with all his senses alert. He watched for signs of a struggle, for footprints, anything. He was open to all possibilities, even to the thought that Garrett had masterminded this entire affair to lure him here.

He did not want to think the exuberant boy he remembered from so many years ago could have become so bitter, so evil as to plot his death, but he could not dismiss that thought either. There were too many holes in Garrett's story.

If the miners wished to discuss something with him, wouldn't they have gone through their foreman? He was always willing to meet with them, to hear their grievances and discuss solutions. Most of them knew that.

Most of them.

As for the others, they tended to quick violence with little premeditation: A gang attack, like the one on Carolly and Margaret so many weeks ago. But would they be prone to violence on a holiday from their work? Right after the festival and in the wake of the Waterloo celebrations? Not likely.

Which meant something highly unusual had caused this circumstance. Or Garrett had lied.

Whichever the case, one thing was certain: Carolly was in danger. The question was: could he trust she was here in the mines where Garrett had indicated? Garrett's clothes and body clearly showed a struggle. From the dirt and grime, James guessed he had indeed been here. In addition, James found an isolated set of deep hoofprints.

Carolly was probably here.

He could only pray she was still alive.

James approached the mine entrance obliquely, searching for someone or something out of place.

Nothing. It looked deserted.

Abandoning that entrance, he rode swiftly to an alternate hole. Garrett had given him specific directions to an unstable tunnel, near the top but abandoned for lack of ore. Although there was only one entrance to that particular tunnel, there were two ways to the corridor just before it.

If there were any hidden booby traps or kidnappers hiding along the route, he would likely bypass all of them by using the separate entrance. It was a slightly longer route, but he reasoned he would make up the time by not searching around every corner for some trap.

He spurred Shadow onto a gallop, fear eating at his reason. He begrudged every passing second away from Carolly, every moment when he could not assure himself of her safety. But he had to move logically, with forethought, or he might very well get them both killed.

Carolly was growing frantic. The rope that bound her wrists was still stubbornly thick. She had barely managed to fray a few of the threads, and yet she was running out of time.

Only a few minutes ago she had heard a noise like a footfall. She hated sitting here in the dark, imagining bugs, rodents, spiders, all sorts of monsters, real and unreal. Her imagination was working overtime. She might have heard a footfall, maybe the echoed sound of someone breathing. Or maybe she'd heard her own gasp as she accidentally scraped her wrist for the thousandth time.

She didn't know.

There was only this oppressive feeling that time was running out.

Working harder at the rope, Carolly gritted her teeth against the pain and felt the bonds grow slick with blood and sweat. Then she chanced to glance up.

Was it lighter to her left? Had the darkness grown the tiniest bit more gray? She couldn't tell, but her mind was working feverishly.

Should she call out? If the light was Garrett returning to

kill her, then she was no worse off. But if anyone else chanced to be wandering the mines today, she needed to grasp this chance.

"Help!" Her voice echoed up and down the tunnels, coming back to her in haunting cries. She bit her lip and tried to slow the frantic beat of her heart as it pounded in her ears. She had to listen, had to hear if someone responded.

"—ly?" Someone had said something. She couldn't make out the words or even the gender of the speaker, but someone else had made that sound.

"Help!" she screamed. "I'm down here." The darkness on the left side of the tunnel was definitely growing lighter, gradually becoming a murky grey.

Then she heard it. James's sweet voice edged with panic. "Carolly! Where are you?"

"Here. Right here. Can you follow my voice? I'm alone. Hurry."

Then suddenly the grey murkiness burst into a bright glow of light. James rounded the corner, keeping his back to the wall, scanning the tunnel before entering.

"Right here!"

"Carolly!"

He was beside her in a moment, wrapping her in his arms, kissing her face even as he scanned her for injuries.

"I'm fine. Mostly. But we have to get out of here. Garrett is going to kill you."

He didn't answer, didn't even recoil at her statement. He simply leaned her forward so he could begin work on the bonds around her wrists. She shifted to accommodate him, realizing as she moved that he must already know about Garrett. She glanced at him, noting the grim lines on his face.

Yes, he already knew.

"We've got to get out of here, James. And he wants you, not me." She waited, but the only response was a taut silence. "James, please."

"What did he say to you?" His voice was low and urgent.

"Just what I told you: That he's going to kill you."

She gasped as he finally loosened her bonds. The rope slipped undone, and her hands began to tingle as the blood flow returned. She tried to move her fingers and nearly cried out at the pain, but her thoughts were on James.

"I can get my feet. Go now, before he comes back."

He looked up from the bonds around her ankles. Beside them, on the floor, the candle threw wild shadows across his face.

"Do you want to die, Carolly? Do you want to become an angel?"

She heard the dread in his voice, but she also heard belief. He understood her now, and the knowledge spread like a warm glow through her body.

"No, James. I want to live my life with you."

She saw joy flash through his eyes; then he leaned forward, giving her a swift and thorough kiss. She arched into it as best she could, then she pushed him away.

"Go now. I can't marry you if you're dead. Go!"

But he only shook his head. "I will not leave without you."

"Well, isn't this a touching scene?"

Carolly froze at Garrett's voice, but James didn't seem to react. He merely bent his head to work at her bonds, his fingers working with lightning swiftness. Still the ropes did not slacken.

Carolly looked up. Garrett stood well down the tunnel from them, his pistol in his hand. He looked mussed and slightly battered, but his hands were steady and his gaze firm.

"Get away from her." Garrett's voice was deadly cold, but James ignored him. "I will shoot you now, James. I swear it."

Carolly flexed her fingers, feeling pain shoot straight up her arms, but at least they moved. She leaned forward, quietly lifting James's hands from her bonds, then bending her own fingers to the task, gritting her teeth against the pain. After a quick glance at her face, James slowly twisted around, keeping his back to her feet, thereby shielding Garrett's view of her actions.

"You don't want to kill me, Garrett."

Garrett shrugged, the movement oddly elegant. "True. I find myself strangely reluctant to watch you die."

Carolly worked feverishly at her bonds, but her fingers were still too clumsy and the ties desperately tight. Meanwhile, James continued to speak with Garrett, his voice smooth and calm.

"Then release us. We can find a solution together."

"A solution?" Garrett mocked. "I have already found my solution, I assure you. I just do not intend to watch it happen. Call it squeamishness." He smiled. Then he bent down, putting his candle to a long thin string.

Carolly felt James tense, and she knew he was prepared to jump his cousin despite the enormous distance between them. She looked up and frowned, knowing she needed to distract Garrett somehow while still working on freeing her legs.

"What are you doing?" she asked, her voice shrill despite her attempt at calm.

Garrett looked up, smiling as he gestured to a dark fissure in the wall. "I am lighting this wick. As you can see, it leads to a rather large pile of gunpowder in that crack. When it explodes, the walls will come down."

"On us." James's voice did not betray any fear, only logic.

Garrett shrugged. "An unfortunate accident."

"Murder." Carolly was grim, and she was pleased to see Garrett flinch. Apparently he wasn't as sanguine about this whole affair as he wanted them to think.

But he still bent to light the wick. And in that moment, James launched himself at his cousin. He didn't have a chance. The distance was too large, the odds too great.

Garrett raised his gun and fired.

The explosion echoed through the tunnels, reverberating like pounding hooves. Carolly screamed as she saw James fall, his head cracking painfully against the wall and a crimson stain spreading about his chest.

Her legs still bound, Carolly began crawling as best she could to James's side. The rock scraped at her knees and bit into her aching hands, but she thought of nothing except his life.

"Yes, hurry, Caroline," commented Garrett. "You shall wish to spend your last moments at his side."

"You monster!" she screamed, frustration curling into a hard knot of anger. Her hand fell upon a rock, and she grabbed it, throwing it with all her might. It hit James's cousin in the face, cutting a gash in his forehead, and blood spilled into his eyes. But it did not stop him from lighting his makeshift fuse.

"For God's sake, Garrett," Carolly begged. "Think what you're doing."

He looked up, his expression slightly haunted. "My apologies, but I am trying my best not to." He bowed formally to her, one hand still trying to brush the blood from his eyes. "Good day, Miss Handren." Then he was gone, disappearing down the tunnel, his erratic footfalls quickly fading into silence. Carolly paid no attention, focusing her efforts on scrambling the last distance to James. When she got to his side, she wadded up her skirt, pressing it where blood oozed sluggishly from his chest.

"James! James, can you hear me?"

He groaned and opened his eyes, his hand going to his head.

"Oh, thank God," she breathed.

He blinked, then his eyes widened. "The gunpowder! Can you stop it?"

Carolly looked toward the tiny glowing light as it wound its way toward the fissure. She already knew the answer. She had, in fact, known the answer when Garrett first lit the fuse. There was no way, even if her legs were free, that she could stop the coming explosion. There was barely an inch left in the wick and even that was disappearing fast.

They had only seconds.

Looking down into his eyes, she bent over him, shielding his body as best she could. "I love you," she whispered.

Understanding and pain mixed in his eyes. But with both those emotions, she saw an overwhelming love. "I love you," he said, his voice rough with emotion. "I want to spend eternity with you."

She smiled. "Eternity."

Then she bent to kiss him. Their lips touched, and the world shattered in a deafening explosion.

No stranger to death, Carolly recognized the process. She felt the glorious lightness, the freedom from body as if an enormous weight had simply faded away. She was familiar with the brilliant light surrounding her and the memories of her incarnation as they reeled past her like scenes in a movie.

As she watched, she fell in love with James all over again. She kissed him, loved him, and married him all in the space of a heartbeat.

Except she had no heartbeat with which to measure the time.

When it was over, she stopped and waited for James to join her. She waited, unable to measure the time except in the aching loneliness of his absence.

Where was he?

He will not come. It is not yet his time.

Carolly lifted her awareness to the one she called Master. She did not know if it was God or Jesus or any of the human terms for the Infinite. She only knew the soul was her teacher and her guide.

"Can he not come, Master? Can he not be with me?"

It is not his time.

"Then am I alone?" Even in the midst of eternity, she felt an expanding emptiness, a hole that even God could not fill.

You have done well, Carolly. You have learned to love, learned to embrace the sacrifice and the pain as well as the joy. I am pleased.

Carolly accepted the statement with conflicting feelings, her satisfaction with her success coming only in the midst of despair. She had lost James.

You have a choice now.

"A choice?" She had difficulty focusing her attention. It all was happening too fast. She had no time to comprehend the Master's words when her heart and mind were still bound to James.

He will live.

Beside her the light changed, coalescing into a grey blanket that shifted into distinct forms and shadows. She saw the mine tunnel choked with dust and debris, rubble everywhere. In the center was James, crouched over her body. His chest still bled, yet he paid no attention to his own pain as he bent over her. She'd been crushed by falling rocks.

James released an anguished cry, and the sound echoed in the shifting light, surrounding her with his torment.

He grieves for you.

"He loves me." And she realized it was true. He had said the words to her, but never before had she felt it so fully. It was like a wall crumbling away from her heart. "I pushed him away for a long time," she said softly.

Yes.

"I didn't believe he could love me. Not who I truly am. I was so prepared for his rejection, I never gave him a chance. I just left." Her words were only an echo of what was happening inside her. Understanding poured like a benediction into her soul as she accepted the truth. She had not allowed him to love her fully, totally, and yet he had done it anyway.

He loved her.

Do you feel his love?

"Yes. Yes!" And she did. For the first time ever, she felt truly and completely loved, without reservation or doubt. She had never thought it could happen, not without conditions, lies, or disappointments. But now she knew James loved her totally, no matter who she was or what she did. "He loves me," she repeated. It was a miracle all its own, and she cherished it with her whole being. "And I love him."

You understand now.

"Yes."

Then you may choose.

She shifted her attention away from James, her mind still reeling from the enormity of feeling loved. "Choose what?"

You may continue on your path. You may become an angel and help others learn as you have learned.

"I can become an angel?" Hope surged within her. Finally her hoped-for fate was a possibility. But even as her mind embraced a future of guiding others to the joy she had just discovered, her attention returned to James and her soul still ached for him. "What happens to James?"

He will continue, will find love as Margaret's father.

The scene shifted, showing her glimpses of James with Margaret. As she watched, time sped away. She watched his body age, his hair lighten to gray then white. She saw James give Margaret away at her wedding, saw him cradling his first grandchild. She saw so much, but through it all, he was still alone. "He will never love another woman?"

Not in this lifetime.

She turned to the Master, sadness filling her at the thought of James spending years alone—a sadness matching her own at the knowledge she would forever be apart from him. "Will he ever find someone? Maybe in another lifetime?"

Perhaps.

She frowned, a thought coming to her. "What about Garrett? Is he going to torment James and Margaret for the rest of their lives?"

Up until now, the Master had never shown an emotion other than loving concern. But this time, his words seemed edged with sadness.

Garrett was caught in his own deceits. The placement of his explosive was ill conceived.

The scene shifted, this time to another part of the mine

where she saw only part of Garrett's coat beneath the rubble. Oddly enough, Carolly felt sadness.

"He did not understand."

No. He will have another chance, in another life, but he will have many reparations to make.

Carolly understood the wisdom of the Master's choice. It was time for Garrett to start over, to try again to learn the lessons she was only now beginning to comprehend.

Then, as she watched, she saw a slim foot appear. It was Margaret, picking her way through the rubble of the mine. Behind her came Wentworth and Mrs. Potherby and many of James's servants.

She will find the collapsed cave and help the others open a passageway for James.

Once again the scene shifted, and Carolly found herself watching James as he held her lifeless body. The ache in her soul, never quite gone, cut at her with renewed vengeance. She tried to turn away from the sight, unable to watch his pain, but she could not do it. She could not abandon him, even though she saw him as if through a thick curtain of glass.

"What is my other choice?" she asked softly.

You may return to him as Caroline Handren. You will remember nothing of your other lives.

She looked back to the Master, hope and surprise flooding her. "I can go back? I can be with him?" She moved forward, already straining toward James.

You will remember nothing. You will be Caroline Handren.

"I will be with him."

Afterwards, you may return as an angel.

She barely heard the words, for she was already pushing through the heavy veil separating her from James. It was a difficult and agonizing process, for with every inch she felt her soul take on weight, limitations, frailty. But she didn't care. She would be with James.

She could love James and accept his love as she had always dreamed.

Immersing herself in her body, she felt pain like leaden bonds, tying her down, and she was thankful for its presence. She felt her injuries heal themselves. Her heart lurched, and she gasped as blood began to flow through her body and dust-choked air filled her lungs.

She lived.

"James?" Her voice was a whisper, raw and thick in her chest, but he heard her nonetheless.

He lifted his head from her chest, his eyes growing wide as he gazed at her. "Carolly? You are alive!"

She was too weak to return his embrace, but she reveled in the feel of him against her, the pulse of life and love that bound them both together.

"I love you, James."

"Oh, Carolly." He kissed her, deeply and thoroughly. When he raised his head, he gazed at her, his heart in his eyes as he touched her face. "I love you. Always."

She raised her hand, and he grasped it, kissing her finger-tips, holding her arm as his own strength gave out, and he lowered himself to the ground beside her.

"You'll be fine," she whispered, knowing she had to tell him what the Master had said before all her memories slipped away. "Margaret is coming. She will open a path through the rubble to save us."

James turned to her, caressing her face even as he frowned. "I told Margaret to stay home."

"Well, thank God she never listens to you."

James touched her lips, his eyes tearing with pain. "I thank God we are still alive, and that you are with me."

Carolly smiled. She thanked God, too, with all her heart. But most of all, she thanked James for showing her what it meant to be loved.

Epilogue

"Janice. Wake up. It's me, Carolly."

Carolly watched as her sister scrunched up her face just like she had went they were kids. She smiled, steeped in nostalgia, as Janice pursed her lips, wrinkled her nose, then rubbed her eyes one after the other. It was almost a ritual, and Carolly loved watching every moment of it.

The only difference was that instead of being six, her baby sister was now twenty-six and a grown woman.

"Janice. Wake up."

"Carolly?" Janice's voice was thick with sleep, but her eyes widened abruptly, then blinked again and again as she tried to focus.

"Don't bother. The picture won't clear whatever you do."

"What?"

"This is a dream."

"What?"

"A dream. Not real." Carolly shrugged. "Sorry, but it's true."

Janice frowned, then sat up, her lush brown hair sliding in a mahogany cascade around her shoulders.

"Wow," Carolly said, awed by the sight. "You've grown into quite a beauty."

"What?"

Carolly laughed. "Can't you say anything other than 'what'?"

Janice propped her hands on her hips. "Okay, how about: Aren't you dead?"

Carolly grinned. "Yup. Well, actually, nope. I'm alive in 1815. Can you beat that?"

Janice shook her head. "I'm hallucinating. Must be the late hours."

Carolly perked up, clapping her hands in delight. "Have you finally learned to party?"

"Party? I'm an ER doctor. Worked a double shift."

"Oh." Deflated, Carolly dropped onto her sister's bed and looked, really looked at her sister. "I was always jealous of you. You know that, don't you? Mom and Dad were so proud of you. You did everything right."

Janice drew her knees up to her chin, her large brown eyes filling with tears. "Not that night. I didn't do everything right that night you got . . . you got . . ."

"Killed?"

Janice nodded, her expression miserable.

Carolly didn't know if she could touch her sister or not. Spanning space and time in a dream was new to her and probably a one-time-only gift. But she tried anyway, leaning forward to clasp her sister's hand. To her surprise, she met warm flesh and, suddenly, they were holding hands.

"Janice," she said softly, "dying was the best thing that ever happened to me."

"What?"

"There's more to dying than you know." Suddenly Carolly felt herself grin. "And there's more to living than I ever knew."

"But—"

"I can't stay, Janice. I just wanted to see you, to find out if you were okay. Mom and Dad, too."

Janice nodded and brushed away her hair. "They're great. And I'm . . . I'm going to get married."

"What?"

Janice grinned, her cheeks turning a soft rose as she blushed. "He came through the ER from a car accident. Only he called it a carriage accident. His name is Bradley, and . . . and he reminds me a lot of you."

Carolly gripped her sister's hand. Her baby sister, getting married. "Do you love him?"

Janice nodded, and Carolly could see the happiness as it suffused her sister's whole body.

"I love him. And let's just say that a visit from a dead sister is only one of the bizarre things I've experienced lately." Janice's smile faded as she dropped to her knees and looked at their clasped hands. "What about you, Carolly? Are you happy? Have you figure it all out?"

"Figured what out?"

Janice raised her eyes until she met Carolly's gaze. "That you deserve to be happy, too."

An image of James flashed through her mind, and Carolly found herself melting just from the thought of her husband. "Yes," she whispered. "I have figured it out. And I'm ecstatic."

Carolly felt her hold on Janice slipping away. Her sister seemed to thin beneath her touch, growing more insubstantial by the moment. With a slight cry of regret, she threw her arms around her sister, hugging her with all her might.

"I love you, Janice. Be happy."

She felt a last tug as her sister returned her embrace, then it faded away as Janice's words became a mere whisper. "We have always loved you. Be happy, Carolly."

"—sorry, my lord. But there's a man outside."

Carolly blinked, then rubbed her eyes as she tried to focus her thoughts. Had she been dreaming? James touched her arm, drawing her back against him in their bed, his voice a low, sensuous rumble against her ear.

"Wentworth, what do I care about some man?"

"James," Carolly interrupted, her thoughts still scattered. "I had the strangest dream."

"Hush, love," he said, dropping a kiss along her brow. "We can talk about it in a moment."

"But . . ." And then it faded. Thoughts and images disappeared, slipping away into the silent parts of her mind. She did not mourn their loss, except in the vaguest sort of way. She knew she would find them again when it was time. As for right now, Wentworth was being unusually persistent for a man who had just interrupted a newlywed couple in their marriage bed.

"My apologies, my lord," he said, and for the first time, Carolly noticed that Wentworth was actually *in* their bedchamber, his red face and puckered lips aimed at the ceiling. "This gentleman appears most insistent."

James cursed under his breath, and Carolly had to stifle a giggle at the crude term. Never would she have thought her formal husband could be so irritated at a simple interruption. After all, they had been married for almost two months now. Surely they could stand one day's interruptions to their typical good morning activities.

"Please, Wentworth," Carolly said with a laugh, "tell us quickly before you lose your job. What does this insistent gentleman wish?"

The dour butler frowned, clearly uneasy with the entire situation. "He claims he has a delivery for you."

"So allow him to deliver it," muttered James, "and send him on his way." Then, to prove the matter closed, James shifted lower on his bed, gently teasing Carolly's body beneath the covers while she gasped and tried to hide the motions from their stiff butler.

"But, my lord!" wailed Wentworth.

James sighed, lifting his head form where he had been kissing the delicate flesh just behind her ear. "What?"

"They're rabbits!"

ATTENTION
BOOK LOVERS!

Can't get enough of your favorite **ROMANCE**?

Call **1-800-481-9191** to:

✴ order books,

✴ receive a **FREE** catalog,

✴ join our book clubs to **SAVE 20%**!

Open Mon.-Fri. 10 AM-9 PM EST

Visit **www.dorchesterpub.com**
for special offers and inside
information on the authors you love.

We accept Visa, MasterCard or Discover®.
LEISURE BOOKS ♥ LOVE SPELL